KU-253-408

Danielle Steel is a descendant of the Löwenbräu beer barons. Her mother is Portuguese and her father is German. Their common language is French, although they all speak eight languages. Danielle's father's family, the prominent banking and brewing clan, has always lived in Munich and the family seat was a moated castle in Bavaria, Kaltenberg. Her mother's family were diplomats and her maternal grandfather was a Portuguese diplomat assigned to the United States for a number of years.

American-born, Danielle lived in Paris for most of her childhood. At the age of 20 she went to New York and started working for 'Supergirls', a before-its-time public relations firm run by women who organised parties for Wall Street brokerage houses and designed PR campaigns for major firms. When the recession hit, the firm went out of business and Danielle 'retired' to write her first book, *Going Home*.

Danielle has established herself as a writer of extraordinary scope. She has set her various novels all over the world, from China to New York to San Francisco, in time-frames spanning 1860 to the present. She has received critical acclaim for her elaborate plots and meticulous research, and has brought vividly to life a broad range of very different characters.

DANIELLE STEEL

THURSTON HOUSE

timewarner
paperbacks

A *Time Warner* Paperback

First published in Great Britain
by Sphere Books Ltd 1983
Reprinted 1983, 1984 (twice), 1985, 1986 (twice),
1988 (twice), 1989 (twice), 1990 (twice),
1991, 1992, 1993 (three times)
Reprinted by Warner Books 1994
Reprinted 1995 (twice), 1996, 1998, 1999, 2000
Reprinted by Time Warner Paperbacks in 2002
Reprinted 2003

ISBN 0 7515 0561 7

Printed in England by Clays Ltd, St Ives plc

Time Warner Paperbacks
An imprint of
Time Warner Books UK
Brettenham House
Lancaster Place
London WC2E 7EN

www.TimeWarnerBooks.co.uk

The House

Who slept here
before I came,
who lived
in this room,
how did it look,
was it
the same?
Was there a girl
or two,
a little boy,
a house filled
with toys
with joys
with dreams. . . .
or was it just
a lonely place
with empty beds
and silent rooms,
was it always
filled
with gloom,
and did the house
long to be
loved?
Was there a girl
who danced
and sang,
a dinner bell
that chimed
or rang,
and did anyone
ever
stand
right here
as I do
now?

Do I know
the name,
have I seen
the face . . .
Was this always
the same sweet
place,
was someone
glad
was someone sad,
was there a dog
a cat,
a horse
a mouse,
who has been here,
who knows this
house,
do they know me
do I know them,
and did they sing
a requiem,
I feel them here
I know their
tears,
I loved them too,
the house was new
was theirs
was different then,
and yet it is
the same again,
and was
and will
and must always be,
and now
the house
belongs
to me.

Book I

Jeremiah Arbuckle Thurston

Chapter One

The sun sank slowly onto the hills framing the green splendour of the Napa Valley. Jeremiah stood watching the hot orange streaks across the sky, followed by a pale mauve haze, but his mind was a thousand miles away. He was a tall man with broad shoulders and a straight back, strong arms and a warm smile. At forty-three years of age, there was more salt than pepper in his hair, yet his hands still had the same strength they had when he had worked in the mines as a young man, and when he had bought his first mine in the Napa Valley in 1860. He had staked the claim himself and was the first to find quicksilver in the Napa Valley. He had been seventeen years old, barely more than a boy, but for years he had thought of nothing except mining, just as his father had done before him. His father had come from the East in 1850, and for him, the promise of gold in the West had been fulfilled. He had sent for his wife and son six months after he arrived, his pockets full of gold, and they had come. But when Jeremiah arrived, he was alone. His mother had died on the way. And for the next ten years he and his father had worked side by side, mining gold, then silver when the gold ran thin, and then when Jeremiah was nineteen, his father died, leaving him a fortune far larger than even Jeremiah had dreamed. Richard Thurston had saved everything for him, and Jeremiah was suddenly richer than almost any man in the state of California.

But for him, it didn't change anything. He went on working in the mines, beside the men he hired, buying mines, buying land, building, growing, mining. His men said that he had the gift of gold, everything he touched succeeded and grew, just as the quicksilver mines he established in Napa, when the silver mines ebbed. He made the transition swiftly and wisely, before others understood what he was doing. But it was the land he loved best. The rich brown soil he would run through his fingers and then hold lovingly in his hand . . .

3

he loved its warmth, its texture, and all that it represented, as he looked as far as the eye could see, at the hills, the trees, the valley, the lush carpet of grass stretching ahead of him. He had bought vineyards too, from which he produced a pleasant little wine. He loved everything that the land produced, apples, walnuts, grapes . . . ore . . . this valley meant more to him than anything . . . or anyone . . . He had spent thirty-five of his forty-three years right here, looking out at the same gently rolling hills, and when he died he would be buried here. This was where he belonged, the only place in the world he wanted to be. Wherever he went in the world, and Jeremiah Thurston had been far, this was the only place he wanted to live, in the Napa Valley, standing here at sunset, looking out over his hills.

And yet, as he stood there, the sky turning a velvety purplish gray, his mind was far from here. There was a business deal in Atlanta he'd been offered the day before, for close to a thousand flasks of quicksilver, and the price was one he liked, but there was something about the way he had been approached . . . for some reason, he had a peculiar feeling about it all, and yet he couldn't understand why. There was nothing wrong with the deal, and he was having his bank investigate the consortium. There was something about the letter he had received, about the man's style that bothered him. He seemed unusually forward and forceful and presumptuous. Orville Beauchamp was the head of the group, and it was stupid to object to the man's flowery prose, but . . . it was almost as though Jeremiah had a sixth sense about him.

'Jeremiah!' He smiled at the familiar sound of Hannah's voice. She had worked for him for almost twenty years, ever since her husband died, right after his own fiancée had died of influenza. She had come to him one day at the mine, glared down at him in her black widow's dress and rapped her umbrella on the floor, 'Your house is a disgrace, Jeremiah Thurston!' He had looked at her in astonishment, wondering who the devil she was, and discovered eventually that she was the aunt of a man who had once worked for him, and that she wanted a job working for him now. Jeremiah's father had built a shack on the far corner of their land in 1852 and Jeremiah had been content to live there with him. He had stayed on after his father died, but by then he had acquired far more extensive lands, annexing them on to what his father had purchased first in the Napa Valley. By the time Jeremiah was twenty-five, he began to think that it was time to

4

take a wife. He wanted children, someone to come home to at night, to share his good fortune with. He couldn't even begin to spend the money he had, and he liked the idea of someone to spoil a bit . . . a pretty girl with gentle eyes and delicate hands, a face he could love, a body to keep him warm at night. Through friends he had met just such a young lady. He asked her to marry him within two months of the day they first met, and he began to build a remarkably handsome house for her. It was in the central portion of his land with a view that stretched as far as the eye could see, beneath four enormous trees that met in a huge, handsome, natural arc, which would keep the house cool in summer. It was almost a palace he built, or so the locals thought, with three floors, two lovely parlors on the main floor, a wood panelled dining room, a big cozy kitchen with a fireplace big enough for Jeremiah himself to stand up in. Upstairs there was a pretty little drawing room; a huge master suite, a solarium for his bride; and, on the third floor, six bedrooms for the large family they would have. There was no point having to redo the house as the children came. And Jennie had taken great delight in the house – in the tall windows with their stained glass, the huge grand piano which she would play for him at night.

Except that she never did. She was struck by the epidemic of influenza which struck the valley in the autumn of 1868, and she died within three days of falling ill. For the first time in his life, Jeremiah's luck had failed him, and he mourned her as a mother would have a lost child. She had been just barely seventeen, and she would have been the perfect wife for him. He rattled around in his house like a marble in a shoe box for a while, and then in despair he closed the house up and went back to the shack he had lived in before, but he was no longer comfortable there. In the Spring of 1869, he moved into the house he had planned to share with Jennie . . . Jennie . . . he couldn't bear to wander through the rooms he had destined for her, couldn't bear to think of what it would have been like if she had lived there. He had visited her parents often at first, but he couldn't stand seeing his own pain mirrored in their eyes, or the hungry way her less attractive older sister looked at him. Eventually, he closed up the rooms he didn't use, and he seldom, if ever, went to the second or third floors. Jeremiah grew used to living on the main floor and he somehow managed to make the two rooms he used look like the old shack. He turned one of the parlors into a bedroom for himself, and never bothered to furnish any of the other rooms. The grand piano had never been used once since it had been touched by Jennie's hands on the day it arrived. He opened the enormous kitchen where he ate, occasionally, with some of his men when they came by to see him. He liked eating with his men, liked knowing that they felt comfortable about stopping by. There was nothing grand or standoffish about him. He remembered from where he had come, from a cold, desperately poor little house in the East, shivering all winter long, wondering if they would have enough to eat, over the trails and the Rockies to the West, to the rivers, and the dirt, and the mines, working at his father's side. And if he had a fortune now, it was thanks to his hard work and that of his father. It wasn't something Jeremiah forgot, or ever would . . . just as he never forgot Jennie . . . never forgot a friend. He had never been tempted to marry again, as the years slid by. Somehow, no matter how appealing a young girl was, she never seemed quite as sweet as Jennie had, nor quite so much fun . . . for years he had remembered the sound of her laughter, her gasps of delight as he showed her the progress on the house. It had delighted him to build it for her, like a monument to their love, and after she died it meant nothing to him. He let the paint chip and the roof leak in the unused rooms. He used every dish and pot and pan he had until there were none clean, and they said that the parlor in which he slept looked no better than a barn. Until Hannah arrived. It was she who changed everything, and cleaned the place up.

'Look at this house, boy!' She had glared at him in disbelief when he'd brought her from the mine to show her around. He still wasn't quite sure what to do with her, but she was determined to come to work for him. She had nothing else to do now that her husband was dead, and Jeremiah needed her, or so she told him. 'What are you, a pig?' she demanded and he had laughed at the outraged look on her face. He hadn't had anyone to mother him in almost twenty years, and at twenty-six, it amused him to suddenly have Hannah. She started working for him the next day. He had come home that night to find the rooms he used spotless and neat, almost distressingly so, and in an effort to make a niche for himself again, he had strewn some of his papers around the room, dropped cigar ashes on the rug, inadvertently knocking over a glass of wine. By morning it looked like home to him again, much to Hannah's dismay. 'I'm going to handcuff you to the wall if you don't behave yourself, boy, and take that damn cigar out of your face, you're dropping ashes on your suit!' She had pried it from his lips and dropped it in the remains of the previous night's wine as Jeremiah gaped, but he was a good match for her. He provided an inexhaustible supply of ashes and disorder and filth, which gave her a constant supply of work. She felt needed for the first time in years, and he felt loved for the first time in longer than that, and by Christmas of that first year they were an inseparable pair. She came to work every day, refusing ever to take a day off. . . . 'Are you crazy? Do you know what kind of a mess I'd find after two days of not being here? No, sir, you're not keeping me out of this house for a day . . . not for an hour, you hear?'

She was tough with him, but there were hot meals when he came home, his sheets were immaculate, his house perfectly kept. Even the rooms he didn't use were spotlessly maintained, and when he brought home a dozen men from the mine to discuss some new plan to expand, or just to drink the wines made from the grapes he grew, she never complained, no matter how drunk they got, or how vile. And in time, Jeremiah teased her mercilessly about her devotion to him, and loved her more than he ever had anyone . . . except Jennie of course . . . Hannah was wise enough never to ask him about her. But when he was thirty she finally began to hound him about finding a wife. 'I'm too old, Hannah, and no one else cooks as well as you.' To which she hotly replied, 'Bull.' She insisted that he needed a wife, a woman to love and bear him sons, but he no longer thought of it anymore. It was almost as though it frightened him, as though if he allowed himself to care about someone that much again, they might die, as Jennie had. He didn't want to think of it, or to build up his hopes. The wound of Jennie's death no longer pained him as it had for years. It was over now, and he was comfortable as he was. 'And when you die, Jeremiah?' The old woman would look pointedly at him. 'Then what? Who do you leave it all to?'

'You, Hannah, who else?' He would tease and she would shake her head.

'You need a wife . . . and babies. . . .' But he disagreed. He protested he had no desire whatsoever for anything different than he had. He was comfortable as he was, he had the biggest mines in the state, land that he loved, vineyards with which he was well pleased, a woman he slept with every Saturday night, and Hannah to keep his house neat. He liked the men who worked for him, had friends in San Francisco he saw from time to time, and when he needed excitement he went on trips to the East, he had even been to Europe a few times. He needed absolutely nothing else, and certainly not a wife. He had Mary Ellen to meet those needs, once a week at least, and he smiled as he thought of her. Tomorrow he would go to see her after he left the mines . . . just as he always did. . . . He would leave the mine at noon, after locking up the safe himself, there was almost no one there on Saturday, and he would ride to Calistoga and let himself in to the tiny house. Years before he had been cautious about being seen, but they were no secret anymore, hadn't been in years, and she had long since hardened herself to what people said. It was none of their business what they said anyway, he had told her that himself, although it was a little more complicated than that, but not much now. And then he would stretch out in front of the fire, and look at the copper in her hair, or they would sit in the swing in her back yard, looking up at the big elm, hidden by the hedge, and he would hold her and. . . .

'Jeremiah!' Hannah's voice broke into his reverie. The sun was lost behind the hill and there was suddenly a chill in the air. 'Damn, boy! Don't you hear when I call?' He grinned at her, she treated him as though he were five years old, instead of forty-three.

'Sorry . . . I was thinking of something else.' . . . someone else . . . he looked into Hannah's wizened old face with a twinkle in his eyes.

'Trouble with you is you don't think at all . . . don't listen . . . don't hear. . . .'

'Maybe I'm getting deaf, ever think of that? I'm almost old enough.'

'Maybe so.' The twinkle in his eyes was met by the fire in hers. She was a feisty old woman, and he loved her that way. She had been giving him a bad time for years, and he counted on it. It was part of her charm, and an essential part of the banter between them. But now her face looked serious as she looked down at him from the porch. 'There's trouble at the Harte mine. Have you heard?'

Jeremiah's brows knit in an answering frown. 'No. What happened? Fire?' It was their greatest dread, all of them, they worked so closely with fire, and it could so easily explode into a costly disaster in the mines, taking countless lives as it ran wild. Jeremiah hated to think of it. But Hannah shook her head.

'They're not sure. Influenza, they think, but it could be something else. It's running like wildfire over there.' She hated to tell him that,

8

hated to stir up the memories of Jennie, no matter how long ago it was. Her voice was gentle as she went on. 'John Harte lost his wife today . . . and his little girl . . . and they say the boy is hard hit too. He may not live the night. . . .' There was a look of pain on Jeremiah's face as he turned away. He lit a cigar, stared silently into the night, and then turned to Hannah again. 'They've closed the mine.' The Harte Mines were the second biggest in the valley, second only to his.

'I'm sorry to hear about his wife, and the girl.' Jeremiah's voice was gruff when he spoke.

'They've lost seven men this week. They say thirty of them are down with it.' It sounded like the epidemic the year Jennie had died. There was nothing one could do. Nothing at all. Jeremiah had been with Jennie's father when she died. And they had sat silently in her parents' drawing room, as upstairs, her spirit fled, and there was nothing they could do except stare at each other in despair. Jeremiah felt his heart sink like a rock at the memory, and he couldn't even begin to imagine the grief of losing a child.

He wasn't fond of John Harte, but he admired him a great deal. Harte had fought hard and well to establish a decent mine, and it wasn't easy with the Thurston Mines breathing down his neck. He had a harder row to hoe than Jeremiah had when he started out. Harte had opened his mine four years before when he was twenty-two, and he had driven himself and his men beyond anything imaginable. He wasn't always kind, and Jeremiah had heard from men who had left him to come and work for him that he was irascible and difficult with a wicked mouth, and quick fists, one of the men who left him had said.

But he had a heart of gold. He was a decent, honest man, and Jeremiah admired him. He had gone to see him once or twice, and he too quickly saw some of the mistakes that the younger man was going to make, but Harte didn't want to hear any of Jeremiah's advice, in fact, he didn't want anything from him. He wanted to make it on his own, and he would, in time. But Jeremiah grieved for him now, at the cruelty Fate had dealt, even crueller than that once dealt to him. He looked at Hannah, not sure what he should do. He and John Harte had never become close friends. Harte preferred to view Jeremiah as a rival, and keep a good distance from him, and Jeremiah respected that. 'Don't fool yourself, Thurston, I'm not your friend, and I don't want to be. I want to beat your mine all to hell. And I'll do it fair and I'll do it clean, but if I can, you'll be closing your doors in a year or two, and everyone from here to New York will be buying from me.' Jeremiah had smiled at the blunt words. The fact was that there was room for both of them, but John Harte refused to see it that way. He was courteous when they met, but he wouldn't give an inch. He had already had two fires and a bad flood, and once, on a whim, Jeremiah had offered to buy him out, in answer to which John Harte had offered to flatten his face if he didn't get off his land by the count of ten. But these cruel strokes of fate had nothing to do with that intense rivalry and Jeremiah made up his mind as he strode suddenly toward his horse. Hannah had known he would. Jeremiah was simply that kind of compassionate man. He had room in his heart for everyone, even John Harte, no matter how impulsive or sharp the younger man's tongue was.

'Don't wait dinner for me.' The words didn't even need to be said as he swung a leg over his horse. She'd be there anyway, if she had to wait all night. 'Go home and get some rest.'

'Mind your own damn business, Jeremiah Thurston.' And then she had a sudden thought. 'Wait a minute!' They would be too frantic to fix much of anything to eat. She ran into the kitchen and threw some fried chicken into a napkin, and put that and some fruit and a piece of cake into a saddlebag which Jeremiah could carry with him. She rushed back outside and handed it up as Jeremiah smiled.

'You'll kill them for sure if it's something you cooked.'

She grinned at him. 'Be sure you eat some yourself, and take care you don't get too close to anyone. Don't drink anything, or eat their food.'

'Yes, Mother!' And with those words, he wheeled his horse and took off into the night, thinking his own thoughts, as he galloped over the hills.

It only took him twenty minutes to arrive at the complex surrounding the Harte Mines, and Jeremiah was surprised to see how much it had grown in the few months since he'd been there. John Harte was doing well, but one could tell that something was wrong now. There was an eerie silence, and no one wandering from house to house, but in each cabin, all of the lights were brightly lit, especially up on the hill. Every room of the main house seemed ablaze with light and there was a string of men standing outside, waiting to pay their respects to John Harte. Jeremiah dismounted and tied his horse to a tree a little distance from them, and carrying the saddlebag Hannah had flung up into his hands, he took his place behind the line of men. He was rapidly recognized, and a whisper went through them . . . Thurston . . . Thurston. . . . He shook hands with those he knew, and it was a little while before John Harte appeared on the porch. His face was ravaged, and there was almost a shudder of sympathy that went through the crowd of men below him. He glanced at them, recognizing each one, nodding as their eyes met, and then he saw Jeremiah at the end of the line, and he stopped and looked at him, as Jeremiah approached and held out a hand. And something in his eyes said that he understood the other man's pain. The others seemed to move back, so as to leave the two men alone, and Jeremiah held out a hand to him.

'I'm sorry about your wife, John . . . I . . . I lost someone I cared about a great deal a long time ago . . . the epidemic of '68. . . .' They were jumbled words but John Harte knew that Jeremiah understood. He looked up at him with eyes bright with tears. He was a fine looking young man, almost as tall as Jeremiah was as they stood facing each other. He had raven black hair, eyes that were almost as black as coal, and huge, gentle hands. In some ways, the two men were oddly alike, despite the gap of almost twenty years between them.

'Thank you for coming, man.' His voice was deep and jagged with grief as two tears ran unashamedly down the younger man's cheeks. Jeremiah could feel an echo of the old pain in his own heart as he saw them.

'Is there anything I can do?' He remembered the food he had brought. Perhaps someone in the house could make use of it.

John Harte looked deep into his eyes. 'I lost seven men today, and Matilda . . . Jane. . . .' His voice broke on the words. 'Barnaby's . . . .' He couldn't finish what he started to say, at the mention of his son. He looked up at Jeremiah again. 'The doctor said he won't live through the night. And three of the other men have lost their wives . . . five children. . . . You shouldn't even be here.' He suddenly realized the risk Jeremiah had run, and was touched by that too.

'I've lived through it before, and I wanted to see if there was anything I could do for you.' He noticed that the younger man was deathly pale, but he suspected that it was grief and not the dreaded flu. 'You look as though you could use a drink.' He pulled a silver flask from the saddle bag he had brought and extended it to John.

He hesitated, took it, and then nodded toward the door of his home. 'Do you want to come in?' He wondered if he was afraid, he should have been, but Jeremiah nodded his head.

'Sure. I brought you some food, if you think you can eat.' John looked at him, both surprised and touched, particularly since the last time Jeremiah had offered his help, John had almost thrown him out. He didn't want any help from him. But this was a different kind of disaster than a fire or a flood at the mine. He sat down heavily on the tufted green velvet couch in his living room, and took a long drink from the flask and then handed it back to Jeremiah, staring at the older man with unseeing eyes.

'I can't believe they're gone . . . last night. . . .' He started to gulp, fighting back his own tears. . . . 'Last night . . . Jane came running downstairs to kiss me goodnight even with her fever . . . and this morning Matilda said . . . Matilda said. . . .' He couldn't hold the flood back anymore, and it came, as Jeremiah held his shoulders in both hands and held him there as he cried. There was nothing he or anyone could do, except be there for him. He looked up at Jeremiah at last, and Jeremiah's eyes were damp too. 'How can I go on without them? How?. . . . Mattie . . . my little girl . . . and if Barnaby . . . Thurston, I'll die. I can't live without them.' Jeremiah silently prayed that he wouldn't lose the boy, but he knew that there was a good chance that he would. He had heard as he stood outside that the boy was pretty badly off. But he looked hard into John Harte's eyes now.

'You're young yet, John, there's a long life ahead, and it's a terrible thing to say to you tonight but you may marry again, have other children. Right now, this is the worst thing that's ever happened to you, but you'll go on . . . you have to . . . and you will.' He handed him the flask again, and John took another sip, shaking his head, as the tears coursed down his cheeks.

And it was less than an hour later, when the doctor came for him. John jumped up as though he'd been shot.

'Barnaby?'

'He's calling for you.' The doctor didn't dare say more, but his eyes met Jeremiah's as John raced up the stairs to his son, and in answer to the question in Jeremiah's eyes, he only shook his head.

Jeremiah sat downstairs, he knew instantly from the terrible moan of pain he heard from the little room at the top of the stairs that the boy was gone. John Harte knelt with the boy in his arms keening for the family he had lost in two short days. With a determined step Jeremiah walked solemnly up the stairs, and gently opened the door to the room. Thurston took the boy from him at last, laid him on the bed, closed his eyes, and led John Harte from the room as he sobbed the child's name. He forced strong drink down his throat and stayed with him until the next morning, when his brother and several other friends came, and then Jeremiah quietly went home, aching for him. He was exactly the same age Jeremiah had been when Jennie had died. He wondered how it would affect Harte, but he suspected from the little he knew of him that the boy would press on.

He grieved for him now, and when he dismounted in front of his own house, with the morning sun climbing high into the sky, he looked out over the hills he loved so much and wondered at the cruel fate which could deal life and death so easily . . . how swiftly life's sweetest gifts are gone . . . he seemed to hear Jennie's laughter ringing in his ears as he went inside, and saw Hannah asleep in a kitchen chair. He said nothing to her as he walked past her into the parlor he never used, and sat down at the piano he had brought so long ago for the girl with the laughing eyes and the dancing golden curls – lovely, she had been. He wondered what it would have been like to be married to her – how many children they might have had – it was the first time in a long time that he had allowed his mind to run along those lines; he thought of John Harte's lost daughter and son, and hoped he would marry again soon. That was what he needed now, a new wife to fill his heart, and new babies to replace the two who had died.

And yet it wasn't what Jeremiah had done. He had remained alone for the past eighteen years, and it was too late now. He would never change that. He had no desire to. But as he sat looking down at the piano keys, yellowing now, never touched, never used, he wondered if he should have done what he thought John Harte should do. Should he have married someone else? Had a dozen children to fill his empty house? But there had never been anyone who captured his heart, no one he liked well enough to marry. No, there would be no children for him. But as he thought the words to himself, he felt a shaft of grief slice through his heart. . . . A child would have been so

13

nice . . . a daughter . . . a son . . . and then suddenly, he remembered the two John Harte had lost, and he felt something inside him close tight. No. He couldn't bear another loss. He had lost Jennie. That was enough. He was better off like this . . . wasn't he?

'What happened?' He was startled to hear Hannah's voice, and he looked up to see her standing in the empty room, as he fingered the piano keys. He stopped and looked at her, tired, depressed. It had been a long, sad night.

'Harte's boy died.' He almost winced as he remembered closing the boy's eyes and taking John Harte forcibly from the room. Hannah shook her head and began to cry. Jeremiah walked slowly to her, put an arm around her shoulders and led her from the room. There was nothing left to say. 'Go home and get some sleep.'

She looked up at him and sniffed as she wiped the tears from her cheeks. 'You should do the same.' But she knew him better than that. 'Will you?'

'I've got some work to do at the mine.'

'It's Saturday.'

'The papers on my desk don't know that,' he smiled tiredly. There was no way he could go to bed and sleep. He would have been haunted by the vision of Barnaby Harte. 'I won't work too long.' She knew that too. It was Saturday. He went to Calistoga on Saturdays, to see Mary Ellen Browne. But she could see that today he wasn't much in the mood.

He poured himself a cup of coffee from the pot on the stove and looked at his old friend. There were a thousand thoughts running through his head after the night before. 'I told him he should get married again, and have more children. Was I wrong?'

She shook her head. 'You should have done the same for yourself eighteen years ago.'

'I just thought of that.' He looked out the window at the hills. He never let her put up curtains anywhere because he loved the view of the valley so much, and there was no one within miles to look in.

'It's not too late.' Her voice was old and sad. She was sorry for him. He was a lonely man, whether he knew it or not, and she hoped that John Harte would not choose the same fate now. It seemed wrong to her. She had never had children herself, but for her it had been destiny not choice. 'You're still young enough to marry, Jeremiah.'

14

But he laughed at the words. 'I'm too old for that now. And he frowned as he thought and met her eyes again. They were both thinking the same thing. 'I never really could imagine being married to Mary Ellen, and there's no one else. Hasn't been for years.' Hannah already knew that he only went to Mary Ellen, but after the night he'd just been through, he needed to talk to her and she understood that too. She was his friend.

'Why didn't you ever want to marry her?' She had always wondered that, although she thought she knew. And she wasn't far wrong.

'She isn't that kind of girl, Hannah. And I don't mean that meanly. She didn't really want to marry me at first, though lately I think she would. She wanted to be free,' he smiled, 'she's an independent little cuss, and she wanted to take care of her own kids. I think she was afraid people would say she married me for what I had, or that she tried to take advantage of me.' He sighed. 'Instead they called her a whore. But the funny thing is that I don't think she minded that as much. She always said that as long as she knew the truth, that she was a decent woman and that there was only me, then she didn't give a damn what people said. I asked her to marry me once.' Hannah looked stunned at his words, and he grinned, 'and she turned me down. It was when those damn women in Calistoga gave her such a bad time, I always thought her mother started that fuss to force my hand, and maybe she did, but Mary Ellen told me to go to hell back then. She said she wouldn't be forced into marriage by a bunch of old bags. And I think she was still kind of half in love with her drunk of a husband in those days. He had left her more than two years before, but she always hoped he'd come back. I could tell by the way she talked.' And then he smiled again. 'I'm glad he didn't. She's been good for me.'

And he'd been good to her too. He had furnished her house, and helped her with things she needed for the kids, when she'd accept the gifts. They had been together now for close to seven years, and her husband had been dead now for more than two. They were used to the arrangement they had. He rode to Calistoga every Saturday night and stayed with her there. The children stayed at her mother's house when he was there, and they were less clandestine about their affair now than they had once been. There was no reason to hide it anymore, everyone in town knew that she was Jeremiah Thurston's

15

woman . . . Thurston's Whore they had called her at one point, but no one dared to say that anymore. Jeremiah had personally taken care of it with one or two. But he also knew that Mary Ellen was just that kind of girl. She was the kind of girl that women would always dislike and be jealous of, she had flashy red-headed good looks, long legs and full breasts. She wore her dresses too low and was too willing to give a passing cowboy a glimpse of leg as she stepped off the curb and lifted her skirts well above her ankles. It was that which had drawn Jeremiah to her at first, and she had proven to be as lovely as he had hoped when he had dispensed with the rest of her clothes. She was so lovely in fact that he had swiftly come back for more, and then again, and then he had discovered how kind-hearted she was, how decent, and anxious to please. She loved her children more than anything in the world, and there was almost nothing she wouldn't do for them. She had been deserted by her husband two years before and had worked as a waitress, a dancer and a chambermaid at the hotel attached to the spa. Even after her alliance with Jeremiah, she had continued to hold down the same jobs. She insisted that she wanted nothing from him. And several times, Jeremiah had attempted to dismiss her from his mind, but there was something so tender and warm about the girl. She filled an empty spot in his heart, and he was constantly drawn to her bed for more. In the early days, he had ridden up to Calistoga several times during the week, but it was too complicated with her children in the house, and they had made their week-end arrangements at the end of the first year. It was difficult to believe that six years had passed since then. Even more so when once in a while he caught a glimpse of her children. Mary Ellen herself was thirty-two now, and she was still a handsome girl, but he still couldn't imagine marrying her. She had been too worldly when they'd met, too brazen, too used, and yet he loved her honesty and her openness and her courage. She had never backed off because of what people said about her involvement with Jeremiah, although he knew that at times it had been difficult for her.

'Would you marry her now?' He didn't shrink from Hannah's question, but even now, after seven years, he couldn't imagine marrying Mary Ellen.

'I don't know.' He sighed as he looked at the old woman. 'I really am too old to be thinking of that sort of thing, don't you think?' It was a rhetorical question, but Hannah was quick to answer.

'No, I don't. And I think you should give it some thought before it is too late, Jeremiah Thurston.' But she herself didn't think that Mary Ellen was the answer, much as she liked the girl. She had known her all her life, and had always thought her forward and at times downright foolish, she had been among the first to call her a fool for her open affair with Jeremiah. She was a good-hearted girl and it was impossible not to like her. But nonetheless she was thirty-two years old, and he needed a young wife who would give him children. Mary Ellen already had three of her own and had almost died when giving birth to the last one. She'd have been crazy to try it again and she knew it. 'I'd like to see a child in this house before I die, Jeremiah,' Hannah said.

He smiled sadly, thinking of the two Harte children who had just died. 'So would I, my friend, but I don't think either of us will ever see that.' It was the first time he had ever said that to her, or to anyone.

'Don't be so stubborn. You've got time. If you looked, you'd find the right girl.' Hannah's words brought Jennie back to mind, and he shook his head, as much to push her from his mind as in answer to her words.

'I'm too old for a young girl. I'm almost forty-four years old.'

'Well, you sound like you're ninety.' She snorted in disgust and he laughed, running a hand over the beard stubble on his face.

'I feel damn close to that some days, look like it too. It's a wonder Mary Ellen doesn't lock the door when she sees me coming.'

'She should have done that years ago, Jeremiah, but you know how I feel about that.' He did, but Hannah was never afraid to repeat her opinions. 'You were both foolish to start that, and you've both paid a damn high price for it.'

It was the first time she had voiced it quite that way and Jeremiah looked surprised. 'Both of us?'

'She damn near got run out of town on a rail, and you've given up the chance to marry someone who'd give you children. You might as well marry her if you're going to do that, Jeremiah.'

He smiled benignly at Hannah. 'I'll tell her you said so.' Hannah harrumphed and picked up her shawl from the back of a kitchen chair as Jeremiah watched her. He was going to shave and bathe before going to the mine, and he needed another cup of strong black coffee. It had been a long, long night with John Harte until his

17

relatives arrived to console him. 'By the way, John was grateful for the food you sent, Hannah. I made him eat it this morning.'

'Did he sleep at all?' Jeremiah shook his head. How could he? 'And I know you didn't either.'

'I'll be alright. I'll sleep tonight.'

She grinned wickedly at him and turned to look at him from the doorway. 'That don't say much for Mary Ellen, does it?' He laughed and the old woman closed the door behind her.

Chapter Two

There was an eerie silence about the mines on Saturday, which pleased him. All was stillness, there were no voices, no shrill whistles, no blasting of the furnaces. There were two watchmen drinking coffee in the March morning, as Jeremiah dismounted and tied up Big Joe in his usual place and strode into his office. The papers he had come in to look at were waiting for him, contracts for the quicksilver they produced, and plans for four more cabins to house the men who worked for him. Already, the mine had the appearance of a small town, with seven houses for the men and cabins beyond for those who had brought their families to live with them. It was a hard life for them, but Jeremiah was sympathetic to their need to be together. It was a decision he had made a long time ago, and the men were grateful to him. Now he sat looking at plans for still more accommodation for them. The complex seemed to be growing by leaps and bounds, as was the production of the mines. He was pleased by the contracts he had before him, in particular the one from Orville Beauchamp in Atlanta for nine hundred flasks of quicksilver, amounting to some fifty thousand dollars. Beauchamp would in turn be supplying most of the South. He was a clever businessman, Jeremiah could tell from the contract. He represented a group of seven men and apparently was their spokesman. The deal was important enough that, in another week, Jeremiah would be travelling to Atlanta to meet the consortium and cement the deal with them.

At noon, Jeremiah looked at his pocket watch, stood up and stretched. He still had work to do but it had been such a rough night that he was suddenly exhausted and hungry to see Mary Ellen. He needed her warmth and her comfort. Again and again, he had thought of John Harte and the family he had lost. The sympathy Jeremiah felt weighed on him like a boulder, and as the morning wore on, the thoughts of Mary Ellen pressed in on him. It was just after twelve when he left the mines that morning and walked outside to where he had left Big Joe tethered.

'Morning, Mr. Thurston,' one of the guards waved to him, and further up the hillside Jeremiah could see a group of children playing in the distance, behind the family cabins he had built for the miners. It made him think of the influenza epidemic at the Harte Mines, and he prayed it wouldn't touch them.

'Good morning, Tom.' There were some five hundred men who worked for him in three mines now, but he still knew most of them by name. He spent most of his time at the first mine, the Thurston Mine, but toured the others regularly, and knew that they were in the hands of extremely competent foremen. And at the slightest suggestion of a problem, Jeremiah was on the spot himself, sometimes for days, if there was an accident or the mines flooded, as they did every winter.

'Looks like Spring is here.'

'It sure does.' Jeremiah smiled. It had rained for two solid months, and the flooding in the mines had been ghastly. They had lost eleven men at one mine, seven at the other, three here. It had been a rough winter, but there was no sign of it now as the sun shone brightly down on them, and Jeremiah could feel it warming his back as he rode old Joe along the Silverado Trail to Calistoga. Jeremiah urged him on, and the big horse picked up his hooves and literally flew the last five miles. As Jeremiah rode, with the wind in his beard and his hair, he thought of Mary Ellen.

As he drove down the main street of Calistoga, there were clusters of ladies strolling together, protected by lace parasols. It was easy to spot those who had come from San Francisco to visit the hotsprings: their fashionable dresses were in sharp contrast to the simpler costumes of the locals, their bustles were pronounced, the plumage on their bonnets was lavish, the textures of their silks noticeable in sleepy little Calistoga. It always made Jeremiah smile to see them, and they were quick to notice him as he rode past them, astride his white stallion, with his own raven hair in sharp contrast. When he was in a particularly playful mood, he would doff his hat and bow politely from his mount, his eyes always dancing with mischief. There was one particularly pretty woman in the cluster today, a woman with reddish hair and a forest green silk dress, the color of the trees on the mountains, but her coloring only served to remind him of

20

why he had come to Calistoga, and he spurred his horse on a little more quickly, and it was only moments later that he reached Mary Ellen's small, tidy house on 3rd Street in the less fashionable part of town.

Here the smell of sulphur from the spa was strongest, but she had grown used to it long since, as had Jeremiah. It was not the spa, or the sulphur, or even his mines he thought of as he tied Big Joe up behind the house and ran quickly up the back steps. He knew that she would be waiting and he opened the door without ceremony with a faint pounding of his heart. Whatever he felt or didn't feel for this woman, one thing was certain, when she was near him she still had the same magical power over him she had had when they first met. There was a kind of breathlessness he felt, a surge of lust he had felt for few women before her. Yet when he was away from her, he was so easily able to do without her. It was for that reason that he never had any serious inclination to change his status. But when he was near her . . . when he felt her presence in the next room, as he did now, all of his senses suddenly raced with desire for her.

'Mary Ellen?' He opened the door to the little front parlor where she sometimes waited for him on Saturday afternoons. She would drop the children off at her mother's in the morning and then return to the house to bathe and curl her hair and put on her prettiest finery. There was a kind of honeymoon aura to their meeting, because they only saw each other once a week, or if something went wrong in one of the mines, or he went away, then it was longer. She hated it when he was gone. Every moment of the night and day, she waited for their weekends together. It was odd how, over the years, she was becoming more and more dependent on him. But she was sure that he hadn't noticed. He was too intent on his physical attraction to her to be aware of her decreasing independence. He liked coming to Calistoga to see her. He was comfortable in the shabby little house, and besides, he had never invited her to stay with him in St. Helena. In fact, she had only seen the house once. 'You sure he's not married?' her mother had questioned her often at first, but everyone knew that Jeremiah Thurston had never been married, 'and probably never will,' her mother growled after the first few years of her daughter's liaison. Now she no longer growled. After seven years of Saturday nights, what was there to say? She said nothing now as she took the children in, her oldest granddaughter at fourteen being almost as old as Mary Ellen had been herself when she got married. The boy was twelve, and the youngest girl was nine. It was she who particularly adored Jeremiah. But they knew enough not to say too much to Grandma.

'Mary Ellen?' Jeremiah called upstairs again. It was unusual for her not to be waiting for him downstairs, and he made his way slowly upstairs to the three tiny bedrooms, one for herself, one for her daughters and the third for her son, and all of them put together smaller than any one room in Jeremiah's house. But Jeremiah had long since ceased to feel guilty about it. Mary Ellen took a peculiar kind of pride in supporting her own, and she wasn't unhappy in this house. She liked it. Probably better than she would have liked living in his. Hers had more warmth to it, or so he thought. His had always remained a large, uninhabited house, ever since he built it. He occupied so few of its rooms. It had been a house built for children and laughter and noise, and instead it had been silent for almost twenty years, unlike this house which showed signs of wear and caring and small fingers dragged along once pink walls until the smudges became part of the decor and one no longer noticed.

Jeremiah's tread was heavy on the stairs, and he thought he smelled roses in the air as he knocked on her bedroom door. He heard the familiar voice humming in the distance. She was there, for one crazy moment he had wondered if today, for the first time in seven years, she wouldn't be there. But she was. And he needed her so badly. He knocked softly, feeling hesitant and young. She had a way of doing that to him. He always felt a little bit breathless when he came to see her.

'Mary Ellen?' This time his voice was gentle and soft, almost a caress, as it reached her.

'Come in . . . I'm in . . .' She was about to say, 'my bedroom', but she didn't need to add the words as he stepped in, his very presence seeming to stop the blood in her veins as she looked up at him, her skin as creamy as the white roses next to her bed, her hair coppery in the sunlight which streamed through the windows. She had just been about to drop a lace dress over the lace corset she wore, tied with pink ribbons which ran through the lace and tied her pantaloons at the knee. She looked like a young girl as he stared at her, and suddenly she blushed crimson and turned away, struggling with the dress as it tangled at her shoulders. She was usually ready when he arrived, but

22

she had taken longer than she'd planned cutting the roses to put in her bedroom. 'I'm almost . . . I just . . . oh for Heaven's sake . . . I can't!' She was all innocence as she fought with the tangles of lace and he walked toward her to pull the dress gently over her shoulders, but as he began, the gesture suddenly changed direction and he found himself slowly pulling the dress back in the direction from which it had come, pulling it past the silky copper hair and over her head, flinging it onto the bed, and pressing his lips down on hers as he pulled her toward him. It was remarkable to him how hungry he was for her each week when he arrived, seeming to drink in the cream of her flesh, and the rose scent of her hair. Everything about her always seemed to be scented with roses and she had a way of making him forget that she had any life but this. The children and the jobs and the struggles were all forgotten as she lay in his arms, week after week, year after year, looking into the eyes that she loved, and that never quite understood how much she loved him. But she knew him as well as he knew himself. He wanted his solitude, his freedom, his vine-yards and his mines, he didn't want an everyday life with an everyday woman and three children he hadn't sired. He was too busy for that, wrapped up in the empire he had built and was still building. And she respected him for what he was and loved him enough not to ask for what he didn't want to give her. Instead she took only what he gave: one night a week, in a kind of abandon they would have never shared had they had a daily life, which enhanced their passion still further. She wondered sometimes if things might have been different if she could have had his baby, but there was no point thinking about that. She couldn't have another one. The doctor said it was too dangerous to even consider, and he didn't seem to want one, at least he'd never mentioned it to her although he was always kind to her children when he saw them. But it was not her children he thought of when he came here. It was what he saw now that filled his mind and seemed to drown his senses, that rose scented skin, as delicate as parchment, the green eyes like emeralds burning into his as he laid her gently on the bed and began to unlace the pink corset. It fell away from her body with surprising ease beneath his expert fingers and the pantaloons slipped away from her long, graceful limbs until she lay naked and gleaming before him. This was what he came for . . . to devour her with his eyes and his tongue and his hands until she lay gasping and breathless beneath him aching for him to take her. And today he wanted her even more than he had in a long time, it was as though he couldn't get enough of her, couldn't quite breathe deeply enough of the heady aroma of her hair and her flesh and her perfume. He wanted to push away the memories of his long dead fiancée, and the grief-filled night he had spent with John Harte and he needed Mary Ellen to help him do that. She sensed that he had had a difficult week, although she didn't know why, and as always she tried to give him something more of herself to fill the void she instinctively felt in him. She wasn't a woman who could have easily put her impressions into words, and yet she had a deep, almost animal, understanding of him.

Lying sleepy and sated in his arms, she looked up at him and gently touched his beard. 'Are you alright, Jeremiah?'

He smiled at how well she knew him. 'I am now . . . thanks to you . . . you're awfully good to me, Mary Ellen . . .'

She was pleased by his words, as though he understood what she tried to give him. 'Was something wrong?'

He hesitated for a long time. What he felt about the night before seemed to be strangely intertwined with feelings about Jennie, and yet that was so long ago, it seemed strange that the feelings should resurface now. But it was all so reminiscent of eighteen years ago. 'I had a rough night last night. I was with John Harte . . .'

She looked instantly surprised, and propped herself up beside him on her elbow. 'I didn't think you two spoke.'

'I went over there last night. He lost his wife, and his daughter . . .' He hesitated and closed his eyes, remembering little Barnaby's face again after he had died . . . '. . . and his boy, after I got there . . . I got there . . .' A tear slid unbidden down his face, Mary Ellen gently touched it and then took Jeremiah in her arms. He was so big and so strong and so much a man, yet he was so gentle and kind. She loved him more for the tear and for those which followed it as she held him. 'He was so young . . .' He began to sob for the child whose eyes he had closed, and he held Mary Ellen close to him, embarrassed at the emotions he could no longer hold back coming from a place deep inside him. 'The poor boy lost all three of them in one day . . .' The flood began to ebb and he sat up in bed and looked at Mary Ellen.

'It was nice of you to go to him, Jeremiah, you didn't have to do it.'

'I knew how he felt.' She knew about Jennie from Hannah when they talked. Hannah had known Mary Ellen since she was a child and they met frequently at the produce market in Calistoga. But Jeremiah

24

had never mentioned Jennie to her himself. 'Something like that happened to me once.'

'I know.' Her voice was as soft as the rose petals beside her bed.

'I thought you did.' He smiled at her and wiped his face. 'I'm sorry . . .' He was embarrassed now, but he felt better than he had all day. She was good for him and she had helped him. 'Poor lad, it's going to be so rough for him.'

'He'll be all right.' Jeremiah nodded and then looked at her.

'Do you know him?'

She shook her head. 'I've seen him around town, but we've never spoken. I hear he's as stubborn as a mule and he can be twice as mean. Men like that don't usually break, no matter what happens to them.'

'I don't think he's really mean. I think he's just very young and very strong and he wants what he wants when he wants it.' Jeremiah smiled. 'I wouldn't want to work for the man, but I admire what he's done.'

Mary Ellen shrugged. She was not greatly interested in John Harte. She was far more interested in Jeremiah Thurston. 'I admire you.' She smiled, and moved closer to him.

'I don't know what for. I'm the old mule you were talking about before.'

'But you're my mule, and I love you.' She liked saying things like that, as much to reassure herself as to say it to him. He had never really been hers, and she knew it, but once a week she was allowed to pretend, and she was satisfied with that. She didn't really have much choice. He had offered to marry her once, but she hadn't wanted to then, and now the moment had passed. He was content with seeing her once a week. Now that Jake was dead, and he was never coming back, she would have married Jeremiah gladly, but she knew that he was never going to offer her marriage now. He didn't want that anymore, and she had long since given up that hope. She had been a damn fool not to press for that from the beginning. But she had thought Jake was coming back then . . . the drunken sonofa-bitch. . . .

'What were you thinking about just then?' He had been watching her face. 'You looked angry.'

She laughed at how perceptive he was; he always had been. 'Nothing important.'

'Are you mad at me?' She was quick to shake her head with a gentle

25

smile. He rarely ever gave her reason to be angry at him. Jake had been a different story. What a bastard he had been. But he was dead now, and she had wasted fifteen years of her life on him, five of them waiting for him to come back when it turned out he'd been living with another woman in Ohio. She'd found that out after he died and the girl came to see her. He'd even had two little boys by her. And Mary Ellen had felt like a damn fool. She had always held back from Jeremiah, thinking her husband would return . . . husband . . . that was a joke . . .

'I'm never angry at you, silly. You never give me reason to be.' It was true. He was a lovely man and he had always been good to her. Almost too good. He was generous and polite and thoughtful, but he also kept a certain distance between them and he held out no hope for the future. There was just today, and next week, and seven years of Saturdays stretched out behind them. But it didn't make Mary Ellen angry, only sad from time to time.

'I'm going away soon.' He always told her ahead of time, it was just the way he was. Considerate and decent and thoughtful.

'Where to this time?'

'The South. Atlanta.' He often went to New York, and once the year before he had gone to Charleston, South Carolina. But he never invited her to go with him. Business was business. And this was something else. 'I won't be gone too long. Just long enough to get there and back, and do business for a few days. Maybe two weeks in all.' He nuzzled her neck and then kissed her. 'Will you miss me?'

'What do you think?' Her voice was muffled by desire and they slid back down into the bed together.

'I think I'm crazy to go anywhere, that's what I think . . .' And he proved it to her again as she lay in his arms, and writhed with pleasure, and her screams of exquisite agony would have been heard by the entire neighborhood if he hadn't had the forethought to close the windows.

By the next morning, he felt like a new man as she cooked him sausages and eggs, a small steak and cornbread on the old stove in her kitchen. He had offered to buy her a new one the previous winter, but she had insisted that she didn't need one. Greed was simply not part of her make-up, much to her mother's chagrin. She frequently reminded her daughter that Jeremiah was one of the richest men in the state and she was the biggest fool that ever lived. But she didn't

26

give a damn. She had everything she wanted . . . almost . . . or once a week anyway, and that was better than every day with a lesser man. She had no complaints, and she was free to do as she chose. Jeremiah never asked what she did with the rest of her time. She saw no one else and hadn't for years, but it was by her own choice. If someone else had come along who was serious about her, she could have pursued it. Jeremiah was careful to demand nothing at all from her.

'When do you leave for the East?' She ate the cornbread as she watched his face. He had wonderful blue eyes, and when he looked at her she felt her soul turn to jelly.

'In a few days.' He smiled, feeling restored. He had slept well, but not before making love to her for several hours. 'I'll let you know as soon as I'm back.'

'Just be sure you don't meet the girl of your dreams in Atlanta.'

'Why would I do a thing like that?' He picked up his mug of coffee and laughed. 'After last night, how can you even say such a thing?'

She smiled with pleasure. 'You never know.'

'Don't be silly.' He leaned over and kissed the tip of her nose, and as she leaned toward him, her cleavage beckoned him. She was wearing a pink satin dressing gown he had bought her on his last trip to Europe to visit the French vineyards. And now he slid a hand down beneath her breasts and felt them grasp his fingers warmly. It sent a shiver through his entire body, which he could not resist, and he put down his cup and walked around the table to her. 'What was that you were saying, Mary Ellen? . . .' His voice was a hoarse whisper as he scooped her up in his arms and headed toward the stairs with his irresistible bundle.

'I said . . . don't go . . .' But he crushed her words with his lips and, moments later, deposited her on her bed again, pulling the satin robe away from her naked flesh with ease. It was difficult to tell where the robe ended and the silk of her flesh began, so smooth did her skin feel to his touch as he pressed his own body against hers and entered her again, and once again their pleasure began and went on until dusk when he rode home on his horse at last, tired, happy and sated. Mary Ellen Browne had served him well, and the sorrows of the night before were all but forgotten as he stabled the horse in his barn in Saint Helena. When he walked inside the house, he barely had the strength to take off his clothes. When he did, he could still smell the roses of her perfume on his flesh, and he went to sleep smiling and thinking of Mary Ellen.

Chapter Three

'Make sure you behave yourself while you're gone.' Hannah glared at him and wagged a finger as though he were a child as Jeremiah laughed at her.

'You sound just like Mary Ellen.'

'Maybe we both know you too well.'

'All right, all right, I'll behave!' He looked tired as he pinched her cheek. It had been a rough week, and she knew it. He had been to the funeral of John Harte's wife and two children. And now there were a few cases of the dread influenza at the Thurston Mines, but so far no one had died, and Jeremiah was forcing everyone to be seen by the doctor at the first sign of a problem. He would have liked to put off his trip to the East, but he couldn't. Orville Beauchamp had insisted, in his response to the telegram Jeremiah sent him, that if he wanted to make the deal, Thurston had to come now. Jeremiah had almost told him to go to hell, he felt like giving the deal to John Harte, but Harte was in no condition to discuss business, let alone go East. So Jeremiah decided to go ahead and take the train to Atlanta, but he wasn't looking forward to the trip. There continued to be something about the man in Georgia which annoyed him.

He bent and kissed the top of Hannah's head as he left, glanced around the cozy kitchen, picked up his leather bag in one hand, and his battered black leather briefcase in the other, his cigar clenched in his teeth, and his eyes squinting from the smoke. There was a big black hat pulled low over his eyes and he looked almost devilish as he walked quickly to the waiting carriage, flinging his bags on and hopped up beside the boy who drove the horses and quickly taking the reins from him.

'Good morning, sir.'

'Good morning, son.' He blew a thick cloud of smoke around him and touched the horses with a flick of the whip. A moment later they were off, moving at a handsome pace down the main highway. He said nothing to the boy as he drove, his mind already involved with the deal he would be completing in Atlanta. The boy watched him with utter fascination, the narrowed eyes, the deep lines beside them, the brow furrowed in concentration, the elegant hat, the broad shoulders, the huge hands, and the sheer cleanliness of him. The boy thought he was too clean to have been a miner, yet they said that he used to work in the mines himself. It was hard to imagine this powerful, enormous man ever squeezing himself into a mine. He seemed bigger than that to the boy as he watched him.

They were halfway to Napa before Jeremiah turned and smiled at him. 'How old are you, son?'

'Twelve.' It was exciting just being here beside him, and the boy liked the smell of his cigar. It seemed pungent and manly to him. 'Well . . . I'll be twelve in May.'

'You work hard in the mines?'

'Yes, sir.' The voice trembled slightly, but Jeremiah wasn't checking up on him, only thinking back to his own life at twelve.

'I worked in the mines at your age too. It's hard work for a boy . . . for anyone for that matter. Do you like it?'

There was a long pause, and then suddenly the boy decided to be honest. He trusted the huge man with the cigar; he had an appealing air of kindness about him. 'No sir, I don't. It's dirty work. I want to do something different when I grow up.'

'Like what?' Jeremiah was intrigued with the boy himself and with his honesty.

'Something clean. Like work in a bank maybe. My Dad says that's a weak man's job, but I think I might like it. I'm good with figures. I can do all my sums in my head faster than most people can write them.'

'Can you?' Jeremiah attempted to keep a serious look on his face, but his eyes showed that he was amused. There was such an intensity about the youth and it touched him. 'Would you like to help me sometime on a Saturday morning?'

'Help you?' The boy looked stunned. 'Oh, yes sir!'

'I come in on Saturdays until about noon, because it's quiet. When I come back, come and see me some Saturday morning. You can help me with some figures and accounting sheets. I'm not as quick with my sums as you are.' Jeremiah laughed. The boy's black eyes were suddenly as big as quarters. 'How does that sound to you?'

'Wonderful! . . . wonderful!. . . .' He practically bounced up and down on the seat beside Jeremiah, and then suddenly subdued himself, remembering to assume a more manly demeanour, and that amused Jeremiah too. He liked the boy. In fact, he liked most children, and they liked him. And as he urged the horses on toward Napa, he found himself thinking of Mary Ellen's children. They were nice and she did a good job with them. There was a lot on her shoulders, and he knew it, yet she never let him help her. And he certainly never had as far as the children were concerned. His only contact with them was for an occasional Sunday afternoon picnic. He wasn't there when they were sick or when they caused trouble in school, when she had to nurse a sick baby, or spank them or hold them. He only saw them in their Sunday best, and that not very often. He wondered if he had failed her by not helping her with the children more, but she didn't seem to expect that from him. She expected nothing more than what she got, his body meshed with her own in exquisite pleasure two days a week in the little house in Calistoga. And then suddenly, as though he thought the boy could read his mind, Jeremiah glanced worriedly over at him as they drove to Napa.

'You like girls, son?' He didn't know the boy's name and didn't want to ask him. He didn't really need to know, and he knew whose child he was, it was one of his most trusted workers at the mines, a man who had nine other children, most of them girls, as Jeremiah recalled. This boy was one of three that worked at Thurston Mines and he was the youngest.

The boy shrugged in answer to Jeremiah's question about girls. 'Most of them are dumb. I've got seven sisters, and most of them are just plain stupid.' Jeremiah laughed at the answer.

'Not all women are stupid. Believe me, boy, a lot fewer of them are than we'd like to think. A *lot* fewer!' He laughed out loud and drew hard on the cigar. There was certainly nothing stupid about Hannah or Mary Ellen or most of the other women he knew. In fact, they were even smart about covering up just how smart they were. He liked that in a woman, a pretense of helplessness and simplicity, when in fact there was a razor sharp mind beneath. It amused him to play the game. Suddenly he realized that maybe that was why he had never really wanted to marry Mary Ellen. She didn't really play the game. She was direct and straight-forward and loving and sensual as hell, but there was no mystery about her. He knew exactly what he was getting, he knew just how bright she was and no more . . . there was no guesswork, no further discovery concealed beneath lace, and that had always been something that appealed to him, though in recent years he seemed to like more complexity than he once had and wondered if it was a sign of old age. The thought amused him. He looked over at the boy again, with a knowing smile. 'There's nothing as pretty as a pretty woman, boy,' and then he laughed again, 'except maybe a rolling green hill with a field of wildflowers on it.' He was looking at one now, and it tore at his heart as they drove past it. He hated leaving this land to go East. There would be a piece missing from his life, from his soul, until he returned here. 'Do you like the land, son?'

The boy looked unimpressed, not sure what he meant, and then decided to play it safe. He had been brazen enough for one morning, and now he had the promise of Saturday mornings to protect. 'Yes.' But Jeremiah knew from the empty way he said the word that he understood nothing of what Jeremiah meant . . . the land . . . the land . . . the soil . . . he still remembered the thrill that used to run through him at the boy's age as he picked up a handful of soil and squeezed it in his hand . . . 'That's yours, son, yours . . . all of it . . . take good care of it always. . .' His father's voice echoed in his ears. It had started with something so small and had grown. He had added and improved and now he owned vast lands in a valley he loved. That had to be born into your soul, bred into you, it wasn't something you acquired later. It fascinated him that it was something not all men had, but he had known for years that they didn't. And it was something that women had not at all. They never understood that passion for a 'pile of dirt' as one of them had called it. They never knew, nor did the boy who rode along beside him, but Jeremiah didn't mind. One day the boy probably would go to work in a bank and be happy playing with papers and sums for the rest of his life. There was nothing wrong with that. But if Jeremiah had his way, he'd have tilled the soil for a lifetime, wandered through his vineyards, worked in his mines, and gone home bone tired at night, but content to the very core of his being. The business end of things interested him far less than the natural beauty and the manual labor it required to maintain it.

It was almost noon when they arrived in Napa, passing the farms on the outskirts first, and then the elaborate homes on Pine and Coombs Streets with their well manicured lawns and perfectly trimmed trees surrounding large, handsome homes which were not unlike Jeremiah's house in Saint Helena. The difference was that Jeremiah's house looked unloved and unused, it was a bachelor's home and somehow that showed, even on the outside in spite of Hannah. It was the place where Jeremiah lived, where he slept, but his mines and his land meant more to him and it showed. Hannah's influence was only felt in the comfortable kitchen and the vegetable garden. Here, in Napa, on the other hand, were homes run by devoted matrons, who saw that the lace curtains at the windows were fresh at all times, the gardens lush with flowers, and the top floors filled with children. The houses were beautiful and it always pleased Jeremiah to drive past them. He knew many of the people here and they knew him, but his was a more rural existence than theirs, and the hub of his life had always been business, not social life, which was far more important here in Napa.

Before going to the boat Jeremiah stopped at the Bank of Napa on First Street and withdrew the money he needed for the trip to Atlanta. He left the boy outside with the carriage, and a few moments later he emerged, looking satisfied and glancing at his pocket watch. They were going to have to hurry to catch the boat to San Francisco, and the boy took special pleasure in urging on the horses for Jeremiah as he glanced at some papers. They arrived at the boat in good time, and as Jeremiah jumped down and took his bags in his hands, he smiled up at the boy for a brief moment. 'I'll see you on the first Saturday after my return. Come in at nine in the morning.' Suddenly, he remembered the child's name, it was Danny. 'See you then, Dan. And take care of yourself while I'm gone.' Jeremiah instantly thought of Barnaby Harte, dead of influenza and felt something catch in his throat, as the boy beamed at him and he walked away and stepped onto the steamer to San Francisco. He had a small cabin reserved, as he always did on his trips to the city, and he sat down quickly and pulled a thick sheaf of papers out of his briefcase. He had plenty of work to do in the five hours it would take to reach San Francisco. The Zinfandel was a particularly fine boat, and Danny watched the paddle wheel with fascination as she left the dock.

At dinnertime, Jeremiah emerged from his cabin and sat at a small table by himself. A woman travelling with a nurse and her four children eyed him several times from across the room, but he appeared not to notice until finally the young matron gave him a haughty look when they left the dining room, embarrassed to have had no effect on the handsome giant. He stood outside on the deck for a while smoking a cigar after that and watched the lights of the city as they docked in San Francisco. His thoughts drifted back to Mary Ellen more than they usually did when he was away from her and he felt surprisingly lonely that evening as the Zinfandel docked and he took the hotel carriage to the Palace, where his usual suite awaited. From time to time he was given to visiting a house of ill repute, with a madam he particularly liked, but now he had no such inclination. Instead, tonight he stood in his room, looking out on the city and thinking back over the years. He had been in a melancholy mood ever since his night with John Harte and it was hard to shake off even now, although here he felt light years away from Napa and its beauty and its sorrows.

The hotel itself was only eleven years old, and offered every possible comfort. And at last, unable to sleep, Jeremiah took a turn around the lobby. It seemed to be filled with expensively dressed people, women flashing handsome jewels, people returning from late dinners, theater parties, and evenings on the town. There was almost a holiday atmosphere downstairs, and Jeremiah went out for a brief walk down Market Street and then returned to the hotel to sleep. He had a full day of appointments ahead of him before leaving for Georgia the following night and he wasn't looking forward to the long confinement on the train on the way to Atlanta. Trains always bored him, and, with a sensual smile before he drifted off to sleep, he wondered why he had never thought of bringing Mary Ellen, but the idea was totally absurd . . . she didn't belong in this part of his life . . . no woman did . . . there was no room for anyone in his business life . . . in his private life . . . or was there? He couldn't determine the answer as he fell asleep and by the next morning he had forgotten the question. He had only a vague sense of malaise as he rang for the valet and ordered his breakfast. It arrived on an enormous silver tray half an hour later, along with the coat he had given them to press the night before and his shoes, which had been shined to perfection. There was no doubt in anyone's mind that the Palace was one of the finest hotels in the country and Jeremiah knew that nothing in Atlanta would compare, not that he really cared. What he dreaded were the six endless days on the train to Georgia.

As there were no private compartments available on the train, he had reserved an entire car for his private use. A small buffet was set up at one end, and there was an area with a desk in which he could work on the moving train and a bed which could be concealed. He always felt like an animal confined to a cage when he travelled by train. And the food they got at the stations along the way was barely worth eating. The only advantage to the trip was that it was a perfect opportunity to work, as there would be no one for him to speak to during the entire six days crossing the country.

He was already desperately tired of the journey as he walked into the station in Elko, Nevada on the second day of the trip. Walking into the restaurant for a brief and predictably indigestible lunch composed of all fried foods like all the other meals they were offered he noticed a startlingly attractive woman. She looked to be in her mid thirties, was small and slight, with hair as raven black as his own. She had enormous almost violet eyes, delicate creamy skin and he noticed that she was very fashionably dressed in a velvet suit which could only have come from Paris. He found himself staring at her throughout his lunch and couldn't resist speaking to her as they left the restaurant at the same time, hurrying so as not to miss the train. He held the door open for her, and she smiled at him and then blushed, which he somehow found endearing.

'Tiresome, isn't it?' he said, as they hurried toward the train.

'More like dreadful.' She laughed, and he noticed from her speech that she was British. She had a large, beautifully cut sapphire ring on her left hand, but he didn't notice a wedding ring. He found himself intrigued, enough so to wander through the train that afternoon, and he found her in the Pullman car, reading a book and drinking a cup of tea. She looked up at him in surprise, and he smiled down at her, feeling suddenly shy. He wasn't sure what to say to her, but he hadn't been able to get her out of his mind all afternoon, which was rare for him. There was something remarkable and magnetic about her and he felt it now as he stood near her seat. She waved to an empty seat across from her. 'Would you like to sit down?'

'You wouldn't mind?'

'Not at all.'

He sat across from her and they introduced themselves. Her name was Amelia Goodheart, and she soon revealed that she had been a widow for more than five years and was visiting a daughter in the South, and her second grandchild, recently born. Her first had been born only weeks before in San Francisco. Amelia Goodheart lived in New York.

'You're awfully spread out, all of you.' He smiled, passing the time, enjoying her smile, watching her remarkable eyes.

'Too spread out for my taste, I'm afraid. Both of my oldest daughters married last year. The other three children are still at home with me.' She was forty years old and one of the loveliest women Jeremiah had ever seen. His eyes were riveted to her as the train sped along. Suddenly, it seemed, it was dinner time. He invited her to dine with him when they stopped at the next town. They left the train arm in arm, and he felt something stir deep inside him, as she walked along at his side. She was the kind of woman one wanted to protect, to shield from all harm, and at the same time, show off, 'look, she's mine!' It seemed unimaginable that she could survive for even an hour alone, and yet she was funny and warm and had a stiletto sharp mind. He felt almost like a school boy as they talked, ready to grovel at her feet. He was instantly infatuated with her, and he invited her back to his private car after dinner for a cup of tea. She spoke of her husband with warmth and kindness as they rolled along, admitting to Jeremiah that she had apparently been totally dependent on him, and she was now, finally, making the effort to get out in the world on her own, in this case to visit her two oldest children. It was quite obvious that this was her first adventure on her own and she seemed greatly amused and wondered why she hadn't done it before. Even the minor inconveniences seemed to trouble her not at all. She was the consummate good sport, and, as Jeremiah looked at her, he felt certain that she was the loveliest woman he had ever seen.

For the first time in years, someone had managed to totally push Mary Ellen Browne from his mind. How different they were. The one so simple and so staunch, so weathered and strong, the other more delicate, more complex, more elegant, more poised, and, in her own way, probably even stronger than Mary Ellen. He was clearly drawn to them both, but it was Amelia who had his attention now. She mentioned that she had brought only a maid along, an elderly cousin had been scheduled to make the trip and had fallen ill, but

Amelia had decided to go anyway. She wanted to see her girls, 'and I didn't really need another woman along. Cousin Margaret would hardly be able to take care of me.' She laughed at the thought and Jeremiah smiled at her. There was something vulnerable about the violet eyes, and he suddenly longed to hold her in his arms, but he didn't dare. Instead they spoke of Europe and Napa, and his wines, his childhood, her children, his work. He wanted to sit and talk to her all night, but at last, after midnight, he saw her stifle a yawn. They had been together for almost eight hours, and yet he hated to walk her to her car and leave her there.

'Will you be alright?' His voice radiated concern and she smiled.

'I believe I will.' And then, with a warmer smile, 'I've had a lovely time. Thank you very much.' She shook his hand and he was intoxicatingly aware of her perfume again. He had noticed it in his private car and he noticed it again when he went back. It was an exotic spicy scent with a dollop of freshness but at the same time, deeply sensual. And it was so much like her that as he noticed it lingering in his private car late that night it was almost as though she were still there with him. He wished she were as they rolled along endlessly through the darkness.

The night seemed to never end as Jeremiah waited for the dawn to come, thinking of the elegant woman he had met, sleeping not far away on the train. It had been a long time since he had been that taken with anyone, and he stepped down hopefully at their first stop, wishing to see her walking along the platform in the fresh morning air, but there were only a few maids with small dogs, one or two solitary men stretching their legs and no sign of Amelia anywhere. He went back to his private car, feeling as disappointed as a small child, and then finally, at noon, he strolled the length of the train and discovered her reading a book and sipping a cup of tea again.

'There you are!' He said it almost as one would to a lost child, and she looked up at him with a broad smile.

'Have I been lost?' He loved the look in her eyes as he smiled down at her.

'You have been to me. I've been looking for you all day.'

'I was right here.' He was impatient to spend time with her and he hastened to ask her join him in his private car. She didn't hesitate as she walked back with him but suddenly he wondered if he were creating an awkward situation for her. He was a single man after all, and one never knew who might be on the train . . . he so seldom thought of things like that, but he didn't want to cause Amelia any harm.

'Don't be silly, Jeremiah, I'm hardly a young girl.' She dismissed his concern with an elegant hand, and he noticed that she wore a remarkably pretty emerald today. He wondered that she wasn't afraid to wear her jewels on the train, but Amelia appeared to be totally unconcerned. He soon learned her mind was filled with pleasanter things than worrying about gossip or jewel thieves, or the fears which filled other women's minds. By the end of the second day they shared, Jeremiah was filled with admiration for her. He was almost sorry he hadn't met her years before and he told her so. And as he said the words, she was touched and her eyes caressed his face.

'What a lovely thing to say. . . .'

'I meant every word. I've never known anyone like you before . . . you've got more spirit than anyone I know, Amelia.' His eyes were gentle on hers. 'Your husband was a lucky man.'

'I was the lucky one.' Her voice was as soft as a summer breeze and Jeremiah held out a hand to her. They sat silently, with the countryside sliding by, looking into each others' eyes, the rest of the world lost to them.

'Have you never wanted to marry again?'

She shook her head with a gentle smile. 'Not really. I'm content as I am. I have the children to keep me happy and busy and fulfilled . . . my house . . . my friends. . . .'

'There should be more than that.' They exchanged another long smile, and he gently touched her fingers again. She had exquisite hands, it was no wonder her husband had given her such magnificent rings. They looked well on her as did the expensive clothes she wore. As he looked at her he found himself wondering what it would have been like to be married to a woman like her. It was odd to think of her in Napa though . . . coming home to her after working at the mines all day long.

'What were you thinking just then?' She loved the look in his eyes, there was a world of depth there.

'About Napa . . . my mines . . . what it would be like to have you there. . . .'

She looked startled at his words, and then she smiled. 'I suppose it would be an interesting life, wouldn't it? Certainly very different

37

than New York.' She couldn't even begin to imagine it. 'Are there Indians where you live?'

He laughed. 'Not the way you mean, but yes, some. But they're all very tame and ordinary now.'

'No hooting and hollering and throwing tomahawks?' She looked let-down and he laughed again as he shook his head.

'I'm afraid not.'

'How disappointing, Jeremiah.'

'We find other ways to have fun.'

'Like what?'

His Saturday nights in Calistoga instantly came to mind, but he forced himself to think of other things. 'San Francisco is only seven or eight hours away.'

'Do you spend a lot of time there?'

He shook his head. 'Honestly, no. I get up at five, have breakfast at six, leave for the mine after that, and come home when the sun goes down, and sometimes long after that. I work on Saturday mornings,' he hesitated, but not for very long, 'and on Sundays I tap my foot, waiting to go back to the mine.'

'It sounds like an awfully lonely life, my friend.' She looked sad for him and it moved him. What difference did it make to her if he worked too hard or was alone? 'Why have you never married, Jeremiah?' She seemed distressed.

'Too busy, I guess. I almost did once, twenty years ago.' He smiled at her and looked unconcerned. 'Maybe it just never was in the cards for me.'

'That's nonsense! No one should grow old alone.' But she would too, unless she married again.

'Is that what it's all about, why people get married, so they won't be alone when they're old?'

'Of course not. Companionship. Friendship. Love . . . someone to laugh with and talk to and share the aches and the sorrows with, someone to spoil and to love and to run home to, and run out into the first snow. . . .' She was thinking of the look in her daughter's eyes as she said the word. She was so in love with her husband and her brand new infant son. Amelia's eyes rose to Jeremiah's again. 'I don't suppose you really know what I'm talking about, but you've missed a great deal. My children are the greatest joy in my life. And it's not too late for you to have that. Jeremiah, don't be a fool. There must be a thousand women standing in line for you, grab one of them, marry her, and have a bunch of children before it's too late. Don't deprive yourself. . . .' He was amazed at the urgency of her words, and something about the way she said it touched his heart.

'You almost make me think twice about the life I've led.' He smiled at her and then sat back against the dark green velvet seat. 'Maybe you'll just have to save me from myself and marry me in the next town. What do you suppose your children would say to that?'

She laughed, but her eyes were kind as she answered him. 'They'd think that I'd finally gone mad, and they'd be right for once.'

'Would they?' His eyes held a tight grip on hers.

'They would.'

'Would it really be such a mad thing . . . you and I?. . . .' She felt an odd tingling run down her spine, there was something serious in his eyes and she didn't want to play with him. They were strangers on a train, and she knew herself that she was very taken with him, but she wasn't completely out of her mind yet. She had a life to live, a house in New York, three children still at home, two daughters and two sons-in-law to answer to.

'Jeremiah, don't tease about something as serious as that.' Her voice was as soft as silk and as gentle as a kiss on a child's cheek. 'I like you too much. I want to be your friend, even after we get off the train.'

'So do I. Marry me.' It was the craziest thing he had ever said, and would be the craziest thing he'd ever done, and he knew it too.

'I can't.' She felt suddenly pale and then flushed and then pale again.

'Why not?' He was serious and that made it worse somehow. She was almost frightened by the look in his eyes.

'For Heaven's sake, I have three children to bring up.' It was a lame excuse, but she couldn't think of anything else to say.

'So what? We can take them to Napa. Other people bring up their children there. It's a respectable place, in spite of the Indians.' He smiled. 'We'll build them their own school.'

'Jeremiah! Stop!' She jumped to her feet. 'Stop saying these mad things. I like you, you're one of the most remarkable, interesting, decent men I've ever met. But we've only just met. You're a stranger to me, and I to you, you don't know if I drink, if I'm half mad, if I gamble, or cheat . . . beat my children . . . if I killed my husband perhaps. . . .' A small smile dawned in her eyes and he held a hand out to her, which she took, and brushed with her lips. 'Lovely man, be kind to me, don't tease me like this. I'll be forty-one years old next Spring, Jeremiah, I'm too old for these games. I married my husband when I was seventeen, and we were happy for eighteen years, but I'm not a young girl anymore, there are no babies left in my womb. . . . I'm a grandmother now. . . . I'm beyond doing something crazy like running to California with you. I'd like to, it sounds like marvelous fun, but that's right now, right here . . . in a few days, you'll be in Atlanta, and I'll be in Savannah looking at my second grandchild. We must behave you and I, lest someone get hurt, and above all, I don't want that someone to be you. Do you know what I wish for you? A beautiful young girl for your wife, a dozen children, and a love like the one I had for eighteen years. I've had mine, but you haven't had yours, and I hope you find it soon.' Her eyes filled with tears then and she turned away. He took one step toward her; without saying anything he enfolded her in his arms, held her close, and sought her lips with his own, and she didn't fight him at all. She kissed him with all the fervour and passion that had been pent up so long and he did the same, and they were both breathless when they sat down again.

'You're a madman, Jeremiah.' But she didn't seem to mind, and he smiled.

'No. Many things but not that.' He looked deep into her eyes again. 'And you're the most spectacular woman I've ever met. I hope you know that. It's not an infatuation, not a whim. In forty-three years, I've only asked two women to marry me. And I would marry you at the next stop this train makes, if you would. And you know what? We'd be happy for the rest of our lives. I know that as sure as I know I'm sitting here.' And the funny thing was that she suspected he was right.

'We might be, and we might not. But I think we'd be wiser not to try.'

'Why?'

'Perhaps I'm not as brave as you. I'd rather have you as my friend.' But he wasn't sure he believed that after the way she had kissed him only moments before, and to break the tension building between them again, he stood up and went to a walnut cabinet where he had put a dozen bottles of his best wine.

40

'Would you like a drink? I brought some of my own wine with me.'

'I'd love that, Jeremiah.' He drew the cork and poured out two glasses of a full-bodied rich red wine, sniffed the glass, looked satisfied and handed the first one to her.

'No one will see you drink this here.' She wouldn't have drunk it elsewhere on the train, but she was suddenly relieved to have a glass of wine, and she was surprised at how fine it was when she took the first sip. Once again, she found herself impressed with him, and she looked sadly up at him as she set down the glass.

'I wish I didn't like you so much.'

'I wish you liked me more.' They both laughed at that, and got off at the next stop to share a quick dinner before getting back on the train. They bought an enormous basket of fruit. Jeremiah had some cheese left over from the day before and they ate fruit and cheese and drank his wine well into the night as they discussed the condition of the human race and slowly began to get drunk as they laughed at it all. Somehow each of them knew that they had found a lifetime friend. Amelia was the wisest woman he had ever met, and for the next few days he drank in every word she said, and shared all of his wine with her. They ate every meal in each other's company, played cards, laughed, told jokes, shared confidences that neither of them had ever told before, and, by the time they reached Atlanta, Jeremiah knew that he was head over heels mad for her, yet he knew at the same time that she would never agree to marry him and he also thought he understood why. In the depths of her soul, she still hadn't given her husband up and perhaps she never would. She kept insisting that Jeremiah needed a young girl, and children of his own. He had told her about John Harte, and the two children who had died, and he had admitted to her that he wasn't sure he ever wanted to take that risk. 'I couldn't bear it if I lost a child. I lost a woman I loved once, Amelia, that was enough. . . .' This was late one night, more than halfway down his second bottle of wine, but Amelia had shaken her head at him.

'You can't live in fear like that. You have to gamble a bit in life, you know that. . . .'

'Not with your heart . . .' Barnaby Harte's face came to his mind again and he closed his eyes. 'I couldn't bear that.' She grabbed his arm. 'You must. Don't miss that chance. You still have a whole life to live . . . do it . . . dammit, don't let it pass you by. I won't let you do that. Find the right girl, go looking for her if you have to, but get what you want . . . what you need . . . what you deserve. . . .'

'And what's that?' He wasn't even sure what he wanted anymore.

'A girl with fire . . . with passion . . . with love in her veins, a girl so alive that you almost have to tie her down to capture her.'

Jeremiah laughed. 'Sounds like you, is that what I should do to you?'

'You'd better not, Jeremiah Thurston. But you know just what I mean, a little fireball to keep you warm and happy and amused.'

'Sounds like a great deal of trouble to me.' But he had to admit, in some ways, the idea appealed to him. 'And where does one find such a girl?'

'Wherever she is. And one looks hard, if one has to. Or perhaps she'll just walk right into your arms.'

'She hasn't yet, or at least not until this trip.' He eyed her knowingly again and she laughed. She had almost allowed herself to fall head over heels in love with him. But she couldn't do that. She had too much left to do on her own, and he deserved more than that.

'Don't forget what I said!' she told him in the last moments of the trip. The train was already pulling into the Atlanta station and his bags were packed. They were standing in his private car, and he had left instructions to leave it on for her and her maid. The journey to Savannah would only take them a few more hours, but she wasn't thinking of Savannah now. She was only thinking of him, and he of her.

'Damn you, why don't you marry me?' He looked down at her tenderly, with grief and passion mixed in his eyes. 'You're a fool.'

'I know I am,' tears suddenly welled up in her eyes, 'but I want something better for you.'

'You're the best there is.'

She shook her head, and the tears rolled slowly down her face as she smiled. 'I love you, dearest friend.' She took him in her arms in a hug that enveloped him and he held her close until the train stopped and then he pulled away to look at her again.

'I love you too. Take care of yourself, my dear. I'll see you in New York sometime soon.'

She nodded, and waved at him as he left the train, and he stood and waved at her as the train pulled away, and he wondered at the fate which had brought her to him and then let her slide away. There had never been anyone like her before . . . and probably never would be again . . . and the damnedest thing was that if she would have let him, he would have married her in a moment. It was strange. He had fallen head over heels for Amelia in a matter of days, moments . . . hours . . . and with Mary Ellen Browne, he would have been content with a lifetime of Saturdays. It was something to think about as he rode to his hotel, watching the sights slide by.

Chapter Four

There was a wonderful quality of elegance about the Kimball House, which dominated the skyline of Atlanta. A fleet of men rushed forward to help Jeremiah alight and enter the richly decorated lobby, where armies of servants seemed to be hovering about. The decor was more that of a grand ballroom than a hotel lobby. It made the grandeur of the Palace Hotel in San Francisco pale by comparison. Jeremiah joined his luggage in his suite, looked around, had a drink, and it seemed only moments later when he heard a knock on the door to his room, and Mr. Beauchamp's footman appeared. He stood impressively tall and black in formal livery and handed him an envelope of rich creamy paper, the envelope closed with a very grand gold seal. Having ascertained who Jeremiah was, the footman extended the envelope in a powerful hand.

'From Mrs. Beauchamp, Suh.'

'Thank you.'

Jeremiah swiftly pulled out the card and discovered that he was expected for dinner at eight o'clock that evening. French hours, he thought to himself, as he thanked the footman, and asked him to reassure the Beauchamps that he'd be there. With a stern nod, the man, resplendent in his livery, disappeared. Jeremiah wandered around the room, thinking of that night. The suite was handsomely decorated, with fine fabrics and French antiques, but to Jeremiah it looked all too empty now. There was a soft knock on the door, and a black maid appeared with a silver tray, bringing him another tall mint julep and a plate of biscuits that smelled freshly baked. Normally, after the long ride on the train, he would have liked nothing better, but now all he could think of was Amelia. In a few hours she would be arriving in Savannah, and she would be busy with her daughter, but all Jeremiah wanted was to fold her into his arms again. It troubled him as he took a long sip of the mint julep the maid had left and strolled out onto the terrace to look at the city. Atlanta had grown a great deal in the twenty years since the war, and in many ways it was a booming city. But much about it was as it had been before the war, and he knew that the Southerners still resented being dragged into the Union. They liked their old ways and were still bitter about losing the war. He wondered briefly what Beauchamp and his friends would be like. He knew that they had plenty of money at their disposal, but he suspected that Beauchamp was newly rich and painfully flashy. It was easy to surmise that from the heavily gold encrusted suit the man's footman wore.

Jeremiah bathed before dinner and attempted to have a nap, but as he lay on the large canopied bed all he could think of was the enchanting woman with the black hair and huge dark eyes, almost as dark as the jet beads on the suit she wore the night that she met him. Why was it that he could remember every detail about her dress? He had never done that before. But she was elegant and so beautiful and sensual that he wanted her desperately and he felt a knot in his throat, which he tried to dissolve with another mint julep, but nothing seemed to chase her from his thoughts and Jeremiah found himself wondering how he was going to do business with his head so full of her. But this evening was just a matter of social amenity. He knew that he wouldn't be expected to begin discussing their business deal until the next day. Southerners were far too correct to mix business with pleasure and this evening would more than likely be a quiet dinner at Beauchamp's home, to show the uncivilized Westerner a little Southern hospitality. Jeremiah smiled at the image as he put on his jacket and looked at the white suit in the mirror. It seemed in sharp contrast to his deeply-tanned skin and dark hair, the same color as Amelia's . . . Amelia . . . Amelia . . . Amelia . . . He wished he had never got off the train as he walked down to the lobby and out to the waiting carriage Orville Beauchamp had sent for him.

The footman was quick to jump to the ground and hold open the door to Jeremiah, and then he hopped up beside the coachman again as elegant ladies swept past them in glittering evening dresses, accompanied by well-dressed men on their way to dinners and concerts and the other social events that made up the night life of Atlanta.

The carriage sped down the broad splendor of Peach Street and into the residential section of the city, to Beauchamp House which stood in small, but stately splendor farther down on Peach Street, as well. It was a relatively new building, obviously built since the war and it was not wildly extravagant, but it was definitely handsome. Jeremiah was suddenly sorry that Amelia wasn't there with him to share the evening. They could have gone back to the hotel afterwards and discussed the various costumes and foibles of the guests and laughed as they sampled more of the wine he had had sent on for him from Napa. And it was Amelia he was thinking of, as he shook hands with Elizabeth Beauchamp, Orville Beauchamp's once pretty but now faded-looking wife. She was a washed-out blonde with pale skin the color of milk glass and eyes that seemed to water with despair. The impression Elizabeth Beauchamp left one with was one of extreme fragility, as though she might not live out the week, and one was not even sure she would care to. She had a plaintive, sad little voice, and talked constantly about the days before the war, and life on her 'Daddy's' plantation. Orville seemed not to hear anything that she said, except that now and then he would snap, 'That's enough, Lizabeth, our guests don't want to hear about life on your Daddy's plantation. That's all gone now,' but the very words seemed to strike her like a whip, and she would seem to subside silently into her own reminiscences. Orville himself was of an entirely different breed, obviously less aristocratic than his wife. He had a rough edge to him, with eyes narrowed constantly as though he had just thought of something important. And it was clear that the only thing important to Orville was business. His hair was as dark as Jeremiah's, his complexion almost swarthy. He explained that his grandparents had been from the South of France and had first come to New Orleans before moving to Georgia. And he made no secret that they had had nothing when they'd come, nor had his father some thirty years later. It was Orville who made the family's first fortune, who profited from the industrialisation of the South during and after the war. He had built himself a small empire, which he admitted was not yet as large as he wanted it to be but would be one day, especially with the help of his son, Hubert, named after Orville's grandfather.

But it was Jeremiah's impression that Hubert was not nearly so bright as his father. Instead, he had his mother's annoying whine and he seemed far more interested in spending his father's money than making any of his own. He talked about a string of race horses he had bought in Kentucky and the brothel he liked best in New Orleans.

46

All in all, it was a tedious evening for Jeremiah. Two of the other members of the consortium he would do business with were there too, quiet older men with strong opinions and uninteresting wives who talked to each other in hushed tones for most of the evening. Jeremiah noticed that they spoke little or not at all to Elizabeth Beauchamp and she seemed to ignore them completely. It was easy to see that she thought them far beneath her, given her aristocratic beginnings on her 'Daddy's' plantation.

Jeremiah also noticed in the course of the evening that the Beauchamp family was singularly obsessed with everyone's fortune, how much who had and how they had made it. Elizabeth had lost everything she might ever have had during the war. Her father had shot himself after the destruction of his plantation, and her mother had died shortly after of grief, perhaps more for the fortune they had lost, Jeremiah thought, than for her husband.

The Beauchamps apparently had a daughter, whom Orville claimed was a 'perfect jewel', but given what he'd seen, Jeremiah sincerely doubted it. She was at a grand ball somewhere that night, 'with every boy in Atlanta nipping at her heels,' the proud papa said, before adding, 'They should be . . . The dress she has on cost me a fortune.' Jeremiah smiled blankly at his words, tired of their obsession with money, and all he could think of as the evening droned on was that he wished he were with Amelia in Savannah, seeing her grandchild for the first time and visiting her daughter. What a different and far more genteel atmosphere that would have been, he thought, and then he laughed at himself. It wasn't the gentility of the scene which appealed to him, but the chance to be near Amelia, to inhale her sensual perfume, kiss her lips, and spend hours looking into her eyes. Just thinking of her brought a smile to his lips, which Elizabeth Beauchamp thought was meant just for her, and she patted his hand limply before getting up to lead the ladies into the other room, while the men stayed to smoke cigars and drink brandy. It was only then that the deal which had brought him to Atlanta was mentioned, and it was almost a relief to talk business after the incredibly boring evening.

Jeremiah was relieved when the first guests left shortly after eleven o'clock, and he was able to seek refuge in the excuse that he was exhausted from the long trip and anxious to return to the hotel to rest before they began negotiations the next morning. The

Beauchamp carriage took him back to the hotel, and half an hour later he was standing on the terrace looking out over the city. He thought back over the hours he and Amelia had shared and it seemed almost like a dream, as he looked out over Atlanta. The Beauchamps were already forgotten. All he could think of was her.

'Good night, little love,' he whispered as he went back inside, thinking of her words again . . . Get married, Jeremiah . . . have babies. But he wanted no babies now. He only wanted her. 'I love you,' she had said to him . . . I love you . . . powerful words from a powerful woman . . . His mind and his heart seemed full of her as he drifted off to sleep in the elegant canopied bed a short while later, feeling desperately lonely.

Chapter Five

Jeremiah's dealings with Orville Beauchamp's consortium were extremely successful and within a week of his arrival in Atlanta, the deal had been made. Nine hundred flasks of quicksilver were to be sent to them for distribution among them, for the manufacturers of bullets and assorted minor war machines, and for mining throughout the South. Jeremiah had made slightly more than fifty thousand dollars on the deal. He was extremely satisfied with the terms, as was Orville Beauchamp, who took a commission off the top for making the deal. In fact, he had made several sub-deals, involving the re-sale of his portion of the quicksilver. Unlike the others, it was not for use in factories of his own. He was more of a middleman and a wheeler dealer in every way, and he was only interested in big money and quick deals. The deal complete, Beauchamp extended his hand to Jeremiah. 'I think we ought to celebrate tonight, my friend.' From the moment the negotiations had begun, their socialising had ceased. Jeremiah had dined each night in his hotel, and the Beauchamps had not extended another invitation to dine, but now there was cause for celebration. The seven Southerners and their wives, as well as Jeremiah, were invited to dine at his home. 'Lizabeth will just be so almighty pleased,' he insisted as he beamed. But Jeremiah couldn't imagine her being anything of the kind, particularly not to have fifteen business people come to dine. But that was Orville's problem, not his, and he was tired after the long week and anxious to get home. He had been unable to get a satisfactory train connection for another three days, and he was trapped in Atlanta through the week-end with nothing whatsoever to do and was less than pleased about it. He wanted to go home now.

Once or twice he had toyed with the idea of going to Savannah for a couple of days while he waited, but he didn't want to embarrass Amelia. She was visiting her daughter and the sudden appearance of a strange man on the scene would have been difficult to explain. So he was faced with cooling his heels in Atlanta and he just hoped he wouldn't have to see Orville Beauchamp much after tonight. It had definitely been a very long week, albeit a profitable one for him.

The carriage picked him up once again at eight o'clock, and this evening he had been asked to wear formal dress. Apparently Beauchamp was going all out. Jeremiah had to admit when he got to their home that everything looked lovely. There were hundreds of candles ablaze in the chandeliers and sconces along the walls, huge bouquets of flowers everywhere, orchids and azaleas and jasmine and heavily scented blossoms that Jeremiah had never even seen before, which seemed to add a heady fragrance to the air as the candles danced and the guests arrived, covered in silks and satins and heavily bejewelled.

'You're looking very well tonight, Mrs. Beauchamp.' But he knew instantly that it had been the wrong thing to say. 'Looking well' was never an effect that Elizabeth Beauchamp strove to achieve. She seemed to enjoy her ill health and her pallor.

'Thank you, Mr. Thurston.' She drawled over the words as her eyes wandered to the next guests arriving. Jeremiah stepped aside and began speaking to one of the men he'd been doing business with all week, and they were joined a few minutes later by Hubert, who was full of some tale of a horse he wanted to see in Chattanooga. Jeremiah wandered aimlessly through the group, chatting with the men and being introduced to their wives. Eventually he was introduced to a pretty young blonde whom Hubert had invited to join them. She was a livelier, healthier, much prettier version of his mother, and Orville seemed to find her particularly attractive as they got ready to go into dinner. It was only then that he noticed that their numbers were uneven and called across to his wife.

'Where's Camille?' His wife looked faintly nervous and Hubert laughed before answering his father.

'Probably out back with one of her beaux!' Neither the laughter nor the comment were tainted by brotherly kindness and his mother was quick to scold him.

'Hubert!' She turned to her husband then. 'She was upstairs dressing, when we came down.' Orville frowned, spoke quietly to his wife. He was particularly displeased by Hubert's remark. Camille was the apple of his eye, a fact which was no secret to those who knew

50

him. 'Tell her, Lizabeth, that we're ready to go into dinner.'

'I'm not sure she's dressed . . .' Lizabeth detested confronting her daughter, and giving her orders, even if they were not her own. Camille did as she pleased at all times, and tonight would be no exception.

'Just tell her we'll wait for her.' The guests didn't seem to object to the opportunity for another mint julep, and Elizabeth Beauchamp disappeared upstairs and returned a few minutes later looking relieved as she whispered something to her husband. He nodded and seemed satisfied with the answer, none of which impressed Jeremiah very much as he strolled about among the guests, catching bits and snatches of conversations as he wandered around. At last, he walked through the handsome double French doors into the garden and stood enjoying the balmy spring air, before going back inside.

But as he crossed over the threshold this time, he stopped, fascinated by what he saw: a tiny delicate young woman with raven hair and skin so white she looked like a snow queen as she stood there. Her eyes were as blue as a summer sky and she wore a matching taffeta gown and a string of blue topazes about her neck which served to enhance the sparkle and the color of her eyes still more. She was the most dazzling-looking creature Jeremiah had ever seen, and the amazing thing was that she was the perfect combination of both her parents, her father's dark hair and her mother's milk white skin and blue eyes. From two perfectly ordinary people had sprung this pocket goddess, this vision who floated between them now, almost dancing as she went, kissing and flirting and laughing. Jeremiah was suddenly aware of the beating of his heart as he watched her. She took one's breath away, and it struck him that she looked a little bit like Amelia . . . the same dark hair, creamy skin . . . She could have been the girl that Amelia had once been, but he concentrated on Camille now as she pranced among the guests and made them laugh, flirting with the men, teasing the women, and linking her arm adoringly into her father's.

'You're still an impossible child!' Jeremiah heard one woman say, not totally without venom. It was easy to see that she made her mother very nervous and was clearly the object of her brother's hatred. But somehow Jeremiah found that amusing as he watched her cavort and he could easily imagine that she had been playing the same games since she'd been old enough to walk. It was equally obvious that her father adored her.

'Mr. Thurston,' Orville Beauchamp pronounced his name as though he were about to give him an award. 'May I present you to my daughter, Mr. Thurston?' He beamed, 'Camille, this is Mr. Thurston from California.'

'How do you do, Miss Beauchamp?' Jeremiah graciously kissed her hand and watched the sparkle in her eyes. She was indeed a naughty little girl, but she had an enchanting quality about her like a mischievous elf, or a slightly wicked fairy princess. He had never seen a creature as devastatingly lovely as she and wondered how old she was, deciding that she couldn't be more than seventeen. In fact, she had turned seventeen in December, and since then her life had been an endless round of parties and balls. Her tutor had been dismissed on the first of the year and Camille was enchanted.

'Good evening, Mr. Thurston.' She curtsied prettily to him, giving him a fine view of her firm young breasts as she did so and knowing full well that she had. There was very little Camille did without planning beforehand. She was witty, wise and canny about her effect on those around her.

Dinner was announced immediately after her appearance, and Jeremiah went in on Elizabeth Beauchamp's arm, feeling as though his whole world had just turned upside down. He was surprised and delighted to find himself seated between Camille and another lady. Even more fortuitously, the other lady being engaged in conversation to her right, Jeremiah found himself with only Camille Beauchamp to talk to. She was bright and amusing and just as flirtatious as he had suspected, but he was surprised to discover that there was something more to her, too. She seemed to have an extraordinary understanding of practical matters and she had an excellent head for business. She asked a number of very intelligent questions about his most recent deal, and he was surprised at how much she knew about her father's business. And how much Orville himself had told her. It certainly wasn't what Jeremiah would have discussed with his daughter, had he had one.

'Has your father taught you all that?' Jeremiah wondered and was startled. It would have seemed that he'd be more interested in teaching Hubert, although he was undoubtedly not as avid to learn as his sister.

'Some of it.' She seemed pleased by his appreciation of her extensive knowledge. 'Some of it I've just listened to.' She smiled with an air of false innocence, which amused Jeremiah.

52

'You've done more than listen, young lady. You've sorted it out and come to some very interesting conclusions.' She had said one or two things which he thought were amazingly perceptive, and he didn't usually like talking business to women, especially very young ones. Most girls would have tittered and stared had he even attempted to discuss one tenth of what had gone on during his 'office' day.

'I like hearing about men's work.' Camille said it matter of factly, as though she had just said she liked hot chocolate for breakfast.

'Why?' He was intrigued. 'Most women find it very dull.'

'I don't. I like it.' She looked him square in the eye. 'I'm interested in how people make money.' It was a shocking thing to say and for a moment Jeremiah was too startled to answer.

'What makes you feel that way, Camille?' What went on behind those bright blue eyes and pretty black curls? Surely not the usual thoughts of a seventeen year old girl. She was surprisingly blunt about her views, and it was actually refreshing. There was no pretense, no hiding behind a lace fan. She said what she thought, even if it was shocking.

'I think money is important, Mr. Thurston.' She said it with an enchanting drawl. 'And it makes people important. And when they don't have it anymore, they stop being important.'

'That's not always true.'

'Yes, it is.' She was brutal in her verdict. 'Look at my mother's father. He lost his money and his plantation and he was no one and he knew it, so he shot himself, Mr. Thurston. And look at my Daddy, he's got money and he's important and if he had more money, he'd be more important.' And then she stared him straight in the eye. 'You're a very important man. My Daddy says so. And you must have an awful lot of money.' She made it sound as though he had barrels of it, on his front porch and in his basement, and the image of what she said made him laugh in embarrassment as much as amusement.

'I have land more than money.'

'That's the same thing. In some places it's land, in other places it's cattle . . . it's different things in different places, but it means the same thing.' He knew what she was speaking of, and wondered if she really did too. It was almost frightening if she did. How could she know so much about business and money and power?

'I think what you're talking about is power. You're talking about the kind of power people get when they're successful or important.' It was a very perceptive thing for a seventeen year old to have grasped, particularly a sheltered, southern girl. She looked pensive for a moment and then nodded.

'I think you're right, and that is what I mean. I like power. I like what it makes people do, how they behave, how they think.' She looked at her mother and then back at Jeremiah. 'I hate weak people. I think my grandfather must have been weak, to shoot himself like that.'

'That was a terrible time in the South, Camille.' Jeremiah spoke softly, lest his hostess hear them. 'It was a tremendous change for most people, and some of them just couldn't survive it.'

'My Daddy did.' She looked at him with pride. 'That's when he made all his money.' It was something that most people wouldn't have cared to mention, let alone brag about. Then, as quickly as she had brought up the forbidden subject, she dropped it, turning to Jeremiah with those summer sky eyes and smiling a smile that would have melted the heart of a man of iron. 'What's it like in California?'

With a smile at the contrasts in her style, he began to tell her about the Napa Valley. She listened politely for a time, and then was obviously bored. This was not a girl who had a passion for the country. She was far more interested in his stories about San Francisco. And then she told him about a recent trip to New York which she had found absolutely fascinating, and if she wasn't married by the time she was eighteen, her Daddy would take her to Europe. He still had a distant cousin in France, and what Camille really wanted to see was Paris. She sounded like a little girl as she rattled on, and as he watched her Jeremiah found himself no longer listening to her words but totally in awe of her delicate beauty. And it was as though he could hear Amelia's words to him on the train . . . find a young girl . . . get married . . . have babies. This was the kind of girl that turned old men's heads, and turned their knees to jelly. Enough. He had not come to Atlanta to find a bride, but to do business. He had a normal, sane life to return to in Napa Valley, five hundred employees in three mines, a housekeeper, a house, Mary Ellen. Suddenly, as though in a vision, he could see Camille dancing among them. It was like a kind of delirium thinking of it and he forced his mind back to the dinner, albeit with considerable effort.

They chatted on throughout the meal and a small group of musicians began to play in the main drawing room after dinner. Jeremiah politely asked Elizabeth Beauchamp to dance, but she informed him that she never danced, and perhaps he would like to dance with her daughter. Camille was standing nearby as she spoke, and there was nothing he could do, but offer his arm, although he felt slightly foolish dancing with a girl of her age. Foolish and at the same time pleased, and embarrassed to realize that he was almost breathlessly drawn to her. He had to fight the power of her charm as they whirled around the floor and he looked into the pale sapphire eyes.

'Do you like to dance as much as you like hearing about business?'

'Oh yes,' she smiled up at him, all Southern Belle and huge blue eyes, 'I love dancing.' It was as though the earlier conversation had never taken place, and all she ever thought about was dancing. He almost wanted to laugh out loud and call her a little minx, which it was obvious she was. 'You're a wonderful dancer, Mr. Thurston.' It was a skill which came to him naturally and which he enjoyed, but he was amused at her extravagant praise and he laughed as they circled the room in each other's arms. He hadn't been this carefree in years, and he wasn't sure he knew why. It was frightening to realize how attracted he was to her.

'Thank you, Miss Beauchamp.'

She saw the twinkle in his eyes and laughed, too, managing to look both sensual and impish all at once, and again he had to fight his own instincts. As the last waltz came to a close, he was suddenly aware of the heat of the room, the brilliance of the candles, the heady scent of the flowers, and then the brilliance of her eyes as she looked up at him again. She looked so delicate that she reminded him of one of the lovely Southern flowers in the huge bouquets decorating the room. He wanted to tell her how pretty she was, but he didn't quite dare, she was only a girl of seventeen after all, and he was more than twice her age. It was an awesome thought as he returned her to her mother's side, and a short while later bid them all goodnight. He held her hand for only an instant as her eyes dove into his and she spoke to him in a soft voice which tore his soul, and at the same time touched something more primitive within him.

'Will I see you again before you leave?' There was a plaintive note in her voice and he smiled. That was all that remained on this trip, to be the object of a young girl's crush and to become ensnared in her spell. If that were the case, he chided himself, it was time for him to go back to California.

'I don't really know. I'll be leaving Atlanta in a few days.'

'What are you doing until then?' She asked him with the open eyes of a young child. 'Daddy said you were all through with your work.'

'I am. But there's no train to San Francisco until the first of the week.'

'Oh,' she clapped her hands happily and looked up at him with a broad grin, 'then you'll have time to play.' He laughed out loud and allowed himself to kiss her cheek.

'Goodnight, little one. I'm too old to play. And much too old to play with you.' He said nothing more, but swung up into the carriage after shaking his host's hand. On the drive back to the hotel, he let his thoughts drift over the evening and the beguiling Camille. She was an outrageous child, but with those huge blue eyes, and sharp mind, she could have had anything she wanted, and undoubtedly did. It was easy to see why her father adored her, but she was obviously a handful too. As he thought of her he felt an odd twinge of something more; he felt almost dizzy as he remembered circling the drawing room in her arms as they danced the waltz. There was something immoral about lusting after such a young girl and he forced her from his thoughts and attempted to replace her with a vision of Amelia, and then Mary Ellen, but no one could push Camille from his mind. At last he sank back into the carriage with a breathless feeling, and had she been sitting beside him, child or no, he would have crushed her to him. There was something about her which was so exotic, so beguiling, so sensual, that it almost drove a man from his senses, and for no reason he could even understand, Jeremiah felt almost frightened. He was suddenly anxious to leave Atlanta and return to California. Because, if he stayed . . . it was impossible to say what would happen. . . .

Chapter Six

The next morning dawned warm and sunny with the smell of spring in the air, as Jeremiah rose slowly from his bed, donned his dressing gown and wandered out onto the terrace of his room. He was determined to attack a stack of papers he purposefully spread out on the desk, but again and again, his thoughts leapt back to the exquisite nymphet he had met the night before. He was furious with himself for it. The worst of all was that he had another two and a half days to wait in Atlanta before catching the train to California.

He pressed the call button in his room, and a porter arrived to take his breakfast order. And half an hour later a tray arrived, covered with sausages and eggs, biscuits and honey, orange juice, coffee, and a basket of fresh fruit, but as he stared at it, he had no desire to eat, only to see Camille, and he slammed a fist on the table just as there was another knock on the door. Surprised, he opened it, to see the Beauchamp's footman standing there.

'Yes?' He was startled and embarrassed at his own pounding on the table, though the footman couldn't have heard it.

'A note for you, Suh.' The footman smiled pleasantly and handed Jeremiah an envelope addressed in a delicate, flowery hand. For a fraction of an instant, Jeremiah hesitated, and then took it from him, as he waited for Jeremiah's response, as he had been told to do.

'It's a lovely day for a stroll in the park,' the note read in an almost childlike hand, 'would you care to join us for the afternoon? We're having lunch at home, and then all of us will go to the park. You'll be quite safe,' she teased, 'and perhaps you could stay for dinner too.' She was a brazen little thing, just as he had known the night before, and he wasn't at all sure what to do. The thought of her tormented him and yet he wasn't in any way certain that Orville Beauchamp would be amused to see his business associate strolling through the park with his seventeen year old daughter. Appearing on their doorstep

57

for every meal seemed more than a little forward too. Yet he wanted to see her and he felt torn as he read the note again. He turned and threw it on the table, as he grabbed a pen and sheet of paper, bemused. He wasn't even sure what to say to a child of her age. He wasn't in the habit of courting children of her tender years, and yet there was nothing childlike about Camille Beauchamp. In almost every way, she was a young and beautiful and very tempting woman.

'If it is agreeable with your Mama, dear Miss Beauchamp,' he answered, 'I will be exceedingly happy for lunch and a stroll in the park with your family and friends,' he wanted nothing to suggest a clandestine or even solitary meeting, 'and in the meantime, I remain, your obedient servant, Jeremiah Thurston.' She didn't know how true the words were, and neither did he, until he saw her again, and felt his heart almost turn loose from its moorings. She was wearing a simple white lace dress, and her shining black hair danced down her back in long graceful curls. They strolled in the garden before lunch, she looked more than ever like an exquisite child and, at the same time, a devastatingly beautiful young woman.

'I'm so glad you decided to come today, Mr. Thurston. It must be terribly boring for you at the hotel.'

'It is,' he was careful with his words. There was nothing boring about Camille. But it also struck him that there was something faintly dangerous about her, not least her very appeal. For the first time in his life, Jeremiah felt capable of unbridled madness. He wanted to grab Camille and pull her into his arms, throw her parasol to the ground and run his hands through her hair. He turned away from her, as though to flee his own thoughts and break the spell, wondering if his recent restraint with Amelia was making him long for Camille now.

'Are you unwell?' She had noticed his pained expression and she looked concerned as she laid a delicate hand on his arm. 'It's so terribly hot here in the South. Perhaps you aren't accustomed . . .' Her voice trailed off and he turned to face her. How innocent she was. He was almost faint with desire for her and deeply shocked by the power of his feelings. She was barely more than a child after all. But no matter how many times he told himself that, he was somehow not convinced. She was so much more a woman than a child. Surely even Orville Beauchamp knew that. . . .

'Not at all, I'm fine. And it's so lovely here in your garden.' He looked at the flowerbeds so as not to look at her, and then suddenly he laughed out loud. It was absurd for a man his age to be so taken with a girl, no matter how lovely she was. He looked at her then, and spoke some of what he felt, hoping to defuse it. 'You know, Miss Beauchamp, you quite turn my head.' The openness of his words somehow helped, and his feelings seemed not sordid but sweet, and she laughed delightedly at him.

'Do I? And you're so very grown up too . . .' It was the perfect thing to say and they both laughed as he took her arm and they strolled in to lunch arm in arm. They chatted about the weather and the parties she had recently attended. She claimed that the young men of Atlanta seemed terribly silly to her. 'They're not. . . .' She frowned as she looked up at him, struggling for the words, 'they're not . . . important, like you and Daddy.' It was her attraction to power which once again surprised him.

'One day they might be far more important than we are.'

'Yes,' she nodded, conceding that he might be right, 'but in the meantime they're very boring.'

'How unkind, dear Miss Beauchamp.' Somehow, he wasn't sure why, she amused him.

'Kind people bore me too.' She twinkled at him, and he roared with amusement. 'My mother is always kind.' She rolled her eyes, and then giggled, and he wagged a finger at her.

'Shame on you. Kindness is a lovely virtue in a lady.'

'Then I'm not sure that's what I want to be when I grow up, Mr. Thurston.'

'How shocking!' He was having more fun than he had in years, as he took his place beside her at the luncheon table, and Orville Beauchamp looked particularly pleased to see Thurston so amused by his daughter. He hadn't seemed at all surprised to see Jeremiah in their midst again, and anything Camille did seemed to meet with her father's approval. Only her mother appeared to be constantly nervous, and in deathly fear of some terrible fate. She was the most uncomfortable looking woman Thurston had ever met, in sharp contrast to her happy, contented daughter.

'Is my daughter behaving herself, Mr. Thurston?' Beauchamp shot the question at him from the other end of the table.

'Most certainly, Mr. Beauchamp. I am enchanted.' And Camille appeared to be too, as she cast brilliant eyes at Jeremiah. She seemed more demure for the remainder of lunch, and it was only when they were walking in the park that she made him uncomfortable again.

'You don't think I'm old enough to take seriously, do you?' She looked him squarely in the eye and cocked her head to one side as they strolled along in the park. He pretended to be unconcerned.

'What do you mean by that, Camille?'

'You know what I mean.'

'I take you very seriously, you're a bright girl.'

'But you think I'm a child.' She looked annoyed. But she wouldn't have been if she could have heard the rush of blood in his veins. 'You're a very charming child, Camille.' His smile was warm, but not as warm as the fire in her eyes. She stared at him, now angry.

'I'm not a child. I'm seventeen.' She said it as though it was ninety-three, but he didn't laugh.

'I'm forty-three years old. I could be your father and then some, Camille. There's nothing wrong with being a child. You'll get old soon enough, and wish that people saw you as young again.'

'But I'm not a child. And you're not my father.'

'I wish I were.' He spoke in soothing tones but her eyes flashed just the same.

'You do not. That's a lie. I saw how you looked at me when we danced last night. But today you keep reminding yourself of who I am, that I'm Orville Beauchamp's daughter and that I'm only a girl. Well, I'm not a child. I'm more woman than you know.' With that, she pressed her body against his, and kissed his lips. He was so astounded that he almost took a step back, but he found that he couldn't move anywhere but closer to her, and without thinking, he let desire take the upper hand and crushed her against himself, kissing her with all the passion he felt for her. When his lips left hers at last, he was aghast at what he'd done. He didn't even remember that it was she who kissed him first.

'Camille . . . Miss Beauchamp . . . I must apologize. . . .'

'Don't be a fool . . . it was I who kissed you. . . .' She seemed not to have lost her sangfroid at all, and as the others rounded the turn in the path, she looked quite in control, and she quietly took his arm. 'We'd best keep walking so the others don't know. . . .' And then dumbly, he let her take his arm, and a moment later he began to laugh. Nothing like it had ever happened before. She was easily the most outrageous girl he had ever met.

'How dare you do such a thing!'

'Are you shocked?' She looked only a trifle concerned, mostly she seemed pleased, and he wanted to stop and shake her until she screamed and then hold her close . . . but he forced himself to listen as she continued talking. 'You know, I've never done that before.'

'Well, I certainly hope not. People might begin to talk.' He was laughing now. Imagine being kissed by a seventeen year old girl, but more than that . . . imagine kissing her back. . . . It was all like a dream, and she looked at him with curiosity now.

'Will you tell?'

'What do you suppose would happen if I did, Camille? You'd be chained to your bed for a week . . . or a year . . . and I'd be tarred and feathered by your father and run out of town on a rail.' She laughed with glee, obviously delighted by the idea. 'I'm glad all of that appeals so much to you. Actually, it's not the way I usually care to leave town myself.'

'Then don't go.' Her eyes almost pleaded with him.

'I'm afraid I must. I have a business to run.' She didn't seem to object to that, but she still looked sad.

'I wish you didn't have to go. There isn't anyone like you here.'

'I'm sure there is. You must be surrounded by young, handsome men, just begging for the sight of you.'

'I told you, they're all stupid and dull.' She sounded pettish as she glanced up at him. 'You know, I've never known anyone like you before.'

'That's a very nice thing to say, Camille.' He could have said the same, but he didn't want to encourage her. 'I hope we meet again sometime.'

'You're just being polite.' Suddenly, she looked almost near tears as they stopped on their walk again and she looked up at him. 'I hate it here.'

'In Atlanta?' He was shocked. 'Why?'

She looked beyond the trees in the park. She knew it well, and knew how different her life was from her mother's when she was young. She had certainly heard enough about it in the course of her life. 'It would be different if we lived in Charleston or Savannah, but . . . Atlanta is different from all that. Everything here is ugly and new. People aren't as genteel here as they are in other parts of the South, and when we go there, people aren't as nice to us. It's like my mother . . . she knows the difference, she tells us about it all the time. It's as if Daddy isn't

61

good enough for her, and she thinks I'm like him,' she made a face, 'and Hubert's worse,' Jeremiah laughed, 'I hate being here. Everybody here thinks like that. They accept Mama . . . but they whisper about Daddy and Hubert and me . . . they don't do that up North, and I'm tired of it here. No matter how much money your Mama and Daddy have, they talk about you all the time, who your grandfather was, where your money came from . . . look at Mama, she doesn't even have a penny to her name, but they still think she's all right, and we're not . . . have you ever heard anything so dumb?' Her eyes blazed as she looked into Jeremiah's eyes. He knew precisely what she meant, but it was a difficult topic to discuss with her. He was stunned that she had brought it up, and so candidly. She really was an amazing girl. Nothing was forbidden to her, not even his lips.

'In a few years, Camille, no one will care. Acceptance comes with time, and perhaps your father's . . .' he stumbled over the words '. . . fortune . . . is still very new. They'll forget in time. By the time your children come along, all they'll remember is who your grandfather was, and how well you've dressed for the last twenty years.' But he didn't quite believe that and neither did she.

'I don't care. I'm going to get out of here some day and go North.'

'Things aren't so different there. People are snobbish in Chicago and New York, and even in San Francisco sometimes, although it's a little different there because everyone is new.'

'It's worse in the South. I know it is.' She wasn't entirely wrong, and their eyes met again as he watched her face. 'I wish I lived in California with you.' It was a shocking thing to say, and he suddenly wondered if she were going to assault him again, finding himself more than half wishing she would.

'Camille, behave yourself.' For the first time he sounded stern, but she liked that too.

'Why aren't you married by now? Do you have a woman in California?'

Things were getting worse. There was no stopping this girl. 'What is that supposed to mean?' He sounded annoyed with her as he looked away.

'It means a mistress. My father has one in New Orleans. Everyone knows that. Do you?'

Jeremiah gasped and looked her firmly in the eye. 'Camille, that is a shocking thing to say.'

'It's true. My mother knows it too.' And then, 'Well, do you?'

'I do not.' He shoved Mary Ellen from his mind, she was not a mistress after all, and this child had no right to know about that. Or about anything. She was a great deal too free.

'What do you know of things like that?' She was far too knowing for a girl of seventeen, and suddenly he disapproved. They began to walk back in the direction they had come and the way she tucked her hand into his arm suddenly warmed his heart again. 'You are a little minx, you know, a vixen, and if you were my child, or my "woman," as you put it, I would beat you every day.'

'No, you wouldn't,' she laughed musically in his ear, 'you'd love me to pieces because we'd have a lot of fun.'

'Would we now, and what makes you so sure of that? I'd make you scrub floors, and pull weeds, and work in the mines . . .' But what was he saying, he was playing her game again. But how could one not? There was something absolutely irresistible about the girl.

'No, you wouldn't. We'd have a maid.'

'Of course not. I'd treat you just like an Indian squaw.' But it was obvious that she didn't believe a word he said, and he found himself standing too close to her as they left the park, aware of her delicate perfume, the rustle of her silks, the warmth of her slender arm, and graceful neck . . . the tiny little ears . . . he felt a wave of lust wash over him again and backed away from her. What on earth was this girl doing to him? She looked up at him with a devilish glance.

'I like you very much, you know.' It was the end of the afternoon and the light in the sky was as soft as her skin.

'I like you too, Camille.'

He thought he saw a tear in her eye and he was stunned. 'Will I ever see you again?'

'I hope so. One day.' They said very little to each other then, and walked home arm in arm. He felt almost a sense of loss when he said goodbye to her and returned to his hotel. All night, as he tossed and turned, he had to push her from his mind. And he was even more upset to realize how relieved he was when Orville Beauchamp sent him a note at the hotel the following day, asking him to dine with them. When he saw Camille again, he realized how desperately he had missed her since the night before, but that was ridiculous, even to him. As his eyes caressed her face she seemed relieved to see him again, as though she had been afraid she never would, and they could scarcely take their eyes off each other during the entire meal. Beauchamp noticed it himself, and his son looked amused, and when at last Orville and Jeremiah were alone over brandy and cigars, Orville Beauchamp looked directly at him. There was no preamble to his speech and Jeremiah felt as though he had been punched in the chest at the sound of her name.

'Thurston, Camille means everything to me.'

Like a youth, he felt flushed. 'I can certainly understand that. She's a lovely girl.' Oh God, what had he done? Did he know that they had kissed? He felt like an errant boy about to get a well-deserved but ferocious scold. And he waited nervously.

'The question I want to ask you,' he looked Thurston right in the eye, 'is just how lovely is she to you?' He didn't mince words, and Thurston almost flinched. He deserved what was happening to him. He had no right to flirt with a girl of her age, yet surprisingly, Beauchamp didn't seem upset, but Jeremiah had to deal now with what he had asked.

'I'm not sure I understand what you mean.'

'You heard what I said. Just how attractive is my daughter to you?' Oh my God . . .

'Very attractive, of course, sir. But I must apologize if I have offended you and Mrs. Beauchamp in any way . . . I . . . there's really no excuse for . . .'

'Hush! Men always behave like fools around her. Old, young, they all go half mad when she turns those blue eyes on them, and she's well aware of her own powers. Thurston, don't delude yourself. I wasn't complaining about any affront. I was asking you a direct question man to man. But perhaps I'd best explain myself first. She's what I love most in this life. If I had to give everything up, business, money, house, wife, and save one thing . . . Camille would be it. She's all I really care about,' he considered his words and then thought better of what he'd said, 'just about anyway.' He grinned, and then his features sobered again. 'And I want to get her out of the South. This is no place for a bright girl. They're all fools here, overbred, overrun, with no money left, and the ones who have the money, like me,' he looked honestly at the man sitting across from him, 'aren't the kind of man I want for her. They're crass and uncouth, unrefined, and more than half of them aren't as smart as she is. She's a remarkable girl in many ways, the best of two worlds, but because of that, she doesn't fit here.

64

The men like her Granddaddy are all weak and whining and poor, the others aren't good enough. Thurston, there is no one good enough for her here. Not in Atlanta, or Charleston or Savannah or Richmond, or anywhere in the South. I was thinking of taking her to Paris next year, and introducing her to the aristocracy.' Jeremiah found himself wondering how Beauchamp would have managed that, although at times it was amazing what money could do. 'In fact, I've been promising her that for a long time. But when you walked into our house last week . . . Thurston, I had an amazing idea.' Jeremiah felt his entire body grow cold. His whole life was about to change, and he knew it too. 'You're the perfect man for her. And she appears to be very taken with you.' Jeremiah instantly thought of the kiss she had attacked him with the day before, which had been far from repugnant to him. 'You're a good man. I've heard it from everyone, and I like you myself. And I trust my instincts above all, and my instincts tell me you'd be good for her. It's not everyone who could handle Camille.' Jeremiah laughed at that. It was really an overwhelming thought, and he found himself staring at his host. 'Well? What do you say? Would you be interested in marrying my daughter, sir?' It was the bluntest question that had ever been put to him, like buying cattle or land or a house, and yet he had an insane desire to say yes. He had to take a deep breath and set down his glass before responding to his host, and the silence sat between them like a boulder in the room.

'I'm not quite sure where to start, or what to say, Beauchamp. She's a remarkable girl, there's no doubt about that. And I am deeply flattered by all that you've said. It's easy to see how deeply you care about the girl, and she's richly deserving of the feelings you bear for her.' Jeremiah could feel his heart pounding again, it seemed as though it hadn't stopped since the first time he had laid eyes on Camille, but what he said now could affect the rest of his life and it was essential that he weighed each word more carefully than gold. 'But I must tell you, Sir, I am almost three times her age.'

'Surely not that much . . .' Orville Beauchamp looked only faintly perturbed.

'I am forty-three years old. She is seventeen. I would think that an age difference such as that would be repugnant to her. In addition, I live some three thousand miles from here, in a place far less sophisticated than this. You spoke of introducing her to the aristocracy of France . . . I am a miner, Sir . . . I live a simple life, in an empty house, ten miles from the nearest town. It's hardly an exciting life for a young girl.'

'If that were the only thing stopping you, you could move to town. To San Francisco. There's no reason why you couldn't run your mines from there. They're established by now. You couldn't be here if they were not.' Jeremiah had to concede that that much was true. 'You could build her a house in town, and she'd get used to your country life in time.' He smiled, 'It might even do her good. Sometimes I think her life is too frivolous here, although I have to confess, I'm partially responsible for that. I don't like her to be bored, so we take her to balls a great deal of the time. But your life might do her good.' Camille's father knit his brows. 'But that's not the point. The real point is, could you care for her?'

Jeremiah Thurston felt a breath whistle through his lungs, as though it might be his last. 'I never thought to hear myself say this, sir, but I think there is a distinct possibility that I already do. In truth, I don't even understand what I feel for her, and I've been fighting it since we first met, if for no other reason than out of respect for you. She's barely more than a child, a young girl, and I am a great deal too old for this. I have a simple, quiet life, as I said, and I've long since given up such dreams' . . . and yet he had met Amelia on the train, and she had touched a place in his soul, and before that he had watched John Harte's boy die in his arms . . . for the first time in twenty years he had to admit that he wanted something he had never had before, a wife to love, and a child of his own . . . something different than just coming home to Hannah every night, and Saturday nights with Mary Ellen Browne . . . and there was Camille, like a vision in a dream, the embodiment of all that he had never had, or even thought he would . . . 'Something's happened to me in the past week,' it was all he could say, 'and I need some time to think about it.' He wasn't sure what he felt anymore, after Amelia and now this.

Orville Beauchamp did not look displeased. 'She's too young now anyway. And I don't want you to say anything to her.'

Jeremiah looked shocked. 'I had no intention of doing so, Sir. I need some time to think myself. I would like to see what happens when I return to my everyday life, my empty house, my mines,' he sighed, suddenly it sounded desperately lonely to him. Suddenly he felt as though he needed her there. And he had never felt that way about anyone before . . . not since Jennie . . . or even then. . . . 'I don't know what I feel for her. Right now, I would ask you for her hand tonight,' his voice was deep and gruff with the power of what he felt for her, 'but I want to be sure I'd be doing the right thing for both of us. How old is she now?' Suddenly his mind was blank, all he could think of were her eyes, her arms . . . her lips. . . .

'Seventeen.'

'I will return in six months to ask you for her hand, if that still seems wise to me then. If not, I will advise you long before that. I will come to Atlanta, if you still agree, and ask her to marry me, then I will return again in six months and take her with me.'

'Why so long? Why not just take her back with you six months from now, if that's what you decide?'

'I want to build her a decent house in town, if she agrees to marry me. I owe her that much at least. Rest assured, Beauchamp, if I marry your child, I will give her a good life in every possible way.' His eyes emphasised his words, and Beauchamp nodded.

'I have no doubt of that. It's why I spoke to you at all. I meant what I said. You'll be the best thing that ever happened to her.'

'I hope so.' Jeremiah's eyes were strangely bright. He felt as though he had just made the biggest deal of his life. The nine hundred flasks agreed to only days before meant nothing to him. But Camille . . . she was a dream come true, and he already knew that he would be back in six months. It made him look differently at her when he and Orville emerged from their seclusion in the dining room.

'What did my father say to you?' she whispered to him. 'Did someone see us kiss?' She didn't seem overly concerned about it though, and Jeremiah was amused. Looking at her now, it was he who wanted to grab her in his arms and plant a kiss on her lips.

'Yes.' He whispered back, teasing her now. 'He's sending you to a convent, to be guarded by nuns.'

'Oh he is not!' She squealed with laughter and shouted at him. 'He'd never do such a thing. He'd miss me too much!' It reminded him of what a sacrifice Beauchamp would make, if Jeremiah married her and took her away, but he was right in a way, it was better for her. In some ways, she would never be accepted in the South, and she knew it herself. Her blood was tainted by Beauchamp's, and they wouldn't be forgiven for that for at least a hundred years, if then. Her brother seemed not to care, but it was obvious that Camille was bothered by it. Even her mother constantly behaved as though there was a

67

bad smell in the house, and she talked of Savannah like a land forever lost to her, no matter how many times she visited each year.

'Actually,' Jeremiah felt oddly relaxed for a man who had just sealed his fate, or as good as, 'we were discussing another deal. I might come back to Atlanta to discuss it with him in another six months.'

Camille looked intrigued. 'More quicksilver?' She seemed surprised. 'I thought the consortium bought enough to last them a year.' He was continually amazed at how much she knew, and more than that, how much she understood.

'It's more complicated than that. I'll explain it to you some other time.' He glanced at his watch. 'But it's getting late now. I should get back to my hotel, to make sure that they've packed my things. I'm leaving in the morning, little one.' He suddenly felt possessive about her, but he didn't want it to show. He turned and said something to her mother then, but she seemed not to be paying attention to him, and she drifted away, leaving them alone again.

Camille looked up at him with big, sad eyes. 'If I have time, before you come back, perhaps I'll write to you.'

'I'd like that very much.' But he wanted time to think as well.

She looked at him strangely then, as though she knew . . . 'Daddy said he was going to take me to France this year, perhaps I won't be here when you come back. . . .' But he knew she would. Or perhaps he should let Beauchamp sell her to some minor count or duke. The idea revolted him. She wasn't an object to be sold, not even to him. She was a woman, a human being . . . a child . . . now, more than ever, he wanted time to think about whether or not she would be happy with him. He wanted to look across his rolling hills and out the windows of the room in which he slept, and try to imagine her there with him. 'California is so far away . . .' Her voice sounded tiny and forlorn and he reached out and pressed her hand.

'I'll be back again.' It was a promise as much to her as to himself, and he wondered if he truly would. His life would never again be the same, but he wasn't sure he wanted it to be. He looked down at the exquisite girl beside him then and said the only words she wanted to hear. 'I love you, Camille . . . remember that . . .' He gently kissed her fingers then, and then her cheek, and then with a firm handshake and a knowing look exchanged with Orville Beauchamp, he was gone, leaving none of them quite as they had been, least of all himself.

Chapter Seven

The boat arrived in Napa bright and early on a Saturday morning, and Jeremiah expected to hire a coach to take him home to Saint Helena. He had wired the mines that he would be back in the office on Monday morning and he had a whole week-end at home to sort through his papers and mail and check on the vineyards. He looked around as he stood on the dock and took a deep breath of the familiar air. The hills in the distance looked even greener than they had three weeks before when he'd left Napa. As he stood there he saw the boy who had driven him to the station, the boy he had promised the Saturday morning job to. Little Danny Richfield.

'Hey, Mr. Thurston!' He waved an arm from his perch on the carriage and Jeremiah walked toward him with a slow smile. It was nice to be met, even by a child he barely knew, and as he walked toward him he realized that the boy was only a few years younger than Camille. It was a strange thought as he flung his bags up and smiled at Danny.

'What are you doing here, son?'

'My Dad said you'd be coming in today, so I asked if I could use the carriage to pick you up.' He hopped up beside the boy and caught up on the news on the drive home. The two and a half hours sped by as Jeremiah looked happily around him. He fell in love with the Napa Valley each time he saw it. 'You look happy to be back, Sir.'

'I am.' He smiled happily at the boy. 'There's no place in the world like this valley. Don't ever fool yourself about that. You may get the itch to wander one day, but if you do, you'll never find a place you'll like better.' But the boy looked doubtful at his words. There were more exciting places in the world, and he knew it. Besides, he wanted to be a banker when he grew up, and how exciting could it be for a banker in the Napa Valley? At the very least, he wanted to go to San Francisco . . . or St. Louis . . . Chicago . . . New York. . . .

'Did you have a good time, Sir?'

'I did.' But as he looked at the boy, once again thoughts of Camille raced into his head. How was she? Where was she now? How would she like it here? Questions had been pressing into his mind during the long trip back, and even more so now that he was back in Napa again. Suddenly, he saw everything as though through her eyes, imagining what it would be like to bring her here for the first time.

He sat for a long moment and looked around as the carriage rolled to a slow stop outside his house. What would she think of this, he asked himself. Somehow, it was difficult to imagine her here. And there was so much he hadn't done over the years . . . planted flower beds, put up curtains, all the things that Hannah had given up badgering him about long since suddenly mattered to him now. But he was jumping way ahead of himself. He had come home to see how he felt about her, not to redesign his entire world to meet her needs, or was that in fact all he wanted to do? He seemed already to have made up his mind, and yet there was something else he had to deal with here. He was well aware of that as he thanked the boy for driving him home and walked quietly into his house. Jeremiah knew full well what day it was, Saturday. And he wanted to go to the mines and see how things were there, but after that . . . he had to be fair to her . . . to whom? To Camille, he asked himself . . . or Mary Ellen Browne? . . . he felt as though his head was too full, he saw Hannah watching him with her familiar frown.

'Well, you don't look none the worse for wear.' There was no rush to give him a hug or a hello and he smiled at her.

'You sure could take a man by surprise, standing there. How's the world been treating you since I've been gone?'

'Not bad. What about you, boy?' He laughed, but he was still a boy to her and probably always would be.

'It feels good to be home.' And actually it did. The valley in which he lived meant more to him than anywhere else in the world. Even if he had come to realize there was something missing there for him. But perhaps not for too long. He looked up and saw Hannah staring at him.

'What have you been up to, boy? You look guilty as hell.' She knew him better than anyone in the world, enough to see that something had happened to him since he left. 'You been up to mischief while you were back East?'

'Some.' His eyes smiled at her.

'What kind of "some"?'

It was almost impossible to explain and he wasn't sure where to begin. 'Well, let's see. I closed a very important business deal.' He was stalling her and she refused to be fooled.

'That don't interest me worth a damn, and you know that ain't what I mean. What else did you do?'

'I met a very charming young lady.' He had decided to put her out of her misery and now the old eyes glowed.

'Just how charming is that, Jeremiah? Did you pay for it, or was she free?' He roared with laughter and she grinned.

'That is an extremely rude question for you to ask, and no, I did not "pay for it". She is seventeen years old, and the daughter of the man with whom I made the business deal.'

'You chasing after children now, Jeremiah? Isn't seventeen a mite young for you?'

His brows knit at that. She was right, and it was precisely what he feared. She had hit a nerve, without meaning to. And he stood up and tried to brush the thoughts of Camille away. 'I'm afraid it is. That's what I told her, and her father, before I left.' But something in his face looked pained and grim, and Hannah grabbed him by the arm before he left the room.

'No, don't go running off like a wounded cow, you damn fool. I don't expect you to be running after an old dog like me. Maybe seventeen ain't all that young after all. Tell me what she's like.' She had an intuition that this could be serious. 'Come on, Jeremiah. Tell me about this girl you met . . . you like her a lot, don't you boy?' Her eyes met his and, seeing it all, she almost gasped. She had never seen so much love in one man's eyes, and yet he couldn't have known the girl for very long. 'Why, Jeremiah . . . This is serious, isn't it?' Her voice was as soft as old burnished wood, and he nodded as he met her eyes.

'I think it is, my friend. I don't know . . . I need to think it out . . . I'm not even sure she'd be happy here. She's accustomed to a very different life in the South.'

Hannah's voice was gruff when she spoke again. 'Well, she'd be a damn lucky girl if you decided to bring her here.' Jeremiah smiled at her prejudice.

'I'd be the lucky one.' And then, 'She's a very special girl, brighter than most of the men I know, and prettier than any woman I've ever seen. You can't ask for more than that.'

'Is she good?' It was an odd question and it caused a peculiar stirring in his soul . . . good . . . that much he didn't know about her. Jennie had been good, decent, warm, loving, kind . . . Mary Ellen was a decent sort, but Camille? Good . . . bright, funny, fun, delectable, sensual, passionate, exciting. . . .

'I'm sure she is.' Why wouldn't she be? She was seventeen years old. But Hannah had brought another thought to mind, and now their eyes met and held.

'What are you going to do about Mary Ellen, lad?'

'I don't know yet. I thought about it all the way home on the train.'

'Have you made your mind up about this girl? It sounds like you have.'

'I don't know that yet. What I need more than anything is time . . . time to myself . . . to make up my mind. . . .' But that meant keeping his distance from everyone. He knew what he had to do, but he cringed at the thought of telling her. He remembered her words on that last Sunday afternoon . . . 'don't find the girl of your dreams in Atlanta.' . . . Don't be silly, he had said . . . don't be silly . . . and yet he had . . . How could he have done a thing like that, and after all these years? He was thinking of turning his whole life upside down in a way he had done for no one else, certainly not Mary Ellen Browne. All he had ever given her was one night a week, and now he wanted to offer his whole life to this outrageous child . . . but he felt something for Camille he had never, ever felt before. A passion that seared through his very soul. He would have walked a hundred thousand miles for her, carried her across the desert, torn his heart out and put it in her hand. Suddenly he saw Hannah staring at him.

'You look sick.'

'I think I am.' He grinned. It was a kind of sickness, an insanity, both miserable and delightful. 'What does one do about something like this?'

'Go after her, if you want her that bad, but first, you've got something else to do.' They both knew he did, and he dreaded it now. Mary Ellen had been good to him, and he didn't want to hurt her after all these years, except that he knew he would. There was nothing else that he could do. He turned away and looked out over the valley then. It was such a lovely place, it was difficult to imagine anyone unhappy there, except there were those who were. He turned back to Hannah then.

'Have you see John Harte?'

72

She shook her head. 'I hear he won't see anyone. Locked his doors and stayed drunk for more'n a week, and now he's working in the mines alongside his men. He lost almost half of them by the time the sickness went.' She looked sadly at Jeremiah then, 'We lost two, you know, but it never hit us bad over here while you were gone.' She told him who the two men were, and he looked at her unhappily. Why was there no way to stop things like that? How unfair life was at times. 'They say John Harte is like a wild man now. He works all night, works all day, shouts his head off at everyone, and gets drunk the minute he leaves the mines. I guess it'll take a while.' It reminded Jeremiah of his lost fiancée again, and now frightened him about Camille. What if she fell ill while he was gone, if he returned to find her dead? A wave of terror swept over him and Hannah read it on his face and shook her head. 'You got it bad, boy.'

'I know.' He could barely speak after the fear of a moment before.

'I hope she's worth it, 'cause she's getting a good man.' She sighed. 'And I suspect Mary Ellen Browne's about to lose the best man she ever had.'

'Don't. . . .' He turned away again. 'Don't, dammit. . . .' Maybe it was wrong to end it now, and yet it would be worse if he went on and married Camille in the end . . . he could give Mary Ellen a choice of course, but that wouldn't be fair to her. He sighed deeply and stood up. He wanted to bathe and change before going to the mine, and then he had to face Mary Ellen again. It was curious, only weeks before he had left her with regret, and now he was going to say goodbye to her. How strange life was. He looked at his old house-keeper and smiled. 'Maybe in the end, what happens will be for the best.'

'I hope so for you.' He smiled at her and left the room, and half an hour later, he was astride his horse and headed for the mine.

Chapter Eight

When Jeremiah tied his horse to the tree behind Mary Ellen's house that night there was no sign of the children anywhere. He went around to the front door and knocked, and she was quick to pull the door open when she saw him. She was wearing a pretty pink lace dress and her coppery hair shone. Before he could say a word she threw her arms around his neck and kissed him hard. For an instant, he held back, and then he felt the familiar surge of passion rush through him and he pressed her to him, enjoying the feel of her body in his arms as he always did. Then, remembering himself, he pulled away. His eyes avoided hers as he walked her into her parlor.

'How've you been, Mary Ellen?'

'Missing you.' Her eyes searched his face. She looked desperately happy to see him as they sat down in the tiny room. They seldom spent any time there, and it made her a little uncomfortable to do so now, as though he were new to her. There was always a little awkwardness when he returned, but she knew that once they went to bed, the familiar feelings would return and things would be as they always had been. 'I'm glad you're back, Jeremiah.' And as she said it, there was an undeniable tug at his heart. It was pain and regret and guilt. Her eyes looked imploringly at him, and he could feel his stomach churn. Suddenly the visions of Camille leapt into his head, and he could hear Amelia's words again . . . get married . . . .She was right, but where did that leave Mary Ellen now?

'I'm glad I'm home too.' He didn't know what else to say. 'How are the children?'

'Fine.' She smiled almost shyly. 'I took them to my mother's in case you came by. I heard you were coming home tonight.' He felt like a beast now. What could he say? There's a seventeen year old girl in Atlanta. . . . 'You look tired, Jeremiah. Do you want something to eat?' She didn't say the words 'before we go to bed', but she might as well have. He heard them loud and clear, and he shook his head.

'No, no . . . I'm fine. . . . You been all right?'

'Fine.' And then, without saying another word, she slipped a hand inside his shirt and gently kissed his neck. 'I missed you.'

'I missed you too.' He took her in his arms and held her tight, as though to soothe her from the pain he was about to inflict, though suddenly he wasn't even sure why he should. Why did he have to say anything? Yet he did. And he knew it. And it was almost as if she knew it too. 'Mary Ellen,' slowly he pulled away, 'we have to talk.'

'Not now, Jeremiah.' She sounded scared, and he could feel the pounding of his heart.

'Yes, we do . . . I . . . I have some things to say. . . .'

'Why?' Her eyes were big and round and sad. She knew what was coming. She was sure. 'There's nothing I need to know. You're home now.'

'Yes, but . . .' And then suddenly she looked at him with genuine fear. Was it more than just the confession of an indiscretion on the trip? Suddenly she sensed that he was going to change her life.

'Jeremiah. . . .' She had sensed it before he left, feared it. She always did. 'What happened?' Maybe she did need to know.

'I'm not sure.' That was worse still. And she saw easily now how confused he was.

'Is there someone else?' Her words were terse, her eyes sad, and looking at her was like putting a knife in his heart. How could he say the words to her?

His voice was gruff when he spoke. 'I think so, Mary Ellen. I don't really know.' He tried desperately not to think of Camille and in spite of that, visions of her filled his head. 'I'm just not sure. In the last three weeks, my whole life has turned upside down.'

'Oh.' She sat back against the little settee, pretending to be calm. 'Who's the girl?'

'She's very young. Much too young.' Those were words that hurt. 'Barely more than a child. And I don't even know what I feel for her. . . .' His words trailed off and Mary Ellen sprang to life, leaning forward toward him, her hand on his.

'Then what difference does it make? You don't have to tell me something like that.' Maybe nothing was going to change after all, but he shook his head.

'Yes, I do. A lot could come of it. I told her father I wanted six months to think. And then . . . I might be going back. . . .'

'For good?' Mary Ellen looked shocked. She didn't understand, but he shook his head again.

'No.' There was nothing to say except the truth. 'For her.'

Mary Ellen reeled back as though she had been slapped. 'You'd marry the girl?'

'I might.'

There was a long pause as they both sat side by side, numb, and then Mary Ellen looked sadly up at him. 'Jeremiah, why didn't we ever get married?'

'It wasn't the right time for either of us, I guess.' They were wise words and his voice was soft in the small room. 'I don't know. It was so comfortable like this.' He sat back with a tired sigh. He was suddenly exhausted. 'Maybe I'm just not a marrying man. That's part of what I want to think out.'

'Is it kids? Is that what you want?'

'I might. I stopped thinking about that a long time ago, but lately. . . .' He looked unhappily at her, 'Mary Ellen . . . I just don't know.'

'I could try again, you know.'

He was so deeply touched that it hurt as he touched her hand. 'You'd be crazy to do that. You told me you almost died the last time.'

'Maybe this time would be different.' But her eyes didn't hold much hope.

'You're older now, and you already have three fine children.'

'But not yours.' Her voice was a caress. 'I'd try, Jeremiah . . . I would. . . .'

'I know you would.' And then, because he didn't know what else to say, he silenced her with a kiss, and she pressed her body against his, until they lay breathless in the small, airless room. It was Jeremiah who finally pulled away. 'Mary Ellen . . . don't. . . .'

'Why not?' There were tears in her eyes now. . . . 'Why the hell not. . . . I love you, don't you know that?' Her voice rang out with a passion that cut him to the quick. He loved her too, with a friendship and compassion born of seven years. But he had never wanted to marry her, to live with her, be with her . . . the way he wanted to be with Camille. He held her close and let her cry.

'Mary Ellen, please. . . .'

'Please what? Please, goodbye? That's what you came here to say, isn't it?' With tears in his own eyes now, he nodded his head. 'But that's crazy, you don't even know this other girl . . . this . . . child! . . . and all you want to do is think about it for six months. If you have to think about it, it can't be right.' She was fighting for her life, but she sounded more strident than living. He stood up, and looked down at her ravaged face as she began to sob, and he scooped her up in his arms again. There was nothing left for him to say. He walked slowly upstairs and lay her down on her bed, stroking her hair, and soothing her like a small child.

'Mary Ellen, don't . . . you're going to be alright.' But she only looked at him with heartbroken eyes. For her, nothing would ever be the same again. Empty Saturday nights without him stretched ahead of her like a long lonely road. And what would people say? That he'd cast her aside? She cringed as she imagined her own mother's words . . . 'I told you he'd do that, you little whore' . . . and that was all she was now. Jeremiah Thurston's Saturday night whore. All those years of pride and now he'd be gone. She should have grabbed him years before, she told herself, but even she knew that he'd never really even come close. They had both been too comfortable with things as they were.

He sat beside her in the room's only chair as she lay on her bed and sobbed. At last she looked at him with big sorrowful green eyes. 'I never wanted it to end like this.'

'Neither did I. And I didn't have to say anything to you tonight, but that wouldn't have been fair to you. I didn't want to tell you in six months, and I really do have to think.'

'What about? . . .' and then with a choked sob, 'what's she like?'

'I'm not really sure. She's very young, and bright,' and he told a lie for Mary Ellen's sake, 'she's not as pretty as you.'

Mary Ellen smiled. He had always been kind. 'I'm not sure I believe that.'

'But it's true. You're a beautiful woman. And there will be other men. You deserve more than just Saturday nights, Mary Ellen. I've thought that for a long time. It was selfish of me.'

'I didn't mind.' But he suspected that she had, and that she had held her tongue. Slowly the tears began to flow again, and it hurt him so to see her cry that he kissed her eyes and drank away her tears with his lips. Her arms reached out to him again, pulling him close, and this time he was unable to resist her. He held her tight and they lay on the bed. He was as desperately hungry for her as he had always been, and tonight, as he fell asleep, his head beside hers, she wore a tiny smile, and kissed him on the cheek as she turned out the light.

Chapter Nine

'Jeremiah!' When Mary Ellen awoke the next morning, he was gone, and she leapt from the bed with a look of fear. 'Jeremiah!' She ran down the stairs, trailing her pink satin robe on the stairs, her lush figure making him turn to stare at her as she stood in the kitchen doorway.

'Good morning, Mary Ellen.' He looked business-like as he set down two full mugs. 'I made coffee so it would be ready when you got up.' She nodded, and looked frightened again. The night before she had been certain that she had changed his mind, and now suddenly she was no longer so sure. Her voice was frightened and soft.

'Are we going to church?' They sometimes did. But now nothing was the same anymore. He nodded slowly at her, took a sip of the coffee and then set it down.

'Yes, we are.' There was a pregnant pause. 'And then I'm going home.' They both knew that it was for the last time, but she hadn't given up the fight yet.

'Jeremiah. . . .' She took a deep breath as she set down her cup. 'You don't have to change anything. I understand. You were decent to tell me about it last night . . . about . . . about her . . .' She almost choked on the word, but she didn't want to lose this man.

'It was the only thing I could do.' He looked hardened now. He knew he was going to cause her pain, and that it was the only thing he could do. He felt stronger than last night, and that frightened her most. 'I care about you. I couldn't lie to you about what was in my thoughts.'

'But you're not sure.' Her voice was almost a whine, and a muscle grew taut in his cheek.

'Do you want to wait until I am? Sleep with me until my wedding night? Is that what you want?' He stood up, and his voice had grown loud. 'Let me do the decent thing. For God's sake, it's hard enough as it is.'

'And if you don't marry her in the end?' It was a pathetic plea, and he shook his head.

'I don't know. Don't ask me that. If I don't marry her, do you really want me back?' He turned away, and she watched his back. 'You'll hate me after this.'

'I could never do that. You've been nothing but decent to me for all these years.' But just hearing her words made him feel worse and when he turned to her again, his eyes were damp, and suddenly he went to her and held her in his arms.

'I'm sorry, Mary Ellen. I didn't mean it to end like this. I never thought it would.'

'Neither did I.' She smiled through her own tears as they held each other tight, and that morning they did not go to church, instead they went back to bed again and made love until that afternoon when Jeremiah finally saddled Big Joe, pulled himself up into the saddle and sat looking at her on the front porch in her pink robe.

'Take care, pretty one.'

There were tears running slowly down Mary Ellen's face as she stood there, 'Come back . . . I'll be here. . . .' She was barely able to speak and lifted a hand, as his eyes reached out to her for a last time as he rode off toward home, without her, without Camille, without anyone. Alone. As he had always been.

Chapter Ten

Summer in the Napa Valley was rich and ripe and hot that year. The flasks of quicksilver went out to the South as had been arranged in Spring, the mines prospered, the grapes grew, and Jeremiah was more restless every day. Time and again he thought of stopping in to see Mary Ellen in Calistoga, and he was lonelier than he had ever been on Saturday nights, but he did not go back again. Instead, he went to San Francisco several times and visited the brothel he preferred there. But there was an ache no one seemed able to reach, and Hannah watched him come and go, with little to say. She noted that sudden look of relief he wore whenever he went to get his mail and found a letter from Camille.

Camille had been writing to him since his return, funny letters about the people she met, the balls she attended, the parties her parents gave, several trips to Savannah and Charleston and New Orleans, and a hopelessly ugly girl Hubert had met and was chasing because her father had the best stables in the South. The letters were rich and funny and perceptive, and it amused him to read the pirouettes of her pen. Always at the bottom were a few crumbs she left there for him ... as though to dangle him along ... to give him hope ... to bring him back. There was no evidence of real passion now, and she let him know that he would have to pursue her when he returned. By August he couldn't stand it anymore, and he made reservations on the train. It had only been four months since he'd seen her, but he knew his mind now, and Hannah knew it too when he left Saint Helena. She was still sorry for Mary Ellen, the girl had been grieving for months, but she was glad too that Jeremiah would be bringing a young bride home, and that the house would soon be filled with the sounds of his children and a laughing young wife.

Jeremiah had cabled Orville Beauchamp to warn him of his arrival but he had also asked that nothing be said to Camille. He wanted to surprise her, to see what her reaction would be. Four months was a long time in a young girl's life, maybe she had changed her mind after all. He could do nothing but think of that on the long trip into the South, and this time there was no Amelia on the train. He barely spoke to anyone at all, and he was nervous and exhausted when he arrived and saw the Beauchamp carriage waiting to take him to his hotel.

He checked into a beautiful suite of rooms, sent a note to the Beauchamps, and an answer was quickly returned. The pleasure of his company was requested for dinner, and Orville Beauchamp assured him that Camille had still not been told of his arrival. It began to amuse Jeremiah to think of her surprise at seeing him again. It was odd though, he felt a ripple of fear at the same time, and by the time he climbed into the Beauchamp coach at eight o'clock that night, his hands were damp, and he could feel his heart jolt as he saw her house again.

He was ushered into the small, lavishly decorated parlor at the front to wait, and Orville Beauchamp was quick to enter the room and pump Jeremiah's hand. He had known when he'd got the cable from the West Coast, that Jeremiah's trip meant good news.

'How've you been . . . good to see you here, man!' He looked genuinely thrilled and Jeremiah hoped that his daughter would be as pleased to see him.

'Very well.'

'I didn't think we'd see you for another two months.' There was a question in the father's eyes. And at this, Jeremiah smiled.

'I couldn't stay away for another two months, Mr. Beauchamp.' His voice was soft and the swarthy little man beamed.

'I thought it would be like that . . . I hoped it would. . . .'

'How is she? She still doesn't know I'm here?'

'No. But you came at just the right time. 'Lizabeth is in South Carolina visiting friends, Hubert is off buying some damn horse. We're alone, Camille and I, and there's precious little going on in town. Everyone's away for the summer months, but she's been kind of peevish this year,' he grinned. 'She waits for the mail a lot, and talks about you to all her friends.' He didn't tell Jeremiah that she referred to him as 'the richest man in the North, my Daddy's friend.' He didn't need to know that, only that she talked about him to her friends.

'She may change her mind when she sees me again.' He had worried about that all the way East. She was young after all, and he was a much older man. Maybe he would seem too old to her now.

'Why would she do that?' Beauchamp looked surprised.

'Girls do, you know.' Jeremiah smiled, but Beauchamp laughed. 'Not Camille. That child has known her own mind since she was born. Stubborn as a mule, and headstrong too,' he laughed again, proud of his only girl child, 'though I don't suppose I should tell you that, but you'll manage her all right. She's a good girl, Thurston, and she'll make you a fine wife.' His eyes narrowed as he looked at the other man, checking. 'That's still what you have in mind?' He assumed that was why Jeremiah had travelled all the way to Atlanta again, and he was right.

Jeremiah spoke softly from his great height. 'Yes, it is. And you haven't changed your mind, Sir?'

'On the contrary. I think it will be a perfect match for you both.' He toasted Jeremiah with his glass, and the two men smiled. Now all that remained was to convince Camille.

It was another ten minutes before she entered the room, the door swung open quickly, and in floated a vision in the palest yellow silk. There were ropes of topazes strung with pearls dancing at her throat, and her hair was loose in a cascade of dark curls, with one perfect yellow rose pinned behind her ear. She sailed into the room looking at her father, and then glanced without interest at his tall friend. It was terribly hot, and she'd been lying in her room for hours. As she saw him she stopped, and he could hear her breath catch as she registered who he was, and then just as suddenly she flew across the room and hurled herself into his arms, burying her face in his chest. When she pulled away again there were tears in her eyes and a huge smile, and she looked more than ever like a beautiful child as his heart went out to her and held fast for good. He had never felt that way for any living being before, and he was breathless as he looked at her.

'You came back!' It was a squeal of joy as her father laughed. They were a lovely sight to see, the huge man, and the delicate girl, so obviously in love, their age mattering not at all. What mattered was the delight one saw in her eyes, the appreciation in his. The passion barely reined in.

'Of course I came back, little one. I told you I would!'

'But it's so soon!' She was dancing about him with glee, clapping her hands, and the rose in her hair fell at his feet. She scooped it up, and curtsied deeply as she handed it demurely to him. And this time he laughed at her. It was laughter born of ecstasy and relief. He could see in her eyes that she still cared for him.

'You're as big a tease as you ever were, Camille. Should I go away and come back if it's too soon?' He tucked her hand into his as she stood looking into his eyes.

'Don't you dare! I won't let you go away again. And if you do, I'll go to France with Daddy, and marry a duke or a prince!'

'That's a charming threat.' But he didn't seem worried about it.

'I will have to leave eventually though, you know.'

'When?' It was a frightened wail and her father smiled. It was going to be a perfect match for them both, and he had no doubt that Thurston loved the girl, and she was obviously quite taken with him. She was flattered by the attentions of a much older man, just as Thurston was enjoying the affection of a young girl. But there was more to it than that, something that burned between them, almost too bright to touch.

'Let's not talk about my leaving yet, little one. I've only just arrived.'

'Why didn't you let us know you were coming back?' She pretended to pout as dinner was announced and they moved slowly toward the dining room.

'I did.' He smiled at Beauchamp and she tapped her father's arm in reproach, with her fan.

'How naughty you are, Father. You didn't say a word!'

'I thought it would be nicer if Mr. Thurston's visit came as a surprise.' And he hadn't been far wrong.

She beamed at them both. 'How long are you here for, Jeremiah?' She looked imperiously at him, suddenly enjoying the power she had, knowing full well that he had crossed the country to see her. He was a very important man, her father had told her so, again and again. And she had told her friends how important he was. That mattered a great deal to her.

He had made arrangements at the mine to be gone for a month. It was the longest he felt he could stay away, but that would give him more than two weeks with Camille, and if she said yes, he'd have to come home and get things organized anyway. There would be plenty to do. He already had a plan, and Hannah had been as nervous as a cat when he'd left, making him promise to write to her and tell her what Camille had said. But his thoughts were not on Hannah now, but on the pretty girl at his side. She was even more beautiful than she had been that Spring and she seemed to have grown up. She asked him countless questions about the mines and complained that his letters never gave her enough news. 'I haven't written to very many girls,' he smiled at her and a little while later her father shooed her from the room. The butler served them both brandy and cigars, and Beauchamp looked at his prospective son-in-law.

'Are you going to ask her tonight?'

'With your permission, I will.'

'You know you have that.'

Jeremiah sighed softly as he lit his cigar. 'I'd like to know where I stand with her.'

'Do you really have any doubt?'

'Some. She could just be playing, with no idea that I'm going to ask for her hand. That could be frightening to a girl her age.'

'Not Camille.' He kept saying that, as though she were different from all other girls, but Jeremiah wasn't so sure. 'Would you like to announce the engagement at once?'

'I would. Before I go back. And then I could start my plans when I return to California.'

'And what plans are those?' Beauchamp eyed him with interest, wondering what he had in mind for his little girl.

'Something that you said before,' Jeremiah was cautious. After all, she hadn't accepted him yet, but he had already given the matter a great deal of thought, and Beauchamp had been right. She'd be unhappy in Napa too much of the time, and he could go back and forth to see to the mines. He would build a house in San Francisco for her, and they would at least spend the fashionable winter months there. He explained his plan to Beauchamp now, who looked pleased. 'And after the house is built, say in five or six months, I'll come back here for the wedding, and I'll take her back to California with me. How does that sound?'

'Perfect. She'll be eighteen in December. That's four months from now . . . think the house might be ready then?'

'That's a little quick, but it might. I was thinking of February or March, but,' Jeremiah smiled and he looked like a boy again, 'I'd prefer December myself.' He was lonely without Mary Ellen now. 'We'll try for that.' And then suddenly, he got to his feet and began to nervously circle the room.

'Don't worry about it, man.' Beauchamp smiled, and then he realized that it was time to let him speak to Camille. He got up to leave, and left Jeremiah to find her in the garden himself. She was sitting on her favorite swing.

'You two took an awfully long time. Are you drunk?' were her first words to him, and he laughed.

'Not too much so.'

'I think it's so stupid that the women always have to leave the room. What did you talk about?'

'Not much. Business, the mines, a little of everything.'

'What did you talk about tonight?' She was a smart girl, and she watched his eyes as she moved slowly back and forth on the swing. His eyes locked into hers and his voice was deep and soft.

'We talked about you.' He felt his heart race and the swing stopped.

'What did you say?' Her voice was a whisper in the thickly scented Southern air.

'That I'd like to marry you.' For a moment neither of them spoke, as she turned huge childlike eyes up to him.

'You did?' And then she smiled at him and he felt his heart melt. 'You're teasing me.'

His voice was deep and serious. 'No, Camille I'm not. I came to Atlanta this time to see you and ask you to marry me.' He heard her catch her breath and suddenly, as once long before, her lips were crushed on his, but his answering embrace took her breath away this time until, at last, he cradled her in his arms and spoke softly to her. 'I love you very much, Camille, and I want to take you back to California with me.'

'Now?' She looked stunned and he smiled at her.

'Not quite yet. In a few months, after I've built a house for you, and you've turned eighteen.' He stood in front of her now, and gently touched her cheek with his hand, and then he knelt at her feet, bringing her face close to his. 'I love you, Camille . . . with all my heart . . . more than you'll ever know.' Their eyes met and held, and his voice brought a shiver to her flesh. 'Will you marry me?'

She nodded, for once bereft of speech. She had hoped for this, but

86

somehow it had always seemed like a distant dream. And then she threw her arms about his neck. 'What will the house be like?' It seemed a funny thing to say and he laughed.

'Whatever you like, my love. But you haven't answered me yet, at least not in so many words. Will you marry me, Camille?'

'Yes!' She shrieked with delight, pulling him close again and then she pulled away with a troubled air. 'Will I have to have babies if I'm your wife?' He raised his eyebrows at the unexpected words. Her question had embarrassed him. It was something she had to discuss with her mother, not with him. And he was reminded again of how young she was, in spite of how grown up she sometimes seemed.

'I suppose we might have a child or two.' He almost felt sorry for her. She was such a child herself. 'Would you mind that very much?' It was one of the things he wanted most. In the past four months he had thought of nothing but that, the babies they would have. But she looked crestfallen now.

'One of my mother's friends died in childbirth last year.' It was a shocking thing to say, and Jeremiah was even more uncomfortable than he'd been before; this was definitely not a subject he wanted to discuss with her.

'That doesn't happen to young girls, Camille.' But of course he knew it did. 'I don't think you ought to worry about that. Things come about naturally between a man and wife. . . .' But she cut him off, unimpressed.

'My mother says it's the price women pay for original sin. But I don't think it's fair that only women pay the price. I don't want to get fat and. . . .'

'Camille!' He was deeply distressed by what she had said, 'Darling . . . please . . . I don't want you to worry about anything.' And as he said the words, he took her in his arms again and she forgot about what her mother said, and their talk turned to the house he would build her instead, the wedding after she turned eighteen . . . announcing their engagement as soon as her mother got home . . . the party her father would give them . . . as far as Camille was concerned, they were all much more important things. And by the time she went to bed that night, she was so excited she couldn't sleep. They had sought out her father to tell him the good news. He shook Jeremiah's hand, kissed Camille's cheek, and when he went to bed that night, he was more than well pleased. His daughter was going to be a very rich, very lucky, very happy girl. And that made him a very happy man. He was happier than ever that he had put the idea in Thurston's head the previous Spring.

And all Jeremiah could think of that night was the tiny, delicious dark-haired beauty who would lie in his arms so soon. And he could hardly wait. He had been lonely for the past few months, and he hadn't seen Mary Ellen again. Nor had he heard anything from Amelia in New York, although he'd written to her a month or two before, and told her about Camille. But he had enough to think of now . . . his bride . . . and the spectacular house he was going to build her. And as for her comment about having babies, he wasn't concerned. It was natural for a young girl to be afraid. Her mother would undoubtedly talk to her before her wedding night and the problem would take care of itself. Think of it, he told himself as he drifted off to sleep, a year from right then, she would probably be giving him a child . . . he went to sleep that night, smiling to himself, and dreaming of Camille and the children they would have, watching them play in Napa, as he and Camille strolled across the lawn. . . .

Chapter Eleven

Elizabeth Beauchamp rushed home to Atlanta as soon as Orville's letter reached her with the news, and Hubert did too, although he had been a little more difficult to reach. But the family assembled quickly, and invitations were sent all over Atlanta inviting their friends to celebrate the couple. And although many people were still away, more than two hundred appeared for the engagement party, and Camille had never looked more lovely as she stood on the reception line in a beautifully embroidered white organdie dress. Scattered across it were tiny pearls and exquisite little beads, and she looked like a fairy princess with her creamy skin and jet black hair, standing at Jeremiah's side, wearing a dazzling smile, and a twelve carat diamond as her engagement ring.

'My God, it's almost as big as an egg!' Her mother had shrieked when she saw the ring, and Camille had danced about the room looking pleased as her father laughed. 'Aren't you a wicked girl,' her mother laughed too, 'and you're going to be so rich, Camille!' She cast a reproachful glance at Orville who chose not to respond to her this time. He was too pleased about Camille.

'I know I am. And Jeremiah is going to build me a beautiful house, with everything most modern in it, and everything I want!' She sounded nine years old and her mother knit her brows.

'What a spoiled girl you're going to be, Camille.'

'I know.' And the only shadow that crossed her face was the prospect of having a child, but maybe that would be a small price to pay. She was going to talk to her mother about that, and ask if there was anything she could do to put it off for a while, she had heard women talk about that, but she didn't want to mention it now. There was still time before her wedding night.

'Do you know how lucky you are?'

'Yes.' And then she scampered off as the maid came to tell her that Jeremiah was downstairs.

His two weeks in Atlanta felt almost like a dream, with parties and picnics and presents and announcements, and stolen kisses with his hands around Camille's tiny waist. He could hardly wait to bring her home, and it tore at his heart to kiss her goodbye this time. But he had a lot to do before he brought her back with him at last, land to buy, a house to build for his bride. He spent the entire trip back on the train making sketches of exactly what he had in mind, and before he even returned to Napa this time he spent three days in San Francisco looking at parcels of land and enormous lots and then he went to several architects to have them start drawing up plans. The morning he went home, he found exactly what he wanted for her. The lot itself was enormous, almost an entire square block on the southern edge of Nob Hill with a view all the way across the city, and as he squinted his eyes, he could imagine just what he wanted. It would be even grander than the Huntington or Crocker residences, that of Mark Hopkins, or even the Tobins. When he went to the architect's office later that morning and described it, he laughed when the man said that within two years he would have just exactly what he wanted.

'Not quite, my friend.' The architect looked puzzled as Jeremiah smiled at him. 'I had a little less than two years in mind.'

'One?' The man blanched and Jeremiah's grin widened. He didn't know Jeremiah Thurston . . . or Camille Beauchamp for that matter. Jeremiah could easily imagine her being just as exacting as he was, when she grew up a little and got used to being Mrs. Thurston.

'I was thinking more like four months, maybe five.'

The architect almost gagged and Jeremiah laughed. 'You're not serious?'

'I am.' And with that he sat down at the man's desk and wrote a check for a staggering sum, but they were the best architects in the city and had been highly recommended to Jeremiah by his bankers. He handed the check to the architect and explained that another like it would be delivered upon completion of the job, in four months, five at the most. It was a sum which no one would have argued with and it even helped to ease the time problem a little. With that amount of money behind them, they could hire an army to put up the house on the lot on Nob Hill, which later that day Jeremiah purchased with a single check. He was an easy man to deal with. And when he got on the boat for Napa at twilight, he was pleased with the day's business behind him. The architect himself would be coming to Napa in a week's time to show Jeremiah his drawings, and with any luck at all, they would be starting construction only days after that. Jeremiah didn't want to waste a moment, and he wanted the house finished when he brought his bride out from the East. He had already decided to honeymoon in New York after their December wedding, and then he would bring Camille home, to Napa, and their beautiful new house in San Francisco. They would live in the city during the winter months, and at the first hint of Spring they would move to Napa until the end of the summer. It sounded like a perfect existence to Jeremiah, and when the architect appeared at the mines the following week he thought that the drawings he presented were equally perfect. The man had correctly understood the importance of Jeremiah's project. He was a man of forty-four years of age, marrying for the first time, and his bride was an eighteen year old girl who fired his heart and his dreams and his soul. It was a house to which one would have brought a princess, a home in which to raise one's children, and which would withstand a dozen generations. It was a veritable palace, with a stained glass dome gracing the central part of the house, over the main hall, and four beautiful little turrets at each corner. There were columns in front and a stern looking façade, extensive grounds and layouts for beautifully manicured gardens, an exquisite gate through which their carriages would pass and a high fence all around. It looked more like a country property than a city dwelling, which pleased Jeremiah immensely, and he was especially excited about the stained glass dome. It would bring in shafts of brightly colored light and give the appearance of sunlight even on a dreary day. It was a gift he especially wanted to give Camille, to whom he wanted to give a lifetime of sunlight. In every way, the designs were perfect. It managed to combine the rococo and the contemporary in a way which pleased the eye and satisfied Jeremiah's soul, and when the architect returned to Napa to take the boat back to the city, Jeremiah sat back at his desk with a huge smile. He could hardly wait until Camille saw it. He could already imagine her strolling in the elegant gardens, or lounging in the lavish suite they had just discussed, with a huge master bedroom, a boudoir, and both a dressing and sitting room for her, and a handsome wood panelled study for Jeremiah. There was to be a nursery on the same floor with a sitting room, and a bedroom for the baby's nurse, and upstairs, six more large, airy bedrooms for the same purpose. Who knew how many children they might have? The drawing room downstairs was the largest the architect had ever designed, and there would be another smaller one, an enormous panelled library, a dining room and a ballroom. The kitchens would be the most modern ever built in San Francisco, the servants' quarters enviable and extensive, the stables would even have filled Hubert with jealousy. The house had absolutely everything they could have wanted, and would boast wood panelled rooms and handsome chandeliers, sweeping staircases, magnificent carpets. The architect assured Jeremiah that his staff would begin searching out these treasures now, and cabinet makers and carpenters would be put to work at once, even before the house was complete. And from now on, Jeremiah would come into the city once a week, to observe the work on the site, and to look over their progress. It was a mammoth project for all concerned, and Jeremiah wondered constantly if it would be ready in time, as letters rained in from Camille, talking of all her preparations for the wedding. The fabric for the dress had been bought in New Orleans and had been woven in Paris, and she wouldn't tell him more than that, but she could hardly wait, and she was as excited about her trousseau as he about their house, about which he said very little to her. He had told her only that he thought they should have a house in San Francisco, he didn't tell her that he was building the largest and finest home the city had ever seen, and that each day crowds stood gaping as the work went forward with vast crews of men attempting to meet his deadline. He had even sent some of the men from the mines to assist them, and on weekends he offered huge bonuses to those who would work in the city on the construction site.

And at the same time he was doing everything he could to refurbish the house in Saint Helena. He had never noticed before how shabby his bedroom had got in nineteen years, and he now realized how barren and empty the house really was. He went on massive buying sprees, both in Napa and San Francisco, and had Hannah making curtains for every room. If he was going to bring Camille to Napa, it was going to be pretty. She was a young girl and needed light, airy, cheerful surroundings. He had fresh gardens planted outside the house, had some of his men paint the house, and by

October, it looked like a new home, and he was surprised himself at how beautiful it was. Only Hannah seemed annoyed by the changes and she snarled at him each time she saw him, until at last she fell silent and said nothing at all until Jeremiah could stand it no longer. He finally sat her down at the end of a long day, poured a cup of coffee for them both, and lit a cigar despite the inevitable protests.

'Alright now, old woman, now we're going to talk. I know you don't like the changes I've made, and I've been whipping everybody's ass for the last two months, but it looks lovely, and Camille is going to love it. What's more, you're going to love her, she's an enchanting child,' he smiled, thinking of the letter he had received from her only that morning, 'and it seems to me that you've been nagging at me for I don't know how long to get married. And I am. So why are you so mad at me?' She had refused several times now to come and see the beginnings of the house in town. 'You can't be jealous of an eighteen year old girl. There's room for both of you in my life. She already knows about you, and she's excited to meet you, Hannah.' He looked troubled, the old woman really had been giving him a bad time, especially in the last few weeks. 'What's wrong? Aren't you feeling well, or are you just angry at me for building a house outside Napa?'

She smiled at that, there was some truth in that. 'I told you, you don't need another house. You're going to spoil that girl before she even gets here.'

'You're right. She's going to be an old man's darling.'

'She's a lucky girl.' They were the first kind words Hannah had said to him in a month, and Jeremiah felt relief sweep over him. He had been genuinely worried about her, and worried too that she was going to be as disagreeable to Camille as she was being to him, and that his fragile little bride from the South wouldn't have known what to make of the chilly reception.

'I'm a lucky man, Hannah.' His eyes met the older woman's, and she could see that he was happy. It was funny how his life had changed in the last six months . . . funny . . . but there was more to it than that. 'I've got a lot to be grateful for.' His eyes were innocent as they bore into hers, and he saw something sad there. 'What's wrong?'

She had to tell him the truth. No matter what she had promised. There were suddenly tears in her eyes as she looked at him. 'I don't know how to tell you this, Jeremiah.'

'What's wrong?' A genuine rush of fear ran through him and he remembered the terror he had felt when they came to tell him that Jennie was dying of influenza. He had the same sinking feeling now as Hannah watched him.

'It's Mary Ellen.'

His heart stopped as a sudden portent of doom ran through him. 'Is she sick?'

Hannah slowly shook her head. 'She's having a baby . . . your baby. . . .' He felt as though someone had punched him, chasing every breath of air out of his body.

'Oh no . . . but she couldn't . . . she wasn't. . . .'

'I told her myself she was crazy when I saw her in Calistoga.' She almost died with the last two young 'uns, and she's no young girl now. She made me swear not to tell you, Jeremiah.'

He nodded, feeling sick for a moment and calculating backwards. It must have happened in April, perhaps the last time he'd been with her. And he had the strange feeling that she had wanted it to happen. She had told him then that if he wanted children, she would have his baby. But she was crazy. The doctor had told her years before that she would die if she ever had another child. And why was she doing this now? . . . Now? Without saying a word to Hannah, he clenched his fist and pounded the kitchen table, as the woman watched his eyes. Then he got to his feet and strode to the kitchen door.

'What are you going to do?'

'I'm going to talk to her, if nothing else. She's a damn fool, and you're a bigger one if you thought I wouldn't do anything about it.' He'd had enough of her stubborn, stupid pride. She had been his woman for seven years, and the least he could do was help her now. But that was all he could do for her. There was no changing the fact that he was getting married. He wasn't willing to change that.

He walked outside and saddled up Big Joe, and he rode to Calistoga with a vengeance, arriving outside with a cloud of dust which startled Mary Ellen's children, who stared at him wide eyed as he marched inside. But the oldest called out to him, 'Ma's not home.'

He returned to the familiar doorway, scowling. He could see that no one was home. 'Where is she?'

'She's working at the spa. She won't be home for a while yet.'

He would have waited, but he wasn't in the mood, instead he grabbed Big Joe and rode towards the main street where the spa was. Damn woman. Everyone in town probably knew she was having his

94

baby. He berated himself every step of the way for having gone to bed with her that night. He had never meant to, but she had been so heartbroken, and, to be honest, he had wanted her as he always did. But it was stupid . . . stupid . . . and he couldn't help wondering if one day Camille would find out about this illegitimate child. That worried him as he tied up Big Joe outside the spa, but in truth he was far more worried about Mary Ellen.

He found her behind a counter, carefully marking names down for appointments, her body hidden behind a desk. At least it wasn't overly hard work for a woman who was expecting a baby. She started when she saw him, and made as though to back away, but he reached out and grabbed her arm.

'I want you to come outside with me right now.' His eyes were blazing with worry and anger, and it irked him to realize how happy he was to see her. She looked prettier than ever, even more so now that she was a little frightened.

'Jeremiah . . . stop . . . I . . . please . . .' She was afraid of making a scene, and she didn't want him to see her figure. She didn't realize yet that Hannah had told him, and she looked so distressed that a male attendant approached, ready to assault Jeremiah.

'Want some help, Mary Ellen?' He prepared his fists and she quickly declined the offer, imploring Jeremiah with her eyes to leave them.

'Please . . . it's better if you . . . I don't want. . . .'

'I don't care what you want. I will carry you out of here if I have to. Get up and walk out to the street with me, or I'll pick you up and do it for you.'

She blushed purple, and looked despairingly around her, grabbing desperately at a shawl on the back of her chair which she wove loosely about her, and followed him outside. The man who had been willing to protect her had promised to take over the desk in her absence, but she had promised not to be away long.

'Jeremiah . . . please . . .' He was pulling her across the street to a small clump of trees and a bench. 'I don't want to . . .' He almost shoved her onto the bench and turned to face her.

'Never mind what you want. Why didn't you tell me?'

'Tell you what?' She looked blank and then her face went pale. 'I don't know what you mean.' But her pallor and her obvious terror made her a liar.

'You know perfectly well what I mean.' He stared pointedly at her midsection and gently peeled away the shawl. There was no denying what he saw. She was six months pregnant. 'How could you not tell me, Mary Ellen?'

She began to cry softly and dabbed at her eyes with a lace handkerchief he had given her long before, making him feel even worse. 'Hannah told you . . . she promised not to . . .' She began to sob, and he sat down and put his arms around her, for all the world to see. He had never been ashamed of Mary Ellen. He just hadn't wanted her as his wife, and that hadn't changed. None of it had, except that things were a good deal more complicated now, if she were having his baby.

'Mary Ellen, what did you do, you foolish girl?'

'I wanted your baby if I couldn't have you . . . I wanted . . .' But she couldn't go on as the sobs overwhelmed her.

'It's so dangerous for you. And you knew that.' He wondered if she thought he would marry her when he found out, but she was quick to deny that. She explained that she had just wanted his child, and she wanted nothing else from him. But that brought him to a quick boil too. 'I don't want to hear that nonsense anymore, Mary Ellen. I've heard too much of that from you, and I should have stopped listening years ago. You're going to stop working right now. Pride be damned. I'm taking care of you and this child, financially, since I can't in any other way. At least I can do that much for you, and if you don't like it, it's too bad. It's something I want to do for my child. Is that clear?' She almost trembled at the ferocity of his words.

'I have three other children to support, Jeremiah.' She said it with quiet pride. 'And I've never failed them.'

'I don't want to hear anything more about it.' He sat down again, with a worried look. It was a matter which wasn't resolved just with a little money. 'Have you seen the doctor, Mary Ellen?' She nodded and her eyes sought his. It was obvious that she still loved him, and he tried not to feel all that he did as he looked at her. He had to think of Camille now. In two months they would be married . . . before this baby was even born. Life really wasn't fair at times. Things might have been different if Mary Ellen had conceived his child before this. 'What did the doctor say?'

'That everything will be fine.' Her voice was soft and gentle, and Jeremiah felt a shaft of guilt so acute that it was almost a physical pain in his chest as he looked at her.

'I wish I believed that.'

'It's true. I survived the other three, didn't I?'

'Yes, but you were younger. This was a foolish thing to do.'

'No, it wasn't.' There was a look of defiance on her face and it was obvious that she regretted nothing. It angered him again to see it.

'What in hell made you do it?' It was something he would never understand. It was a foolish thing to do, for a thousand different reasons.

'It's all I have left, Jeremiah . . .' Her voice was soft and sad and it tore at his heart to listen to her. 'You're gone now, and you'll never be back and I know it. You're marrying that girl, aren't you?' He nodded, with a frown between his eyes and she looked even more determined. 'Then I was right to do it.'

'You risked your life.'

'It's my life to do as I want with.' She stood up and he thought that she had never been more beautiful. She had pride and guts and she had done just as she wanted . . . not unlike what Camille would do . . . but Camille had even more spunk and style than this woman, and he acknowledged it. He didn't regret his choice now, seeing Mary Ellen again, but he regretted what she had chosen to do. It was going to make life difficult for them all, including the child, and he knew it. Sooner or later word would get out, Camille would find out, and eventually his children would know. Napa was too small a county to allow for that kind of indiscretion without being discovered, and more than anything he didn't want to hurt his bride. Imagine if she heard about the birth of his bastard, a month after their wedding? He cringed at the pain it would inflict on her.

'I wish you hadn't done this, Mary Ellen.'

'I'm sorry you feel that way, Jeremiah.' She tilted her chin up and he wanted to kiss it. 'I always thought you wanted a child.'

'But not like this. There are better ways to do this.'

'Not for me, Jeremiah. Not now. I wish you happiness with your bride.' But he knew that she wished him nothing of the sort. She knew too that he was refurbishing his Napa house and building a veritable palace in the city. Everyone within a hundred miles knew of the house he was building for Camille.

'What are you going to do now?' He was thinking neither of his bride, nor of the house he was building for her.

'Just what I've been doing up until now. I got the job at the spa, and it's decent. I don't get too tired working there, and when the baby comes, the girls can help me take care of it when I go to work.'

'You should stay home with your children.' He sounded disapproving, which wasn't like him. He had never said anything like that to her before, but now one of her children was his, which was different. 'I'll see to it, Mary Ellen.' The next day he would go to his bank in Napa and make arrangements. There were ways to handle this sort of thing, and he was going to see to it. Maybe he should have done something for her years before, but it wasn't too late to do it now.

'I don't want you to do that, Jeremiah.'

'I'm not asking you, just like you didn't ask me about this. Now I'm making the decisions.' Secretly, she was disappointed that he wasn't more moved by the impending birth of his baby, but his mind was filled with other things now . . . and other babies than hers. Mary Ellen sighed. In some ways, she had made a mistake and she knew that too, but she stubbornly refused to regret it, as she had told Hannah several times before. This was what she had wanted. 'I want you to stop working at the spa.' He was looking at her in an almost fatherly fashion.

'I can't do that.'

He glared at her now. 'Either you give them notice or I will. Your life is going to change right now. Is that clear? You are going to stay home with your children and my child, and save what's left of your sanity and your health. If you kill yourself over this baby, what's going to happen to the others? Have you thought of that?' Her eyes overflowed at his words, and he regretted the vehemence with which he had said them. 'I'm sorry . . . I just don't . . . this is difficult for us both. Let's make it as easy as we can. Let me make it easier for you. Won't you?' Her eyes looked deep into his and slowly she nodded. She wanted to tell him that she still loved him, but there was no chance, and she had to go back to work in a few minutes, and she was starting to feel sick, she had been wearing her corsets so tight so that no one would notice. At least if she stopped work for a while, she wouldn't have to wear those corsets. . . .

'Maybe for a little while, Jeremiah.' She was suddenly very tired. 'Just until after the baby.'

'No.' And then he simply patted her arm. 'Let me work it out.' He would send his banker to talk to her. It had been done before. She would cry, and he would reason, and every month she would be paid a stipend, which would support herself and her four children, comfortably, for as long as she needed it. It was the least he could do for her. He wasn't going to marry her, and that was the end of that. The dream of that was long gone. Instead, he was building a palace for the girl from Atlanta.

Jeremiah stood up then, and walked Mary Ellen back to where the young man was waiting, suddenly wondering if there were more to his protectiveness of her than first met the eye, but if that was the case, Jeremiah didn't want to know about it. He had no doubt that the child was his, he trusted her and knew there had been no one else, and if there was now, she still had a right to some comfort. He had Camille after all.

'You'll quit your job then?' She nodded, and then her eyes sought his.

'Will you come back and see me again sometime, Jeremiah?' She tore at his heart with her words, but something deep inside told him not to.

'I don't know. I don't think I should, for all our sakes.'

'Not even to see the baby?' Her eyes overflowed again and he felt like the biggest monster alive.

'I'll come to see you then. And I want to hear from you before that if you need anything at all.' He wasn't afraid that she would take advantage of him. She never had before, and even now when other women would be clawing at him, she was being very decent. 'I'll be gone . . .' he hesitated with embarrassment 'after the first of December.' He was getting married in Atlanta on the twenty-fourth, but there would be two weeks of parties before that, and he had promised Camille he would be there. And now this woman in Calistoga was having his baby. How strange life was. He couldn't help thinking that as he rode slowly home, thinking of how much his life had changed in the past six months. And stranger still, it was possible that within the next year, he would have two children. He had to smile at the thought as he tethered Big Joe in his stables . . . two children . . . one by Mary Ellen . . . and one by Camille . . . and it didn't even seem peculiar to him, in light of all the other goings on, that there was a letter from Amelia Goodheart waiting for him on the kitchen table. It was the first time he had heard from her since he had left her on the train, on her way to Savannah. She wrote to him now to tell him that she had received his letter and that she was happy for him about the young lady in Atlanta, a little jealous too, she admitted with a smile he could almost see, but she told him that he was doing the right thing, and she hoped to meet her if they ever came to New York. And in the meantime, her daughter in San Francisco was expecting another baby, and she would undoubtedly be out sometime in the next year to see her. Her letter filled Jeremiah with a kind of warmth, and he found himself thinking of the three women and how different they were as he heated up some dinner Hannah had left for him. Curious how life was, women and babies, and wild flings on transcontinental trains, and in another nine weeks he would be married to the delicate little girl with creamy skin and rich black hair, with the teasing lips and dancing eyes, his whole body seemed to shiver as he sat in the quiet kitchen thinking of her.

Chapter Twelve

When Jeremiah left for Atlanta on the second of December, work on the house on Nob Hill had gone at a pace even he could scarcely believe. He was due back in San Francisco around January 15th, and he had no doubt in his mind that the house would be complete by then. They had already put up a small brass plaque in the outer wall with 'Thurston House' engraved on it in carefully engraved letters. Thurston House, and Camille knew almost nothing about it. He had kept it a carefully guarded secret, but there was no doubt in his mind that she would love it. The turrets were in place now. The trees and gardens were planted. The exquisite wood panelling and chandeliers were already done, and a marble floor had been designed from marble shipped down specially from Colorado. There would be every modern convenience ever made and the woods and the fabrics and the crystal were the best anyone could buy. The place was almost a museum before anyone had ever lived in it, and he laughed to himself as he took a last look around before catching the train to Atlanta. It was going to take a lot of children to fill it.

The trip to Atlanta seemed interminable this time, he was so excited to arrive, and he was bringing with him the most beautiful pearl necklace they had ever seen at Tiffany's in New York, with pearl and diamond earrings to match, and a very handsome bracelet too. They had sent him drawings of the pieces and they had arrived just in time for him to take them to Atlanta. There was also a very pretty ruby pin for Mrs. Beauchamp and a spectacular sapphire ring he was going to give Camille when they got to New York for their honeymoon. And he had written to Amelia, hoping to see her, and to introduce her to Camille when they were in New York. She had finally begun to write to him and he enjoyed the correspondence with her almost as much as he had enjoyed the hours they had shared on the train. He had taken Amelia's advice after all, and he was so proud of his bride, he could hardly wait to show her off to everyone he knew.

He thought of Amelia now, on the trip East. It had been less than a year since they met, and since he saw her last, and he still remembered the striking, elegant beauty. It struck him again that she looked vaguely like Camille, but it was Camille who was foremost in his mind now, the graceful arms, the tiny face, the long fingers, the delicate ankles, the shining hair; he could hardly wait to hold her again and kiss her lips and listen to her laughter as he held her in his arms.

She was waiting for him at the train station in Atlanta this time, complaining because the train was four hours late, but it didn't seem to dampen her spirits and she flung herself into his arms with a squeal of glee, and a kiss and a burst of laughter. She was wearing a deep green velvet cape with a matching hood and a muff, all of it lined in ermine, and beneath it a green taffeta dress, which she had meant to save for her trousseau, but didn't because she wanted to wear it to meet him at the station. He could hardly keep from squeezing her too hard as they rode to the Beauchamp home where he greeted the entire family and drank champagne before going to the hotel and settling in for the two weeks before their wedding day.

The next two weeks were a ceaseless, breathless round of parties, with balls, dinners and lunches and every possible kind of feast and celebration. The Beauchamps gave a large dinner themselves the day before the wedding for Camille's closest friends, as a sort of goodbye before she left Atlanta. And there were tearful greetings and tearful goodbyes, and Jeremiah thought he had never seen so many pretty young women in one room, but the prettiest by far was his fiancée. She swirled around the dance floor in his arms, and danced until dawn every evening, never seeming to tire, and always alive and excited again by the next morning.

Jeremiah laughed to his future father-in-law one day: 'I'm beginning to worry about keeping up with her. I'd forgotten that that was what youth meant.'

'It'll keep you young, Thurston.'

'I hope so.' But he wasn't really worried. He had never been happier than he was now, and he was looking forward to their trip to New York and their return to San Francisco, when he would show her the house he had built for her. He had to assume that all was going well in his absence, and even if some of the finishing touches had to be completed later on, the overall effect was already spectacular. He had told Orville about it when he arrived, and Camille's father looked well pleased by what Jeremiah had done for his daughter. It was quite a tribute to his Camille, who was already enjoying her fiancé's lavish gifts, as was Mrs. Beauchamp . . . 'so much the gentleman . . . so very kind . . .' She looked ever more the relic of the old South, unlike her daughter, who brazenly proclaimed how much she enjoyed Jeremiah's extravagant gifts, and showed them off to all her friends, 'twelve carats' she said again and again of the diamond ring, and now she was showing everyone the pearl necklace, which was indeed a remarkable piece of jewelry, with pearls of up to 28 mm. in diameter. 'They cost him a fortune, I'm sure,' she added once and was instantly scolded by her mother, but her father was only amused, and Jeremiah said nothing. He was growing used to the Beauchamps' ways, and knew that inwardly, Camille was different from them.

The wedding was held at six o'clock in the evening on Christmas eve in St. Luke's Cathedral on the corner of North Pryor and Houston Streets. The wedding was performed by the Reverend Charles Beckwith, a cousin of the Bishop, and there were several hundred friends present to watch the couple exchange their vows and several hundred more that had been invited to the reception at the hotel where Jeremiah was staying. It made it easy to slip away at last, and bring his bride to the suite where her bags were already waiting. They would spend the night here, and then lunch with her parents the next day before catching the train to New York early that evening. And by the time Camille and Jeremiah reached his room, they were both exhausted. It had been a long long day for them both, a longer two weeks, filled with excitement and parties, and even a family Christmas party that day at lunch. Jeremiah felt as though he had never in his life been to so many parties. And now he looked at his tiny bride, draped languorously across the room's pink velvet settee, her magnificent ivory lace wedding dress spread around her like a collapsed tent, and he thought again how much she meant to him. He had waited more than half a lifetime for her, and he had no regrets now. She had been worth waiting for, worth the heartbreaks that had come before, the disappointments, the lonely years . . . in the end, she was even worth causing Mary Ellen pain. Not for anything in this life would he have given up marrying Camille. He adored her in every possible way, and knew that she would be the perfect wife for him, with all her brilliance and her fire and her outrageous flirtatious ways and her passion. But she didn't look particularly passionate now, as she lay sprawled out in her wedding dress, her eyes suddenly glazed with exhaustion. It had indeed been an endless two weeks of constant celebration and he had worried more than once that the festivities would prove to be too much and she might fall ill. But she didn't look ill now, only childlike and terribly tired.

'Are you all right, my love?' He knelt at her side and took her hand and kissed her palm as she smiled at him.

'I don't think I can move, I'm so tired.'

'I'm not surprised. Shall I call for the maid?'

Her eyes held his, and he liked what he saw in there. Lately, she had often said the wrong thing, talking of some expensive dress her father had bought her for her wedding clothes, or the enormous diamond which had been Jeremiah's engagement gift to her, but what he saw in her eyes now pleased him to his very core; he saw love and joy and trust. It was only her upbringing at her father's hands which had made her so aware of the money people spent. But after a month or two in the Napa Valley, he knew that her mind would be filled with simpler pleasures, the grapes from his vineyard, the flowers in the garden Hannah was planting for her, the babies they would have . . . and even though the house in the city was a veritable palace, the most valuable thing about it was the love with which it had been built for her. It was a monument to their love, which was precisely what Jeremiah was going to tell her when she first saw it. For the first time in his life, he felt totally fulfilled, and now as he looked at his exquisite little bride, lying so quietly in her wedding dress, he felt as though his heart would burst from the sheer happiness of it.

'Well, Mrs. Thurston . . . how does that sound to you?' He kissed the inside of her wrist and something in her stirred as she smiled voluptuously at him. She was too tired to move, but not too tired to want him near her now. She never tired of having him close by, and just looking at him always made her ache with desire. She had never known she would feel that way about any man, and certainly not one as old as Jeremiah Thurston. She had always secretly suspected she would marry some terribly dashing young man, maybe a Frenchman from New Orleans, or one of the French counts her father always talked about . . . or a very rich banker from New York with smoky eyes . . . but Jeremiah was more handsome than any of the visions she had conjured up, and there was a rugged maleness about him, which she liked, and which frightened her only a little now. He was terribly appealing to her, and in spite of what her cousin had said, somehow she couldn't bring herself to think that what he was going to do to her was disgusting. She could see it in his eyes now, the same lust he had looked at her with from the first, but she liked to tease him and bring it out in him, and she did so again now, kissing his neck, and then his ear, and at last his lips, as she could feel him strain toward her.

And then, without saying a word, he began to undo the tiny buttons up her arms, revealing the creamy flesh and kissing her as he did so. And then, removing first the heavy ropes of pearls he had given her, he began to undo the myriad tiny satin buttons down the front of her dress, showing off the exquisite cleavage, covered by the perfectly sculpted satin slip, and finally the lacy corset. He seemed extremely adept at it all, and released her ravishing young body from the clothing which bound it, and she stood before him unafraid, and unadorned, in her naked splendor, with only her creamy silk stockings still on. One by one he peeled them from her, and then he quickly cast aside his own clothing, marvelling at her lack of shyness with him, her openness and her courage . . . covering her with his lips, with his hands, bringing her more pleasure than she had ever dared hope for . . . her cousin had been wrong . . . wrong . . . she thought of her as she moaned . . . this was precisely as she had dreamed it . . . and even when he lay her gently on the bed and parted her legs, entering her at first with his tongue, and then his fingers, and then finally plunging into her with his full desire unleashed within, she moaned not with pain but with pleasure . . . He brought her an exquisite agony she had never even dreamed of, and she brought him to heights so pure and so lovely that he almost cried in her arms, as he lay there, spent, with his head cradled on her bosom.

He looked at her sleepily then, and was happy to see her lying softly beside him, almost purring with pleasure. The expected pain had been brief, and so artful was he that she had barely noticed it. He whispered softly to her, 'You are mine now, Camille.' And she smiled up at him, looking more like a woman than she had only an hour before. This time she reached out for him, and when he took her again, she shouted with pleasure and almost keened as he held her, until at last, released, she fell soundly asleep in his arms as he held her, and it was only a few hours later when she woke again, begging him for more . . . and it was he who cried out this time, at her hands, at her mercy, totally under her spell. There was a magic to her he had never divined, and the wisdom of his choice, and the richness of his luck occurred to him again and again as they made love that morning. He almost had to drag her out of bed to get to the luncheon at her parents the next day on time, and she teased and giggled and pretended to seduce him again, which she carried out with relish and rapture once they were on the train. And they scarcely came up for air all the way to New York after they had said farewell to her parents. They were at Grand Central Station before Jeremiah came to his senses again and he looked like a very happy man as they rode to the Cambridge Hotel where he always stayed. There were moments when he thought he would die of pleasure in her arms, but he didn't really care. If he was going to die, he couldn't think of a better way to go than while making passionate love to his sweet Camille. She was truly the girl of his dreams. And his life was at long last complete.

Chapter Thirteen

Jeremiah and Camille reached New York the day after Christmas and a blanket of snow covered the ground, as the bride leapt from the train clapping her hands with delight. Her eyes sparkled in the cold air, and her face was set off by the splendid sables and matching muff Jeremiah had given her for Christmas. She looked like a Russian princess as she stepped down from the train, one tiny gloved hand held in his as he looked at her with pleasure. She adored all the beautiful things he gave her, and frequently thought how lucky she was to have left Atlanta. He was almost as good as one of the princes or dukes her father had promised her for so long. And she could hardly wait to see his home in the Napa Valley, which she assumed was even grander than a plantation.

They drove to the Cambridge Hotel on Thirty-Third Street. There was no lobby, and Walmsby, the desk clerk, was diligent about keeping press away, which Jeremiah had always liked about the place. He valued the privacy he always had there, the exquisite suites, and Walmsby was always full of amusing stories. Camille strode into the suite ahead of Jeremiah as though she had been checking into hotels with him for years, which made him laugh as he swept her off her feet and threw her on the bed with all her finery and sables.

'You're a brazen little thing, you are, Camille Thurston.' The name still sounded funny to them both, but she did not deny the accusation. And he did not tell her that he'd been startled by her chill manner to his old friend the desk clerk. She had been playing grand lady, and poor Walmsby looked crushed when he had proferred a hand and she ignored it.

'How rude,' she said loudly as she walked past him. 'Who does he think he is?'

'My friend,' Jeremiah had whispered softly. But once alone in the suite with him, she kissed him so hungrily that he forgot all about Walmsby, and as they were dressing for dinner, he smiled to himself thinking of the house he had built her in San Francisco. He could hardly wait until she saw it. He had scarcely mentioned it to her since he'd first arrived in Atlanta, and whenever she inquired about their home, he just brushed her questions off and told her it was decent and she that might like to make a few changes when she arrived.

But for the moment, she was far more interested in what they were going to do in New York. They went to the theatre several times, the opera once, and dinner at Delmonico's on their first night, and the Brunswick on their second, where Jeremiah had a dinner of duck and game hens. The 'horsey set' ate there a lot, and many of the patrons were British. On the third night, Jeremiah had accepted an invitation from Amelia. He had done so with a feeling of excitement. He was so anxious to introduce Camille to her and happy to see Amelia again too. The correspondence they'd struck up had totally turned his infatuation to firm friendship. Amelia's invitation had been so warm that he had accepted with delight, though in the carriage on the way to her home on Fifth Avenue with his bride, he began to have misgivings. Camille was being pettish and spoiled. She had been rude to the maid at the hotel while she was dressing, and it was beginning to annoy him.

Camille was wearing a black velvet cloak and her profusion of sables. The huge diamond ring glittered on her left hand, and the sapphire he had just given her sparkled on her right, and beneath the velvet mantle from Paris she wore a white velvet dress, with little ermine loops at the shoulders and all around the hem. It was an exquisite creation and had cost her father a king's ransom, as he had been only too happy to inform Jeremiah before they left Atlanta.

'You look like a little queen,' he had said to her before they left the hotel, and he took her little kid gloved hand in his own now, as he attempted to describe Amelia to her. 'She's a very special woman . . . intelligent . . . dignified . . . beautiful. . . .' He thought of their harmless flirtation on the train to Atlanta and felt a warm glow. Amelia was a lovely woman and he knew she would be gracious to Camille when she met her.

But Camille was difficult from the moment they entered Amelia's house. It was as though she resented Amelia's obvious breeding, her good taste, her exquisite clothes, even her genteel manner, and it instantly brought out the worst in Camille, much to Jeremiah's embarrassment.

Amelia had a rare grace and gentle charm that made everyone who saw her want to embrace her. Jeremiah himself had forgotten how really lovely she was, with the translucence and sparkling clarity of a very fine diamond, her brilliant eyes, her delicately carved features, the way she moved, the discreet elegance of her very fine jewelry, the ravishing gowns made in Paris. He had never seen her really at her best, only on the train to Atlanta, and yet this friendship had been born there, a friendship he knew he would never relinquish, as he watched her seem to float through the halls of the splendid house Bernard Goodheart had left her. There were liveried footmen everywhere, and the candlelight danced in the most beautiful chandeliers Jeremiah had ever seen, over intricately laid marble floors, patterned in the shapes of flowers scattered from one end of the hall to the other. The decor of each room was unmistakably French, except for the dining room and main library which were impeccably English, and the entire house had the beauty of a museum, and within it danced this gem of a woman. But now, it was obvious that Camille was devoured by jealousy as she observed Amelia's gracious manner. It was as though she couldn't bear anything the older woman did. She resented her every word, every smile, every movement.

'Camille, behave yourself!' Jeremiah urged her in a whisper, as Amelia left the room for a moment to see about selecting another bottle of champagne for them after dinner. 'What's wrong with you tonight, aren't you well?'

'She's a whore!' she hurled at Jeremiah in a stage whisper, 'and she's after you, and you're blind if you don't see it!' Her Southern accent seemed thicker than ever, and he would have been touched by her attack of possessive devotion if she hadn't been as rude to his friend, but she was truly unbearable as the evening wore on, making pettish remarks in response to almost everything Amelia said. Still Amelia treated her with the determined calm of an extremely able mother, accustomed to handling difficult children. But Camille was no longer a child, and Jeremiah was furious with her as they rode back to the Cambridge.

'How could you behave like that? It was a disgrace. I was mortified!' He chided her as he would have an errant child, and he wanted to shake her as she stormed out of the carriage at the hotel.

She slammed the door of their suite hard enough to wake all the guests. 'What's got into you, Camille?' She was like a madwoman tonight, and though she had been rude to various people for days, he had never seen her behave that way before, but he had never seen a great deal of her anyway. He wondered if this was some aspect of her behavior he had overlooked; if so, he was going to correct it.

'I'll behave anyway I damn well please, Jeremiah!' She shouted at him now, and he was shocked.

'You most certainly will not. And you will apologize to my friend, Mrs. Goodheart. You will write her a letter tonight, which I will have delivered in the morning. Do you understand?'

'I understand that you're crazy, Jeremiah Thurston! I'll do no such a thing.' He startled her then by grabbing her arm and forcing her into a chair with one quick, sharp gesture.

'I'm not sure you understand me, Camille. I expect you to write a letter of apology to Amelia.'

'Why? Is she your mistress?'

'What?' He looked at her as though she were crazy. Amelia was far too respectable to be anyone's mistress. And he had almost asked her to marry him once. He nearly told Camille as much, but decided that that would only make matters worse. 'Camille, you've been intolerably rude, and you are my wife now. You are not some spoiled child who does as she pleases. Is that clear?'

She stood to her full height then and stared at her husband. '*I* am Mrs. Jeremiah Thurston of California, and my husband is one of the richest men in the state of California, hell . . . in the country. . . .' She looked at him with an expression that horrified him, 'and I can do anything I damn well please. Is *that* clear?' It was like watching a transformation take place before his eyes and Jeremiah was determined to stop her.

'That kind of behavior, Camille, will win you the utmost contempt and hatred everywhere you go. And may I suggest to you now that you become extremely humble before you reach California. I live in a simple house in the Napa Valley, I grow grapes, and I am a miner. That is all I am. And you are my wife. If you feel that this is reason to be rude to our friends or our neighbors or the people who work for us, then you're sorely mistaken.'

She suddenly laughed and grabbed a handful of her sables. She had what she wanted now. She loved him, but she also loved what he had and what he represented. And now she represented it too. And no one was going to look down at her for what her Daddy was anymore. If her aristocratic mother hadn't been enough to cancel out her father's humble beginnings, then she had done them all one better. She had married right out of their league, and got herself the richest man in the state of California. And no one was going to look down on her again. Now she had the position to go with the money, and more money than she'd ever had before or even dreamed of in Atlanta. She heard the people whispering everywhere they went, and she knew what they were saying. Her Daddy had told her. Jeremiah was one of the most powerful, most important men in the country. 'Don't tell me you're "just a miner," Jeremiah Thurston. That's garbage and you and I both know it. You're a lot more than that, and so am I.' It was hard to believe she was just eighteen. She seemed a great deal older as she stood there, glaring at her husband.

'And what happens if we lose it, if the mines fail, if I lose it all, Camille? What happens then? Who are you if you've hitched all your importance to all that? You're no one.'

'You're not going to lose a damn thing.'

'Camille, when I was a little boy in New York we barely had enough to eat, and then my Papa struck gold in California. It was everyone's dream back then, still is, I suppose. And I was lucky too. But that's all it is. Luck. Good fortune. Some hard work. But it can go just as easily as it comes, and you have to stay who you are no matter what happens. I married a wonderful little girl from Atlanta, and I love you . . . now don't suddenly turn into someone else because you married me. That's not fair. Most of all it's not fair to yourself. You don't need to do that.'

'Why not? People have been doing it to me for long enough. Even my Mama did it.' There were suddenly tears in her eyes as she said it, and she sounded like a defiant child as she told him. 'She always acted as though I weren't good enough, because I was part of my Daddy . . . as though he was trash . . . well, she married him, and even if he was trash, he made good, and he was good enough for her, and rich enough for her, after her father shot himself. But people have been looking down on me and Hubert all our lives. Hubert doesn't give a damn, but I do, and I'm not going to take it anymore, Jeremiah. And she was just like the rest of them, so damned aristocratic and fancy. I know them. I've seen that type all over the South, they're charming as hell and then they let you have it.'

He looked shocked. What an undeserved attack on Amelia, and yet he suddenly understood some of Camille's pain. He had never been so aware of it before, yet now he knew, and he felt for the many slights she must have suffered as she grew up. Now he understood what Orville had meant, when he said he wanted to get her out of the South. It mattered to her a great deal, and it mattered to Orville. 'But Amelia didn't say anything like that to you, darling.'

'She would have done!' There were tears running down Camille's cheeks now, and Jeremiah came and took her in his arms.

'I would never, ever let anyone do that to you, my love. No one will ever slight you like that.' He was suddenly glad he had built the house for her in San Francisco. Perhaps it would give her the self-confidence she apparently needed. 'I promise you, no one is going to treat you badly in California. And I know Amelia wouldn't have either. You should have given her a chance.' He held her close like a frightened child. 'Perhaps next time.' He took her to bed then, and held her tight as though to console her, and when morning came, she didn't write the letter that he wanted, and he didn't want to upset her by insisting. Instead he sent Amelia an enormous arrangement of white lilac, almost unheard of in the dead of winter, and he knew that she would love it and understand.

Jeremiah and Camille spent the rest of their stay shopping and buying pretty baubles for Camille, paintings for their new house, a rope of black pearls, a diamond and emerald necklace that she insisted she couldn't live without, and trunks and trunks and trunks of fabrics and feathers and laces, 'in case I can't find what I like in California'.

'It's not Africa, for Heaven's sake. It's California.' But he was amused by what she bought and let her buy it all and when they entered their private railroad car to return to California, it was more than half-filled with Camille's trunks and boxes with all her treasures. 'Do you suppose we bought enough, my love?' He looked amused as he lit a cigar and they rolled out of Grand Central Station. He had managed to speak to Amelia once before they left, and she insisted that he shouldn't be upset by Camille's behaviour. 'She's young, give her a chance to adjust to being your wife, Jeremiah.' And he had every intention of doing just that. They spent most of their time making love on the trip to California. And for a girl with what he assumed was a very straight-laced Southern upbringing, she had a wonderful sort of abandon about her when they made love. He had never been happier in his life, and she was growing rapidly adept at the ways which pleased him most. She was an extraordinarily exotic young lover.

At last when they arrived, Jeremiah could barely contain his excitement anymore. He was dying to show Camille the house . . . their house . . . Thurston House . . . in all its splendour, though he was still playing it down for her. 'No, it's not terribly big, but it'll do for us, and the first baby.' The first ten babies, he laughed to himself . . . wait until she saw it! He helped her down from the car they'd ridden in for seven days and guided her toward the carriage that had come to meet them. It was a brand new one, brown with black trim, drawn by four perfectly matched jet black horses, a pretty little set up he had bought especially for Camille just before he went to Atlanta for their wedding.

'What a pretty rig, Jeremiah!' She seemed impressed as she laughed and clapped her hands and she looked up at him adoringly as he lifted her inside. There was a second coach for their trunks, and both carriages bore a scrollwork with his initials. JAT. Jeremiah Arbuckle Thurston. 'Is the house far from here?' She looked around the station with a faint degree of concern, and Jeremiah laughed.

'Far enough, little one. Were you worried that I'd set up house for you down here?' She laughed at herself, and he hopped in beside her for the drive north across San Francisco. He pointed out landmarks to her as they went, the Palace Hotel where he had so often stayed before he built the new house, St. Patrick's Church, Trinity Church, Union Square, the Mint, and Twin Peaks in the distance. As they finally began to climb Nob Hill, he showed her Mark Hopkins' home, the Tobin Residence, the Crocker House and the Huntington Colton House, all of which they passed on the way to Thurston House. She was particularly impressed with the Crocker and Flood Houses. They were finer even than anything she had seen in Atlanta and Savannah.

'Finer even than New York!' She clapped her hands. San Francisco wasn't so bad after all, she hadn't been so sure at first, and now she was even more excited to see their house, but he had warned her that it would be small, and they were driving into a little park now. They had passed through an enormous set of gates, and the horses picked up speed as they drove around a maze of trees and hedges. 'Is the house in here?' She looked confused. She saw only trees and no house, but perhaps he was giving her a little tour before taking her to their house, and then she saw the largest house of all, a spectacular edifice with four turrets and a sort of cupola on top. 'Whose house is this?' She was fascinated. It was the grandest house she'd ever seen. 'It looks like a hotel or a museum.'

'It's neither.' Jeremiah looked very serious as the carriage stopped, and she didn't know him well enough to read the mischief in his eyes. 'It's probably the largest house in the city. I wanted you to see it before we went home.'

'Whose house it it, Jeremiah?' She spoke in a whisper of awe. It was even larger than some of the churches they'd passed. 'They must be very rich.' She said it in awed tones, and he laughed.

'Would you like to see the inside?'

'Do you suppose we should?' She was hesitant but curious at the same time. 'I'm not really dressed to pay a call.' She was wearing a tweed suit and a fur cape, with one of the pretty hats he'd bought her in New York.

'You look fine to me. This is San Francisco after all, not New York. In fact, I think you look very elegant.' And then, before she could say more he walked her right up to the front door and struck the large brass knocker, and almost instantly a liveried servant swung open the door and stared at Jeremiah. Everyone had been warned about their arrival, and that if the master behaved strangely, they were to take no notice. He strolled right past the footman now, as Camille gasped, having explained nothing at all, and he pulled Camille in beside him. Together, they stood beneath the enormous stained glass dome, and she gasped again. It was the most beautiful thing she'd ever seen, and she stared at it in fascination as it cast lights and patterns on the marble floor beneath.

'Oh Jeremiah . . . it's so lovely. . . .' She stared up at it with her enormous eyes, and he smiled down happily at her. This was what he had wanted.

'Do you want to see the rest?'

'Shouldn't you let them know we're here?' She looked worried. People couldn't be that informal in San Francisco. It was certainly different from the South. Her parents would have been horrified to find people wandering around their home, even friends, but on the other hand they didn't live in a palace like this. She didn't know anyone who did. Even Jeremiah's woman friend in New York had a house that was less grand than this, and Camille was suddenly glad. Whoever these people were, they had outdone Amelia. 'Jeremiah. . . .' The footmen didn't seem to be taking any notice of him, and he pulled her slowly up the grand staircase.

'You've got to see the upstairs, Camille. It's the handsomest suite of rooms you've ever seen.'

'But Jeremiah . . . please. . . .' This was awful. What would the people say when they saw them? But before she could say another thing he had pulled her right into what appeared to be the master bedroom, all done in the most extravagant swathes of pink silk she had ever seen. She had never seen so much fabric in one room, and there were two beautiful French paintings on either side of the bed, and another over the mantle across from the bed. From here, he led her into a tiny French boudoir with hand painted wallpaper obviously brought directly from Paris, and a dressing room full of mirrors and the largest pink marble bathroom she'd ever seen, and, beyond it, another in dark green marble, presumably for the master of the house. They passed through a wood panelled study, and then suddenly they were back in the master bedroom again. And however uncomfortable she was to be in someone else's house, she was so overwhelmed by the beauty of their house that she almost didn't mind it. It was like eating chocolates and not being able to stop until you devoured the whole box, all before your hostess came back into the room. It was like a dream and a nightmare all at once and she stared at Jeremiah now, in absolute rapture. 'Who lives here?' Not that she'd know the name, but she'd remember it now. She would never forget this house, the exquisite rooms, the rich fabrics, the treasures scattered everywhere. 'Who are they? How did they make their money?' The last question was whispered so softly he could barely hear her.

'In mining,' he whispered back.

'There must be a lot of good mines out here.' She whispered again and he smiled.

'Enough.'

'What's their name?'

'Thurston.' He whispered matter of factly, and she nodded, and then stopped and looked at him again.

'Thurston? Are they relatives of yours?'

115

'More or less.' They were still whispering. 'My wife lives here.'

'Your *what*?' She looked horrified. What kind of joke was this? And she would have begun to cry, but she was too frightened. Did he have another wife? Had he played a cruel joke on them all? He saw everything that was running through her mind and turned her around slowly to look in one of the long mirrors. He pointed at her reflection with a smile. 'That wife, silly girl. Do you know her?'

She spun to face him now, with a look of total amazement. 'What do you mean, Jeremiah, is this your house?'

'Our house, my darling.' He pulled her into his arms, feeling all the pleasure there was to feel in the world well up inside him at once. 'I built it for you. And there are probably a few unfinished corners, but we'll finish them together.' He held her tight and she pulled away from him after a moment and shrieked in amazement, and then she began to laugh.

'You tricked me! Jeremiah Thurston, you tricked me! I thought you were crazy roaming around someone else's house!'

'But you were willing to do it!' he teased.

'It's the prettiest house I've ever seen, and I didn't want to leave until I saw more. . . .'

'Then I'll show you the rest, and you don't ever have to leave my darling, it's yours, from top to bottom.' Now the footmen who saw them were smiling and a cluster of maids had come out to see the new mistress. They had been hired just before Jeremiah left for Atlanta, and he scarcely recognized them himself. Everything was so new here. He showed her the kitchens and the pantries, and the nursery and children's room upstairs, the view from almost every window and the discreet plaque on the front gate that said 'Thurston House'. He showed her everything there was to see and at the end of the tour she collapsed on their huge canopied bed with an equally huge grin on her face and stared at him.

'It's the most beautiful house I've ever seen, Jeremiah. Any-where.'

'And it's all yours, my darling, enjoy it.'

'Oh, I am!' She already had visions of the dazzling parties she was going to give, and she could hardly wait to start using the ballroom. 'Wait until I write to Daddy!' That was the highest praise, Jeremiah knew. Daddy was godlike to Camille's eyes, but Jeremiah was rap-idly gaining the same importance. And now he had truly impressed

116

her. Even the enormous diamond hadn't impressed her this much. This really did it, and she grinned at him now. 'This must have cost you a fortune, Jeremiah. You must be even richer than Daddy thought!' But the prospect of that didn't seem to depress her.

He was thrilled by her delight in the house, vague about her questions about how much things cost, and disappointed at her reaction when he took her to Napa. After the elegance and modern marvels of their house on Nob Hill, she was unimpressed by the house he had refurbished in Saint Helena. She was disturbed at how far they were from town, how negligible a town it was, and how long it took to get to San Francisco. It was still an all day affair by carriage and steamer, and she found the house in Napa depressing. She had heard that he had built it for a love who died, and that annoyed her too. She wanted to go back to the grandeur of Thurston House and show off her new clothes. Now! And the fact that he had lived there for the last twenty years didn't interest her at all, the valley itself held no magic for her whatsoever, and the only thing that seemed to interest her at all were the mines and how much money he made there. Every day she asked him a thousand questions, but they were so mercenary and so pointed that he was noticeably vague with his answers. It embarrassed him to discuss money to that extent and he had too much work to do to be able to spend much time with her after his long absence. He needed a month in Napa to set things to rights, and Camille detested every moment he spent away.

He was in the process of devising an elaborate system that would allow him to live in San Francisco for most of the time, as he had promised her father, but communications between Thurston House and the mines would have to be perfected. He had already promised his bride that from February until June they would stay in the city that year, and after that she had agreed that they would move to Napa for the summer. It was a compromise which he wanted to make work, but there were other compromises he would have liked to work out, too. For the moment, Hannah and Camille were not getting along, and on his second night home from the mines, Jeremiah wondered which woman he would find waiting for him when he got home. It seemed unlikely that they would both survive their encounter.

Camille thought Hannah slovenly and forward, much too familiar by half, as she had dared to call Camille 'girl', instead of Mrs.

117

Thurston. Worse than that she had eventually called her a brat, and a spoiled one at that, and Hannah told Jeremiah in a total uproar that the little vixen had actually thrown something at her. She held the offending object aloft, as though to prove her point. Camille had apparently thrown a small hat box at her, and the old housekeeper had effectively dodged it.

'She's so old, Camille, that it really doesn't seem fair to turn her out.' Jeremiah attempted to cajole Camille. His wife had demanded the old woman's head on a platter by morning. 'I just can't do it.' He couldn't think of anything worse.

'Then I will.' She had never sounded more determined nor more Southern and Jeremiah realized that he had to take a stand before things got totally out of hand between them.

'No, you won't. Hannah stays. You'll have to get used to her, Camille. She's part of how I'm used to living in Napa.'

'That was before you married me.'

'Yes, it was. And I can't change everything overnight. I refurbished this house just for you. It was a mess before that, and I'll hire more servants if you need them, but Hannah stays.'

'And if I leave and go back to San Francisco?' She looked at him haughtily and he pulled her down on his lap without further ado.

'Then I'll bring you back here, and spank you.' She smiled in spite of herself and he kissed her. 'There that's better, that's the woman I love, smiling and sweet, and not throwing hat boxes at old women.'

'She called me a vixen!' Camille looked angry again, but she also looked very lovely, and he felt a strong urge to take her to bed again.

'Apparently you were a vixen if you threw that thing at her. Behave yourself, Camille. These are good country folk up here, they're simple people and I know you're terribly bored here, but if you're good to them, they'll be true to you forever.' He was thinking of Mary Ellen's long years of loyalty to him as he said it, and wondered if she'd had her baby.

Camille looked petulant again as she got up and walked around the room. 'I like it better in the city. And I want to give a ball.' She was like an anxious child, and she wanted her birthday now, no matter what!

'All in good time, little one. Be patient. I have to do some work here first. You wouldn't want to be in the city without me, would you?' She shook her head but she didn't look pleased and he kissed her again, making her forget any place but his lips, and a moment later he had her in bed beside him, and the issue of Hannah was temporarily forgotten until the next morning, when she attempted to revive it, but he wouldn't let her. He told her to go for a long healthy walk, and he'd come home to see her at lunchtime. That prospect didn't appease her a great deal, but there was nothing much she could do about it. He left the house a few moments later and she was left alone with Hannah, who said barely two words to her all day until Jeremiah came home, and then she seemed to have plenty of conversation for him, questions about the mine, gossip about people in town whom Camille didn't know. It bored her just to listen. In fact, the whole damned Napa Valley bored her. She wanted to go back to San Francisco, and she told him so again after lunch when he saddled up Big Joe again and got ready to go back to the mine. But this time he shook his head and spoke frankly to her.

'We're here until the end of the month. Get used to it, Camille. This is the other side of our life. We live here too, not just at Thurston House. We have a life here too. I told you that. I'm a miner.'

'No you're not. You're the richest man in California. Now let's go back to San Francisco, and live like it.' What she said annoyed him and he tried repeatedly to reason with her to no avail.

'I had hoped you would like the Napa Valley, Camille. It's important to me.'

'Well it's ugly and boring and stupid. And I hate that old woman, and she hates me.'

'Then read a book. I'll take you in to the library in Napa on Saturday.' It would mean missing his Saturday morning session with Danny, but Camille was more important just now. He wanted her to settle down to his country life in Napa. He couldn't be in San Francisco all the time, and he wanted her with him always.

But as things turned out, he spent Saturday morning with neither Camille nor Danny. On Friday afternoon, there was a flood at the mine, which happened every winter. They lost seven men and fought like dogs to save thirty others. Jeremiah was right down there with the rescue teams, covered with mud, and fighting desperately to bring the men out of pockets where they were digging, barely able to breathe, like bats in caves, waiting to be rescued. It was a tense and terrible time as Hannah explained to Camille when she heard the news and Jeremiah didn't come home. She knew he wouldn't be back until the last of the men were found, dead or alive, and he would go to see the widows before he came home to his own wife. Camille was subdued when she heard about it, and when he rode slowly in on Big Joe at noon the next day, she knew how grim it had been from the look on his face.

'We lost fourteen men,' were his first words to her, and she felt her eyes fill with tears as though she understood the pain of those women.

'I'm sorry.' She looked up at him with eyes full of tears, tears for how much he cared as much as for the women who were widowed.

They had lost Danny's father in the flood and Jeremiah particularly felt his loss. He had told the boy himself, holding him in his arms as he sobbed. And he would be a pallbearer at the funeral on Monday. It was difficult to explain these things to Camille. Though they were the realities of his life, she was so young and so new to it all. To her, the only thing real was the beauty of the house he had built her. But there was much, much more than that. And now she was learning.

Hannah went to run him a hot bath, and Camille went to pour him a cup of the hot broth Hannah had been making. She had none of those skills herself, nor any inclination to learn them. But she poured him the soup now, as Hannah stood alone with him upstairs in the bathroom. She looked at him for a long moment, and then shook her head.

'I know this isn't a good time to tell you . . .' She hesitated for only a fraction of a second. 'Mary Ellen's been in labour for two days. I found out yesterday morning, but I never got a chance to tell you. And I heard at the market this morning, she's still at it.' They both knew what that meant. She could die. Countless others had before her. 'I don't know if you want to do anything about it,' there was no reproach in her voice. It was a matter of fact statement. 'But I thought I should tell you.'

'I'm glad you did.' But he didn't look it, as Camille entered the room with the cup of soup, and glanced suspiciously from one to the other. She instantly sensed that Hannah had been telling him a secret, something about her she assumed incorrectly.

'What was she telling you?' she asked Jeremiah the minute the old woman left the room.

120

'Some local gossip. One of my men needs some help. I'm going to go out as soon as I get cleaned up.'

'But you need some rest.' She looked shocked; he was so tired he was numb. He had worked all night in the freezing wet mud, though for the men they had saved, it was worth it.

'I'll rest later, Camille. Can you bring me some more soup, please? And a cup of coffee?' She did, and found him sitting in the bathtub. He drained both cups and stood up. He still had the powerful, solid body of his youth. His years of working in the mines in his youth had stood him in good stead. He was a beautifully built man even at forty-four, and she looked at him now with admiration.

'You're beautiful, Jeremiah.'

He smiled at her. 'So are you, little one.' But he was quick to slip into his clothes and get ready to leave, and as she watched him, she had an uneasy feeling.

'Why are you going now?'

'I have to. I'll be back in a little while.'

'Where are you going?' It was the first time she had quizzed him this way and he wondered why.

'To Calistoga.' He met her eyes without wavering, but inside he felt a tremor. He was going to assist at the birth of his child, or to at least be there if Mary Ellen died, if she hadn't already.

'Can I come?'

'No. Not this time, Camille.'

'But I want to.' She sounded petulant again, and he pushed her aside.

'I don't have time for that now. We'll talk about it later.' And before she could say another word, he was gone again, on Big Joe, this time moving at considerable speed across the hills, and she wondered just where he was going.

Chapter Fourteen

The big white horse lumbered down the road and up the valley with Jeremiah pressing him onward. All he could think of were the men they had lost the night before and once or twice he felt himself nodding off to sleep, but Big Joe seemed to know where they were going. The white horse was silent as Jeremiah tied Big Joe to a tree, and he went around to the front, knocked, and let himself in. There was no sound at first, and he suddenly wondered if Mary Ellen had gone to her mother's house to have the child, and then from above he heard a terrible moaning. He stopped, wondering if she was alone, and then walked softly up the stairs, not quite sure what to do, or why he had come, except that he knew he had to be there. It was his child she was struggling with, and all along he had been afraid it would kill her.

He stood outside her bedroom for a long moment until the groans ceased, and then all he heard was a soft wail and a man's voice speaking softly. It was an awkward situation for Jeremiah, and he felt fatigue in every bone of his body. He felt foolish for having come, but he knocked anyway. Maybe if nothing else, he could go in search of the doctor, he decided. But it was the doctor who opened the door to him, his sleeves rolled up, his eyes haggard. Blood was smeared all over the front of his shirt, but he didn't seem to notice.

'I'm sorry . . . I was wondering if . . .' He felt more than awkward now. He felt wicked to have left this woman alone to deliver his baby. He looked at the doctor and asked bluntly, 'How is she?' He didn't introduce himself, but there was no need to. The doctor knew who he was. Everyone in the county knew Jeremiah Thurston. He closed the door softly behind him, and came out into the hall to speak to Jeremiah.

'She's not good. She's been laboring since Wednesday night, and we just can't get that baby out. She's trying like a dog, and she's just

122

about wore out.' Jeremiah nodded, afraid to ask if she might die. He already knew the answer. 'Do you want to come in?' There was no judgment in his eyes, and maybe it would make a difference to the woman. It couldn't do any harm, and she was in so much pain, and had been for so long that she probably wouldn't care who saw her now, and it was his baby.

Jeremiah hesitated in the hallway. It was unheard of to attend a woman's childbirth, but the doctor didn't seem shocked at the suggestion. 'She wouldn't mind?' ·

He looked at Jeremiah honestly. 'She may not even know who you are. She's pretty far gone.' And then he hesitated and seemed to be looking deep in Jeremiah's eyes. 'Can you take it? Ever seen anything like it before?'

Jeremiah shook his head. 'Only livestock.'

The older man nodded. It would do. Without saying another word, he opened the door and walked into the room, with Jeremiah just behind him. There was a sweet, heavy scent in the room, that of bodies and rose water and damp sheets, and there were no windows open. She lay on her bed, covered with two blankets, and from her waist down she was surrounded by blood soaked sheets. It looked as though someone had been murdered in her bed. Her legs hung like those of a ragdoll and her entire body trembled, and then suddenly, as he watched her, feeling guilt and sorrow wash over him, she was racked by what looked to him like a convulsion. She gave a soft jagged moan, which rose slowly to a scream as she thrashed about in the bed, rolling her eyes, and clutching at the air. She spoke incoherently and the doctor went quickly to her. It was easy to see that she was barely conscious, and a huge gush of blood shot from between her legs. As she screamed, the doctor plunged his hands into her womb, but there was no progress as he pulled them out again and wiped them on a blood soaked towel. She whimpered horribly then as she lay there, and Jeremiah slowly approached the bed and looked down at the ravaged face. Had he not known who she was, he wouldn't have recognized her.

The doctor spoke softly to Jeremiah, even though he knew she couldn't hear him. She seemed to doze now between contractions. 'She's lost too damn much blood. Something's sprung loose in there, you can see it by that gush of blood she just had, but I can't stop it, and the baby's turned the wrong way. All it's doing is pushing its shoulder out. We won't get anywhere that way.' He looked aggrieved as he said it, and the question was plain in Jeremiah's eyes. 'We could lose them both,' he glanced at the exhausted woman on the bed, 'her for sure if we don't get it out soon. She ain't got much more left in her.'

'And the baby?' It was his child after all, but all of his concern was for Mary Ellen now. It was as though he had never left her, and Camille had never existed.

'If I could turn it around, I might get it out, but I can't do it alone.' He stared at Jeremiah. 'Can you hold her?' He nodded, afraid to cause her more pain, and she was awake now, screaming with the beginnings of another contraction, as she looked up, she seemed to see Jeremiah, but it was obvious that she thought she was dreaming.

'It's alright,' he smiled gently down at her, and touched her face as he knelt on the floor beside her. 'I'm here. You're going to be fine.' But not for a moment did he believe it, and he had already seen so much death in the past twenty-four hours, he didn't want to see more now, but he feared that he would as he watched her writhe and convulse, and more blood flowed from her.

'I can't ... I can't anymore. ...' She was gasping for air, and instinctively he took her shoulders and held her, and then suddenly her head lolled back against his arm. She had fainted, and her complexion was a pale gray. The doctor took her pulse then and looked at Jeremiah.

'I'm going to try and turn it and pull it out the next time. You hold her. Don't let her move.'

Jeremiah followed his orders, speaking softly all the while to Mary Ellen, but her screams were so acute that she couldn't hear him and she fainted again before the doctor had accomplished what he wanted. Jeremiah felt a sweat break out on his brow, and he was stunned when he glanced at his watch and realized that he had already been there for four hours. 'She can't take much more, doctor.'

'I know.' He nodded, and waited for the next contraction, preparing an evil looking tool which he was going to use to pull out the baby once he turned it. And then suddenly they both watched her convulse and wake up again, this time with wild eyes as Jeremiah held her mercilessly against the bed and the doctor reached into her as far as he could, grappling with the baby. Her screams were a

124

sound he knew he would never forget, and it took four more attempts before he had turned the baby to his satisfaction, and another five with the wicked tool he plunged between her legs, as she howled in Jeremiah's arms. It was a sound which was no longer even human, and then suddenly the doctor gave a ferocious grunt as the sweat poured from Jeremiah's brow, and he was suddenly aware of a change in Mary Ellen's body. She sank into his arms almost as though she had passed through them and she was a pale grayish green, her breathing so soft and irregular that he wasn't even sure she was still breathing. But as he turned frantically to the doctor, he saw what had happened. The child had finally sprung from her limbs, and lay dead between her legs, and she was haemorrhaging badly. It was a painful scene to take in all at once, and the doctor silently cut the cord and wrapped the baby in a clean sheet, as he quickly attempted to staunch Mary Ellen's bleeding. Jeremiah felt a quick surge of defeat in realizing that his firstborn was stillborn, but now all he could really think of was its mother, clearly dying in his arms, and there was nothing he could do to stop it. The doctor made several desperate attempts, and then covered her with blankets and came to the head of the bed to pat Jeremiah's shoulder.

'I'm sorry about the baby.'

'So am I.' His voice was hoarse. He had seen too much that night and the night before, and he was still deathly afraid for Mary Ellen. 'Will she be all right?' He looked pleadingly at the doctor, who looked uncertain.

'There's nothing more I can do. I'll stay here with her, but I can't promise you anything.' Jeremiah nodded and kept his vigil by her bedside, and it was well into the night before she stirred again, groaning softly and turning her head from side to side, but she didn't open her eyes until morning.

'Mary Ellen . . .' He whispered her name softly. The doctor was asleep in the corner. 'Mary Ellen. . . .' She turned to him with a look of confusion.

'Are you really here? I thought it was a dream. . . .' And then she looked at him with the question in her eyes that she feared most. 'Jeremiah . . . the baby? . . .' But instinctively she knew, and she turned her face from him as tears poured down her cheeks and he held her hand and stroked her hair.

'We saved you, Mary Ellen. . . .' There were tears in his eyes now, he had been so afraid she would die. He wanted to tell her that he was sorry about the baby too, but there was a lump in his throat the size of a fist and he couldn't do it.

'What was it?' She turned her eyes to his again and saw that he was crying.

'A boy.' She nodded and closed her eyes, and then she slept and when she awoke again, the doctor declared himself pleased and said he would leave her for a while and return that afternoon to see her. In the hallway, he told Jeremiah that if she didn't lose any more blood, she would make it, and personally he thought she'd survive.

'She's a tough gal. But I told her years ago not to try it again. It was a foolish thing to do,' he shrugged, 'accident, I guess.' And then he looked at Jeremiah. 'I'll send my wife over to stay with her if you have to be getting home.' He didn't want to pry, but he knew from the grapevine that he had a young wife in Saint Helena.

'Thank you. I'd appreciate that. I was up all the night before with floods in our mines.' The old doctor nodded, he had respect for this man. He had been a great help through the long night.

He held out a hand to Jeremiah. 'I'm sorry about the baby.'

Jeremiah nodded. 'Thank God you saved her.' The doctor smiled, touched by his devotion. He wasn't the first man in the valley to have both a mistress and a wife and children by both, and he seemed like a decent man.

'I'll send my wife around in a little while.' And when he did, Jeremiah took his leave of Mary Ellen.

'I'll be back tomorrow. You just rest and do what the doctor tells you.' Then he had another thought, 'And I'll send Hannah to you in a little while. She can stay with you for as long as you need.'

Mary Ellen smiled weakly and held the big warm hand. 'Thank you for being here, Jeremiah. . . . I'd have died without you.' She had almost died with him, but he didn't say that to her.

'Must be a good girl now.' She closed her eyes on the words and was asleep again before he left the room, and as he rode Big Joe back to Saint Helena, he felt every fibre in his body slump with exhaustion. He looked as though he had been beaten and dragged through ditches when he dismounted in front of his house. Hannah rushed out to see him. She wanted to hear before Camille came outside, looked silently and expectantly at Jeremiah, and for the same reason he was quick to answer and spoke in a low, husky voice. 'Mary

Ellen's alright, but the baby was stillborn.' And then, with a deep sigh, 'We almost lost her. I told her you'd come to her today and stay with her for as long as she needed.' He suddenly wondered if he had been too free with his offer, but the old woman nodded.

'I'm glad you did. I'll get my things right now.' And then, with a searching glance, 'How is she?'

He shook his head, and the agony of the night seemed to still be with him. 'It was awful, Hannah, the worst thing I've ever seen. I don't know why women would ever want to have babies.' He was deeply impressed by all that he'd seen, and he wasn't sure that he could have gone through it.

'Some don't.' She glanced knowingly over her shoulder, and then encouragingly back at Jeremiah. 'It's not always like that, son. She knew she was going to have a hard time. The last one was almost like that. The doctor warned her.' There was faint reproach in her voice, but more sympathy, especially for Jeremiah. 'Were you with her?' He nodded, and she looked at him with renewed respect. 'You're a good man, Jeremiah Thurston.' And with that Camille walked out onto the front porch with a look of exasperation.

'Where were you all night, Jeremiah?' She didn't care that Hannah was there, listening.

'With one of my men who got wounded at the mines.' It explained the blood on his sleeve and the stubble on his face. He had been awake for two nights now and he was exhausted. 'I'm sorry I didn't come home, little love.'

She glared at him peevishly and turned on her heel and slammed back into the house as Hannah watched her.

'That's what I like,' the old woman said acidly, 'an understanding wife.' She patted Jeremiah's arm and went up the steps to get her things. 'I'll be going in a few minutes, Jeremiah. You don't worry about anything. Get some rest. I left some soup and some stew on the stove for you.'

'Thank you, Hannah.' He strode quietly inside and poured himself some soup in the kitchen before going upstairs to find his wife in their bedroom.

'Where were you?' She reeled to face him again.

'I told you where I was.' He wasn't anxious to talk about it. He had watched his first child die that night, and his mistress of seven years almost going with him.

127

'I don't believe you, Jeremiah.' She looked beautiful and immaculate in a pale pink voile dress, and beside her he felt exhausted and filthy.

'I don't think you have much choice, Camille. I was with one of my men.'

'Why?'

'Because he almost died, that's why,' he snapped the words at her and sat down with his bowl of soup at a table near the fireplace, but she was still fuming as she paced the room.

'You could have let me know you weren't coming home.'

'I'm sorry.' He looked openly at her. 'There was no one to send.' The answer seemed to satisfy her and she turned away again but it intrigued him that she had such a strong sense that he was lying. She was even brighter than she knew, but he couldn't tell her that, he just went on eating his soup, with fresh respect for her sharp mind and intuitive senses.

'I suppose you're going to bed now.' She sounded a little less angry as she sat down in a rocking chair nearby.

'I'd like to go to church, after I get cleaned up.'

'Church?' She almost shrieked the word. She hated church, always had. Her mother liked to go to church, but she had never thought much of her mother. 'You never go to church.'

'I do once in a while.' If he hadn't been so exhausted, he would have been amused by her reaction. 'And we just lost fourteen men at the mines, Camille.' That, and his only baby. 'You don't have to go if you don't want to, but it would look better if you did.' She glared at him in obvious annoyance.

'When are we going back to town?'

'As soon as I can.' He stood up and walked towards her. 'I'll do my best to get you back to San Francisco soon, little one, I promise.' That seemed to mollify her, enough so that she changed her dress and accompanied him to church an hour later. And when they returned, he slept the sleep of the dead until dinnertime and only woke up to eat another bowl of soup and sleep again until the next morning, when he had to rise to attend the funeral of the men who had died in the mine on Friday. But this time Camille didn't join him. She stayed home and complained to him later that Hannah hadn't come in. And he explained that she was tending a sick friend.

'Why didn't she tell me that?' Camille fumed. 'I'm the mistress of this house. She works for me now.' Jeremiah didn't like the way she said it, but he didn't want to enrage her further.

'She mentioned it to me on Sunday morning when I got home.'

'And you let her go?' She was livid.

'I did. I was sure you'd understand.' He tried to embarrass her into silence, but found that he couldn't. 'She'll be back in a few days.' However, it was almost a week before Hannah returned, and she reported to him that Mary Ellen was still feeling poorly but she was back on her feet now. He nodded, and was satisfied that she knew there was no hurry. He had sent her a note several days before, assuring her that the death of his child changed nothing. He would not remove the stipend she had already been receiving for several months. He had already informed his bank that it would be permanent, and he told her that he hoped she wouldn't go back to work now. She could stay home, take care of her children and get her health back. She had wanted to send him a note thanking him, but she hadn't dared, for fear that it would fall into Camille's hands. Instead, Hannah thanked him for her. 'You're sure she's all right, Hannah?'

'She's still weak as a cat, but she's getting stronger.'

'Probably your good cooking.' He smiled his thanks at the old woman and warned her that Camille had been upset during her absence.

'Did she cook for you herself?'

'We managed.' And then he told her that they'd be going back to San Francisco in a few days. The prospect of their departure didn't please Hannah.

'It'll be lonely around here, Jeremiah.'

'I know. But I'll be coming back and forth to see to the mines.'

'That's hard on you.' But it was only fair to his bride. He couldn't build her a palace in the city and then condemn her to country life, which she apparently hated.

'It'll be all right. And we'll move up here for the summer months, probably June till September or October.' But if he had his way, he would have moved up in March, and stayed till November. 'If you need anything, just let me know, between times.'

'I will, Jere.niah.'

'What was that?' A waspish little voice behind them took them both by surprise, and Jeremiah wondered how much Camille had heard before she made herself known. 'Did I hear you say "Jeremiah"?' She was addressing herself to Hannah, and they were both startled.

'You did.' Hannah looked as though she couldn't figure out what Camille meant, and neither could Jeremiah.

'I will thank you to refer to my husband as *Mister* Thurston, from now on, he is not your "boy", nor your "lad", nor your "friend". He is *my* husband and *your* employer, and his name is *Mr.* Thurston.' She had never sounded more Southern or more vicious and Jeremiah was furious at her. He said nothing in front of Hannah, but he followed his wife upstairs, and slammed the door to their bedroom.

'And just exactly what was that all about, Camille? That was unnecessary, and you were rude to Hannah.' The same old woman who had just nursed his mistress back to health after the stillbirth of his baby! He was still feeling sensitive about all of it, but Camille didn't know that, and she was in for a surprise now. She had rarely seen him angry. 'I won't tolerate that, and I want you to know that right now.'

'Tolerate what? I expect respect from our servants, and that old woman acts as though she were your Mama. Well she isn't, she's an ugly old woman with a sharp tongue and forward ways, and I'll whip her if I hear her call you "Jeremiah" again.' She looked evil in her fury and suddenly he wanted to shake her. Instead, he grabbed her by the arm and pulled her halfway across the room.

'Whip her? *Whip* her? This is not the South, Camille, and these are not the days of slavery. If you lay a hand on her, or are ever rude to her again, I'll *whip* you, mark my words. Now go down and apologize to her right now.'

'What?' She shrieked at him in disbelief.

'Hannah's worked for me for more than twenty years and she's decent and loyal, and I'm not going to have her abused, not by some spoiled brat from the South, and you'd damn well better apologize to her right now, or I'll tan your hide for you!' He was serious but he was already beginning to calm down, unlike his wife, whose eyes blazed with tears of anger.

'How dare you, Jeremiah Thurston! How dare you! I'll do no such thing, apologize to that scum. . . .'

But this time he'd had enough. He reached out and slapped her, and she caught her breath and reeled backwards, catching herself

130

with a hand against the mantle. 'If my Daddy were here, he'd whip you to within an inch of your life.' She spoke in a low, venomous voice, and Jeremiah instantly sensed that things had gone too far between them.

'That's enough, Camille. You were rude to a trusted servant, and I will not tolerate that. But that's enough talk of whippings and threats. Behave yourself from now on, and this won't happen.'

'*Behave* myself? Behave myself! Damn you, Jeremiah Thurston. Damn you, and damn you, and *damn you*!' And with that she stalked out of the room, and slammed the door, and she did not speak to him again until they returned to San Francisco. She was all icy politeness and distance, but as she walked in the front door of their magnificent home on Nob Hill, it took her breath away again, and for an instant, she forgot herself and threw her arms around her husband. She was so happy to be back that she forgot how angry at him she had been, and he laughed with pleasure as he carried her upstairs to her bedroom and made love to her.

'Well, you survived the month in Napa, little lovebird,' he joked but he was still discouraged about how she felt about the valley he loved so much. 'All we have to do now is have our first baby.' The sting of loss over Mary Ellen's child was still with him, and it only spurred him to want another one quickly, this one by Camille, his wife. He thanked God that she was young and healthy, and hopefully would never undergo an ordeal like Mary Ellen's. They had been married for two months now, and he was anxious for her to get pregnant.

'My mother says it takes a while sometimes, Jeremiah. Just don't think about it.' But he was growing impatient. And talking about it made her uncomfortable. She didn't want a baby yet. She was eighteen years old, and they had a magnificent house, and she wanted to give lots of parties, not get fat and feel sick and stay home and die in childbirth.

And all through the spring months, as she ensconced herself in San Francisco's social scene, Jeremiah did not get his wish, but she had never been happier in life. She had reached the status she wanted so badly and they gave parties and balls and dinners, went to operas and concerts. She gave a beautiful picnic in their enormous gardens in May, and she rapidly became known as the city's most glittering hostess. The balls she gave rivalled those at Versailles, and Camille was ecstatic at their life. Jeremiah was slightly less so. He was commuting back and forth to Napa as much as he could, and most of the time he was exhausted. She teased him when he fell asleep at one of her sumptuous dinners, and she insisted that they go out every night when he was in town, and went out without him when he wasn't. It was a constant social whirl, and she almost went into mourning when he reminded her that on the first of June they were moving back to Napa.

'But I wanted to give a summer ball, Jeremiah,' she wailed sadly at him, 'can't we go in July?'

'No, we can't. I have to spend some time at the mines, Camille, or there'll be nothing to support all your parties.' But he was only teasing, he was still the richest man in the state, and they had no financial worries. But he did want to spend more time at the mines, and in summer he liked being near his vineyards, and he had lived long enough in the city. They had been there since February, and he was ready to go home to his valley. He had told Hannah as much when he'd spent the night there the week before.

'And no baby yet, Jeremiah?' she had asked. She had agreed to humour Camille and call him Mr. Thurston within her hearing, but when they were alone, she still called him Jeremiah, and always would.

'Not yet.' He was disappointed about that too, and hoped that when he got her away from the city and her constant parties, she would get pregnant. She needed a taste of country life, he told himself, but Hannah pursed her lips with disapproval.

'Well, we know it's not you.' And then she frowned. 'Maybe she can't have babies.'

'I doubt that. It's only been five and a half months, Hannah, give her time.' He smiled at the old woman, 'Give her some good Saint Helena air, and she'll be pregnant in a month's time.' And then his brow clouded as he remembered Mary Ellen. 'How is she?' he asked Hannah. He hadn't been to see her again since the night their baby died. Somehow, he just didn't want to. It didn't seem right to Camille, and she was far too intuitive for him to lie to her very often.

'She's all right. It's taken her a long time to get back on her feet though. I'd say she's fine now.' And she decided to tell him the rest too. He had a right to know after all, he'd been decent to her. No one could say he hadn't done the right thing. Jacob Stone at the bank had told everyone how generous Jeremiah had been. 'She's seeing some man who works at the spa, he looks nice enough, works hard,' Hannah shrugged, 'but I don't think she's too crazy about him.'

'I hope he's a nice man,' Jeremiah said quietly and turned the conversation to other things. They would be moving up to Napa soon, and there was plenty to keep Hannah busy, getting the house ready for their arrival.

But when Camille arrived in Saint Helena, with all her bags and trunks and belongings, she did nothing but find fault with what Hannah had done, and the old woman was so frustrated with Jeremiah's shrewish young wife that she turned to her one day with a gust of passion and suggested that it was a damned shame he'd married her, and not the woman he'd been seeing in Calistoga before she came along, which only infuriated Camille further. She began a campaign to try to find out who the woman was, but neither Jeremiah, nor Hannah, who was filled with remorse for her indiscretion and had clammed up at once, would tell her who the woman was, or confirm that what she'd said was really true. And the more she dug, the less she found out, until one day, for the fun of it, she went to the spa in Calistoga with a group of her friends who were staying there, for the mudbaths. She had agreed to meet them for lunch at the hotel, and as she waited for them, she saw a man in the spa's white uniform stroll along with an attractive redhead in a green dress that caught Camille's eye. There was something about the girl which held Camille's attention. She held a lace parasol carelessly resting on one shoulder and she was laughing up into the man's eyes, and as she did so, something in the distance seemed to catch her attention, and she instinctively turned toward Camille, feeling her gaze upon her. The two women's eyes met, and Mary Ellen instantly realized who Camille was, she looked exactly as she'd been described to her by Hannah and others who had seen her, and at the same moment it was as though someone had shouted in Camille's ear or put a sign up over Mary Ellen's head. She knew instantly who she was and what she had been to Jeremiah. She half rose in her seat and then sat down again, feeling flushed and breathless, as Mary Ellen walked quickly away on her friend's arm, and for the rest of the day, Camille was haunted by her. She was the prettiest girl she had seen in the Napa Valley, and she instinctively knew now that this had to be the woman Hannah had inadvertently referred to . . . with all of

Jeremiah's trips back and forth to the mines during the winter and spring months, who knew if the liaison hadn't continued. She stewed about it all the way home in the carriage, and when Jeremiah returned from the mine office that evening she pounced on him with a venom that both alarmed and amazed him.

'You haven't fooled me for a minute, Jeremiah Thurston.' He was totally taken by surprise, and at first thought that she had to be teasing, but it was clear very quickly that she wasn't. 'All those trips up here this winter . . . I know what you were up to . . . you're just like my father with his mistress in New Orleans.' Jeremiah almost gasped. He hadn't looked at another woman since he married Camille, and had no desire to, as he attempted to tell her. 'Balderdash, and what about the redhead in Calistoga?' Oh my God, Mary Ellen. His face went pale. Who had told her? And had someone told her about the baby too? But all that Camille observed was his obvious shock. She sat down with a look of frigid satisfaction. 'I see by your expression that you know whom I refer to.'

'Camille . . . please . . . there has been no one since we've been married, my darling. Absolutely not a soul. I wouldn't do that to you. I have too much respect for you and our marriage.'

'Then who is she?' He could have denied it, but he didn't dare. She would never have believed him.

'Someone I used to know.' It was honest and his face showed it.

'Do you still see her?'

Her question angered him and that showed too. He was not accustomed to being interrogated by an eighteen year old girl. 'I do not, and I consider that a highly inappropriate question. I also consider this entire subject most unladylike for you to discuss, Camille.' He decided to hit a grand slammer. 'Your father would not approve of your behaviour.' She blushed at this, knowing full well that her father would be horrified if he thought she knew about and, worse yet, discussed, his mistress.

'I have a right to know.' Her face was beetroot red. She had gone too far and she knew it.

'Not all men would agree with you, but as it so happens, I do. And let me assure you, before we close this very distasteful subject, that you have nothing to fear from me, Camille. I am faithful to you, have been since the day we got married, and intend to stay that way until my dying day. Does that satisfy your concern, Camille?' He spoke to her as a stern and disapproving father, and she was genuinely embarrassed. She only brought it up again once, in bed, later that evening.

'She's awfully pretty, Jeremiah. . . .'

'Who is?' He was already half asleep.

'That woman . . . the redhead in Calistoga. . . .' He sat bolt upright in bed and glared at her.

'I will not discuss that with you again.'

'I'm sorry, Jeremiah.' Her voice was very small as he lay down again and closed his eyes and she put a tiny hand on his shoulder, and a little while later she mollified him with the passion that always enthralled him. It had been an ecstatic six months for him in their marriage bed, and he knew that Camille was happy in that regard too. The only disappointment for him was that she continued not to get pregnant. But Hannah shed fresh light on the subject for him in late August, as she stood in front of him at breakfast one day, before he left for the mines, while Camille was still asleep upstairs.

'I have to talk to you, Jeremiah.' She sounded like an angry mother hen, and he looked up from his eggs and sausages in surprise.

'Is something wrong?'

'Depends on how you look at it.' And then she glanced upstairs. 'Is she up yet?'

'No.' He shook his head and frowned. Had there been another altercation between the two women? He didn't attempt to deny anymore that there was no love lost between the two and he no longer even attempted to sing either one's praises to the other. It was a hopeless venture. 'What is it Hannah?'

She locked the kitchen door from the inside, something she had never done, approached Jeremiah, and dug a hand deep into her apron pocket, bringing out of it a wide gold band, rather like the rim of a small dresser knob, or something one would use to hang curtains except that it was smoother, and fine and exceptionally well made. 'I found this, Jeremiah.'

'What is it?' The mystery did not seem particularly interesting to him, and he was irritated to have to play games at this early hour of the morning.

'Don't you know what it is, Jeremiah?' She seemed surprised. She had never seen one quite this fancy, but she had seen simpler ones. But he shook his head now, both mystified and bored, and she sat down across the table from him. 'It's a ring.'

'I can see that.'

'You know . . . a *ring* . . .' She was embarrassed to explain it to him, but she knew she had to. He'd been had. 'Women use these contraptions so . . . so . . .' She got red in the face, and went on, for his sake, '. . . so they don't get babies, Jeremiah. . .' The full portent of her words took a moment to sink in, and then hit him with the impact of an entire building falling on his chest.

His voice instantly shook as he grabbed at the offending object. Maybe the old woman was just making it all up, to cause trouble for Camille. It was unlike her, but anything was possible, given the two women's hatred for each other, and Camille had tried to get her fired more than once. 'Where did you get that?' He stood up as though he couldn't bear to sit down any longer.

'I found it in her bathroom.'

'How do you know that's what it is?'

'I told you . . . I seen them before. . . .' And then, blushing again, 'They say they work real good, Jeremiah. As long as you're careful with it. It was wrapped up in a handkerchief, and I took it to wash it, and . . . it just fell out. . . .' She suddenly wondered if he was angry with her, but she knew better than that. 'I'm sorry, Jeremiah, but I thought you had a right to know.'

He glared at her, unable even to reassure her, he was so furious with Camille, and hurt and disappointed. 'I don't want you to say anything to her. Is that clear?' His voice was still harsh and she nodded, and then he strode to the door, unlocked it, and went outside to saddle Big Joe. And a moment later, he took off for the mines, at a gallop, with the ring still in his pocket.

Chapter Fifteen

What Jeremiah had learned from Hannah that morning troubled him all day, and he couldn't concentrate on his work for a moment. The ring in his pocket burned through his heart like a torch, and finally in the middle of the afternoon, he left, and went to seek out the doctor who had delivered Mary Ellen's baby in Calistoga. He showed him the object and wanted him to explain it. And when the old man did, Jeremiah almost shuddered.

'I gave her one myself. She didn't tell you that?' The doctor looked surprised and Jeremiah looked shocked.

'My wife?' Now it was the doctor's turn to look shocked, he didn't think that Jeremiah and Mary Ellen had got married, but you never knew with rich men like him. They did what they wanted and they moved quickly.

'Didn't know you'd married her . . .' His voice trailed off and Jeremiah understood.

'No . . .' And then he explained. 'This was in my wife's bathroom.'

'Is she pregnant now?'

'No.'

Slowly the old country doctor understood. 'I see . . . and you've been wanting her to get pregnant.' Jeremiah nodded honestly. 'Well she's not likely to with that. They work pretty well, as well as anything.' He shrugged, and then looked pointedly at Jeremiah. 'It makes sense in some cases though, like Mary Ellen. She has no choice but to use that. Might as well shoot herself in the head than try again and I told her as much.' Jeremiah nodded quietly, it wasn't his problem anymore, but he didn't tell the old man that. He was only interested in Camille. 'Did your wife tell you she was using this?' The doctor was intrigued now.

'No.'

There was a long silence as the doctor soaked it all in and Jeremiah sifted through his own thoughts. 'Not very nice of her, was it?' the doctor said, and Jeremiah shook his head and stood up.

'No, it wasn't.'

He shook hands with the old man and returned to Saint Helena, where he found Camille sitting in her chemise and pantaloons, fanning herself in her bedroom. And without further ado, he dropped the gold ring in her lap. She just glanced at it at first, not sure what it was, and hoping it was another piece of jewelry, and suddenly when she saw what it was, she recoiled as though from a snake, and her face grew pale. She had been looking for it for days and was afraid that she'd lost it.

'Where did you find that?'

He stood looking down at her from his great height and for once there was no kindness in his eyes. 'More to the point, where did you find it, Camille? And why did I know nothing about it?' It was obvious that he knew what it was and that it was hers. It would do her no good to deny it and she knew it.

'I'm sorry . . . I . . .' Her eyes instantly overflowed and she turned away from him. And he wanted to stay angry at her but he couldn't. He knelt beside her on the floor and forced her to look at him.

'Why did you do that, Camille? I thought something was wrong that we didn't . . . that we couldn't . . .'

She shook her head as fresh tears flowed and hid her face in her hands . . . 'I didn't want a baby yet . . . I don't want to get fat and . . . and Lucy Anne says it hurts so much . . .' The memory of Mary Ellen shot into his head and he forced it from his mind. 'I can't. I can't . . .' She was just a baby and he saw that now, but she was a woman too, and his wife, and he wasn't getting any younger. He didn't have five or ten years to wait, and he told her as much, in a gentle voice, and chided her for protecting herself from him in secret. 'I couldn't help it, Jeremiah . . . I was scared . . . and I knew you'd be angry . . .'

'I was. But I was hurt too. I always want you to be honest with me.'

'I'll try.' But she didn't tell him that she would.

'Now, do you have any more of these?' She began to shake her head, and then, looking mortified, she nodded. 'Where?' She led him to her bathroom where she showed him a carefully concealed box. She had two more and he took them.

'What are you going to do with them, Jeremiah?' She was in a panic, but he was unrelenting. He crushed all three rings in his huge hands, rendering them useless and then breaking them before dropping them into a wastebasket, as she began to sob. 'You can't do that! . . . you can't . . . you can't!' She began to flail at his chest and he held her tight as she cried, and then he gently took her to the bed, laid her down and left her there with her own thoughts. He went outside for a walk in the garden, still feeling betrayed by what she had done, and they were both quiet that night when they went to bed. Jeremiah was still hurt by the discovery of the treacherous ring, and Camille said not a word as he turned off the light, and she kept well to her side of the bed, which was unusual for her. More often than not, it was she who had approached him. The ring gave her the freedom to enjoy cavorting in bed with him, and now she lay in deathly fear, keeping her distance. But tonight it was Jeremiah who sought her out, reaching out to her as she trembled and attempted to push him away. 'No . . . no . . . Jeremiah . . . don't . . .' But for once, he was relentless, partly in anger for what she had done to him, and partly because he had a right to her. He forced her legs open and took her, and tonight she did not moan with pleasure, instead she cried softly, and when she had stopped, he took her again. And then again the next morning.

Chapter Sixteen

In September, Camille and Jeremiah returned to the city, as he had promised, and Camille almost instantly began her usual round of parties, but by the second week in September, Jeremiah found her sitting wanly in her dressing room one morning. She had her hairbrush in her hand and she looked green when he stopped in to say hello to her.

'Is something wrong?'

'No . . .' But it was obvious that she was feeling poorly, and within another week or two, Jeremiah suspected the nature of her illness, as did Camille, and she was less than ecstatic when she finally told him that she thought she was probably expecting. He had thought as much himself, and he was thrilled by the news. He had been waiting with bated breath for her to say something. And that afternoon when he came home to Thurston House, he had a handsome leather jewellers' box with him. But even that didn't spark much interest in her eyes. She was feeling absolutely ghastly. And for the next two months she was scarcely able to go to any parties and she gave none at all. It was not at all the way she had planned to spend the 'season' in San Francisco.

And when Amelia arrived to visit her daughter in October, and Jeremiah told her the news, she was delighted for them, and mentioned that her daughter was expecting her third child the following Spring, which Camille later told Jeremiah she thought was disgusting. The girl had had three children in three years, and that was not what Camille intended to do. She silently mourned the sacred rings he had destroyed, and if that old witch of a woman in Napa hadn't told him about them, she told him once, she wouldn't have been in the predicament she was in.

'Is that how you see it?' he asked her sadly. He was so happy about the baby and it saddened him to see how unhappy she was about it. He hoped that once she saw the baby she would feel differently about it all. It was easy to understand that she was of two minds about it now, feeling as ill as she was.

There was no denying that she was having a hard time of it, throwing up, and feeling ill, and she had fainted several times when he took her out. He absolutely refused to take her to the opera again, despite all her protests, and now suddenly none of her dresses fit, and she detested the adjustments she had to make. She envied the girls who claimed they didn't show until the seventh or eighth month, but because of her diminutive stature, she was not one of those, and by Christmas, when he gave her a little birthday party, it was quite obvious that she was pregnant. He gave her a new sable cloak to hide her girth, and a beautiful little watch circled with diamonds. 'And when it's all over, little love, we'll go to New York and buy you lots of pretty clothes. And afterwards, we'll take you to Atlanta for a visit.' She could hardly wait for that time to come. Pregnancy was even worse than she had anticipated. She hated getting fat, hated feeling ill, detested everything about it, and Jeremiah most of all for getting her into that condition. And in February, she was angrier still when he announced to her that he was moving her to Napa for the rest of her confinement.

'But it's not until May!' Her eyes filled with tears and her voice rose in protest. 'And I want to have the baby in San Francisco.' Gently, he shook his head. That wasn't what he had planned. He wanted her leading a quiet life in the country, not trying to race from luncheons to tea parties to balls, exhausting herself and complaining of how ill she felt, and fainting in crowds. He wanted her leading a quiet life in the country, and he assured her that her parents would agree with him. This was a time in her life when it was important for her to rest, and breathe fresh air, and do very little. But she was convinced that he was doing it to torment her, and more than once she screamed at him in frustration and slammed the door to her sitting room, shouting at him, 'I hate you!' She had been touchy and rebellious since the very day she got pregnant, and he wondered if things would have been different between them if he had allowed her to continue using her rings. But this was what he wanted, and he wasn't young enough to allow her more time. He felt certain that he had done the right thing, but he was far from popular with his wife when he moved her to Saint Helena in the midst of the winter rains. The hills were already turning green and the grass was sharp and spiky and bright on the rolling hills, but it was depressing for her to sit through the rainy afternoons with no one to speak to except Hannah.

In an effort to amuse her as much as he could, he came home earlier from the mines, told her of his work there, of the men, brought her little trinkets to delight her. But she was uncomfortable and unhappy and bored, and it was small consolation to her that she was healthy, according to the doctor in Napa. Jeremiah had chosen him to assist Camille with the delivery because he had been highly recommended, but Camille insisted that he was rough with her and rude and she smelled liquor on his breath, and by the eighth month of her pregnancy, she was in tears most of the time, and insisted that she wanted to go home to Atlanta.

'As soon as the baby is born, little love. I promise. You'll spend the summer resting here, and in September we'll go to New York and Atlanta.'

'September!' She hurled the word at him like a boulder, ready to explode in his lap. 'You never told me I'd have to stay here all summer!' She was sobbing again, and she looked as though she wanted to kill him.

'But we spent last summer here, Camille. The weather is awful in San Francisco in the summer, and you'll be tired after the baby's born.'

'I will not! I'll have been stuck here all winter. And I *hate* it.' She threw a vase to the floor and left the room as its splinters flew across the floor. Hannah came in to help him pick it up.

'I wouldn't say that childbearing agrees with her much,' Hannah stated drily. Camille had been unbearable since the day she'd arrived, and by April she was driving them both crazy. The weather had improved and it was a particularly lovely Spring, but she seemed not to notice it at all, as she stormed around the house brooding and complaining. Even getting the nursery ready seemed not to give her much pleasure, she embroidered a few shirts, and bought the fabric for the curtains, but Hannah did the rest, knitting and sewing, and even making a beautiful wicker cradle for the baby. Every night, Jeremiah would take special delight in walking into the cheerful room, and handling the tiny socks and shirts, watching in wonderment as everything was readied. But as the time drew closer, again and again, he found himself haunted by the memory of Mary Ellen. He had an unspoken terror that this child would be stillborn too, and Camille would torture him by doing everything he asked her not to do, walking alone by the creek, swinging from an old swing in a tree behind the house, and three weeks before the baby was due, she horrified Hannah as she took off in a fury one day, saddling a mule Jeremiah had long since retired from the mines and riding out into the neighboring vineyards because she was bored and tired of walking. Hannah was so upset that she told Jeremiah when he came home, and he rushed upstairs to berate Camille, but when he reached their bedroom, he realized there was no point. She was lying on their bed, strangely pale, and as he approached the bed, he saw her wince and her teeth were clenched as he bent to kiss her.

'Are you all right, little love?' He was instantly worried. She didn't look right, and there was a thin veil of perspiration on her brow.

'I'm fine.' But she didn't look it. She staunchly insisted on joining him at the dinner table that night, but she barely ate, and both Hannah and Jeremiah watched her. He sent her upstairs afterwards to relax and this time she didn't argue with him, instead she seemed grateful to go, and she was halfway up the stairs when she suddenly stopped and sank to her knees with a low moan. With a few short bounds, he was on his knees beside her, and took her swiftly in his arms, as Hannah ran up the stairs behind him.

'She's in labour, Jeremiah. I knew it this afternoon. But when I asked her, she said she wasn't having pains. It's riding on that old mule that did it.'

'Oh hush up . . .' She snapped at Hannah, but not with her usual spirit, and Jeremiah suspected that Hannah was right. He lay Camille down on her bed and took a good look at her. She was deathly pale, and her hands were clenched, and she wore a strange, unfamiliar expression, as though she were in pain but didn't want to admit it. And then, as though to prove it to them both, she attempted to get off the bed, but as soon as her feet touched the floor, her knees buckled beneath her and she cried out in pain, reaching wildly for Jeremiah who scooped her up again and laid her on the bed, turning to address Hannah.

'Ride Big Joe over to where Danny lives. He told me he'd ride for the doctor in Napa.' And suddenly Jeremiah regretted selecting a physician so far away. No matter how competent he was, if he didn't get there in time, he wouldn't do them any good, but it had never dawned on him that they would need him quickly. Hannah took off on swift feet, and in half an hour she was back, reporting that Danny had left for Napa. That meant that the doctor would be with them in five or six hours, and in the meantime, she went downstairs to boil water and roll clean rags and make a pot of strong coffee for herself and Jeremiah. She didn't feel sorry for Camille; she was young and, however painful it was, she would survive it, and there was a feeling of excitement in the air. The baby Jeremiah had waited for so long was finally coming, and he seemed to feel the excitement too. He looked down at Camille with a tender smile as she clutched at his arm.

'Don't leave me, Jeremiah . . .' She was panting now, and her face was contorted with the contractions. 'Don't leave me with Hannah . . . she hates me . . .' She began to cry, and it was obvious that she was frightened. It was so different from Mary Ellen on her bed of pain, but she had been through it three times before and she had been so much older than this girl. Camille looked like a child now as she writhed in pain with each contraction. 'Oh make them stop . . . Jeremiah! . . . I can't . . .'

He felt sorry for her, but there was nothing he could do. He put damp cloths on her head until she threw them off, and she was clawing at his arm now. It had been four hours since Danny had left for Napa, and Jeremiah began praying that the doctor would come quickly. It didn't seem as though it was going to go on much longer. And then suddenly, with horror, he remembered Mary Ellen, and the three days she had lain in childbirth. But that couldn't happen to Camille. He wouldn't let it. He began to look at his watch now, every few minutes, and Camille was holding his arm with one hand and clutching the brass headboard on the bed with the other, shrieking whenever the pains came, which was most of the time now. And Hannah finally came up with more coffee for him, but Camille didn't even seem to notice her now.

'Don't you want me to stay with her?' she whispered. 'You shouldn't be in here.' She looked disapproving, but he had promised her he would stay until the doctor came and not leave her to Hannah. And he wanted to be there. It was a relief to be in the room and know what was going on. He would have gone mad if he'd had to wait outside. But when Danny returned three hours later, Jeremiah looked strained and exhausted.

'The Doc's in San Francisco.' He looked grim as he reported to

Jeremiah. Camille was clutching Hannah's hands upstairs and screaming that she couldn't bear the pain a moment longer, as Hannah tried to soothe her. 'His wife said your baby is early.'

'I know that,' he snapped at Danny. 'What the hell is he doing in San Francisco?'

The boy shrugged. 'My ma sent me for the doc in Saint Helena, but he's in Napa delivering a baby.'

'For chrissake . . . isn't there anyone who could come?' And then he remembered the doctor in Calistoga and sent Danny in that direction, but that could take another hour, and as Jeremiah bounded up the stairs, he could hear Camille screaming. It was a horrendous gutteral sound of pain, like a wounded animal keening, and he tore open the door and looked at Hannah with grim eyes.

'Where's the doctor?' she whispered with worried eyes.

'He's not coming. I sent the boy to Calistoga to find the one up there. Good God, I hope he's at home.' Hannah nodded as Camille howled again, tearing at her nightgown and thrashing on the bed in the warm night. But the three of them were already bathed in sweat from the tension.

'Jeremiah . . . I think something's wrong. Having them sharp as she is, the baby should be coming, and I looked, but I don't see anything there.' Jeremiah pursed his lips and watched his wife thrashing on the bed. There was no one coming to help, at least not for the moment, and he had no choice, he had to help her. Between the next pains, he gently spread her legs apart and she started to fight him, but she forgot his presence as soon as the next pain came, and he took a good look, hoping to see the head of their baby. But what he saw instead made him catch his breath, it was one tiny hand reaching down, where its head should have been pressing. The baby was turned around, just as Mary Ellen's had been, and it might already be dead, or would be soon, if he didn't do something. He remembered what he had seen the doctor do in Calistoga, and carefully instructed Hannah, who held Camille down mightily through the next few pains, as the girl shrieked as though she would die, and Jeremiah felt sure that he was killing her, but he had to do what he could to save their baby, and slowly, slowly, as he pressed the baby back up inside and felt for its head, he turned it. Its shoulder had been pressed at the opening, and now he could feel the head coming towards him. The bed was bathed with blood and Camille was almost too weak to

145

scream, but she did, as the baby shot from between her legs and into its father's hands, giving a lusty wail as it did so.

There was a tangle of cord around it and for a moment Jeremiah couldn't tell if he had a son or a daughter, and then through the tears in his eyes, he saw more clearly. 'It's a girl!' he shouted to Camille as she lifted her head wanly and began to cry, more from the horror of what she'd been through than any particular tenderness for the baby. She lay on her bed and moaned as Hannah attempted to clean her up, and she refused to hold the baby. And when the doctor came a little while later, he told Jeremiah he had done a fine job, and he gave Camille some drops which made her sleep, as Hannah crooned to the baby.

'Got rid of them rings, I guess.' The doctor chuckled to Jeremiah as he left, and the proud papa laughed as he thanked the doctor and handed him a gold coin. He had planned to give it to the doctor from Napa, but with the stillbirth and now this, this man had earned it. It was thanks to his experience with Mary Ellen that Jeremiah had known how to turn this baby. And the doctor told him in no uncertain terms, that he had saved the child's life, although he admitted that doing something like that was rough on the mother. But it couldn't be helped, and Jeremiah tried to explain that to her as he soothed her when she woke up. She was still half hysterical from what she'd been through, and she still didn't want to hold the baby. Jeremiah slipped a huge emerald ring on her finger, which he had been saving for this occasion. And he showed her the necklace and earrings and brooch that went with it, all perfectly matched, but she didn't care. All she wanted was his promise that she'd never have to go through it again. It had been the worst experience of her life, and she told him, sobbing, that it would never have happened if he hadn't raped her. It saddened him to see her reaction, but he knew that in a few days she'd be more herself again. Hannah wasn't as sure, she'd never seen a woman refuse to hold her baby for the first three days. Her daughter was four days old before Camille finally agreed to hold her, and a wet nurse had to be found in town, because Camille flatly refused to nurse her.

'What'll we call her, my love?'

'I don't know.' She sounded indifferent, and nothing he said seemed to cheer her. She refused to participate in the selection of names, never picked the child up, and feeling sorry for the little thing, Jeremiah almost constantly held her. He didn't care that she wasn't a son, she was his child, his flesh, the baby he had waited for, for so long, and suddenly he knew what Amelia had meant when she had urged him to get married and have babies. It was the most meaningful experience of his life and he adored the tiny bundle he held as often as he could. He would sit and stare at her in fascination, mesmerized by the delicate hands and the tiny features. He couldn't tell who she looked like but before she was a week old, he knew he wanted to name her Sabrina, and Camille didn't seem to object. They christened her in Saint Helena, Sabrina Lydia Thurston. It was Camille's first outing, and she wore the emerald ring and a green summer dress, but she still felt weak and she was furious that she couldn't get into most of her dresses. Hannah told her it was much too soon to expect that, in an attempt to console her, but Camille brushed her off and ordered her from her room, telling her to take the baby with her.

You could have cut the tension in the air with a knife during most of that summer. Camille was like a lionness in a cage, in the house in Saint Helena, and the vision that Jeremiah had had of her crooning lullabies to their child was far from the reality of the nervous young girl, itching to get back to city life as she watched the weeks tick by. He had promised her a trip to New York and Atlanta, but when her mother fell ill in July, her father wrote and said that they had best wait until Christmas, and as was her habit now, Camille flew into a rage and threw a lamp to the floor before stalking off to her room and slamming the door. She hated everything and everyone, the house, the country, the people, Hannah, the baby, and even Jeremiah fell prey to her ill temper. It was a relief for everyone when they packed up in September, and Camille finally left for the city she had so desperately missed. She felt as though she were being let out of prison.

'Seven months,' she breathed in disbelief as she walked into the front hall of their city home. 'Seven months!'

'We missed you!' her friends said.

'It was the worst time of my life,' she told them in return, 'a nightmare!' And unbeknownst to Jeremiah she went to a doctor and acquired some more rings and a special rinse, as well as a good supply of slippery elm which was an effective contraceptive too, and nothing he would ever say again would deter her from using those precautions. She had not, in any case, resumed having intercourse with him since Sabrina's birth, and she was in no hurry to do so. She didn't want to take any chances. The baby was four months old now, bright

147

and pretty and alert, with soft blonde curls, and big blue eyes like Camille's and Jeremiah's, and tiny chubby little hands with grasping fingers, but it was seldom that Camille visited her child, and she had opted not to use the handsome nursery on the same floor as her rooms, but had put the baby on the third floor instead.

'She makes too much noise,' she had explained to Jeremiah, who was disappointed not to have the baby nearer to their rooms. But he wasn't shy about going upstairs to see her. He adored the child, and made no secret of it. The only one who appeared not to was Camille. She brushed it off when Jeremiah said something to her, but by the time the baby was six months old, he was genuinely worried. Camille had never warmed up to her, and as the child grew older, she would know it. It was unnatural for Camille to show so little feeling for her child, yet she seemed really to feel nothing for her. All she cared about was the time she spent with her friends, the parties they gave or the small festivities she organized at Thurston House when Jeremiah was in Napa. He had told her he didn't like her friends, so she saw them alone now, and ever since he'd got her pregnant, her feelings toward him seemed much cooler. There were times when he wondered if she would ever forgive him.

'Give it time,' Amelia told him when he confessed his concern during her next visit. She held Sabrina and cooed and laughed with her, and the difference between the two women struck Jeremiah like a rock. 'Maybe she's afraid of little babies.' She saw the look in his eyes. 'I have three grandchildren here after all.' The third had finally been a boy and there was great rejoicing in her daughter's household, but she still found time to visit Jeremiah and Camille, though Camille was out when she came this time, as she was most of the time now. She seemed to have no time at all to spend with her husband and daughter. The only times she was at home at all was when she was giving a party or having a ball, and Jeremiah was getting tired of it. She liked the public role of being Mrs. Jeremiah Thurston and the attendant comforts and grandeur, but none of the private duties that went with it. Jeremiah was getting tired of not sleeping with his wife. Claiming that she still felt ill, she was sleeping in her dressing room now and had been since they returned from Napa. But she was never too ill to go to parties. Jeremiah didn't dare tell Amelia all of it, but she sensed it from the things he didn't say, and she felt sorry for him as she kissed him goodbye. He deserved better than that . . . she would have been happy to give him far better than that, had things worked out differently. But she had been too old for him, or so she thought, and she was happy that he had Sabrina.

At Christmas time, Jeremiah drew the line. Camille told him in November that she wanted to give a huge ball then, for six or seven hundred people, 'the biggest ball ever given here,' she said cheerfully and he looked at her and shook his head.

'No.'

'Why not?' Fury walked slowly into her eyes. She was Mrs. Jeremiah Thurston, and she wanted everything that went with it.

'We're going to Napa for Christmas.' Her mother wasn't better yet, and her father didn't think they should come to Atlanta. Camille didn't seem particularly concerned about her mother. It was no secret that she didn't like her. But she would have liked going to Atlanta to play the grand lady and thumb her nose in their faces.

'Napa?' she shrieked. 'Napa? For Christmas? Over my dead body.' There were those by then who would have thought that a pleasure, but Jeremiah was not yet among them.

'I have to be near the mines, there've been floods again . . .' Recently John Harte had lost twenty two out of the 106 men who worked for him and Jeremiah had gone to help him. Harte, who had finally begun to mellow, was thankful.

She cut him off. 'Then you go to Napa. I'll stay here.'

'For Christmas?' He was shocked. 'I want the three of us to be together.'

'Who? You, me and Hannah? Count me out, Jeremiah.'

'I was referring to our daughter,' he grabbed her arm in an unfamiliar show of frustration, 'or had you forgotten we have one?'

'That's an unnecessary remark. I see her every day.'

'When? On your way out the door as she comes in from the garden?'

'I'm not a wet nurse, Jeremiah.' She looked haughtily at him from her diminutive height, and for once the dam broke in Jeremiah.

'You're not a mother either. Or a wife for that matter. Just exactly what are you?' And with that she reached out and slapped him. He stood watching her. Neither of them moved. It was the beginning of the end of their marriage and they both knew it. Camille was the first to speak, but not to apologise to her husband. Something in her had snapped months before, when she had the baby, or when she was trapped in Napa, as she saw it. In truth, she would never forgive him for making her have Sabrina. But there was more to it than that. She

149

had wanted to share the excitement of his business life, only to discover that there was no room for her at the mines in Napa. It was an exclusively male world and he didn't even tell her about it. In exchange, she wanted his presence at her constant round of parties, and he failed her there, shying away from social life, as he always had, and refusing to show off with her. Camille had none of what she had wanted, except the grandeur of Thurston House.

'I am not going to Napa, Jeremiah. If you spend Christmas there, you'll be alone.' She'd had enough of the place to last a lifetime and it reminded her now of the worst moments of her life.

'No, I won't go alone.' He smiled sadly at her. 'I'll be with my daughter.' And he was as good as his word. On the eighteenth of December, he packed up Sabrina and her nurse and they left for Napa. Hannah had a warm welcome for them in Saint Helena. It took her two days to mention Camille's absence, and when she did, Jeremiah made it clear that he didn't want to discuss it. He was hurting terribly over what Camille was doing, but had he known the rest, he would have hurt more. She had actually dared to go ahead and give the ball she had threatened to give. The invitations had gone out without his knowledge, and he read about it in the newspaper two days after the party. He correctly assumed that she had charged everything to him. Instead of spending Christmas with her husband and daughter, she had chosen to spend it surrounded by her friends, the elite, and the grand, the nouveau riche and the showy. They were not a group that Jeremiah would have been happy in, but Camille was in ecstasy, playing the grande dame of Thurston House at the age of twenty, trying to forget that anyone had ever thought her less than aristocratic in Atlanta or that she had been forced to have a baby she didn't want or live in the Napa Valley, which she so desperately hated. She knew that if Jeremiah ever forced her to get pregnant again she would kill herself rather than have the baby. And as far as she was concerned, he deserved everything he got now, for doing what he had done to her body. In her mind, pregnancy was the worst nightmare of all and childbirth a torture which defied description. She remembered every agonizing moment each time she saw him, or even seemed about to approach her, and Sabrina was a living monument to nine months of hell. It was easier simply to avoid him. And she did, closing her heart to all she had once felt for Jeremiah, and whatever she might have learned to feel for her daughter.

Chapter Seventeen

Jeremiah did not return from Napa immediately after Christmas, as Camille suspected he was going to. He was calling her bluff, and he wasn't returning until the middle of January, a note to her read, but he would be happy to see her in Napa. Just reading his words annoyed her. She had no intention of going to Napa now, missing all the balls and parties in the city. She explained his absence to her friends with casual ease, and she continued to attend every party in town, including one given by a couple Jeremiah particularly disliked, a nouveau riche pair who'd come out from the East the year before, and were known for their more than slightly improper parties. With Jeremiah in town she had never been allowed to go, so she seized this opportunity to attend the ball they gave on New Year's Eve and was pleasantly surprised by the people she met there. They were an amusing group, far more fun than the people she and Jeremiah usually saw, in particular a man who had just arrived in town, a French count named Thibaut Dupré, who seemed to embody all that was decadent and European and aristocratic. He was exactly what she would have expected to meet, had she gone to Paris with her father. He was tall and handsome and blond with green eyes and fair skin, broad shoulders and slim hips, a delightful accent and a way with words, and he seemed to spend most of New Year's Eve kissing Camille's neck which shocked no one at the party. He spoke English as well as French, and he had a chateau in the North of France, and another in Venice, or so he said, but he was noticeably vague about the details. He made his way over to Camille as the party began, and he remained at her side throughout most of the evening. He mentioned that he had heard she had a magnificent house, and he would be interested in seeing it, just to compare it to his own, of course. Americans had such different ideas about architecture, he insisted as he whirled her around the floor, his arm tight around her

151

waist, his eyes locked in hers. He was a strikingly handsome man, with a great deal of charm, and open, ingenuous ways, and she couldn't see any harm in showing him the house the next day. She saw no harm in it at all, until he pressed his body against hers and kissed her in her boudoir as she showed him the painted French wallpaper there.

But as he touched her, and her body began to blaze beneath his fingers, she realized how long it had been since she felt a man's touch. Suddenly she was seized with a burst of passion for the languid French count, who played her body like a harp and had her almost begging within moments for him to take her. Coming sharply to her senses, she begged him to stop, but her words were garbled by his lips, and he only kissed her again, certain that she had fully understood his intentions when he'd asked to see her home. He had understood the night before that her husband was away and almost always was. But she drew away from him now, and almost ordered him to come downstairs with her. She amused him with her fiery eyes, her pretty lips, her raven black hair, and in the ensuing weeks, he showered her with gifts and trinkets and bouquets, inviting her to lunch, taking her for drives, and all the while Jeremiah did not return from Napa. She insisted that Dupré's behaviour was practically an affront, but she said it in her delectable Southern drawl, and he spoke to her in French, and offered her more fun than she'd had in months. Jeremiah was so serious, and she was so tired of hearing about floods in his mines. He had been delayed in Napa again, this time four men had died in yet another flood. Thibaut didn't talk about things like that to her. He just told her how beautiful she was, how remarkable that she'd ever had a child, and she told him how much she had hated that, and he won her heart by the fervour of his words.

'I think it is a cruelty to ask women to have babies. Barbaric!' He looked outraged. 'I would never ask such a thing of a woman I loved.' He stared meaningfully at her and she blushed.

'I'd never do it again,' she confessed. 'I would rather die.' And then he pleased her by admitting that children had never appealed to him.

'Appalling little brats . . . and they smell!' She laughed and he touched her lips with his own again, and she never quite understood how, but on the divan in her own dressing room, he made love to her after they had shared almost a full bottle of champagne from

Jeremiah's cellars. She was just grateful that she was wearing a ring again. She had put it in after New Year's Eve, just to see if it fit, she told herself . . . and she had left it in, in case Jeremiah came back, she pretended to herself. But it had nothing to do with Jeremiah at all. And it had everything to do with Thibaut Dupré now.

They carried on their clandestine affair for four weeks until Jeremiah returned. Dupré came to Thurston House, and she went to his hotel, which she knew full well was a shocking thing to do, but it was less dangerous than letting him into her home, which she did late at night, and then they would both giggle and tiptoe upstairs hiding in her rooms and drinking champagne and making love until dawn. With him she found the passion she had known before Sabrina's birth, and she found him more exciting than even Jeremiah had been. He was tall and thin and exotic and he spoke to her in French, and he was wicked and erotic. He was only thirty-two, but most of the time he seemed even younger than that, younger even than she at twenty-one. He wanted to frolic and play all the time, and make love from morning till night, and he didn't want her to have a baby. He was delighted with her ring and he even told her of other more exotic methods they had in France. He began talking of her going back to Europe with him.

'You could come with me to the South of France . . . and we could visit my friends . . . parties that last all night . . .' and he almost seared her ears by telling her the kinds of things they liked to do. Better still, he showed her, and as the days wore on, she felt something peculiar happening to her, as though she had discovered a drug, and could no longer live without him. She almost felt as though she were addicted to him, and night and day she longed for his touch, ached for his limbs, needed him to fill her very soul. It was almost painful to peel her flesh from his as she left his bed, and she needed his body on hers, his hands, his lips, his tongue . . . there was a heady perfume about everything he did, and she found herself constantly needing and wanting more of him. She began to feel desperate about Jeremiah coming home. And when he did, she scarcely got Dupré out in time, and while Jeremiah was upstairs seeing to the child she found an empty bottle of champagne under the bed and hid it quickly in her boudoir. She felt dishevelled and indiscreet, tainted and confused and when she saw Jeremiah, she began to cry, and he mistook it for relief to see him. But she cried because she was so desperately confused. And for an instant, just an instant, as she held her child for the first time in six weeks, she caught a glimpse of what life might still have been but in truth no longer was. It could have been just Jeremiah and Sabrina and herself, and for a moment she regretted not going to Napa with him. She would have been safe there, but instead she had cast herself adrift. She had strolled into the garden of Eden, and she no longer remembered the way home. She lay beside Jeremiah that night, hopelessly still, tortured with her own thoughts, and when at last he put a hand on her thigh, she trembled. The most terrible part of it was that she no longer wanted him. And she was already longing for Thibaut by the next morning. They met secretly in his hotel room, and when she returned home that afternoon, she felt as though her mind and soul were possessed by him, almost in a demonic way. She couldn't even imagine what her father would think of him.

He planned to stay in San Francisco for a few months, and she knew that by the end of that time she would be at least half mad from the confusion of it all. Already she didn't know what to say to Jeremiah at night, and she had moved back into her dressing room. She never had time to see Sabrina now, and when she and Jeremiah went out, she looked everywhere for a glimpse of the Count, who stood staring hungrily at her and once dared to caress her breast as she walked past him on the way into a restaurant. She had felt her whole body shiver with lust for him. Jeremiah had thought she was cold, and for an instant she felt sick with guilt.

And still, Thibaut talked of taking her back to France with him.

'But I can't! Don't you understand!' He made her feel crazed with his wild eyes and dancing tongue. 'I'm married! I have a little girl!' And there was more to it than that, a whole way of life, security, Thurston House. She was someone important here. She couldn't just run out on that.

'You have a husband who bores you to tears, and you don't care two pins about the child. So what else is there, my love? Do you not wish to be my countess in a chateau in France?'

'I do ... I do ...' She sobbed, and he was driving her mad by tempting her. She was so confused. She didn't know what to do. And within a month or two, Jeremiah had noticed how pale and wan she looked. He thought she was still recovering from Sabrina's birth and urged her to see the doctor again. But she put him off every day. She

154

had other things to do. She had to meet Dupré in his hotel room . . . where he talked of his chateaux . . . his father . . . his friends . . . all Marquis, and Counts, Princes and Dukes. It turned her head as she listened to him speak and dreamed of the balls in his friends' chateaux all over France. It was all like the dream her father had promised her before Jeremiah came along. She could be a countess now, if she wanted, all she had to do was give up her life here, as Thibaut whispered into her thighs and she thought she would go crazy. 'I can't bear it anymore!' she told him once. 'I'm too confused.' But he didn't care. Like her with him, he was addicted to her flesh, and he wanted more of her, he wanted her for his own, and he wouldn't relent until she gave in. He wanted her to come back to France with him and he assumed somehow that at least some of the fortune she evidenced was her own.

And day by day, Jeremiah saw her slip away, he knew not to where, until at last in April, a friend told him what he had seen. Camille had come out of the Palace Hotel with a tall blond man, and they had kissed before he hailed a carriage for her. Jeremiah felt his heart sink like a stone as he listened to the man's words and he wanted to believe him wrong, but as he watched her day by day, he began to suspect that his friend was right. There was something distant in her eyes every time he spoke to her, and she insisted that they go out every night. She seemed relieved when he left her to visit his mines, and he could never get her to sleep with him again.

He sank deeper into depression as the Spring wore on, and feared what would happen when he tried to move her to Napa again in June. He didn't want to confront her for fear she'd snap, but then, as it turned out, Fate handled things for him. He was leaving his banker's club late one afternoon, after discussing some business matters with him, when a carriage rolled slowly by and he saw Camille locked in the arms of a blond man. Jeremiah stood there on the corner for half an hour, feeling as though his world had shattered around him. He confronted her that night, quietly, in her dressing room.

'I don't know how it began, Camille.' There were unshed tears in his voice but he held them back now. 'And I don't want to know. Someone saw you a while back, and I wanted to think it wasn't true, but I suppose it is.' The tears stood out in his eyes as he looked at her. He loved her so much, and he wondered if he'd lose her to the man he'd seen kissing her in the carriage. He didn't care what she had done, as long as she stopped now. They could still salvage what they'd had, if she was willing to. It depended on her, more than on him. He was willing to forgive and carry on with her. But he didn't realize the confused state of mind she was in.

'How do you know it was I?' She looked sadly at him, bereft of her usual fight, as they both knew it had been she.

'There's no point arguing over that. The point is that I want you to stop.' His voice was as gentle as his love for her. 'It has to stop now, Camille. I'd like for us to leave for Napa next week, and maybe we can put the pieces together there, with Sabrina.' His eyes were damp now and she squeezed her own lids closed. If he had offered to drown her, it would have upset her less than moving to Napa the following week. She couldn't bear the thought, and she couldn't give up Thibaut yet. Not yet. She needed him. Jeremiah's next word was only a whisper, but it was heartfelt. 'Please. . . .'

She opened her eyes again, 'I'll see . . .' But it was as though she felt a hand at her throat, and she snuck out again that night, just to meet him on the street for a kiss and a few words. Jeremiah thought that she was downstairs, speaking to the cook, and he never knew the truth, as she stood desperately on the street, beyond the gardens, whispering to Dupré, while he begged her to join him at his hotel. He was a totally decadent man, with no conscience at all, and he would do everything he could to take her away with him. After all, why not? She was beautiful, sensual, almost as debauched as he by now, an expert in the art, although she was only twenty-one years old. He also knew from what everyone said, she was a very rich girl, and Dupré needed that. He'd heard that she had money of her own, and of course there was whatever Thurston had given her, presumably quite a lot, from the look of her jewels and furs.

But the following day, she met Thibaut in his hotel room, and sobbing as she spoke, she told him that their affair had come to an end. She had reasoned it out. She wasn't willing to give up what she had for him.

'Have I done something wrong?' He looked shocked, the immorality of it had never troubled him at all. It was something he had been playing at for years, other men's wives, they were good sport and this one was the best he'd had by far. And he had no intention of letting her go, not this one. She was too juicy, too sweet. And now she was his.

'It's I who've done something wrong,' she explained. 'I couldn't help myself, but now I have to stop. My husband knows.' She expected him to gasp and was startled when he didn't. Instead, he only looked concerned.

'Did he beat you, mon amour?'

'Not at all. But he wants me to go Napa with him next week.' She could barely go on, so oppressed did she feel at the thought. 'We'll be there for almost four months, and. . .' She was sobbing as she spoke, 'you'll be gone when we get back.'

'I could not come to Napa with you? To stay in a hotel nearby . . . .' It was a shocking thought, but she didn't reproach him for it, she wanted him just as desperately.

'No, that's not possible there.' He shook his head and wiped his eyes, and then he looked at her.

'Then you must come with me. You must make a choice. Now. This week.' He looked decided. 'We must go back to France. It is time for me to go home anyhow, we can summer in my chateau in the South,' if his father took him in, 'go to Venice perhaps for the summer balls,' that much was true, 'and then back to Paris in the fall.' It appealed to her a great deal more than Saint Helena but she knew she had no right to any of it. She was Jeremiah's wife and she had a life to lead in California. Besides there were benefits to that.

'I can't go.' She was barely able to force the words out.

'Why not?' You would be my Countess, ma cherie. Think of that!' She did, and it tore her heart in two. Her Daddy had always promised her a count or a duke.

'And my husband? And my child?'

'You care nothing for them. I know that, so do you.'

'That's not true. . . .' But she had behaved that way, and the life Thibaut dangled before her eyes was so much better suited to them both. She didn't want more babies, didn't want to be a respectable wife . . . didn't want to have a child, she never had wanted that . . . the only thing she liked about Jeremiah was Thurston House, and Thibaut was offering her two chateaux . . . Then in horror, she recoiled from her own thoughts. Did it amount to that? Who had the larger house . . . she was appalled at herself suddenly. What was it all coming to? 'I don't know what to do,' she sat down in sobs.

He poured her a glass of champagne. 'You must choose, my love. But choose wisely and well. When you rot in Napa for the rest of your life, you will regret the opportunity you missed . . . when he rapes you and gets you pregnant again. . . .' She shuddered visibly at the thought. 'Think of that! I will never ask that of you.' And she knew that sooner or later Jeremiah would. But it wasn't right . . . she was his wife . . . she drank the champagne and began to cry and Thibaut held her in his arms and made love to her again, and that night when she went home, she walked upstairs to the nursery and stood watching her child at play. She was a year old now, she said a few words, she had begun to walk, but Camille was no part of the child's life. She had chosen not to be. And now she wanted to put her face in her hands and sob, she really didn't know what to do. That night, when Jeremiah reminded her that they were leaving in five days, she thought she would go mad. She met Thibaut again in his rooms the next day, but this time he made up her mind for her. He pinned on a huge diamond brooch which he said was a family heirloom and pronounced them engaged before making love to her again half a dozen times. This time when she went home, she had a beaten look about her. She knew that however kind Jeremiah had been, she could not go back to Napa with him, could not bear him another child, could not even give herself to the one they had. It simply wasn't in her. Thibaut had shown her that, not with the diamond brooch, but with his words, and now she was going to Paris with him. She was going to be a Countess. Perhaps that was what she had been meant to be.

Jeremiah listened to her in shocked disbelief, and when she had finished what she had to say, he went to Sabrina's room, and tiptoed past the nurse to look at the sleeping child. It was inconceivable to him that her mother was leaving her, more painful still to think of her leaving him. And the agony of what he felt was impossible to put into words. He thought of her keening as she gave birth to their child, and it was what he felt now. He remembered John Harte losing his wife and child several years before. And now he knew something of what he had felt. He had never felt greater pain, and he wondered if that was what Mary Ellen had experienced when he left her. Perhaps this was retribution for his past sins. He lay his head in his hands and silently cried before leaving the sleeping child and going back to the loneliness of his bedroom.

It took Camille two days to pack, and a pall fell on the house as the rumour spread. Jeremiah said nothing to anyone at all, and the morning before she left, he grabbed her by both arms and pulled her close to him as tears ran down his face.

'You can't do this, Camille. You're a foolish child. You'll wake up and wonder what you've done. Don't think of me . . . think of Sabrina . . . you can't leave her now. You'll regret it all your life. And for what? Some fool with a chateau? You have all this.' He waved at Thurston House, but she shook her head and she was crying too.

'I was never meant to be here . . . to be your wife. . . .' She choked on a sob, 'I'm not good enough for you.' It was the first kind thing she had said and he held her tight.

'Of course you are . . . I love you . . . don't go . . . oh God, please don't go. . . .' But she only shook her head and hurried from the house, running through the gardens as she went, her dress flying out behind her, a vision of blue and white silk and flying black hair as Jeremiah watched blindly from upstairs. Thibaut was waiting for her with a carriage at the front gate, and a coachman came for her things that night. Jeremiah found a single note, with her jewels, 'For Sabrina . . . one day . . .' And another note in his dressing room, 'Adieu.' She hadn't known when she left the jewelry behind that Thibaut would be furious with her.

Jeremiah felt like a dying man as he went from room to room that night. He couldn't believe she was gone. It was an insane thing to do. She would change her mind, would come back, would cable from New York. He put off his departure for Napa for three weeks, hoping that she would return, but she never did, never came, never called out to him. He never saw her again, except in his dreams. He wrote to her father eventually, and explained what little he himself understood, and the answer came back that she was a wicked child, and she was dead to them now, dead to them all, as she must be to him, her father urged. It seemed an unkind way to think of her, yet what other way was left? She never even wrote to him, she disappeared into the night with a stranger who had taken her to France with him.

Her father had no sympathy for her, even though he was partially responsible for what she had done. He had taught her to want too much, to count too heavily on material things. He had filled her head with dreams of princes and dukes. But the difference was that when he saw Jeremiah, he had recognized a good man, a good marriage for his child, and he had done the right thing. Camille had gone too far, and her father couldn't forgive her that. She wrote to him eventually, and he told her that she was dead to him. She would inherit nothing from him, or her mother, who was too ill to have any contact with her now. The only one left was Hubert, and he was of a selfish bent and had never had much interest in Camille.

And in California, Jeremiah told everyone that she had died of the still dreaded flu. There had been a recent epidemic of it, and Camille had been wise enough to keep it quiet when she left. It seemed that no one knew that they had gone. Thibaut Dupré left an enormous outstanding bill at the Palace Hotel, so he was anxious to keep his future whereabouts unknown. He had told no one that he was taking Camille Thurston with him. They simply left, and for more than a week, Jeremiah told everyone in town that his wife was desperately ill. The knocker was draped in black crepe after that and everyone was shocked. A small notice appeared in the newspaper, and the house was closed up, almost sealed. Jeremiah left for Napa after that. Everyone there believed her dead of influenza, as well. He explained that her body had been sent back to Atlanta for burial in her family plot, and there was a small memorial service in Saint Helena, attended by pathetically few. Almost no one knew her there, and those who did were understandably not fond of her. Hannah came, looking strangely stiff in a black dress, some of the men who worked at Jeremiah's mines, out of respect for him, and Jeremiah was touched to see that John Harte had come too. He had never forgotten Jeremiah being there for him when his wife and children had died. He hadn't married again and he still dreaded going home at night to his empty house on the hill. But he shook Jeremiah's hand with a look of sympathetic grief.

'Be grateful that you've got your little girl.'

'I am.' Jeremiah's eyes met his. The younger man was twenty-nine now, but he seemed older and wiser than his years. There was a lot of responsibility on his back and he carried it well. In an odd way, Jeremiah was fond of him. He was touched that he'd come, and shook his hand warmly before he left. And then he went home to Sabrina, who had no mother now. He still couldn't understand what Camille had done, or why. How could she have run off with him? But one thing was sure in Jeremiah's mind. There would be no divorce. He wanted no one to know that Camille hadn't died. There was to be no record of that. He was going to perpetuate the myth of her death as long as he lived, especially to his child. As far as everyone was concerned, Camille Beauchamp Thurston was dead. And only Jeremiah and Hannah knew the truth. All of the servants at Thurston House had been let go, and the house was closed for good. Perhaps he would sell it one day or keep it for Sabrina, but he would never live there again. There were still some of Camille's clothes hanging there, the things she didn't want. She had taken all of her expensive clothes and her evening gowns, and her beautiful sables with her. She'd packed almost everything, except the old and the used, and there was precious little of that. She had filled her trunks well when she left, and if she ever came back, she would find herself still married to him, but Sabrina would grow up thinking her mother had died of influenza as so many others had in years past, and she would find nothing whatever to deny that tale, no trace of anything that might suggest the truth. No letter, no explanation, no divorce. There would be no such thing. Camille Beauchamp Thurston was simply gone. Rest in peace.

Book II

Sabrina Thurston Harte

Chapter Eighteen

The carriage pulled up at the mines just before lunch, and out bounded a slender young girl, her silky dark brown hair neatly tied in a blue satin ribbon, and her pale blue linen skirt and middy blouse made her look even younger than her thirteen years as she bounded across the yard outside the mines, and waved to the man just emerging from the office. He stopped for a moment, shielding his eyes against the sun, and shook his head. But he was smiling as he did so. Only the week before he had told her not to come riding helter skelter over the hills on his best horses, so instead she had taken the carriage out and driven it herself. He wasn't sure whether to be amused or angry, except that generally it was a decision he easily made. Sabrina was not an easily repressed child, never had been, and growing up alone with him, she had picked up certain peculiarities. She adored the smell of his cigars, knew all his quirks and needs and catered to them constantly, she rode his horses as well as he, and knew every man at all three of his mines by name. She had even come to know more about making wine from his grapes than he did. And none of it displeased him. Jeremiah Thurston was proud of his only child, prouder than he liked her to know, but secretly she knew it. He had never laid a strap on her or spanked her once in the past thirteen years, he taught her everything he knew and kept her with him every moment. When she had been very small he had scarcely ever left Saint Helena, but stayed with her constantly, reading her bedtime stories at night, soothing her when she was sick, cradling her when she was sad, and, more often than not, taking care of her himself, instead of letting Hannah or the maids he hired do it.

'It's not natural, Jeremiah!' Hannah had scolded him more than once in the early years. 'She's a girl child, barely more than a baby, leave her to me and the other women.' But he couldn't do it, couldn't bear to have her out of his sight for more than a little while. 'It's a wonder you still go to the mines every day.' And after a while, he began to take her with him. He would gather up a few toys, a warm sweater, a blanket, sometimes a pillow, and she would play in a corner of his office, and lie cozily on the blanket by the fire when she grew sleepy in the afternoons. Some people found it shocking, but more often than not, they found it touching. Even the hardest-hearted men he dealt with couldn't resist the little pink face tucked in beneath the blanket, the brown curls cast across the pillow, and she always awoke with a smile and a tiny yawn, and then would come running to kiss her father. It was a love which startled some and filled most who saw it with envy, a rare consuming passion, an understanding for each other's ways. In thirteen years, she had given him no grief, in fact she had given him nothing but pleasure and sunshine and affection. In the lavishness of her father's love, Sabrina felt no pain at the loss of her mother. He had told her simply one day that her mother had died when she was a baby.

'Was she pretty?' she asked.

His heart clenched a little as he nodded. 'Yes, she was, love. Like you.' He smiled, but in fact, Sabrina looked more like him than her mother. She had the sharpness of Jeremiah's features and it was obviously early on that she would have his height. If anything, what she had taken from Camille was a sense of mischief. Now and then she played pranks on him, and she was a terrible tease, but it was all good fun, and she had never shown any sign of her mother's spoiled, pettish behaviour. And in all her years, no one had ever hinted to her that her mother hadn't died but had deserted them both instead. There was no reason to tell her. It would only confuse her and hurt her, as Jeremiah had told Hannah long before. And in thirteen years, there had been nothing but joy in Sabrina's life. She had a happy, easygoing existence and she went everywhere with her adoring father. When she was old enough for him to hire a tutor for her, she waited patiently through the day, feigning interest in her lessons, and then she would fly to the mine to be at his side and spend the rest of the day following him there. It was there that she learned all that she wanted to know.

'I want to work for you one day, Papa.'

'Don't be silly, Sabrina.' But secretly, he wished that she could have. She was daughter and son all rolled into one, and had a fine head for business. But it would be impossible for her to work at the mines, no one would ever have understood it.

'You let Dan Richfield work for you when he was just a boy. He told

166

me so himself.' But he was twenty-six years old now, a married man with five children. How long ago it seemed that he had begun working for Jeremiah on Saturday mornings.

'That was different Sabrina, he was a boy. You're a young lady.'

'I'm not!' In rare moments of petulance, she did indeed remind him of her mother, and he would turn away so as not to see the resemblance. 'Don't turn your back on me, Papa! I know as much as any man about your mines!'

He would sit down and take her hand in his with a gentle smile. 'That's true, my love, you do, but it takes more than that. It takes a man's hand, a man's strength, a man's determination. You'll never have those.' He patted the cheek he so dearly loved. 'We'll just have to find you a handsome husband.'

'I don't want a husband!' Even at ten, she had been outraged at the thought, and at thirteen she was no more interested than she had been then. 'I want to live with you forever!' In a way, he was glad of that. He was fifty-eight years old now, still vital and strong and alive and full of ideas about how to run his mines and his vineyards. But the pain Camille had caused him had taken its toll. He hadn't felt like a young man in years. He felt old and worn and tired, and there was a part of him that he would never open up again, just as he would never again open up the palatial house in the city. He had had numerous offers over the years, from people who wanted to buy it, even one man who wanted to turn it into a hotel, but he had no inclination to sell it. He had never set foot in the house again, and probably never would. It would be too painful to see those rooms he had built for Camille, the home he had hoped to fill with half a dozen children. Instead, he would leave it to Sabrina, and if she married, he would give it to her then. Instead of his children, it would be for hers, it seemed a suitable end to the home he had built with such loving intentions.

'Papa!' She called out to him as she ran across the yard, leaving the carriage safely tied up. She knew more than most boys about mines and horses and coaches. And yet her femininity had remained intact, as though hundreds of years of Southern ladylike traditions were bred into her so deeply that they would always be a part of her. She was female to the very tips of her toes, but in all the gentle, loving ways that her mother wasn't. 'I came as soon as I could.' She ran up to him breathlessly, tossing her long curls over her shoulder as he laughed and shook his head in mock despair.

'So I see, Sabrina. When I suggested you drop by this afternoon when your tutor left, I didn't mean to steal my best coach to do it.' She looked suddenly remorseful and glanced over her shoulder.

'Do you really mind, Papa? I drove it very carefully.'

'I'm sure you did. It wasn't that which concerned me. But you make quite a spectacle of yourself driving a rig like that, my girl. Hannah will surely tan both our hides. If you did it in San Francisco, they'd run you out of town on a rail and say you were "fast" and behaved in a most unseemly manner.' He was teasing her now, and she shrugged her shoulder with obvious indifference.

'Then they'd be silly. I drive better than you do, Papa.'

This time he frowned in mock outrage. 'That's a downright rude thing to say, Sabrina. I'm not totally over the hill, you know.'

'I know, I know,' she blushed slightly, 'I just meant. . .'

'Never mind. Next time ride your sorrel over here. It's a little less conspicuous.'

'But you told me not to run hell for leather over these hills, to come in the coach, like a lady.'

He bent toward her and whispered in her ear. 'Ladies do not drive coaches.' And then she began to laugh. She had had a wonderful time driving over, and the truth was that there wasn't a great deal for her to do in Saint Helena. She knew no children her own age, she had no siblings or cousins, and she spent all of her time with her father. So she played pranks when she got bored, or hung around the mines. And now and then, he took her to San Francisco. They always stayed at the Palace Hotel, and he took rooms for her adjacent to his own. When she was younger, he would take Hannah with them, but now the poor woman was too crippled by her arthritis and she did nothing to hide the fact that she hated going into the city. And Sabrina was old enough to go alone with her father.

They had often driven by Thurston House, and once he had unlocked the gate and they had strolled through the gardens together, but he had never taken her inside, and she suspected why. It was too painful for him since the death of her mother. But she had always been curious about the inside of the house. She had asked Hannah about it, and had been disappointed to learn that the old woman had never been inside it. She had pressed Hannah about what her mother was like, too, but she never got much information and early on deduced that Hannah had not been overly-fond of her mother. Though she wasn't sure why, she never quite dared press her father about it. Something so ravaged and sad and angry came into his eyes when her mother's name came up that she preferred not to cause him any anguish by asking him about her. So there were mysteries and holes in her life, a house she had never seen, a mother she had never known . . . and a father who adored her.

'Did you finish all your work, Papa?' She pressed him as they walked toward the coach arm in arm. He had finally agreed to let her drive him home, with his horse tied to the back of the coach, and a shudder for what people would think if they saw them.

'Yes, I did, you little minx. You know, you're a shocking child.' He attempted to glare at her as he took his seat beside her. 'If anyone sees us, they'll think I'm mad to let you do this.'

'Don't worry about it, Papa.' She patted his hand in a motherly fashion. 'I'm a very good driver.'

'And a very brazen girl, you little hussy.' But it was obvious how much he loved her, and a moment later she renewed her question about his work. She had an ulterior motive and he knew it. 'Yes, I did, and I know why you're asking. And yes, we are going to San Francisco tomorrow. Does that satisfy you?'

'Oh yes, Papa!' She beamed at him and rounded a bend in the road without looking, almost turning over the coach as her father gasped and reached for the reins, but she corrected the problem swiftly and deftly herself and then smiled demurely at him as he roared with laughter.

'You're going to be the death of me yet, one way or another.' But that was something she didn't like to hear, even in jest. Her face clouded over, as it always did, and he was sorry he had said it.

'That's not funny, Papa. You're all I have, you know.' She always made him feel remorseful when he said something like that to her, and he tried to lighten the moment now.

'Then kindly attempt not to kill me with your driving.'

'You know perfectly well I seldom make a mistake.' And as she said it, she rounded another corner, this time with mathematical precision. She looked at him with glee. 'That was better.'

'Sabrina Thurston, you're a monster.'

She bowed politely from her seat. 'Just like my father.' Except she wondered now and then if she were actually more like her mother . . . what had she been like? . . . whom had she resembled? . . . why did she die so young? . . . she had a thousand unanswered questions about the woman. There wasn't a single portrait of her in their house, not a miniature, not a sketch, not a photograph, nothing. And her father had said only that she had died of influenza when Sabrina was a year old. Full stop. End of story. He said that he had loved her very much, that they had been married on Christmas Eve in Atlanta, Georgia, in 1886, and that Sabrina had been born a year and a half later in May of 1888, and a year later, her mother had died, leaving him grief-stricken. He explained to her too that he had built Thurston House before marrying her mother, and now some fifteen years later, she knew that it was still the largest house in San Francisco, but it was a relic, a tomb, a place which she would enter 'someday', but not now, and not with him. And at times, as they drove through San Francisco, her curiosity almost overtook her. So much so that she had developed a plan, and the next time she went to town with him she was going to try it. 'Are we still going to the city tomorrow, Papa?'

'Yes, you little villain, we are. But I have meetings at the Nevada Bank all day, and you'll have to keep yourself amused. In fact, I told Hannah that I didn't think you should come with me this time,' she began to object before he even finished his sentence and he held up a hand for silence, 'but I knew that that was exactly what you'd say, so I told her that for my own peace and quiet, I was taking you with me. You'll have to make it up with your tutor next week, Sabrina. I won't have you avoiding your lessons by running around with me.' For a moment he sounded stern, but he wasn't really worried. She had always been an excellent student, and they both knew that she often learned more by being with him. Normally, he might even have offered to let her go to the bank with him, but a full day of meetings would be too much for her. 'Take some books with you. You can study a little at the hotel, and we'll go out when I get home. There's a new play I thought you might like to see. I wrote and asked the bank president's secretary to get tickets for us.' Sabrina clapped her hands and then grabbed at the reins again as they pulled into their own driveway and the horses slowed down.

'That sounds lovely, Papa.' And she knew exactly what she was going to do when he was at his meetings. 'And you can't complain, I got you home safely.'

He scowled at her and drew on his cigar. 'The next time you take out my best coach, I would be grateful if you would be so kind as to ask me.' She jumped lightly to the ground with a smile, enjoying the pungent smell of his cigar.

'Yes, sir.' And with that she bounded into the house, and greeted Hannah with a shout and the report that they were going to the city the next day.

'I know, I know . . .' She clapped her hands over her ears. 'Lower your voice. My goodness, you're loud, girl. Your father don't even need to send them fancy cables of his from the mine. You could just hang out the window and shout all the way to Philadelphia for him.'

'Thank you, Hannah.' She curtsied teasingly, kissed the old woman's leathery cheek and raced up the stairs to her room to wash her hands before dinner. She was always spotlessly clean and instinctively well-dressed without anyone saying anything to her. There was indeed something of Camille Beauchamp in her. And Hannah looked at her retreating back now and spoke to Jeremiah.

'You're going to have your hands full in a few years, Jeremiah.'

He smiled at Hannah and hung up his coat. 'She tells me that she's going to live with me forever, and work for me at the mines.'

'That's a ladylike prospect.'

'So I told her.' He sighed and followed Hannah into the kitchen. He still liked talking to her, they had been friends for more than thirty years, and in some ways she was his closest friend, as he was hers. And she adored Sabrina. 'The truth is she'd be wonderful with the mine, it's a damn shame she's not a boy.' It was seldom that he said that.

'Maybe she'll marry some fine young man whom you can teach all you know, and you can leave it all to your grandkids.'

'Maybe.' He wasn't ready to think about that yet, and it would be years before Sabrina married. But on the other hand, he wasn't getting any younger, and the year before he'd had a problem with his heart. It had terrified Sabrina when she had found him unconscious in his dressing room, but he was fine after that, and they had all tried to forget that it had happened. But the doctor reminded him often to slow down, a piece of advice which made Jeremiah smile, and Hannah knew too. He wondered who would speed up to make up for his slowing down.

'You're getting old, Jeremiah. You'd best start to be thinking about your future,' she nodded her head in the direction of the stairs that led to Sabrina's room, 'and hers. You're still hanging onto that house in town, ain't you?'

He smiled a sad half smile. 'Yes. And I know you think I'm crazy, you always did. But I built it with love and I'll give it to Sabrina with love. She can sell it if she wants. I don't ever want her to turn to me and say "Why didn't you save that for me, Papa?" '

'What will she want with a house ten times bigger'n a barn, and in San Francisco to boot?'

'You never know. I'm happy here. Maybe she'll want to live in the city when she grows up. This way she'll have that choice.' He fell silent and they both thought of Camille. She had never deserved all the kindness he had showed her, and he had never heard from her again, not a word, or a sign, or a letter. But he was still married to her legally anyway. Her father had written him a few times, apparently she went to live in Venice for a while, and then moved to Paris, and she had stayed with the man she had fled with. Called herself Countess and pretended to be married to him. They had no money, and France was having a hard winter. Orville Beauchamp had broken his resolve and was going to see her. His wife had died, and Hubert had married a girl in Kentucky. And Jeremiah was determined never to let him see Sabrina. He wanted no reminder, no one who could possibly tell Sabrina something different than what he himself had told her for years. Orville Beauchamp had no one else. He was all alone now, and went to Paris to see his little girl, who was apparently living in squalid conditions in a house outside Paris, and she had given birth to a stillborn son, but when he attempted to bring her back to the States, she refused to go with him. He described her as 'crazed by a passion he couldn't understand. She clung to her worthless lover and refused to leave him.' Jeremiah also read between the lines that she had begun drinking, and was probably playing with absinthe, but whatever her problems, they were no longer his. Orville Beauchamp had died a few years later, and Camille had never come home. Jeremiah had no further news after that, and he was relieved not to. He wanted no contact with her to taint Sabrina's life, no chance that someone would tell her her mother hadn't died of influenza when he said she had. For Jeremiah and Sabrina, the door was closed, and Camille would never pass through it again.

There had never been anyone like her in his life again, never

172

anyone he cared for as much, or behaved as foolishly for, never anyone, except of course Sabrina. She was the love in his life now, his reason for living. And there were others who kept his senses alive, when that was what he wanted. There was a house of women in San Francisco that he visited, when Sabrina wasn't with him, and a teacher in Saint Helena he had dinner with from time to time. Mary Ellen had long since married and had moved to Santa Rosa, and whenever Amelia Goodheart came to town to see her daughter, Jeremiah and Sabrina delighted in seeing her. She was as marvellous as ever and Sabrina adored her.

Though she was well into her fifties now, Amelia was still the most dazzling person Sabrina had ever seen, and she came to San Francisco once a year to visit her daughter and grandchildren. There were six of them and she had brought them all to Saint Helena once to visit Jeremiah and Sabrina. Sabrina loved her more than any woman she had known. There was a gentleness and a warmth to her, and at the same time a brilliance and a style which delighted Sabrina. She always brought the most extravagantly beautiful clothes with her, and jewellery that took Sabrina's breath away.

'She's the loveliest woman in the world, isn't she, Papa?' Sabrina had said in awe and her father smiled. He still thought so too and there were times when he regretted not insisting she marry him that first time on the train to Atlanta. It would have been a mad thing to do, but as it turned out, no madder than marrying Camille Beauchamp in Atlanta. In fact, years after she was gone, on a trip to New York with Sabrina, he had asked Amelia to marry him again and she had ever so gently turned him down.

'How can I, Jeremiah? I'm too old. . . .' She had been fifty then. 'I'm set in my ways, I have my life here in New York . . . my home . . .' For her, he would have opened up Thurston House again, and he told her, but she was firm in her resolve to remain unmarried, and in the end he suspected that she had been right. They each had their separate lives, their children, their homes. It was too late to bring it all together under one roof, and she would never have been happy living away from New York. It was the centre of her existence. But he saw her each year, when she came to San Francisco to visit, and once or twice a year when he went to New York on business. In fact, unbeknownst to Sabrina, the last time he had stayed with her.

'At our age, Jeremiah, what harm is there? Who will speak badly of us, except to whisper in admiration that we still have this much passion left,' she had giggled like a girl, 'and you can't get me pregnant.' It had been a glorious two weeks in her home, the happiest he remembered, and when he left, he gave her an exquisite sapphire brooch and choker with a diamond clasp, and on the back an inscription which made her roar with laughter, 'To Amelia, with passion, J.T.' 'What will my children say when they divide up my jewels, Jeremiah?'

'That you were obviously a very passionate woman.'

'That's not a bad thing.' She had escorted him to the train, and this time it was she who stood on the platform, waving a huge sable muff in his direction, as the train pulled out slowly. She was wearing a magnificently cut red coat trimmed in sable with a matching hat, and he had never seen a more beautiful woman. Had he met her on the train again, he would have been just as taken with her as he had been before he met Camille. '. . . if I still had the strength . . .' He had told her before he left, but they both knew he did. He had proved it night after night during his visit to New York and returned to San Francisco feeling renewed and in extraordinary good humor.

'What're you smiling about, Jeremiah?' He had been thinking about her over his coffee, as Hannah prepared dinner. 'That woman in New York, I'll bet you a nickel.'

'Then you'd win,' he smiled at Hannah. He thought of Amelia often, and was still as excited as a schoolboy before her visits. But she wasn't due in San Francisco for another six months, and he wasn't going to New York for three or four, so it would be a long wait until he saw her.

'She's a fine looking woman, I'll grant you that.' In fact remarkably, Hannah not only approved of her, she liked her. Amelia had won her heart when she rolled up her sleeves and helped cook dinner for Jeremiah, Sabrina, and her six grandchildren. In fact, she had cooked most of the dinner, and it was better than Hannah liked to admit . . . flashing her diamonds as she worked, her hands flying, with an apron over her fancy New York dress, 'and she didn't even care when she spilled gravy down the front.' She had won Hannah's admiration forever.

'She's more than that, Hannah. She's a very special person.'

'You should've married her, Jeremiah.' She looked reproachfully at him from the stove and he shrugged.

174

'Maybe. Too late for that now. We have our lives, our children. We're comfortable like this.' Hannah nodded, there was truth in that too. The time for foolishness was past. It was Sabrina's turn now, or would be soon, and she only hoped that she chose wisely, more wisely than her father.

'You going to the city tomorrow for sure?'

He nodded. 'Just for two days.'

'Mind that Sabrina doesn't get into mischief while you're working.' She still thought the girl should stay in Saint Helena.

'I told her the same myself. But you know Sabrina.' He fully expected to see her driving a borrowed coach down Market Street one day, brandishing the whip and grinning broadly as she waved at him and flew by. The image made him laugh as he went to wash his hands before dinner.

Chapter Nineteen

Jeremiah and Sabrina left for the city early the next morning, taking the train to Napa, as they always did now, and from there the familiar steamer that Sabrina loved. It had always seemed like an adventure to her to take the boat to San Francisco and she teased and laughed and amused her father all the way into the city, which they reached by nightfall. Jeremiah watched her as they shared a late dinner in the dining room of the Palace Hotel. She was going to be a beautiful girl one day, when she grew up. And even at thirteen, she was already as tall as most of the women in the room, and taller than some. But she still had a childlike air about her, except when she furrowed her delicate brow and began to talk to him about business. One would have thought that he was talking to a business associate, had one only listened to them and not seen who Jeremiah's companion was. Right now she was concerned about a mite that seemed to be affecting the vines in his vineyards. He was amused at her seriousness as he watched her expound her theories to him, but the vineyards had never been his primary concern. The mines held his attention more closely and she scolded him for it now.

'The vineyards are just as important to us, Papa. They'll make as much money as your mines one day, mark my words.' She had said the same thing to Dan Richfield the month before and he, too, had laughed at her. There were indeed vineyards in the valley that were beginning to make money, but it would never compare with mining for profit, everyone knew that, and Jeremiah reminded her of that now. 'Years from now that may not be true. Look at the fine wines they produce in France, and all of the vines come from there.'

'Just watch out you don't turn into a little tippler on me, young lady. You seem mighty interested in those grapes.' He was teasing her but she wasn't amused and she glared at him with all the seriousness of her thirteen years.

'You should be more interested in them, too.'

'I'll leave that to you, since you're so interested in the vineyards.' It was a little less unseemly than letting her interest herself in the mines, although it was a shame not to let her do that too. She had a remarkable head for business.

And he was reminded of it again the next day when they shared breakfast in his room, before he left for his meetings with the President of the Nevada Bank. Sabrina spent the entire time quizzing about the business he was going to do, and it was obvious that she wished she could go along, but she seemed less wistful than she usually did about such things.

'And what are you going to do today, little one?'

'I don't know,' she looked pensively out the window as she spoke, so he couldn't see her eyes. He knew her too well and would suspect some mischief afoot. 'I brought some books with me. I thought I might read this afternoon.'

He stared at her for a moment and then glanced at his watch. 'If I had time to think about that, it would probably worry me, young lady. Either you're sick, or you're lying to me. But you're in luck, I'm late and I have to get going.' She smiled sweetly at him and kissed his cheek.

'See you tonight, Papa.'

'Be a good girl.' He patted her shoulder and then squeezed it gently. 'And stay out of trouble, Sabrina Thurston.'

'Papa!' She sounded shocked as she escorted him to the door. 'I always do!'

'Ha!' He roared as he went out the door, and she spun around on one heel, with a grin. She was free for the entire day, and she knew just exactly what she was going to do. She had brought a little money with her from Napa, and her father always gave her enough to have lunch and take care of herself while he was out. Now she stuffed her coin purse in the pocket of her grey skirt and she quickly changed a pink blouse for the old cotton middy she'd brought along. She pulled on a pair of old boots that she wouldn't mind getting scuffed, and half an hour later, she was comfortably seated in a carriage on her way to Nob Hill. She had given the driver the address, and when they arrived, she paid her fare and stood breathlessly outside the front gate, feeling her heart pound with excitement. It was almost too exciting to believe, and she had waited months, no, years, for this moment. She didn't know what she would do once she climbed the gate. She had no real intention of going inside. Just being on the grounds would be enough. But she was inexorably drawn to this house which her father had built for her mother.

Thurston House stood in silence, buried in its park, as Sabrina stood staring at it for a long moment, and then, as though taking her courage in her hands, she began climbing the gate, in a spot where her efforts were somewhat hidden by a large tree, and as she rose, she prayed that no passerby or neighbour would report her to a policeman. But she was still adept at climbing gates and trees and, a moment later, she was sliding down the other side, feeling her heart pound even faster than it had before. She let herself drop the last few feet to the ground, and then she just stood there for a moment, enjoying the fact that she had made it. She was inside the hallowed grounds of Thurston House, and she quickly moved deeper into the gardens so she wouldn't be seen from the street. The bushes and trees were so overgrown that it was like moving into a jungle and she was quickly hidden from the street as she followed the driveway toward the house, feeling as though she were being pulled by a magnet.

And it was impossible not to think of her mother as she did so. How much he must have loved her to build this house, and how happy she must have been there. Sabrina couldn't help wondering what her mother had thought the first time she'd seen it, she knew that her father had built it as a surprise and she couldn't imagine anything more lovely. It made her sad now to see the huge door knockers tarnished almost beyond recognition, the windows boarded up, the waist-high weeds pushed between the front steps. The house had been empty for twelve years and it looked mournful and unloved. She would have liked to press her nose to a window, to look inside, to see the rooms they had moved in and danced in and lived in together. It was almost like coming to see her mother to be here, as though in being here she could absorb some greater sense of what the woman had been like. Her father said so little about her, and Hannah was even more taciturn on the subject, and Sabrina was desperately hungry for any crumb, any morsel of knowledge of what Camille Beauchamp Thurston had been like.

Slowly, without thinking of why she did so, Sabrina circled the house, climbing over the weeds, glancing at the shutters. She could see where the flowerbeds had been, and there was a pretty Italian statue of a woman with a babe in her arms in a garden behind the house. There was a marble bench, too, and Sabrina sat down there, wondering if her parents had sat there, holding hands, or if her mother had sat there with her baby in her arms on sunny days. She had so much more of a sense of her mother here than she did in Napa, for some reason. That house seemed so much a part of her father somehow, and she knew that he had lived in it long before he married her mother. But here, everything was different. It was a love palace built for her mother, she giggled to herself at the thought as she continued her meanderings. She felt faintly disappointed as she did so. Somehow she had expected to see more once she was here, and although it was exciting just being within the main gate, it was unsatisfying not to even be able to peek in through the window. But then, just as she was about to turn back toward the statue of the woman and child, she saw that one of the shutters was broken. It had a large crack in it, and one of the boards was sagging into the bushes. It was the perfect opportunity she had longed for, and she pressed through the bushes until she could press her face against the window. But the window led only into a dark hallway and she could see nothing. She wrestled with the board then and tore it loose. She didn't even know why she did it, but she found that she could open both shutters once she did so. Instinctively she pulled against the window, and much to her amazement, it gave beneath her weight and swung toward her with a sharp jerk. She stood holding the open window, looking stunned. But only for a moment. Without hesitating further, she climbed the window sill and hopped in, pulling the window shut behind her. The hallway looked no more revealing than it had when she pressed her nose to the window, but she stood in the darkened hall in absolute awe now. She was inside the house she had dreamed of and wondered about for her whole life. Thurston House. She was here now.

She wasn't sure whether to go right or left, and she realized in a moment that she was in some kind of a service pantry. Everything was neat and tidy, but very dark with all of the windows shuttered. And she knew that although no one had been in the house in twelve years, it had been so well sealed that there was surprisingly little dust around her. For an instant, she had feared that it would look like a haunted house, but instead it only looked empty and deserted. But there was no turning back now. She had waited too long for this moment.

Sabrina walked stealthily to the end of the hall, opened a door and gasped as she did so. What she saw above her looked like the gate to Heaven. She had walked into the main hallway and above her was the spectacular stained glass dome Jeremiah had designed for Camille. Its rainbow colors and intricate design shot a myriad brilliantly-coloured lights at her feet as she looked up in awe and delight. From there she wandered up the main staircase and into the bedrooms. She found what had been her nursery, but there was nothing there now. Everything had been removed to Napa. But in the master bedroom she sat down on a chair and looked around. It was as though she could feel her father's sorrow of twelve years before overwhelm her. The room was so totally like her mother must have been, so feminine and lovely. The pink silks had faded with the years but the room was still like an endless bed of flowers on a spring day, and a perfume hung on the silks, mixed with a musty smell now, but still there, and it almost overwhelmed Sabrina as she walked into her mother's dressing room and began opening the wardrobes. Jeremiah had thrown nothing away before abandoning the house. Camille had left tiny delicate kid shoes, and red satin evening pumps she had worn to the opera with Jeremiah, an old fur cape, and row after row of dresses. Sabrina took them out now, feeling the expensive fabrics, and sniffing the perfume she recognized now. The beautiful old clothes brought tears to her eyes, it was like visiting the mother she had never known and finding that she was gone forever. But she knew as she stood in the pretty pink silk room that this was why she had come here, to find the woman who had been her mother, some piece of the puzzle, some fragment of what she had been. As she had grown up and become a woman herself, she had longed for some piece of her mother to cling to. Now she felt overwhelmed as she roamed free in the house they had lived in, the house she had come to when she was four months old and left again, never to return, when she was a year old, after her mother's death, or so she thought.

She went into her father's study. She sat at his desk, spun round in his chair, and wondered why he missed none of the things he had left there. There were handsome prints on the wall, some interesting ornaments on the desk, there was row after row of beautiful crystal downstairs, china, silver. He had left it all, simply closed the house and gone to Napa, never to return here again. He had often said that it would be hers one day, but she had imagined Thurston House as a house with some old furniture under dust covers, she had never imagined it like this, a home that looked as though the people had left in a hurry and then died before returning to sort out their things. There were even some books on her mother's night table and a stack of lace handkerchiefs in her drawers. He had thrown nothing away before he left, and Sabrina saw it all now. And what she wanted most of all was to throw back the shutters and let the sunlight into the rooms, but she didn't dare. She felt in some ways as though she had intruded into a private world, someone else's private pain, and she could see now why he didn't want to come back here. It was like visiting his wife's tomb, and he had let it all lie for too long to be able to come back now. Here, he would have to see her clothes, feel her presence, smell her perfume, he would remember the agonies and the joys and the pain he must have felt at her death, Sabrina felt sure, and she cried for her father as she stood in his rooms for a last moment, and then walked solemnly down the stairs in a dignified way. The house filled her with even greater tenderness for Jeremiah than she had had before, and a renewed sense of the delicacy and beauty of her mother. As in Napa, there were no portraits of her mother here, but there was something far greater than that, a sense of where the woman had been, how she had lived. As Sabrina stood beneath the stained glass dome in the front hall again, she knew that once, years before, her mother had stood in the same spot, and perhaps looked up at it in the same way. She had touched the same door handles, looked out the same windows. It was an awesome thought, like a journey back in time, one felt the hand of those who had come before touching one's own. They were benevolent ghosts, but they were nonetheless a powerful presence, and Sabrina was almost relieved as she pushed open the window in the back hallway again, and pushed the broken shutter back in place after she closed it. She had come to a place where she didn't belong, and yet she was glad that she had come here.

She walked pensively back out through the overgrown gardens, walking slowly this time, absorbing what she had seen. And she turned back once or twice to look at the house again. It was a magnificent home, and she would have loved to have seen it before, with the gardens handsomely trimmed, and her mother's carriage wheeling swiftly in. And it was exciting to think that she had been there too, a part of their life and the beauty of that house. It would be hers one day, but it would never be quite the same as it had been . . . and the beautiful girl from Atlanta would be long gone, along with the man who had loved her more than anything. It would never be the same again. The thought saddened her as she climbed back over the gate and landed on her feet. She realized that she looked a fright as she glanced around. She had torn her skirt, and her middy was filthy, her hair was dishevelled, her hands were dirty too and there was a long bloody scratch on her arm, either from climbing the fence or wrestling with the broken shutter. But she regretted none of it as she walked hastily back toward the Palace Hotel. It was not a very long walk, and she needed the air after her day in the musty house. She almost felt as though she had seen too much, and yet she was glad she had seen it, and she slipped quietly into the hotel and went upstairs to take a bath before her father came home from his meetings.

She was ravenous at dinner that night, she had had no lunch that day, and he took her to Delmonico's where they both ordered steak. In spite of the hearty appetite he noticed, she seemed strangely quiet.

'Something wrong?'

'No.' She smiled, but she seemed vague. But if she had looked him in the eye, she would have begun to cry. She was haunted by the sadness of the empty house, and all of her mother's things he had so carefully left in place when he left. How much he must have loved her. She had a vision of a broken man, fleeing to Napa with his infant child, barely able to cope with the loss of his young wife, dead at such an early age, and after she had been so greatly loved.

'What's bothering you, Sabrina?' He knew her too well, but she only shook her head and forced a smile, pushing the melancholy thoughts from her head, but she wasn't herself all evening, and at last before she went to bed, she knocked softly on his door and came in when he bid her to do so. 'Goodnight, little love.' He kissed her on the cheek, but he quickly saw the troubled eyes. They had worried him all night. He invited her to sit down and she did so gladly. She had come to make a confession. She never lied to him, and she didn't like doing so now. She had decided to make a clean breast of it. 'What's wrong, Sabrina?'

'I have something to tell you, Papa.' She looked all of five years old as she sat down in her nightgown and her wrapper, her pink feet peeking from beneath the lace hem. 'I did something today, Papa.' She didn't say something 'bad', because she didn't think it really was, but she knew that it would upset him. Yet she also knew that she had to tell him. He would probably never find out what she had done if she didn't confess, but they had trusted each other for too long to begin lying now. In that way, she was very unlike her mother.

'What was it, little one?' His voice was gentle as he watched her. Whatever it was, he knew that it had upset her greatly, and he was anxious to know what it was. He felt a flutter of concern as he waited.

'I went . . .' she gulped, almost sorry that she had come to tell him, but she had to go on, 'I went . . . to Thurston House.' It was a barely audible whisper, and he imagined her standing outside, looking up at the sturdy gates.

He smiled gently at the confession and came to touch the silky hair, neatly arranged in braids. 'That's no sin, little one. It was a beautiful house once.' He sat down beside her, thinking of the mansion he had built so long ago. 'It was a beautiful place.'

'It still is.'

He smiled sadly. 'Sadly neglected, I'm afraid. But one day, before I give it to you and your groom, I'll have it all put to rights again.'

'There's nothing wrong with it now.' She sounded strangely certain and he looked at her.

'Everything's probably faded and dreary in there by now, little lamb. It's been twelve years since anyone set foot in the place. There must be ten inches of dust everywhere.' She shook her head, her eyes on his face, and he looked puzzled. 'Did you look inside?' And then, in confusion, 'Were the gates open?' He'd have to see to it if they were, he didn't want the curious wandering onto the grounds, or worse yet, someone breaking into the house. He still had a great many valuable things there. He had a patrol go by there every once in a while, and miraculously there had never been any trouble so far.

Sabrina took a deep breath. 'I climbed over the gate, Papa.' So this was what she had looked so woebegone about, thank God the little minx had a conscience and had told him.

He looked serious as he addressed her. 'That's hardly a ladylike thing to do, Sabrina.'

'I know, Papa.' And then she went on to tell him the rest. 'And there was a broken shutter. . . .' Her face went pale, and she spoke to him in a frightened whisper, 'and I pushed my way inside . . . I looked all around . . .' Her eyes filled with tears and overflowed. 'Oh . . . and Papa . . . it's such a beautiful house and you must have

183

loved her so much . . .' She began to sob and she hid her face in her hands as he put an arm around her. He was stunned that she had gone there.

'But why? Why did you go there, Sabrina?' His voice was troubled and gentle. What had drawn her to that place? He couldn't really understand it. She couldn't remember living there herself, so it hadn't been a return to anything familiar, and it had to have been more than just mischief. He wanted her to explain it to him. 'Tell me . . . don't be afraid, Sabrina. You were brave to tell me that you'd been there, and I'm glad you did that.' He kissed her cheek and took her hand. He was surprised himself that he wasn't angry at her, but he was troubled.

'I don't know, Papa. I've always wanted to see it . . . to see where you lived . . . what she was like . . . I thought there might have been a picture of . . .' She stopped, afraid to hurt him, but he understood and finished the sentence for her.

'Of your mother.' He was saddened that Sabrina cared so much. Camille hadn't been worth it. But there was no way he could ever tell Sabrina. 'My poor baby . . .' He took her in his arms and held her as she cried. 'You shouldn't have gone in there.'

'Oh but Papa . . . it's so beautiful . . . that dome . . .' She looked up at him in awe, and he smiled. He hadn't thought of that dome in a long, long time, and she was right. It was extraordinary, in some ways he was glad that she had seen it.

'It was a beautiful house in its day, Sabrina.'

She said something that startled him then. 'I wish we still lived there.'

'Don't you like Saint Helena, little one?' He looked down at her, wondering if, like her mother, she would come to dislike Napa, but it had always been her home.

'Of course I do . . . but Thurston House is . . . it's so very beautiful. It must be very elegant living there.' The way she said the words made him laugh, and she smiled through her tears.

'When you're older, you can live there. I've told you that before.' But now it was different, she knew what the house looked like. And she was aggrieved by his words.

'You know I don't want to get married, Papa.'

He had a thought as they were speaking. 'Then maybe we'll have to take you there for some other reason.'

'You mean it, Papa? Like when?' Her eyes were enormous in the firelight.

'We could give a ball there when you turn eighteen. I've kept you out in the country all your life, and it'll do for a few more years. It might even help to keep you out of mischief, young lady,' he waggled a finger at her, 'but when you're eighteen, you should meet the right people in San Francisco.'

'Why?' She looked surprised.

'Because one day you might decide to broaden your horizons a little.' He didn't mention marriage to her again, she was too young for them to worry about it anyway, but in a few years, a ball in San Francisco would be just the thing. He had never thought of it before, but he liked the idea now. It struck him that she would be nearly the same age then that Camille had been when they'd met, and he would be the proud father now. 'You know,' he forced his mind back to his daughter, 'that might be a nice idea. We could come to San Francisco then, and open Thurston House just for you. What do you think of that?' She looked stunned. A ball just for her? Open the house she had seen . . . 'We could have the party right in our own ballroom.' She had seen the ballroom that morning, and she squinted, trying to imagine her parents dancing there, her father, fifteen years younger, with the delicate Southern beauty in his arms.

'What was she like Papa?' She had already forgotten the ball and was thinking of her mother again. He looked down at Sabrina with a sigh. In many ways, he wished that she hadn't gone to the house today. He wondered what she had found, and how intensively she had searched for some clue of their past and her own.

'She was very pretty, Sabrina.' He decided, as he said it, to tell her some small part of the truth. 'And very spoiled. Southern girls often were then. Her father wanted her to have everything.'

'Did he see the house?'

Jeremiah shook his head. 'Her parents never came out here. Her mother got sick after we were married, and she died shortly after . . . your mother's death.'

'They would have loved the house.' She looked up at him with childlike adoration. 'She must have, too.'

'I suppose so.' And then suddenly he remembered the constant round of parties. 'She loved to entertain there.' He remembered too the ball he had forbidden her to give, and later the parties she must

185

have gone to with Dupré, whenever he was in Napa. 'She liked to go out a great deal.'

'She must have, she had such pretty clothes.'

He knit his brows. 'How do you know that, Sabrina?'

She looked momentarily embarrassed. 'I saw her clothes today, Papa. They're all there.' They weren't 'all' there, but she couldn't know that and he didn't tell her.

He sighed again. 'I suppose I should have done something about all that when . . . when she died . . .' Sabrina noticed that he always seemed to have trouble saying the words, as though they still pained him too much. He looked at his daughter now. 'You shouldn't have gone there, Sabrina.'

'I'm sorry, Papa. It's just . . . I've wondered about it for so long.'

'But why? We have a good life in Saint Helena.'

'I know,' she hung her head, but her thoughts instantly went back to the beautiful mansion, and when she looked at him again, her eyes were hopeful. 'Will you really give me a party there one day? Can we stay there?'

'I told you I would.' He smiled at her, and pulled gently at one of the long plaits. 'If that would make you happy, princess, then it's a promise. For your eighteenth birthday.'

'I'd love that.' Her eyes shone in the soft light.

'Then it's a promise.' And they both knew that he always kept his promises.

He didn't say anything further about her wanderings in the city house the next day, but he spoke to his friend at the Nevada Bank, and had him send over some men to look for broken shutters and board the house up further if necessary, and on the way back to Napa he extracted a promise from Sabrina.

'I don't want you to go there again, little one. Is that clear?'

'Yes, Papa.' She was surprised that he hadn't been angrier about it. 'But couldn't I go there one day with you?' He shook his head.

'I have no reason to go there again, Sabrina.' And then he smiled. 'Until the ball on your eighteenth birthday. I made you a promise, and you know I'll keep it. We'll go there then, and spend some time in San Francisco together that spring, if you like. But in the meantime, you're not to go climbing over fences, and climbing through windows to go through old wardrobes and other people's clothes.' She flushed scarlet at his words. And in truth, that was what had bothered him most of all, that she had been hungry for some distant glimpse of Camille, even through the clothes in her wardrobe. He wondered if that was the only reason she had gone there, and that really cut him to the quick. So much so that his voice was harsh on his next words. 'You could have fallen and gotten hurt, and no one would have known where to find you. It was a stupid thing to do.' He frowned and stared out the train window, and Sabrina said not another word until they pulled into the station at Saint Helena.

Chapter Twenty

'Well, Hannah, take care of the place while we're gone.' The old
woman harrumphed and limped painfully down the front steps with
them. The carriage was loaded with what looked like all of their
belongings, but was actually only Sabrina's new dresses. Jeremiah
was smiling down at the old housekeeper now. He had wanted to take
her with them, but she'd insisted that she didn't want to go. And at
eighty-three years of age, she had a right to decide what she wanted to
do. She thought it a lot of foolishness anyway. 'It's only for two
months anyway.' And he had promised her years before. It was a
promise he hadn't even been sure Sabrina would want him to keep.
But he'd been surprised when he had broached it to her several
months before, she thought it would be fun. He had promised to
open up Thurston House for her, and give her a ball for her eighteenth birthday. 'Maybe there's a little of her mother in her after
all,' he had teased when Amelia had come to town. But Amelia had
thought it a fine idea, she was only sorry not to be able to come back
to San Francisco for it. But she had already been twice that year, once
for her oldest granddaughter's wedding to one of the Floods, and the
second time to stay with her daughter when her son-in-law died. She
couldn't come back again, and, as they were officially still in mourning, it wouldn't have been appropriate to attend a ball. But she had
given Jeremiah all the advice she could about the party.

She had even gone with him the first time they opened the house,
and she had felt a shiver run through him as he stood next to her. She
had turned sympathetically to him and touched his arm.

'You don't have to do this, you know. The Fairmont Hotel should
be finished by then. You could give the ball there, Jeremiah.' She
had often wondered why he hadn't sold the house, she knew just how
painful it was for him, and yet he had stubbornly held onto it for
Sabrina.

'I want to do it here.' She had watched his jaw tense, and together they had gone through the house with a crew of newly-hired servants. There was an incredible amount of work to do, repairing, and rehanging, and cleaning and painting, but actually, the place was in surprisingly good condition. But Amelia felt particularly sorry for him when they reached the master suite. It seemed so painful for him to be here. Amelia had dared to urge him to sleep in another room and he was grateful for the idea. She stood beside him as they opened the wardrobe in Camille's dressing room. She was going to suggest to him to throw everything away, but he told the servants to put everything in boxes in the basement.

'Why would you want to keep those things? She didn't even want them when she left.' Amelia looked puzzled as they made their way back downstairs. It was going to be a mammoth job readying the house for Sabrina's ball, but Amelia thought it an exciting project.

'Sabrina may want her mother's things one day.' He told her then about Sabrina's escapade five years before, when she was thirteen, when she had climbed the gate and come in through a back window. 'I realized then that there's a piece of her missing, because she never knew Camille, and I've never said a great deal about her. I think Sabrina feels that the subject is taboo, she thinks I'm still in mourning for her death.' He sighed and smiled at Amelia. They had known each other for twenty years now and he took as much pleasure as he once had in seeing her. She was always vibrant and alive, and kind, and a pleasure to be with. And even at sixty, she was still a beautiful woman and he told her so each time he saw her.

'What outrageous lies you tell, Jeremiah. And how glad I am that you do!' She laughed, and he kissed her.

She had given Sabrina a beautiful pearl necklace in advance of the party, and had told her again how sorry she was not to be there.

'We'll miss you too, Aunt Amelia.' Sabrina had kissed her warmly and promised to wear the pearls to her ball. Amelia had helped her pick out an exquisite white satin dress with clusters of pearls embroidered on it. It was a spectacular gown, and at the same time, Amelia had helped her to design and order three more dresses to wear to the other parties with her father. One in particular Sabrina was excited about wearing. It was more sophisticated than any dress she'd ever owned, and she and Amelia had debated lengthily over it. It was a soft metallic gold fabric, and it was absolutely exquisite with her creamy skin and black hair. Together, she and Amelia had decided that she could get away with it, if the dress was simple enough. They chose a design which was not terribly low cut, and when the dress arrived in Saint Helena, Sabrina had absolutely gasped in delight, and wouldn't let her father see it till she wore it. She had already decided to wear it to the opera in San Francisco with him. The New York Metropolitan Opera Company was coming to San Francisco, and her father was taking her to see Carmen with Fremstadt and Caruso. She was immensely excited, as much about what she'd be wearing as about the opera.

The dress was in her trunk now, as the carriage rolled onto the grounds of Thurston House. For an instant, she remembered the first time she'd been there, after climbing over the gate, and now here she was, rolling up to the house in grand style, in her father's new carriage. For the last half hour they had been discussing the blight on the grapes in the Napa Valley which had ruined the crops for several years, but suddenly she could think of nothing but the excitement of moving into the elegant house. She stood in the front hall under the magnificent dome, and again remembered the first time she had seen it. But there was nothing clandestine now, the house was spotless and there were flowers everywhere, the silver was polished, the brass shined, and as she turned toward her father, he felt a knife pierce his heart for an instant. She momentarily looked so much like her mother as she stood there. He remembered the first time he had brought Camille here, and her sheer delight to learn that the house was theirs. Jeremiah had given orders that Sabrina be given the master suite. He didn't want to sleep there anymore, and with fresh fabrics everywhere in soft silks and bright pinks, it was the perfect room for her. She was the same age as her mother had been when she had lived there, only she was not a married woman, but a young girl, and she was very different from Camille Beauchamp.

'Papa, everything looks so lovely!' She didn't know where to look first. He and Amelia had done a spectacular job ordering new fabrics and curtains. The ballroom had been freshly painted and everything shone. It was another three weeks before her party, and she could hardly wait, but there was plenty for them to do in the meantime. They were going to the opera in two days, and the following week, the Crockers and the Floods and the Tobins had invited them to dinner. Her father had renewed friendships he had neglected for years, in order to present Sabrina to everyone he knew. He wanted her to have a glittering two months in San Francisco, and then they would return to Saint Helena for the summer. In October, he would bring her back to the city again until Christmas. It was not unlike the life he had led with her mother, but unlike Camille, Sabrina was grateful for every moment in the city, and equally happy to return to Saint Helena. She took an active interest in his mines, and was desolate over the disaster that had struck the vineyards. She was intrigued by the fact that the lethal mite had mainly affected the European vines, and she had a theory that their native vines would survive and become resistant to the plague which had all but destroyed them. Her father admitted goodnaturedly that she knew far more about it than he now. The vineyards had been her passion for years, but she was equally attentive to what went on in the mines. He often teased her that when he died, she could run it all perfectly well without him.

'That's a terrible thing to say, Papa.' She always scolded him, she didn't like to think of his dying. And at sixty-three, he was still in relatively good health, although from time to time his heart gave a whisper of trouble. But she and Hannah took as good care of him as he would allow, and the doctor said he would live for at least another twenty years. 'And you'll have to live that long if you plan to marry me off and have me mother to a dozen children.' She still loved to tease him, but the fact was that she knew a great deal about his business. She had spent too many hours at his side, watching what he did, and listening carefully, not to, and she was an unusually bright girl. But he didn't want her thinking about any of that now. He just wanted her to have a good time, and enjoy her 'first season'. This was a special time for her, and he wanted everything about it to be perfect.

There were huge vases filled with pink roses in her room, and by the next day she felt quite at home there. For a moment, as she lay in her bed, she had thought to herself that her mother had once slept there, looked up at the same ceiling, glanced out the same windows, sat in the same bathtub, and she smiled to herself. It gave her a feeling of kinship with the mother she had never known, just to be here. Over the past months, she had been in the house several times, discussing with her father whatever changes were going to be made, and what they needed in the way of modern conveniences to live there. A great many things had changed in the twenty years since he'd built it, and although it was still one of the largest mansions in the city, it was no longer the most modern. But it was certainly comfortable now, as Sabrina dressed to go to the opera with her father.

The gold dress lay spread out on the bed, and she had had gold shoes made to match from the same delicate metallic fabric. She would wear the pearls which Amelia had given her before she left, and the pearl and diamond earrings her father had given her for Christmas. She dressed her hair carefully after she took her bath, applied a tiny bit of rouge and powder to her face and then carefully put on lipstick. It served only to enhance the striking beauty of her complexion and features, and finally she carefully put on the gold dress, with the assistance of one of the new maids. And for a moment, Sabrina felt as though her mother were watching, and she wondered if she would approve. Undoubtedly, Sabrina had deduced, she had been a great beauty, and she couldn't help wondering what her mother would think of her now. She would never know the answer to that, but it was obvious what her father thought as she walked slowly down the main staircase beneath the stained glass dome. There were tears in his eyes, as he watched her, speechless.

'Where did you ever get that dress, little one?' She smiled at the fond words, but there was nothing little about her now. She had grown to a considerable height, and was tall for a woman, but not too much so. She had stopped growing just in time, and she had a long graceful neck, and long thin, well-shaped arms, which showed well in the elegant dress. 'My word, child, you look like a goddess.'

She glowed in the warmth of his love as she smiled up at him. 'I'm glad you like it. Amelia helped me pick out the material when she was here. I ordered it just for tonight.'

And when she arrived at the opera house on Mission Street with her father, she didn't regret it. Metallic fabrics and sequins in a riot of colours were the fashion, and her dress was subtler than most, but as beautiful as any dress there. The women of San Francisco had gone wild in wearing their largest jewels, their finest gowns, and all their best plumage for the occasion. The opera had actually opened the night before, but tonight, with Caruso's performance of 'Carmen', was the greatest social event, and there were balls planned at the Palace, Saint Francis, and Delmonico's afterwards. The

Thurstons were planning to join a group of their friends at the Saint Francis, but Sabrina was excited enough now, just seeing the crowds of elaborately dressed women going in and again at intermission. It was a long way from their quiet life in Saint Helena, and she suddenly realized that these were going to be the most exciting months of her life, and she was thrilled that they had come to San Francisco.

As they left the opera several hours later, she gently pressed her father's arm, and he looked down at her to see if something was wrong, but instead he saw her beaming up at him looking like a fairy princess.

'Thank you, Papa.'

'What for?' he asked as they reached their carriage.

'For all this. I know you didn't want to come back to the city and open the house. You did it for me, and I'm loving every minute.'

'Then I'm glad we did it.' And the funny thing was that he really was glad. It was exciting being out in the world again, he had forgotten how pleasant it could be at times, if it wasn't excessive. And there was something wonderful about presenting his only child to the world. She was graceful and intelligent and kind, poised and lovely. . . . He beamed to himself, there weren't enough words to describe just how lovely she was. He looked down at her happily as she looked out the window in fascination as they rode to the Hotel Saint Francis. And the ball they attended was absolutely splendid. Everyone imaginable was there, including Caruso himself at one point, and there seemed to be a festive air all over the city, as people went from one ball to another and then on to smaller parties. The opera had been a major social event, and Sabrina was glad that her ball wasn't for another three weeks. It would give people time to calm down again, and get ready for some more excitement. It would have been impossible to compete with the glitter of the evening of 'Carmen.'

It was three o'clock in the morning when they got home, and Sabrina could scarcely conceal a yawn as she walked slowly up the grand staircase of Thurston House with her father. 'What a beautiful evening, Papa. . . .' He agreed that it had been, and then Sabrina giggled. 'If Hannah could only see us now, coming home at three in the morning.' They both laughed, imagining her frown and sharp scolding. She would have thought it decadent and indecent. Sabrina laughed again, 'And she would have told me that I'm just like my mother. Whenever she doesn't like what I'm doing, that's what she says. Those two must have really hated each other.' Sabrina grinned and Jeremiah smiled. It was funny now, but it hadn't been then. Very little that Camille had done had seemed funny at all.

'They did hate each other. They had some awful fights when I first brought your mother to Napa.' And then, for the first time in twenty years he remembered the ring Hannah had found. Thank God, she had, if not, there would have been no Sabrina, he reminded himself. But like others, it was not a story he would ever tell his daughter, and he was grateful that Hannah hadn't either. She was a decent woman and had been a good friend, for a long, long time.

Father and daughter kissed goodnight outside the master suite which was now Sabrina's, and when she walked into her bedroom, she looked out the window at the beautifully-manicured gardens. How different they had been five years before when she'd climbed the fence. It was a jungle out there then, she smiled to herself, and she thought of her mother looking out those same windows late at night when she came home from some ball or party. She felt the house alive around her, as it had been twenty years before. It seemed right that she should be here now, and it seemed right too that this beautiful house had come back to life. It had seemed so sad and empty five years before as she crept around it for the first time. She smiled at her reflection in the mirror as she took off Amelia's pearls and then the gold dress she had enjoyed wearing so much. And as she looked at her reflection and then glanced at the enamel clock on the night table, she noticed that it was already almost four in the morning. A faint thrill ran through her, she had never been up so late, except maybe once when there was a flood at the mine and her father hadn't come home until morning, but never just for fun. And this had been the most fun evening of her life. She could hardly wait for her ball, she thought to herself, as she went to bed and turned out the light. She lay trying to go to sleep for almost an hour, but she was much too excited by everything she'd seen and the parties they'd been to. She wondered if her father was awake too, and finally she got up and wandered into her little dressing room. She didn't want to go to bed, instead she wanted to stay awake and watch the dawn. She didn't want to miss anything going on, she felt more alive than she ever had before, and as she slipped a white satin dressing gown on and looked for her slippers, she decided to go downstairs for a cup of warm milk, but halfway down the grand staircase, she felt a strange swaying sensation, as though she were on an ocean liner and they had just hit a swell. It was as though the house rose and sank, but it seemed to go on moving for an endless period of time and suddenly it registered what was happening. They were having an earthquake, and as she dashed down the front stairs toward the front door, the entire stained glass dome exploded in a shower of coloured panes and splinters on the floor beneath it. She just missed being cut to shreds as she stood trembling in the doorway, not sure what to do. Her father had often spoken of the quakes of '65 and '68, but all she could remember was that you were supposed to stand in the doorway, and now she stood there, with the door open, shivering in the chill April air as the house began to shudder again, but this time it subsided more quickly. Everything in the house suddenly seemed to be askew. Small tables had fallen over, glass had shattered, silver had crashed to the floor, and as she looked around at the rubble she realized that her arm had been cut by a piece of falling glass from the window beside her. There was a dark stain of blood spreading across the shoulder of her nightgown, she heard a door open above her and her father's voice shout into the darkness. He had already looked for her in her bedroom and couldn't find her.

'Sabrina! Sabrina, are you there?' He saw her standing in the open doorway then and came rushing down the stairs to find her, just as the servants seemed to explode out of their rooms from the top floor. Two of the women were hysterical, the others were crying, and even the men seemed shaken up as another jolt hit them, and this time they all felt a mounting wave of panic. Noise from the street was beginning to reach them now, people shouting, and crashing sounds as though pieces of houses were falling into the streets. Sabrina realized later that many of the brick chimneys had come tumbling down, and when she ventured out with her father an hour later, after he had bandaged her shoulder, they saw bodies lying dead in the streets, beneath the bricks from the fallen chimneys. It was her first glimpse of death, and she was shocked at what she saw. Everywhere, there were people in the street, the earthquake had done considerable damage, and there were injured people, stunned and limping through the rubble, but what became obvious by mid-morning was that the city's greatest problem was the fires the earthquake had ignited and most of the water mains had been broken, so the firemen had no water to fight with. Worse still, the alarm systems no longer worked, and the Fire Chief himself had been killed in the collapse of a fire station. There was panic in the air, but everyone was still hopeful that the fires would be isolated shortly. The worst fires of all were burning south of Market, beyond the Palace Hotel. The hotel itself had its own well and was able to put out whatever fires threatened it at close range. But the columns of black smoke which began to cover the city by that Sunday afternoon began to fill all of San Francisco with terror. Mayor Schmitz asked General Funston at the Presidio to assist him, and the army were doing all that they could by that evening. A general curfew had been ordered and no one was to wander the streets from dusk to dawn. Strict orders had been issued forbidding indoor cooking.

On Nob Hill, Jeremiah and Sabrina had thrown open their gates and were allowing everyone in to camp in their gardens, use their home, and cook in one area which had been set aside to meet the neighbourhood's needs. And Jeremiah himself was in the old Hall of Justice at Kearny and Washington with the Committee of Fifty, which was attempting to organise the city to survive the disaster. By the next day, they had been driven out of their location and had gone to Portsmouth Square, and this time Sabrina insisted on coming with him.

'You stay here.'

'I will not!' She eyed him with determination. 'I'm coming with you. I want to be with you, Papa.' And she was so stern about it that he relented and let her come. There were other women on the committee, and together they were doing what they could to help the dying city. It was a ghastly moment in the history of San Francisco, and Jeremiah could scarcely believe it as he looked around him. Later that day he was told that all of the mansions on one side of Van Ness had been dynamited, in an effort to save the West End of the city. Worse yet, the Committee of Fifty had to leave their location at Portsmouth Square and then move its headquarters to the almost finished Fairmont Hotel, where they stayed until the fires reached Nob Hill, and they left just in time as the flames leapt around them and gutted the inside of the hotel and then roared along to the Flood mansion. Jeremiah urged the Committee to Thurston House then, where they met for a last time before having to abandon Nob Hill completely. The hill itself seemed to be in flames, and the fire darted where it chose, destroying some houses, leaving others intact, burning some to the ground and gutting others. When the Committee of Fifty left the house at the end of the third day, Thurston House itself was still intact. The gardens were badly charred, and the trees along the front of the property had all fallen, but the façade itself was barely touched by the flames, and all of the damage inside had been done by the earthquake and not the fire. As Sabrina stood in the doorway looking into her beautiful home, she couldn't believe the destruction that had been wrought in three days. It was like a nightmare which refused to end, since the first moment she'd felt it, standing on the stairs. She looked up now at the empty place where the dome had been, and all she saw was a dark sky filled with smoke. She was surprised to realize that it was already nightfall. She wasn't even sure what day it was, she just knew that the holocaust had been going on for days, and the streets had been filled with screams and shouts and dead and dying people. She had bandaged hundreds of arms and faces and legs, led lost children to shelters, helped women search for children who could not be found, and now she slumped down on the staircase of Thurston House with a sigh of exhaustion. The servants had all fled, either to lend assistance or go in search of family or friends, and she knew that her father was upstairs. He had looked exhausted every time she'd seen him and she thought now of going to see how he was. Perhaps he needed a brandy or she should go to one of the collective kitchens on Russian Hill for something for him to eat. He was not a young man and the past few days had been a tremendous strain for them all.

'Papa!' She called out as she walked up the stairs. Her legs felt like tree trunks as she lumbered up the steps, almost falling with exhaustion. She could still hear the shouts from outside and knew that the fires on Nob Hill weren't extinguished yet. She suddenly wondered if they ever would be. 'Papa!. . . .' She saw him sitting slumped with tiredness in a chair in his private sitting room. He had his back to her but she could see that he was as tired as she felt. She hadn't seen him look like that since the last flood in the mines, and she went to him with a gentle step and bent to kiss his head. 'Hello, Papa.' She sighed deeply and sat down on the floor at his feet, reaching quietly for his hand. How much they had been through that night, and in some ways how much they had been spared. Neither of them had been hurt, the house was damaged but still there, and she had heard that the chandelier at the Opera House had gone crashing to the floor. Imagine if the earthquake had happened the previous night. 'Do you want something to eat, Papa?' She looked up at his face, and suddenly stared. He was looking straight at her with unseeing eyes, and, feeling terror leap at her throat as it never had before, she was instantly on her knees and touching his face. 'Papa! Papa! Speak to me!' But there was no sound there, no voice, no words, no life. He had come home from the meeting of the Committee of Fifty at the Fairmont Hotel, led the meeting in his home, and come upstairs when the Committee departed . . . 'Papa!' It was a shriek in the empty, silent house, and she began to shake him now, but his body slowly slid to the floor where he lay and she held him close, the sobs overtaking her as the fires had overtaken the town. He was dead. Quietly, without a sound, he had come to this room, to this chair, and sat down . . . and died, at sixty-three years of age, leaving Sabrina an orphan, entirely on her own, two and a half weeks before her eighteenth birthday.

She sat staring down at him in shocked terror long into the night. The fires raged across Nob Hill, gutting almost everything around them, but miraculously sparing them. Sabrina wouldn't leave Jeremiah. She sat holding his hand and sobbing long into the night, as the flames raced to the front door and then suddenly changed direction, and when morning came, she still sat there, holding the hand of the man who had been her father. Most of the fires in the city had been put out, and the earthquake was over. But for Sabrina life would never be the same again, without him.

Chapter Twenty-One

Sabrina brought her father's body back to Napa on the steamer, and on to Saint Helena, in a somber cortège. The carriage from the mines was waiting for them at the pier along with a small, sober faced party of miners, each wearing the only suit he had. It was only when the carriage reached the private road to Jeremiah's home that she saw them all, five hundred strong, lining the road, five and ten deep, quietly waiting for the man they had loved and for whom they had worked so hard. For years, he had fought for them, dug them out in the floods, pulled them from the mines in the worst fires, cried when they died . . . and now they wept for him. Many cried openly as they doffed their hats as the carriage rolled slowly past them. Hannah stood on the front porch, her weather-beaten face awash with tears, her eyes blinded by grief, as the casket was lowered from the carriage, and eight men carried it into the front hall and then into the parlor where he had slept for the twenty years before he married.

Sabrina went wordlessly to Hannah and took her in her arms and the old woman sobbed on her shoulder, and then Sabrina went outside briefly to shake hands with some of the men and thank them for coming. They had little to say, and couldn't have found the words to tell her what they felt. They just stood there and eventually turned away and left, in large, silent groups. Their hearts would be buried with the man they had respected and loved. There would never be another man like him.

Sabrina walked back into the house, and felt a catch in her throat as she caught a glimpse of the mahogany box they had set down in the parlor. Hannah had woven a blanket of the wild flowers he had loved so much, and they laid it carefully over the casket now, as suddenly Sabrina could bear it no more, and she turned and buried her face in her hands, and she was surprised to feel a pair of strong arms take her in their grip, and she looked up into Dan Richfield's face. He had been in charge of her father's mines for years now and he had been invaluable to Jeremiah.

'We all feel terrible, Sabrina. And we want you to know that we'll do anything in this world we can for you.' His eyes were as shattered as hers, and he didn't even try to conceal that he'd been crying. He took her in his arms again then, and held her, but a moment later, she pulled herself free, and stood at the window staring out at the valley Jeremiah had loved so deeply. She spoke as though to herself, the scent of the wildflowers on the casket hanging heavy in the air, and Hannah's sobs clearly heard from the kitchen.

'We never should have gone to San Francisco, Dan.'

He looked at her pretty form, as she stood there, with her back to him. 'Don't torture yourself, Sabrina. He wanted to take you to town.'

'I shouldn't have let him.' She turned to face the man who had been almost a son to her father. He was thirty-two years old, had worked for the Thurston Mines for twenty-three years, and he owed everything to her father. Without him, Dan would have been digging ditches somewhere, but thanks to Jeremiah, he ran the biggest mines in the state and was responsible for some five hundred men, and he did his job well, as her father had often told her.

'He belonged here, and so do I.' Her voice caught again, she had been consumed with guilt ever since she found him. 'I never should have let him take me to town. If I hadn't, he'd be alive now. . . .' The sobs choked her and overtook her again, and Dan was quick to comfort her again, holding her close to him, but each time he did, Sabrina felt as though she needed air. He held her too close, even though she knew he meant well. Perhaps it was his own grief which oppressed her. 'Oh God. . . .' She walked around the room, looking back at Dan with heartbroken eyes, 'what'll I do without him?'

'You have time to think of that. Why don't you get some rest?' She hadn't slept in two days and she looked it. Her face showed the ravages of her grief, and her eyes looked like bottomless pools of sorrow. 'You should go upstairs and lie down. Have Hannah bring you something to eat.'

Sabrina shook her head, and brushed the tears from her cheeks with one hand. 'I should be taking care of her, she's in worse shape than I am, and I'm younger.'

'You have to take care of yourself.' He stopped and looked at her for a long time, and their eyes held. There were things that he wanted to ask her, but they had to wait. It was too soon now, with her father lying there in the parlor. 'Come on, do you want me to take you upstairs?' His voice was soft, and she smiled and shook her head. She could barely speak, she was so overcome by all that she felt. She couldn't imagine a life without her father.

'I'll be alright, Dan. Why don't you go home?' He had a wife and children to think of, and there was nothing he could do here. They had already made all the arrangements for the funeral the next day. Sabrina wanted her father buried quickly. He would have wanted that himself, no fuss, and a simple ceremony. He would have been touched by the men lining the road when they arrived, and by the men who came one by one that night, just to stand staring at the heavy mahogany box in the front parlor, their heads bowed, their eyes damp. Sabrina came downstairs again and again, to shake their hands and to thank them. And Hannah kept a huge pot of coffee on the stove, and she had made huge trays of sandwiches to feed them. She had known they would come, and she was glad to see that they did. Jeremiah Thurston had been the finest man they'd ever known, and they owed him the homage they now paid him.

It was after nine o'clock that night when a man walked up the front steps, wearing a dark suit and a tie. He had gray hair and black eyes, and a rugged face with well-etched features. He seemed to hesitate before he came in, although Hannah noticed that he had an air of command about him, and when suddenly she realized who he was she went to tell Sabrina.

'John Harte is here.' He had remained her father's arch rival, but there had never been any ill-feeling between them. John Harte kept his distance from everyone, that was just his way, and he never lost sight of the fact that he was in constant competition against the Thurston Mines, but he never forgot Jeremiah's kindness either. The two men seldom met, but when they did, there was always a quiet look that passed between them, and when a disaster struck in one mine or the other, the other always showed up, or sent his men to offer assistance. John Harte no longer had a chip on his shoulder about Jeremiah Thurston. In fact, he admired him more than most men knew. And he was sorry now that he was gone. He had only met Sabrina a few times over the years, but she knew who he was and she walked toward him now, her black dress making her look taller, slimmer, and much older than her eighteen years. Her hair was pulled back in a tight knot, and her eyes were huge in her pale face, and she looked more like a woman than a girl as he shook her hand.

'I came to pay my respects to your father, Miss Thurston.' His voice was deep and smooth, and their eyes held for a long moment. His own daughter would have been only slightly older than she, had she lived. She had been three when she died, two years before Sabrina was born. He had never married again, although everyone knew that he had had the same woman for the last ten years. She lived with him at the mine, and she was an Indian of the Mayacoma tribe. She was an exotic looking woman and someone had pointed her out to Sabrina once. She was about twenty-six years old and she had two children of her own, but none by him. He wanted no more children, and no wife. He had sealed that part of his life forever, and Sabrina thought she could still see a hint of the old pain in his eyes as he looked at her. It was as though being here with her brought it back to him again, and she wasn't far wrong. He spoke in barely more than a whisper as they stood in the parlor, side by side, looking at the casket where Jeremiah lay. It brought painful memories back to him, and he had a lump in his throat when he spoke. 'He was with me . . . when my boy died. . . .' He glanced at Sabrina, and wondered if her father had ever told her about that, and of course he had.

'I know . . . he told me . . . it made a great impression on him.' Her voice was gentle as the wind, and he watched her eyes, liking what he saw there. She was a strong, intelligent girl, with unassuming ways and eyes that seemed to take everything in. He felt as though she were searching him as he wondered how old she was, and knew she couldn't be more than eighteen. He didn't think Thurston had been married when Matilda and the children died, and that had been twenty years ago that Spring.

'I never forgot his being there with me. . . . I barely knew him then.' He sighed. 'We never knew each other very well. But I admired him. And his men thought a lot of him too. People in this valley have nothing but kind words to say about Jeremiah Thurston.' He tore out her heart with his words, and her eyes filled with tears as she turned away and brushed them from her cheeks with her slender fingers.

'I'm sorry . . . I shouldn't have. . . .'

'Not at all. . . .' She smiled through her tears and took a deep breath. It was so unbelievable that he was gone. How could he be? She loved him so . . . she had to fight back a sob, and reminding herself that she wasn't alone, she looked up at John Harte. He was almost as tall as her father, and his hair was as dark as Jeremiah's had once been, although the gray had crept into his as well. He was forty-six years old, and still handsome, just as Jeremiah had been right till the end . . . the end . . . the end . . . she couldn't bear the words. 'Would you like some coffee, Mr. Harte? Hannah has some in the kitchen.' She waved vaguely toward the doorway.

'No, I should let you get some rest. I know you came up from San Francisco today. Is it as bad as they say?'

'Worse. There are bread lines everywhere, rubble in the streets, toppled chimneys, everywhere you look charred buildings. . . .' The tears rose in her throat again and she shook her head, unable to speak for a moment. 'It was just awful. And my father. . . .' She forced herself to go on, as John Harte watched her, aching for her. '. . . he was on the Committee of Fifty, to save the city . . . it was just too much for him . . . his heart, you know. . . .' She didn't know why she was telling him all that. But suddenly she had to say the words, had to tell someone, even though she barely knew the man. 'I'm sorry. . . .'

He held her shoulders in his powerful miner's hands. 'You have to get some rest. I know what you're going through. I did the same thing. I wandered and I ranted and I stayed on my feet until I almost went crazy. It'll only make it worse, Miss Thurston, believe me. Get some rest. You're going to need it for tomorrow.' She nodded, the tears unchecked now on her cheeks. Suddenly she could no longer dam the flow. He was right. She was exhausted and half hysterical with grief. She just couldn't believe her father was dead, but when she looked into John Harte's eyes, she saw something comforting there. He was a nice man, in spite of what they said about him, that he was standoffish and proud and something of a libertine, living with his Indian mistress. Perhaps that was why her father saw him so seldom. Sabrina correctly assumed that her father hadn't approved of John Harte's companion.

'I'm sorry, Mr. Harte. I'm afraid you're right. It's been a terrible few days.' And she was going to need her strength for the funeral the next day.

'Is there anything I can do for you tomorrow?'

'No, thank you. Our manager is going to drive me to the funeral.'

'He's a good man. I know Dan Richfield well.'

'My father would have been lost without him, or so he said. Dan's worked for him since he was eleven.'

John Harte smiled sadly at her. So much was going to change for her now, and he wanted to talk to her about it, but he didn't want to do it too soon. He had already mentioned it to Dan, and they had agreed that he should wait a week or two. She was still too much in shock to think about the mine, and Richfield could run it for her in the meantime. 'If there's anything I can do for you, Miss Thurston. . . .'

'Thank you, Mr. Harte.' She shook his hand again, and he left, riding a big black stallion back to his mine, and his exotic Indian mistress.

Sabrina found herself wondering about him after he left, and what his mistress was like. All she remembered was a girl with jet black hair and a delicate dark brown face swathed in white furs the winter before when they had met somewhere. Sabrina had been intrigued, and her father had hastened to drive on, signalling only the briefest of greetings to John Harte, and ignoring the Indian girl in the white furs completely. Sabrina could still remember her questions to her father. . . . 'Who is she, Daddy?'

'No one . . . some squaw. . . .'

'But she's beautiful. . . .' Sabrina had been fascinated by her, as though she knew that the alliance was clandestine and improper, which of course it was, except that John Harte had made no secret of it for more than nine years. As he saw it, he owed nothing to anyone, and he had a right to do exactly what he wanted. That was what he always had done, and he wasn't a man to mince words, or hide an Indian squaw somewhere out of the way. She was his woman and he was a free man, so what the hell. 'She was so pretty, Daddy. . . .'

'I didn't notice.'

'Yes, you did. I saw you looking at her.'

'Sabrina!' He pretended to be annoyed, but Sabrina knew him better.

'Well, you did. I saw you. And she is a beautiful girl. What's wrong with that?'

'Two things, child, to put it to you bluntly: they're not married and she's not white. Therefore we are supposed to pretend that she doesn't exist, or that if she does, she isn't lovely to look at. But the fact is, she is. She's a damn fine looking girl, and if she suits John Harte, then so much the better for him. It's none of my business who he goes with.'

'Would you invite them to our house?' Sabrina was intrigued. He never had. But John Harte and her father had never been close.

'I would not.' He didn't sound angry, but he sounded firm.

'Why not?' She didn't understand.

'Because of you, little one. That's why. It wouldn't be proper. If I lived alone, I might, because I've always liked him. He's a good man and he runs a good mine, not as good as ours of course,' he had grinned at her and she laughed, 'but it's a good one.'

'Do you suppose she's smart?' Sabrina was still fascinated by the Indian girl.

'I have no idea.' And then suddenly he laughed at the innocence of his daughter, and he patted her cheek with a gentle smile as he answered. 'I don't suppose that's what he loves her for, Sabrina. Not all women are smart. Not all women have to be.'

'I think they should at least try, don't you?' She was so earnest, it always touched his heart.

'Yes, I do.' There was some of Camille in her after all. Camille had been so damn smart, and so interested in men's things, particularly business. She would have loved to know more about his mine, if he had let her. But he hadn't thought it seemly for his wife to be involved in his business deals. And yet with Sabrina, it was all so different. He taught her everything, and showed her everything he did, almost as though she had been his son, and he was proud of how much she knew about the vineyards, the mines, the deals he made in the East. She seemed to understand everything, and a day didn't go by that he didn't share more of it with her. But times had changed, and he had grown old, and without Camille he had been lonely. Sabrina had been his companion for eighteen years, and now . . . she was alone . . . remembering the past . . . hearing his voice in her ears. As she lay in her bed that night, she still couldn't believe he was gone. How could it be? And yet he was.

And she knew it for certain the next day as the pallbears carried his casket to his grave, as they all stood in the Spring sun, and it was lowered into the dirt, and each of five hundred and six miners and one hundred and three friends shovelled a little dirt on top of him.

Even Mary Ellen had come and stood at the rear of the crowd crying softly, and at last Sabrina stood looking down at him, her back straight, her head high, her face wet with tears, and she squeezed her eyes shut for one long moment as she clutched Dan Richfield's hand, dropped a handful of dirt on her father's grave and moved on. They stood watching her as she rode home, and she felt as though her world had come to an end as she walked slowly up the front steps and sat down in his favorite kitchen chair. Every inch of her felt numb and Dan Richfield was watching her. His wife hadn't gone to the funeral, his wife was expecting again. Sabrina rarely saw much of her, she was one of those women who were unattractive and pale, and kept breeding every year, and Sabrina had never had the impression that she was overly fond of Dan. They just kept having babies, and he lived with her, but one barely even felt that they were friends, now.

Sabrina looked at him. 'I still can't believe he's gone, Dan. I keep expecting to hear his footsteps on the porch, hurrying up the stairs. . . . I keep thinking I'll hear his horse. . . .' Her eyes were dry now as she stared emptily at him. 'It's hard to believe I'll never see him again.'

'You will. In your mind's eye. He's so much a part of all of us that he'll never really be gone.' It was a nice thing to say and she reached out and touched his hand with a small, wintry smile.

'Thank you, Dan. For everything.'

'I haven't done enough. And one of these days, we'll have to talk, but now's not the time.' It was still too soon for her, and he knew that. But she looked surprised at his words.

'Something wrong at the mine? I mean, did anything special happen this week? I haven't paid attention to anything but myself since. . . .' She couldn't say the words, but he'd known what she meant.

'No, of course not. Nothing's wrong, except that there are going to be a few changes now of course, and you'll have to tell me what you want.' He had of course assumed that he'd be running the mine, unless she sold it of course, and he had already covered his bases by talking to John Harte about that. Whatever happened, he'd still be running the Thurston Mines, whether John Harte bought her out or not. And of course he'd run them for her if she decided not to sell, but personally he thought she should. It was actually going to be better for him now. Jeremiah had always been a major presence at the mine, not just a figurehead, he still ran the entire empire himself, but Dan had worked very closely with him. And he was prepared to take over now, and to run the mines well for her. He was perfectly trained, and had been taught by the best, as was she, and he noticed her looking at him now.

'What changes did you have in mind, Dan?' Her voice was very soft, her eyes hard. It was a combination he had seen often before, in her father, and it made him smile now.

'You look just like your father when you look like that.' She smiled at him then, but the eyes didn't soften, only the mouth. 'I just meant that sooner or later we'll have to talk about what you're going to do, whether you're going to keep the mines or sell.'

She looked shocked, and sat up straighter in her seat. 'What in hell made you think I'd consider selling ever? Of course I'll keep the mines, Dan.'

'All right, all right.' He was trying to keep her calm, but there was something about the look in her eyes that he didn't like. 'I can understand how you feel, and it really is too soon for you to make up your mind.' She didn't like the gist of his words at all and she suddenly narrowed her eyes and looked at him.

'Just what exactly did you have in mind. Dan? That I'd sell the mine . . . like maybe to you?' Her eyes blazed and he was quick to shake his head.

'Hell, no, I could never afford to buy them from you. You know that.'

'Did you make a deal with someone?' Her eyes were relentless now, piercing right through him, and he shook his head again.

'Of course not. For Chrissake, your father's only been gone for two days, how could. . . .'

'Never mind that. Vultures move quickly sometimes, I just want to be sure you're not one of them.' She sounded strangely grown up as she shot the words at him, and she looked far older than her years as she stood up and walked around the room, thinking and then looking at him. 'I want to make something very clear to you. I'm not selling my father's mines. *Ever.* Do you understand? And I'm going to run them myself, from now on, just as he did.' Dan looked at her as though he might faint from the shock, but nothing wavered or softened in her face. 'I'm coming in on Monday, and I'll look over what's there, but the truth is, he's been preparing me for this for years. It's almost as though he knew I'd have to run them someday myself.' She stood with her hands on her hips, and he looked at her as though she were mad.

'Are you out of your mind? You're just turning eighteen, you're a child . . . a little girl, in fact . . . and you're going to run the Thurston Mines? They're the biggest quicksilver mines in this state, and your father wanted them kept that way. You'll be the laughing stock of every client he had, and in less than a year you'll destroy everything he built, Sabrina. You're out of your mind. Sell it, for Chrissake. Make yourself a bundle of money, put it in the bank, find yourself a husband somewhere and go have babies, but don't kid yourself that you can run your father's mines because you can't. It's taken me more than twenty years to learn everything I know. At least let me run it all for you.' She knew that was what he had in mind, and she needed his help, but that wasn't what she was going to do.

'I can't, Dan. I do need your help. But I have to run them myself. That's what I was born to do.'

He looked at her with something she had never seen in his face before. It was fury born of jealousy and thwarted plans, and he strode up to her now and shook his fist in her face. 'You were born to spread your legs to the man you're married to, and nothing else! Do you understand?'

Her eyes narrowed into bullets which could have killed him on the spot. 'Don't ever speak to me that way again! Now get out of my house, and I'll forget what you just said. I'll see you in the office on Monday.' She was shaking as she stood staring at him. She knew how disappointed he was, but she had to take a stand now. She couldn't let anyone push her around. And he hesitated for just a fraction too long. 'And if you get out of hand again, you'll be working at another mine, Dan.'

He glared at her and strode to the front door. 'That might be just what I need. And it might serve you right too.' He slammed the door behind him as he left, and for the first time in her life, Sabrina poured herself a drink. She took a shot of brandy, neat, and tossed it down. But she felt better after she had, and she walked slowly upstairs to her bedroom and sat down. She knew now what she was going to be up against . . . 'you were born to spread your legs to the man you're married to' . . . was that what they all thought? What they would all think? Dan . . . John Harte . . . the men who worked for her now . . . She knew now just how rough it was going to be; she thought she did.

She rode to the mine on Monday morning at six o'clock. She wanted some time to herself before she talked to the men. She read everything on her father's desk, and she had kept so abreast of all that he did that she found few surprises there. The only surprise she found was an unopened letter from some girl at 'a house' in San Francisco's Chinatown. She was thanking Jeremiah for his generous gift the last time he'd been there, but Sabrina wasn't shocked. He had a right to do whatever he did. And he had left everything in order at the mine for her. His attorney had read her his will the day before and it had been a simple document. It left everything to his only child, Sabrina Lydia Thurston: his investments, his real estate, his houses, his land, his mines. He had specifically mentioned that no other person was to inherit his holdings or his fortune. He had left it all to her, and the vehemence of his words had struck Sabrina as odd. Who else would even have tried to inherit something from him? She was all he had. And he had left a handsome gift to both Hannah and Dan, and they had each been pleased by the amounts. She was hoping that Dan would be sufficiently mollified to behave himself today. She needed his support here. She imagined that it would come as a shock to the men too, that she was planning to take her father's place. She knew that she could handle it; he had taught her so much in the past eighteen years, that she felt confident. But now she had to convince them of that, and she knew that working for a woman could prove awkward for them too, particularly one as young as she was.

She knew what she was up against, or so she thought. But the reaction she got was far worse than she feared, as she rang the big mine bell, signalling an announcement at the office. Three rings would have meant an emergency in the mine. Four a fire. Five a flood. Six a death. But she rang it once, and then stood quietly on the office porch waiting for them. She waited quite a while and rang it again. And eventually they came one by one or in groups, talking and chattering, carrying axes and tools. Even that early in the day, they were already filthy from head to foot, they looked like what they were, hardworking men. There were more than five hundred of them standing there, listening to her. It was a breathtaking sight, the men who worked for her now, and she had to admit, she felt a thrill run up her spine. The empire was hers now . . . the Thurston Mines. . . .

'Good morning, men.' She was their leader now. They worked for her, and she would stand by them as her father had. She felt a wave of warmth reach out to them. She would do everything she could for them. She would never let them down. She wanted to tell them that now. 'I have a few things to say to you.' She was holding the same bullhorn her father had used, and they crowded around so they could hear what she said, and Dan Richfield watched her from where he stood. He knew how they would react. They wouldn't take this non-sense from her, at least he hoped not. He was counting on them to play into his hand, and he hoped that they would. 'I want to thank you all for being there when I brought my father home last week. That would have meant everything to him.' She paused, fighting back tears. 'You all meant everything to him. And he would have done anything for you.' They nodded assent. 'I'm going to tell you something now which may come as a surprise.' There was a look of sorrow on the faces of those closest to her, and she realized instantly what they thought. And one man called out 'You're selling the mine'. But she shook her head. 'No. I am not selling the mine.' She could see that they looked pleased. They liked their jobs, were happy at the Thurston Mines. Things were going to be all right. Richfield would carry on. Most of them had hoped he would, and there had been a lot of talk in the past few days, in the bars in town. There were even some healthy bets. And they all waited to hear what she would say to them now. 'The mine is going to stay exactly as it was, gentlemen. Nothing is going to change for you. I'm going to see to it myself, and in fact, I promise that to you.' A cheer went up as they looked at her adoringly, and she held up a hand and smiled. Things were working out better than she had feared. 'I am going to be running the mines myself, just as my father did. With the help of Dan Richfield, just as he helped my father run these mines. I will maintain the same policies he did. . . .' But they weren't listening to her now, they were beginning to shout and jeer at her. . . .

'Run the mines yourself? What kind of whores do you think we are?'

'. . . . Work for a woman? . . . she has to be nuts! . . . Hell, she's nothing but a kid! . . .' The shouting grew into a din and drowned out the reassurance in her words, and she fought to keep them from becoming a mob.

'Listen to me, please . . . my father taught me everything he knew. . . .' They laughed openly at her now, and only a few stood listening to her, but it was more in disbelief than respect. 'I promise you. . . .' She rang the bell again, but pandemonium had broken loose, and Dan Richfield had joined the crowd. She stood looking at them all in despair, and after another fifteen minutes of fighting them, she gave up and went back inside, and she sat at her father's desk with tears running down her cheeks. 'I won't give up! I won't . . . damn them all. . . .' She whispered to herself. But she refused to be beaten by them, even if every one of them quit.

By the next day that was exactly what most of them did. They threw their picks and their tools through the windows of the office where she worked, and she found a mountain of debris heaped around her desk, their names signed on a single sheet of paper, headed by the words, 'We quit. We ain't going to work for no girl.' And then they signed their names, three hundred and twenty-two of them, which left her a hundred and eighty-four men to run three mines, which was clearly an impossibility. It was only enough to run one adequately, the other two would have to be shut down temporarily, but if that was what she had to do, she would. She wouldn't give in to them. There were other miners who needed work, and in time they would see that she knew how to run a mine. They'd be back, and if not, others would take their place. But it was frightening anyway. She called in five men to clear up the mess around her desk, and she was besieged all day with men lining up for their final paychecks before they left. It was a nightmarish way to begin but she would never give up. She wasn't that kind of woman – she was her father's child. He wouldn't have given up in her place, although she suspected that he would have been astonished at her. And Dan knew it too. At six o'clock, he looked at her with folded arms and a look of disgust.

'It's a good thing your father's not alive to see what you've done.'

'If he were, he'd be proud of me.' At least she hoped he would. It was a moot point. If he were alive, this wouldn't be happening to her. 'I'm doing the best I can, Dan.'

'And it ain't bad. I thought it would take you longer than this to run the place all to hell. Instead it's only taken two days. What the hell do you think you're going to do with a hundred and eighty-four men, Sabrina?'

'Close down two of the mines for now. We'll get more men

begging to work here soon.' She sounded nervous but brave. And she was a brave girl, and what's more she was right. Her father would have been proud of her.

'Congratulations, lady. You've managed to turn the biggest mine in the West into the smallest show in town. And do you have any idea what you have left working for you? Some old men Jeremiah was just keeping on to be kind, but he could afford to do that, he had hundreds of others backing them up, some kids, boys, who don't know any more about this place than you do, and a few cowards who couldn't afford to give this up because they have too many children to feed. . . .'

She looked him dead in the eye. 'Does that include you, Dan?' Touché. 'Just why did you stay on? Maybe it's time you made that clear.'

He flushed beetroot red, and looked at her angrily. 'I owe a debt to your old man.'

'Then let's imagine that debt's been paid. You worked twenty odd years for him. That's enough to pay any debt. I set you free, like Lincoln with the slaves. Want to go? You can walk right out that door and never come back,' she waited silently and there was not a sound in the room, 'but if you stay, I expect you to be on my side, to help me run this place, to help me re-open the other two mines again. I don't want to have to fight you, too.'

He came right to the point. There was no reason to play games with her now. She was never going to let him run the mines. He already saw that. She was a damn fool, and as stubborn and power hungry as her father had been, at least that was how he saw her now. His eyes had been opened in the past two days. He had stuck around for more than twenty years so that one day he could run this place, and in two days she had blown his plans all to hell. Now she had to sell out. John Harte would let him run the mines. He had promised Dan that, if Dan could help him make a deal with her, and he was going to see to it now. 'Sell to John Harte, Sabrina. They'll never let you run this place. You'll lose everything you have.'

'No, I won't. My father taught me more than you want to admit. And I'm sorry it's turning out like this. I thought you and I could work together, just as you worked for him.'

'And just why do you think I did that, you little fool? Because I loved him so much? Hell, I thought I'd be running this place one day, not you.' He wasn't going to mince words with her. He hated her guts. He should been Thurston's son, not this damn girl. And who was she anyway? The daughter of that whore who'd run off and left him eighteen years ago, at least that was what he thought. They said she had died, but he had never believed that. He had heard rumors about her lover in town years before, but he was only a kid then and what did he care. He looked angrily at Sabrina now, hatred spilling from his eyes.

'I'm sorry you feel this way, Dan.'

'You're a damn fool. Sell out to John Harte.'

'You've already said that, and you know I won't. I'm not going to sell out to anyone. I'm going to run it myself if I have to go down in the shafts myself. I'll work 'til I drop, but I'm going to keep what my father had, I'm going to be just as good to his men as he was, and the Thurston Mines are going to be here a hundred years from now, if there's still any quicksilver left here. I'm not going to let someone like you scare me out now, and I'm not going to sell to John Harte, or give in because a bunch of bastards up and quit. Do what you damn please, Dan, but I'm staying right here.' She was just like her old man, and he suddenly wanted to slap her face. He had meant to stay calm with her, to urge her gently to sell out, but she had pulled the rug out from under him. She had taken over, cut off his balls publicly, she had shown everyone that he was nothing more than a hired hand, and he wasn't going to put up with it, and suddenly as he looked at her in the silence of the office they shared after dark, he reached out and grabbed her by the hair, and lost control of himself. He shook her until her teeth rattled in her head but she didn't scream, and twisting her hair around his hand, he brought her to her knees, 'You little whore! . . . little slut . . . you can't even begin to run this place. . . .' And with that he grabbed her by the throat and suddenly he realized exactly what he wanted to do, he grabbed the collar of the blouse she wore and tore it from her back, and she stood in her corset, her skirt, her stockings, pantaloons, and boots. She never took her eyes off of him, and he was leering at her now, fondling her breasts with one hand, as he held her captive with the other hand, still clutching her long, dark hair.

'Let go of me, Dan.' Her voice was far calmer than she felt. She was terrified of what he was going to do. And there was no one to help her now. They were alone at the mine. The last of the men had left, and the watchman they kept on duty at night would be too far away to hear her screams, and she didn't want them to see her like this. She had to win their respect and if they saw her getting raped by Dan, it would be all over for her. 'If you lay a hand on me one more time, you'll wind up in jail for the rest of your life. . . . if you kill me, you'll hang.'

'Are you going to tell, if I lay a hand on you, Sabrina dear?' His eyes looked half-mad, and his voice whined in her ear. And she had already realized what he was thinking. How could she admit it if he raped her? Then they wouldn't respect her at all . . . it would be her fault . . . and God only knew who would try it next . . . the very thought was terrifying and suddenly she flung herself away from him with all the strength she had, and ran across the room, pulling open her desk drawer as she went. She knew what her father kept there and so did Dan, they struggled for the small pistol she grabbed, and it went off into the floor, and suddenly they both stood there, immobilised as though realizing for the first time what had happened. He looked at her in sudden horror, and she looked up at him in shame and disgust. He had almost raped her, and a week before he had been their friend, hers and her father's. Her eyes met his now, and her hand trembled as she still held the gun.

'I want you to get out right now and stay out. You're fired.'

He looked stunned for an instant, as though only then realizing what he'd done, nodded and walked toward the door. He wanted to help her put her shirt back on, but he didn't dare. It was just that she had destroyed his dream of two decades. But that was still no excuse. He couldn't understand what he had done, or why. 'I'm sorry, Sabrina. I really am. . . .' He looked at her in despair, and felt sick at what he'd done. And yet she was so wrong to try to run the mines. He had been right about that. 'You've got to sell out, you know. This will happen again. If not with me, with someone else. And someone else may not come to their senses next time.'

She turned to him, indifferent to the way she looked, her hair tangled, her shoulders bare. 'I'll never sell, Dan. Never. And you can tell your friend John Harte that, too.'

'Tell him yourself. I'm sure you'll have the chance.'

'I have nothing to say to anyone. And I'm going to hire any of his men that I can.' She knew that Dan would probably go to work for him. But she didn't care about that now. She never wanted to see

Dan Richfield again. He was an evil man. Her father would have killed him for what he had almost done. Thank God he had stopped in time. He looked at her one last time, standing there in the ill-lit room, and she looked remarkably beautiful with her silky hair falling around her face, and her huge, sad eyes. What a difficult coming of age it had been for her.

After he left she slowly put on her torn shirt, put the gun back in the desk and tidied the room, and at last she turned off the lights and left the mine. It was a relief to feel the cool night air on her face, and suddenly as she did, she felt her whole body shake. She had almost been raped by a man she had known all her life. She couldn't even walk to where she had left her horse, and she had to sit on the office porch for almost half an hour, until she could walk again. And at last, when she pulled herself into the side saddle she used and rode home, with the wind in her hair, a huge sob flew from her like a large bird and she cried out into the night. She was suddenly angry at her father for the first time. How could he leave her? She wanted to ride as hard and long and far as she could, but her faithful mount took her home, and she rode right into the barn, straight to her horse's stall, and slid down and nestled her face in the horse's neck, wondering how Jeremiah could leave her so alone, when she needed him so much.

'Dan Richfield is right.' She jumped at the sound of the familiar voice. Hannah had seen her ride into the barn, and had walked up. 'You're out of your mind.'

'Thanks.' Sabrina turned so Hannah wouldn't see the tears on her face. She had already had enough for one day. 'I needed that.'

'Your father never intended for you to run those mines.'

'Then he should have provided for something else. But since he didn't, I'm all I've got.' She looked her straight in the eye. She didn't feel like taking any more nonsense from anyone.

'You've got Dan.'

'Not anymore.'

'He quit?' Hannah looked shocked.

'I fired him.' She didn't tell her that she had almost been raped, and the jacket she wore hid the torn blouse.

'Then you're a bigger fool than I thought.'

'I'll tell you what.' Sabrina deposited her saddle in the usual place, and turned to look at the woman who had nursed her since she was born. 'You look after the house, I'll look after the mines. It seemed to work when you and Daddy worked it like that. Why don't we try the same thing?'

'Because he wasn't an·eighteen year old girl. My God, what will people think if you try to run those mines?'

'I don't know, and I don't care. And I'll be sure not to ask.' And with that, she turned off the light in the barn and strode purposefully into the house.

Chapter Twenty-Two

When Sabrina went back to her office the next day, there was an eerie quiet about the mines. The loss of three hundred and twenty-two men was making itself felt, and at mid-morning, she rang the mine bell, and made an announcement about closing down the two smaller mines. She reassigned all the men to the largest network of shafts in the biggest mine, and told them just exactly what she expected of them. There was now a harshness about her that hadn't been there before, and they saw something different in her eyes than they had the day before. One of the men mentioned it as they went back to work, and the others shrugged. Like the men who still ran her father's vineyard, they didn't give a damn what went on in her head, as long as she kept paying their salaries on time. That was why they had stayed, not for love of her, or out of devotion to her old man. They figured they didn't owe her a damn thing, they needed the work, and they made a good wage working for her. The rest they didn't really care about, although when word reached them that Dan Richfield had quit, too, they began to worry about that.

'Do you think she knows what she's doing up there?'

'Can she sign a check?'

'I guess.' The men grinned.

'Then I'll stay. She pays better than John Harte, at least her old man did.' And there had been no mention of a decrease in pay. In fact, she was planning to give them all a rise the next week. Her father had been planning to that Spring, and she could afford to now, with two-thirds of the men gone. She had to concentrate her efforts on recruiting more men now, and she was making some notes on that, that afternoon, when her office door slammed and she looked up to see John Harte striding across the room. She looked up at him but she didn't move and she didn't smile when he reached her desk.

'Unless you're here to buy quicksilver from me, Mr. Harte, you're wasting your time and mine.'

'That's one of the things I like about you.' He did not seem put off as he looked down at her. 'There's something very warm and welcoming, I knew it the first time we met.' In spite of herself she smiled and moved back in her chair, waving to a chair on the other side of her desk.

'I'm sorry, it's been a rough couple of days. Sit down.'

'Thank you.' He did, and pulled a cigar from his suede coat, and she suddenly remembered the Indian girl. She wondered if he still lived with her, not that it mattered to her. But the pretty little Indian squaw had stuck in her mind. There was something so delicate and sensual about her, it was an odd insight into this rugged, almost gruff, man. 'I hear you've had an interesting week. Mind if I smoke?' It was an afterthought. It was difficult thinking of her as a lady here. She was in a man's world and he half expected her to light one herself, although she was a remarkably pretty girl. But she had put herself in a tough spot, and he wanted to offer her a way out.

'I don't mind. And yes, it's been an interesting few days.'

'I hear two-thirds of your men have quit.' He wasn't going to play any games with her, and she smiled tiredly.

'Looks like it. I imagine by now, most of them are working for you.' Even though he had a far smaller mine than she.

'Some. I didn't need them all. I took what I could. They were good men.'

'Apparently not.' She looked at him defiantly, and he admired her for her guts.

'You took on a mighty tough horse to tame, Miss Thurston.'

'I know that. But it belonged to my father, and now it belongs to me, and I'm going to break this horse even if it kills me first, Mr. Harte.' And she meant just that.

'Is it worth it to you to do that?' His eyes were kind, but she didn't want kindness from anyone now. She was going to fight her own fight, without the Dan Richfields of the world, or the John Hartes, or anyone. She was alone now. And she'd make it on her own, no matter how unorthodox that was.

'It's worth it to me, Mr. Harte. I'm not going to give this up.'

'Then I guess you were right.' He sighed with a smile.

'About what?'

'I'm wasting my time.' He put the cigar down and leaned closer to her. He wanted to make her see things sensibly. He wasn't trying to steal anything from her, but she had to be reasonable about this. What she was doing was wrong. Even her father wouldn't have approved, and he was prepared to say that to her. 'Miss Thurston, you are a very intelligent, very decent, very charming young girl, and from all I understand, you were the apple of your father's eye.'

Her face hardened into a frown. 'You're wasting your time. . . .'

'Hear me out!' This time his words were harsh. 'You know what I want. I want to buy this mine, all of it, all three, that's obvious to both of us, and I'll pay you a handsome price, and if you turn me down, I'll survive, I have plenty on my hands as it is, and I'm making a damn fortune over there, so I don't really care, but what I hate to see is waste. You're wasting this mine hanging onto it, you've already had to close two of your mines down, but more important than that, you're wasting yourself. You're a young girl.' He looked around the dingy room. 'What in hell are you doing here? Is this what you want to do with your life? You're not a man, you're a girl. What are you trying to prove?' He sat back with a sigh and shook his head. 'I didn't know him well, but from the little I knew, I can tell you that this isn't what your father wanted for you. No one in their right mind would. It's a lonely, ugly, filthy, tiring life, grinding away, digging dead men out of mines, fighting fire and floods, keeping drunks in line. How the hell do you think you're going to do all that and you don't even have Dan Richfield now?' He looked genuinely distressed for her, but she was wary of him now. She was wary of everyone.

'How do you know that?' He had only left the night before.

He was honest with her. 'I hired him today. He's a good man.'

She smiled scornfully. 'At least he won't lay a hand on you.' There was a sudden silence between them and a look of instant fire in his eyes.

'He did that?'

She hesitated and then nodded her head. There was no reason to protect him now, and she knew John Harte wouldn't do the same thing. He wasn't that kind of man, and besides, he had the Indian girl. 'Yes, he did. Fortunately, he came to his senses in time.'

John Harte shook his head, and covered his eyes before looking at her again. 'If you were my daughter, I'd have killed him for that.'

She smiled gratefully and then remembered who he was. 'Well, I'm not, and my father's dead, and it sounds like you have a new foreman at your mine, Mr. Harte.' She was hardened to everyone now. And she stood up and held out a hand. She didn't want to hear anymore. 'Thank you for your vote of confidence, and your interest in our mines. If I ever decide to sell, I'll be sure to let you know.'

'Don't do this to yourself.' He looked deep into her eyes. He meant every word he said. 'It'll break your heart, and eat up your whole life.' She wondered if that was what it had done to him, and he sounded like a sad man. But that wasn't her problem, and she had plenty of her own.

'Don't come here again to see me, Mr. Harte. You have no business here.' She didn't want to be rude to him, but she didn't want him visiting her at her mines again. She still remembered his visit to pay his respects to her father the week before . . . was it only a week? . . . it was difficult to believe as she looked at him now. 'My mines are not for sale, and won't be for a long, long time.'

'You're giving up marriage and a family then.' He was pushing her hard and she wanted him gone.

'That is *not* your concern.' Her eyes flashed at him.

'You can't do both, you know.'

'I'll do what I damn well please!' Her voice suddenly lashed out at him and she came around the desk. 'Now get the hell out of here, Harte!'

'Yes, ma'am.' He doffed his hat at her and strolled slowly toward the door. He had to give her credit for the guts she had, but he still thought she was dead wrong, and he was sorry she wasn't willing to sell the mine to him. He would have liked to incorporate the Thurston Mines with his own. But the one thing that bothered him most was what she had told him about Dan . . . 'at least he won't lay a hand on you' . . . he had tried to rape her then? The damn fool . . . he would have to warn Spring Moon about him then. He didn't want the man anywhere near her, but he didn't even like the idea of him 'laying a hand' on Sabrina Thurston, as it were. It was desperately unfair to take advantage of the girl, as crazy and headstrong as she was to take on her father's mines, and when he went back to his own office that afternoon, he was particularly harsh with Dan, much to his new employee's surprise. He couldn't imagine what he had done so soon to incur his new boss's wrath. The truth was that it was a bitch working for anyone, and it tightened his guts just thinking about Sabrina again. If it weren't for her, he would have been running the Thurston Mines.

John Harte wanted to tell him to never go near Sabrina again, but he didn't want to tell him he knew what had gone on. Instead, he just warned Spring Moon and she laughed at him.

'I'm not afraid of him, John Harte.' She always called him that, and usually it made him smile, but not this time.

'Look dammit, listen to what I say. He's got a pale, ugly wife, and a house full of kids . . . maybe he's hungry for a tender litle morsel like you. I don't know who or what the man is. All I know is that he worked hard at the Thurston Mines for the past twenty years, but I don't want him giving you any trouble. Is that clear? Watch out for him, Spring Moon.'

'I'm not afraid.' She smiled, and with a single gesture, a long sharp knife fell from her sleeve. She wielded it so quickly that one could barely see the blade, and this time John Harte grinned.

'Sometimes I forget how cunning you are, pretty one.' He kissed her on the neck and went back to work, but he wasn't thinking of his mistress when he did. He was thinking of the girl, who was almost a child, attempting to run her father's mines, with barely a skeleton crew of men, and he was almost sorry he couldn't lend her a hand. But that wasn't the plan he had in mind. Dan and he had already discussed it more than once. He was going to sit back, let her fail, and then buy her out, and they both knew it wouldn't take long, no matter how much she thought she knew about her father's mine. She was still only a girl.

And two weeks later, watching the men work in one of the shafts, she turned eighteen. She had given them the promised rise, and still they seldom if ever, spoke to her. The two smaller mines were closed, and she was running the main mine at full power, and she had promoted one of the newer men as her new foreman to replace Dan. He wasn't any fonder of her than the others were, but he liked the pay, and she liked that about him. She played him like a violin, promising him rises which made him drool, if he could recruit new men for her so that she could open the number two mine again. And by November of that year she did, just in time to have it flood and kill five of her new men. But she was there in the pouring rain, helping to dig them out, and it was she who knelt beside them and closed their eyes, she who rode soaking wet and bone-tired to tell their wives, she who helped bury them as her father had done, and she who opened the third mine in the Spring. It had taken her a year to recover from the blow of losing more than three hundred men, but they were working at full force and full profit again. It made Dan Richfield sick every time he thought of it.

'You have to hand it to her, Dan. She's as tough as her old man and twice as smart.' John Harte could barely believe what she'd done.

'Little whore . . .' He said nothing more as he slammed out of the room, and Harte watched him go. He had learned a lot in his years at the Thurston Mines, but there was nothing decent or likable about him, and John was surprised Thurston had kept him on for so long. Perhaps he had guarded his tongue more in those days. He had had a profitable end in mind, which no longer mattered now. But John Harte thought of it again and he approached Sabrina for the second time.

He walked into her office one day, and took her totally by surprise. For the last year, she hadn't even thought of him, and she was proud of what she had done at her father's mine. She knew the men weren't fond of her, and probably never would be, but they worked hard for her and the pay they earned.

'Did you come to shake my hand, Mr. Harte, or to work in my mines?' Her eyes laughed at him as he approached her desk.

'Neither one. I'm bolder than that. Not unlike you.' He admired her more than she knew, and he saw that she was pleased with herself. She had a right to be. The war wasn't over yet, but the first battle was won. The mine was at full strength again, though whether or not she could keep it that way was another thing. He doubted that, and so did Dan, and perhaps he was wrong to return to her so soon. He could wait until she began to fail, but he didn't want to now. He had a plan to expand that year, and it included buying at least one of her mines from her, perhaps two. 'You can spare that. Sell me the smallest one.'

She looked at him like a snake ready to strike. 'No. Not one. Nothing. On the other hand,' she smiled carefully, 'I would be happy to buy yours, Mr. Harte.' She had just turned nineteen and she looked far more womanly now. It had been a long, arduous year for her. It was still a fight every day, and there was no one to make it easy for her. 'I'd be happy to buy your mine, Mr. Harte. Have you considered that?'

He smiled at the sheer nerve of her. 'I'm afraid not.'

'Then we've reached a stalemate again, haven't we?'

'You're a stubborn little cuss. Were you like that when your father was alive?'

'I suppose I was.' She smiled, thinking back to only a year before, which seemed like a lifetime ago. 'Maybe I didn't have as much reason to be.' She had fought for her own survival every day for the past year, and no one had supported her. When she went home at night, she had to listen to Hannah berating her. She almost hated to go home now, but she didn't have the heart to send Hannah away after all these years, so she stayed late at the mine every night, and she had lost a great deal of weight. Even John Harte noticed it, but he said nothing of it to her. He just felt sorry for her. She would have been wiser to sell out to him.

'I'm sorry you won't reconsider this year.'

'I told you. I never will. The Thurston Mines will be put up for sale when I die, and not before, Mr. Harte. Of course, if I say that loud enough, I'm sure there will be plenty of people who'd be happy to oblige you.' It was a sad thing to say, but she meant every word of it. She had no friends here, a few who were coming to respect her perhaps, but still too few. She had more than five hundred men working there again, but only a handful who cared if she lived or died, they were the ones who had worked with her in the flood, or seen her do her damnedest in the mines herself, trying to learn every aspect of what they all did. But they had no real love for her, not as they had had for Jeremiah only a year or two before. She looked at John Harte with few illusions now. She had grown up. And he thought she had paid a high price for it. He felt sorry for her. He held out a hand and she shook his but there was no warmth in her eyes for him. Too many people had hurt her in the past year, too many people had tried to do her harm, starting with Dan. Harte wasn't all that pleased with him himself. Dan's wife had died in childbirth the year before. And ever since, he had been out carousing every night, leaving his nest of children hungry and filthy and ill-clad. John had warned Spring Moon again, but she had only laughed and flashed her knife at him.

'I'm sorry you feel that way,' and then as he hesitated before he left, 'I can't help thinking you'd be better off without the burden of this.' It only sounded like another smooth line to Sabrina to relieve her of her mines and he saw her glance at the door with a tired look. 'I understand.' She almost wondered if he did, but he couldn't possibly. He couldn't know how desperately she would fight to keep it all. She would never let the mines go. Never.

The vineyards were thriving as well and she had joined the

winemakers cooperative in the past year, being determined to help them better their lot and improve their wines, though here again she was barely tolerated by the men involved. But she was used to it by now. She was used to being unwelcome everywhere, to seldom being spoken to, to being shunned and abused, to being the first one the other owner's spent their fury on, but she gave it back to them when she needed to. She had developed a handsome temper in the past year, born of constantly being under stress and John Harte saw that in her face now, and he thought her even more beautiful than the year before. There was something about her which made him want to take her in his arms. But that made no sense at all. She was a woman who wanted no help from anyone. She would climb the mountain alone, and one day she would sit there by herself. That made him sad for her, and in a way, she had chosen the same fate that he himself and her father had. Neither he nor Jeremiah had ever chosen to marry again, they had run their mines alone. He with Spring Moon at his side, his Indian squaw, and Jeremiah with his child, but she had no one at all. The thought pained him as he rode back to his mine, thinking of her, but Sabrina wasted no thought on him, she had work to do. She seldom allowed herself random thoughts these days. Her life was a constant fight just to survive, and it wasn't an accident that she had reopened the two defunct mines again, she had done it with hard work, endless hours, long nights at work and months and months of sweat.

And now she was working just as hard to force the business to grow. She had just sold seven hundred flasks to a firm in the East, and she had promised the men a bonus when the flasks were shipped. She knew how her father had operated the mines, there was no secret to how he had operated it, and in keeping with his philosophy she shared some of her profits with her men if they worked hard. And if they didn't like her, they knew at least that she was decent with them. That was all they asked, and all she asked in return, but it wasn't always what she got, although she expected more now. And if any man wasn't civil with her, he was out of a job within the hour, if it took that long. She could afford to be harder with them and they respected her for it.

'She's still a bitch, snotty little thing.' Dan Richfield was shooting off his mouth in a bar one night with some of her men when John Harte walked in, and Dan didn't see him as he stood at the end of the bar. 'She thinks if she wears pants for long enough, she'll grow a dick.' The men laughed and John Harte spoke up quietly from the end of the bar.

'Was that what you were looking for when you tried to rape her last year?' There was a sudden silence and Dan went pale and wheeled around, shocked to see his boss, and even more so to realize that Harte knew what he had almost done.

'What's that supposed to mean?'

'I don't think you should be talking about Sabrina Thurston like that. She works as hard as the rest of us, and these men still work for her, unless I'm wrong.' Suddenly, one or two of them looked ashamed. John Harte was no friend of hers, but he was right. She did work damn hard, you had to give her credit for that. The men shuffled off and Dan Richfield stayed, his eyes blazing, his fists itching to roar, but he didn't dare, instead he drank his whiskey with a surly look at John, but it was Sabrina he wanted to get his hands on. She had ruined all his dreams. And now that his wife was gone, he could have used a piece like her. It burned him for days, especially thinking about what she must have told John, and late the following Monday night, drinking at the same bar, he decided to ride past the Thurston Mines. He stopped when he saw Sabrina's horse there. It was nine o'clock at night, and he figured she must have left him there. He stopped, and tied up his own mount, walked slowly up the steps, and was startled to see her there. He looked through the window, and saw her at her desk, head bowed, her dark hair pulled back, her pen flying as she wrote. She was there until almost midnight every night, and it was still early for her. He suddenly grinned as he saw her, and although he didn't quite realize it, he had come back to finish what he had left undone the year before when she'd fired him. But as he walked across the porch, a board creaked, and without lifting her head, she pulled open the desk drawer, and had the small pistol in her hand before he reached the door, and her first shot flew through the window pane and whizzed past his arm as he stood transfixed with shock, staring at her as she quietly looked up and spoke out loud enough for him to hear.

'You come through that door, and you're a dead man, Dan.' And he could tell that she meant every word. She didn't look surprised or afraid. She was prepared for anything now, and she wasn't afraid of him. She stood up and levelled the gun at his head, and without saying a word, he turned and walked away. She rang the bell for one of the watchmen then. They were assigned to guard the mines, she had no real need of them where she worked, but she called for them now to check the grounds and make sure that Dan was nowhere around.

And the next day she sent a warning to John Harte, suggesting that he keep better control over his men. If she found one on her grounds again, she would assume he was sent by Harte himself to harass her into selling her mines and she would kill him on the spot.

She informed Harte that she had chosen to spare Richfield this time, but she wouldn't again. And he was not pleased to learn that Dan was bothering Sabrina again. He warned him of it that day and Richfield's jaw clenched as Harte spoke, but he said not a single word. And afterwards, John laughed to himself. Sabrina was not unlike Spring Moon, so sure of her trusty blade, and apparently she had a fine hand with a gun. He was only sorry she had a need for it, but she lived in a man's world. And John Harte did not make her another offer that year.

Chapter Twenty-Three

'Well, girl, you're twenty-one, what you gonna do now?' Hannah looked at her over the cake she had baked and she wanted to cry as she saw Sabrina's face. She had grown into womanhood now and she was a beautiful girl but as hard as rock. She ran a mine of nearly six hundred men and had stepped into her Daddy's shoes, but for what? She had been rich enough before, and now she led a lonely life, working 'til midnight every night, ordering her men around, firing them on the spot if they got out of line. So what? She was losing her gentle ways and Hannah suspected that it was destroying her. Amelia had said as much when she had come to visit the previous year, but she had also realized that there was no changing her mind, and she had told Hannah to back off and give her time. 'She'll grow tired of it in time,' the wise woman had smiled, 'perhaps she'll fall in love'. But with what? Her horse? She was already in love with her work, and when she wasn't killing herself at the mines, she was at the vineyard co-op fighting with another group of men.

'I can't understand what made you like that.' Hannah looked at her in despair. 'Your Daddy didn't even love his mines as much as you do. He was more interested in you.'

'That's why I owe it to him.' She was always definite about that, and Hannah shook her head and served her a slice of the gooey chocolate birthday cake. It was the same cake she had been baking her for twenty-one years, and this time Sabrina smiled at her old friend. 'You're awfully good to me, Hannah.'

'I wish you were good to yourself for a change. You work even harder than he did. At least he came home to you. Why don't you think about selling that damn mine and getting married instead?' But Sabrina only laughed. Who would she marry? One of the men at the mines? The new foreman she had hired when the old one left? Her banker in town? There was no one who interested her, and she had too many other things to do.

'Maybe I'm more like Daddy than you think.' She smiled. She had told Amelia the same thing. 'After all, he didn't marry till he was forty-three.'

'You can't wait that long.' Hannah growled.

'Why not?'

'Don't you want babies one day?'

Sabrina shrugged . . . babies . . . what an odd thought . . . all she could think about were the seven hundred flasks she had to ship East in two weeks . . . and the two hundred and fifty flasks to the South . . . the paperwork she had to do . . . the men she had to fire and keep in line . . . the floods they might have . . . or the fires they had to guard against . . . babies? How did they fit into the scheme of things? They certainly didn't now, and they probably never would. It seemed no loss to her. She couldn't imagine herself with a child. Not anymore. She had too many other things on her mind, and as soon as she finished her cake, she went upstairs to pack. She had already told Hannah that she was going to San Francisco for a few days.

'By yourself?' She always said the same thing.

'Who would you like me to take?' Sabrina smiled. 'Half a dozen men from the mine to chaperone me on the boat?'

'Don't be fresh, girl.'

'All right,' she had said it a thousand times by now, 'I'll take you.'

'You know that damn boat makes me sick.'

'Then I'll have to go alone, won't I?' And she didn't mind at all. The trip to San Francisco always gave her time to think, and it was a rare chance to visit Thurston House. It still pained her to walk into the room where her father had died, but it was a beautiful house now that all the quake damage had been repaired and it was sad never to use it at all. She kept no help there, and she would open it herself and tend to her own needs for the few days she was there. 'Think Hannah, now everyone may think me odd, but in a few years, think how acceptable I'll be. I'll be that crazy old woman who's been running those mines for years. And no one will think it strange when I take a trip alone, or get on a steamer, or go into town without a maid. I'll be able to do absolutely anything I want to do,' she laughed, and for an instant she sounded young again, 'I can hardly wait.'

'It won't be long,' Hannah looked sorrowfully at her. This wasn't

228

what she had wanted for the child she had raised. 'You'll be old soon enough, and you'll have wasted all these precious years.' But to Sabrina they weren't wasted years. She felt victorious most of the time, and satisfied with what she had done. It was only from others that she seldom won approval or acclaim. They just thought her pushy and independent and very odd, but she was used to that by now. She held her chin a little higher than she had before, and her tongue was sharper than it had once been. She was quicker with a retort and faster on the draw with her little silver gun. But in her heart of hearts, she knew she had done well, and she was pleased. She secretly thought that her father would have been too. Perhaps it hadn't been what he wanted for her, but he would have respected how far she had come in three long, long years. It was amazing to Sabrina to realize that it had been that long. And she had worked hard. She thought about it again now as she came downstairs with her bag, and her cloak over her arm.

'I'll be back in three days.' She kissed Hannah's cheek, and thanked her for the birthday cake, and as the old woman watched her start her car, she had tears in her eyes. The girl would never know what she had missed, but for all her strength and her independence, there was a hole in her life the size of the barn out back, and Hannah was sorry for her. This was no life for her, and hadn't been for three years.

Sabrina drove to Napa herself, and left her car at the stables near the dock, just as she always did. She had been one of the first people in Napa to have a car, and like everything else she did, it had caused comment for months. But she didn't care, it was an enormous convenience for her. She still rode her old horse over to the mine most days, but she enjoyed using the car when she went any further than that, and especially when she went to Napa to catch the steamer into town. It saved her a lot of time. She boarded the familiar boat now, and spent the four hours in her cabin reading papers she had brought along. She wanted to speak to the bank about some more land she wanted to buy, and she already knew that she would have to listen to their usual advice, that she would be wiser to sell the vineyards and the mines, or hire a man to run them both. It never dawned on them that there were very few men who could have done what she had, and she was used to their advice. She smiled politely and then went on with the business at hand, and they were always amazed at the

229

soundness of her ideas. 'Who advised you on this?' they almost always asked, or 'Was this your foreman's idea?' It was useless to explain to them that it was her own, it was truly beyond their ken, and she knew it would be again now when she went to them the next day. But somehow they would get through it all, and she would get what she wanted from them. They had learned to trust her in the past three years, like her men, although they seldom understood what she did or why. And she had learned it all from Jeremiah himself.

She closed her briefcase as she felt the boat bump against the dock, and she hadn't left her cabin this time. After Hannah's enormous birthday lunch, she hadn't wanted to eat, and she had had so much work to do. And now she was anxious to relax in a hot bath at Thurston House. It would take time for the water tank to heat up, but that would give her time to make sure that everything in the house was sound. She hadn't been to town in several months, and she was the only one who ever went there, although the bank had the authority to check it from time to time, and she had given them a spare set of keys.

She fit her own key into the lock, when the carriage dropped her off. First she had to open the enormous gate, and then they rolled down the drive and deposited her in front of the house. There was no light anywhere, and when she stepped inside she had to fumble to put the light on, and when she did, she brought her bag inside and shut the door. She was tired tonight, and she stood and looked around, and suddenly she felt tears in her eyes for the first time in a long time. She was twenty-one years old and there was no one to share it with her, and this was the house in which her father had died . . . somehow it seemed sad to her to be here tonight, all alone, and she missed him more than she had in years. She was almost sorry she had come, and as she sat in the deep bathtub in her suite later that night, she thought back over the past three years, how difficult they had been, how many people had done her wrong, wished her ill, caused her pain, even Hannah had often been angry and unkind. No one understood the sense of duty or the drive which kept her running the mines, instead they all wanted to see her fail, or to take them from her. At least John Harte had finally stopped trying to buy the mines from her, and that was a relief. She wondered if Dan Richfield still worked for him, she imagined he did, he had been six months before, and what a disappointment he had been, but he hadn't come to bother her again at the mines, not since the time she had shot at him through the window pane. And at the thought, she glanced over at the pink marble sink where she had left her little silver gun. She never left it very far from her, and kept it on her bedtable at night as she slept. She would have put it under her pillow but the trigger was too quick, as Dan Richfield had seen. In some ways, she led a life of constant strain, but she was used to it now. And in a way, when she came to San Francisco, she got away from it totally. San Francisco was so cosmopolitan, so urbane, and almost no one knew who she was. No one whispered or stopped to point, as they did in Napa, or Calistoga, or Saint Helena now . . . look . . . that's the woman who runs the mines! . . . the Thurston girl . . . crazy as a march hare . . . she runs the mines you know! . . . she's tough as nails . . . mean as fire . . . there were a thousand unkind ways to describe her now and she thought she had heard them all, but here nobody cared. She could even allow herself to pretend that she wasn't who she was, wandering down Market Street, or in Union Square, or stopping at a flower shop to buy herself a rose to pin on her lapel or a bunch of white violets to tie in her hair. She didn't have to worry about what her men thought of her when she went to the mines. She could almost pretend that she was just a frivolous young girl.

And that was what she did after she went to the bank that day. She strolled home slowly, and bought herself a bunch of fragrant flowers to put in a vase in her room in Thurston House, and with a sudden gesture as she walked home, she pulled the pins from her hair, and let her long dark hair flow free in the summer breeze. She walked home with a smile on her face. It was easier being here, she thought to herself, and she still loved Thurston House, in spite of the tragedy that had happened there. As she walked up Nob Hill, she was humming gaily, happier than she'd been in a long time, when she suddenly saw a car stop just in front of her. The driver sat staring at her and then laughed.

'Good God, Miss Thurston. I would never have recognized you. Is that you?' It was John Harte at the wheel of a car and he appeared to be having a good time too.

'It is. Did you just steal that car, Mr. Harte?'

'I did. Would you like a ride?' This was neutral ground for both of them, and she looked at him with a happy smile and then decided what the hell. If he asked to buy her mine again, she could always get

231

out and walk. He wasn't going to kidnap her, and no one would have paid the ransom anyway.

'Sure.' She was amused at the car he had bought. It was the same Model A she had had for two years, except that this was newer and a little more elaborate of course. They seemed to add a whole new bunch of gadgets every year. 'How do you like your new car?'

'I think I'm in love.' He grinned, glancing at the dashboard, and then out the window at the hood before looking back at her. 'Pretty, isn't she?'

Sabrina laughed, unable to resist the urge to prick his balloon. 'Almost as pretty as mine.' She grinned and he looked shocked and then laughed out loud.

'Do you have one of these?'

She laughed. 'I do. I don't use it in Saint Helena much though. My old roan horse seems more appropriate somehow.' She had finally sold the black stallion her father had loved. She never rode him and he was growing old. 'But I drive the car when I go any further than that.'

He looked at her then as though seeing her for the first time. 'You really are a remarkable girl. It's a shame we're arch enemies in a way. If we weren't, I suspect we'd be friends.'

'If you'd stop trying to buy my mine from me everytime I run into you, maybe we could be anyway.' And then she wondered if his mistress would object, but she couldn't say something like that to him.

'You're still not going to sell, are you?' He smiled. For once he seemed unconcerned and she shook her head.

'I told you before. The Thurston Mines won't come up for sale until I'm dead.'

'And your vineyards, what about them?' He was curious now, and he liked the sparkle in her eyes and her hair loose and the fragrant flowers caught up in it. She was a remarkably pretty girl, a fact he had never really noticed before, and she was certainly a match for any man. He knew that much, but that had to be a handicap for her in many ways. He wondered what she did when she wasn't working at the mines, and he watched her now as she answered him.

'My vineyards will go to my grave with me too.'

'You don't seem concerned about having heirs to leave them to.'

She shrugged and looked at him. 'You can't have everything in life, Mr. Harte. I have what I want . . . the mines, the grapes, the land. My father loved it all, I would feel untrue to him if I gave any of it up. It was what he loved most in this world. Selling any of that would be like selling a part of him.' So that was what was at the root of it. Had he known that he would have understood how little chance he had of buying any of it from her years before.

'You must have been very devoted to him.'

She smiled at Harte as he reached Nob Hill. 'I was. And he was very good to me. It only seems fair that I carry on now for him.'

His eyes were gentle on hers. 'But what a painful burden it must be for you sometimes.'

She nodded slowly, feeling a sudden need to be honest with him. She had to tell someone. 'It is, at times. It's been difficult.' She sighed and looked out into space. 'But I suppose there's a certain victory in surviving it, and doing well. It was frightening that first year. . . .' Her voice grew soft at the memory, 'when all those men quit, and Dan Richfield left. . . .' She shrugged again and looked at him. 'But that was three years ago, and everything's all right now,' she smiled again, 'so don't get any ideas about buying me out.'

'I may have to try again sometime, Miss Thurston. It's the nature of the beast, I'm afraid.' He laughed with her, and she directed him toward Thurston House.

'Just as long as you expect to be turned down again.'

'I think I'm used to that by now.'

'Good. There, that's it.' She pointed at the gate she always kept locked and hopped out of his car to unlock it for him, and then she came back and looked up into his eyes. It was odd meeting him like this. Things were so much less intense here. They weren't rivals meeting here in town like this, they were just two people going about their lives harmlessly. She was wearing flowers in her hair and he had bought a new car and was delighted with it. It was like being different people than they usually were, and Sabrina was feeling light hearted again as she looked at him. 'You don't have to drive me in, I can walk from here.'

'Why not let me drive you to the door in my new car, Miss Thurston?' He was being very gentlemanly, an element which had never entered into their relationship before. They had been arch enemies for most of the past three years, and then finally just faded from each other's lives. Now there John Harte was again, but harmlessly, and she wasn't in the mood to be angry at him or even to think about her mines. Napa was too far away, and she was twenty-one years old and just happy to be alive.

'All right, if you insist, Mr. Harte.' She allowed him to drive her right to her front door, and then with a small smile she turned to him. 'If you absolutely promise not to mention my mines even once, or make me an offer of any kind, I'd be happy to invite you in for a cup of tea or some port. But you have to promise first!' She was teasing now, and they were laughing when he promised solemnly and he followed her inside. But he was in no way prepared for what he saw there. It was the most splendid house he had ever seen, and in his forty-eight years he'd seen a few, but Thurston House was spectacular, and like everyone who saw it for the first time, he stood in awe beneath the dome. She had had all of the stained glass replaced three years ago, and all of the earthquake damage had been repaired. She had even had to replace the front door, which was badly singed by the fire, which had miraculously turned and fled right at their threshold.

'My lord, how can you live away from this?'

She grinned. They had promised not to speak of the mines, and she was determined not to be the one to break the vow. 'I have other fish to fry.'

He laughed at the answer she gave. 'Indeed you do. But I think if I owned this house, I would abandon everything else just so I could live here.'

She looked at him in mock dismay. She was in an unusually good mood. 'Are you trying to break your promise and make me an offer, Mr. Harte?'

'I am not. But I've never seen anything as wonderful as this house. When was it built?' He vaguely remembered hearing about it, but he had never actually seen it before, and now Sabrina told him some of the details, and showed him some of the more unusual features of the house, while giving him its history.

He shook his head. 'No . . . it's not as if I didn't know, but hearing you say it like that . . . do you realize what it's like for a man my age, to realize that his arch competitor, in truth his largest competitor, is only twenty-one years old? You are twenty-one, aren't you?'

She smiled at him, looking perfectly poised and very beautiful. 'Yesterday.'

234

His voice was quiet and soft, and it seemed as though the war between them might be off. 'Happy birthday then.'

'Thank you.' She walked him back into the living room and they both sat down and sipped their sherry again. She had had nothing stronger to offer him, but he seemed satisfied with what she had. He looked perfectly happy in fact. More so than he had in years, and so did she.

'What did you do on your birthday?' He looked at her with interest now. There was so much to this girl, so much strength, so many quiet things, and an inner depth he had never really noticed before, although he saw it so clearly now.

'Nothing much. I came to town.' She shrugged. 'Did you expect the men at the mine to bake me a birthday cake?' He laughed but he felt sad for her. This girl actually had no one at all, except the men who worked for her, and he knew that they still resented her, and always would. She would have had to die heroically in a fire at the mine for them to really think well of her. Anything less than that wouldn't have been enough.

John Harte was looking quietly at her. 'You're so young to have so much on your back, Miss Thurston. Don't you ever want to just run away?'

She looked at him honestly. 'Yes. That's when I come here. You must feel that way too sometimes.' He nodded and smiled at her. His life had been so much longer and fuller than hers. It seemed unfair that she should be trapped at her mines, and how unkind they were to her. He still heard it from his own men, and now and then someone she had fired or had refused to hire came to him. But they always went to the Thurston Mines first because she paid so well. She couldn't afford not to pay them well, they disliked working for her so much. It was nothing personal, but it hurt their dignity to work for a woman, even more so a young girl. As he had felt before, he suddenly wanted to protect her again, yet here she was, in her enormous, lovely house. She had her house in town, her vineyards, she had everything, and yet nothing at all. His little Indian squaw, Spring Moon, had more. She had peace, respect, security and at least she had him.

'It's funny that we should wind up competitors, isn't it?'

She smiled and shrugged. 'I suppose everything in life is like that. It's all so coincidental, so unexpected and so odd. Like meeting you today.' She smiled.

'I almost didn't recognize you, with your hair like that.'

This time she laughed. 'I can't very well wear it this way at the mines, then they'd really give me a bad time . . . can you imagine the things they'd say?' She began to laugh even harder then and suddenly he was laughing too. There were times when she was just a very young girl, and no more complicated than that. She was wonderfully unassuming and uncomplicated, very down to earth, and then one realized who she really was, and it was startling. She was a dozen people woven into one, and yet she seemed so simple and so direct. It was confusing and delightful all at the same time, and it enchanted him.

'You know, I like you like this.' He was smiling at her, and without a second thought, he reached out and touched her hair with his hand. In Napa, he would never have dared to do a thing like that, yet here she was almost a different girl, and there was no harm in it, and for an instant, he even forgot Spring Moon.

'Thank you.' She blushed as she said the words, and his hand drifted from her hair to her cheek, and then suddenly she pulled back. She wasn't used to anyone being that close to her, not since her father had died, and it startled her now. She got up to pour him another drink, but his eyes never left her face, and when she returned he spoke gently to her.

'I didn't mean to frighten you.'

'It's alright . . . I . . . it doesn't matter.' She sat down and looked at him earnestly. 'It's difficult to be two people at once. I think I had to harden myself in order to run the mines . . . I think I forgot that I was ever anyone else . . . and before that, actually, I was only a child.' She was barely more than that now, and he was aware of it, but on the other hand, he was also aware of something more. And he also sensed how trusting and foolish she was. He had the vague feeling that there was no one else in the house with them. He saw no evidence of servants anywhere, and on the one hand she was so guarded and so careful, and on the other hand, she had trusted him, which she shouldn't have done. His brows knit as he looked at her, feeling suddenly fatherly.

'Do you stay alone in this house, Miss Thurston?'

She smiled at him. She always had, since her father died. 'It doesn't frighten me. I like coming here alone.' She was a strange, solitary girl, but he thought her foolhardy here.

'You're not in the country here. I think it's very dangerous.'

'I can defend myself.' She smiled, but he wasn't so sure.

'I wouldn't depend on that. What if you can't find your gun?' He remembered hearing about the shot fired at Dan.

'It's never very far from me, Mr. Harte.'

'That's reassuring,' he smiled at her and she laughed.

'I'm sorry . . . I didn't mean to suggest. . . .'

'Why not?' His face was serious again. 'You shouldn't have trusted me either, you know.'

She looked at him very seriously. 'I have several times been very angry at you, but you have never behaved improperly toward me, Mr. Harte.' She still remembered his condolence call when her father had died and he had been nothing but kind to her then. 'I think I have a good sense of people by now.'

'You shouldn't rely on that. Why don't you bring your house-keeper with you when you come to town?'

'She gets seasick on the boat,' she smiled, 'and really, I'm perfectly all right here. If I'm safe at the mines alone until almost midnight every night, what can happen to me here?'

Now he really looked concerned. 'Do your men know that?'

She shrugged. 'Some of them. I've always worked late, just as my father did. There's a lot of work to do in a day, and I don't like to fall behind.' He did the same thing at his own mines, but it was dangerous for her to be alone like that, no wonder Dan had come to bother her. It was fortunate he hadn't come again, at least Harte didn't think he had and he didn't want to ask her now.

'I just think you should be more careful than that. Bring your work home with you.'

She smiled, touched at his concern. Other than Hannah, bellowing at her, no one had done that in a long time, and she told him that. 'I really am all right though. And I appreciate your concern.'

'It would be easier for you if you just let me buy you out one day.' A flicker of anger danced across her eyes and he held up a hand. 'That was not an offer. It was a statement. It *would* be easier, and you know it too. But easier doesn't appear to be what you want.' He stood up then and bowed, as she felt her ire subside. 'I bow to your wishes.'

She grinned at him, suddenly mischievous again. 'Too bad you didn't think of doing that before, Mr. Harte.'

'Now, now, Miss Thurston. I had to try after all. And now, I

237

withdraw.' But she still wasn't sure she trusted him. 'Maybe now we can be friends.'

'That would be very nice.' She smiled at him and he looked at her with something serious in his eyes. This was the man whose child had died in her father's arms, she reminded herself. He was not just a greedy miner trying to buy her out. And her father had thought well of him, perhaps he had even been worthy of that. She wasn't sure about him now, except that she respected him. He was intelligent, and he ran his business decently and well.

'I would like to be your friend, Miss Thurston.' She nodded, looking sadly at him. She had never had a friend, other than the little girls she had gone to school in Saint Helena with. But they were all married now, and had children of their own, and they no longer spoke to her. She was far too outrageous now that she ran her father's mines. She needed a friend, someone to talk things over with. She wondered how his Indian girl would feel if she rode over to the Harte Mine to talk to him from time to time. She was weighing it in her mind as he watched her face and then she looked at him with cautious eyes.

'I'd like that, Mr. Harte. I wonder if that would be possible once we're back at our respective mines.'

'We could try it sometime, I'll come and visit you. Would that be acceptable?' There was no one else to ask. No mother, father, aunt, or chaperone. And he was actually asking her something she didn't understand. He wasn't even sure he understood it himself, but he had seen her walking along the street, and she had taken his breath away, and now they had sat there for two hours like two people who had never met before, and he found himself so taken with her that he didn't want to lose her again, no matter who she became when she went back to the mine. He knew that this girl would be hidden there somewhere, and he didn't want to forget what she had been like tonight. She had said nothing unusual to him at all, but the look in her eyes had touched him to his very core. Matilda had looked a little like that, but she hadn't been nearly as beautiful, nor as intelligent. And now that he was sitting there with her, it struck him how remarkable it was that at twenty-one, this girl ran one of the country's greatest mines. She was rare in a thousand different ways, all of which struck him now, and he had to tear himself away when he left. As she closed the door and listened to his car drive away, Sabrina felt a stirring in her soul that she had never felt before. She kept remembering the look in his eyes, or something he had said to her, and his image haunted her as she sat in the garden the next day, thinking of him. She was taking the steamer back to Napa that night, and it was ridiculous that she should be so taken with him. She had seen him dozens of other times, even as a child, and for three years she had detested him, and yet now . . . she could barely force him from her mind. There was a quiet, subtle strength to him, a force, and yet a warmth, she felt totally safe whenever he was around. And she was aware now that she had felt that about him before, but she had been too busy being angry at him to pay much attention to him. But it was ridiculous that she should think of him so constantly now. He bothered her all afternoon, and again on the boat going North, and again as she drove home. As she rode to the mines the next day, she was still thinking of him, just as he was thinking of her. And when he reached his mine, he heard the news from Dan that she discovered as she walked in her office door. The toll was written on a chalk board sitting on her desk, and she suddenly realized that she should have noticed it the instant she arrived. There had been an explosion deep in the mine, and the damage to the shaft had been minimal, but more than thirty men had died. Thirty-one to be exact, as she told John Harte when he came to visit her the next day, and she looked at him with grim eyes.

'They could at least have sent me a telegram. Instead, they said nothing at all, and there I sat with flowers in my hair. . . .' Her eyes were red-rimmed and she was furious at herself.

'You have a right to more than just this in your life, you know. They go home too at night. They have children and wives and they get drunk. What the hell do you do?' He was angry at her for being so hard on herself.

'I'm responsible for all of them.' She shouted the words at him and he grabbed her arm.

'You're responsible for yourself too, goddamit, Sabrina.' It was the first time he had called her by her first name, and she liked the sound of it on his lips. 'You owe yourself a lot more than just this pile of dirt. Don't you understand that, you damn thickheaded bitch?' And as he said the words, she smiled at him. Something strange had happened to them as they sat in Thurston House. After all these years, they had become friends.

And then her eyes looked sad again. 'I understand that thirty-one of my men are dead, Mr. Harte. And I wasn't here.'

'Would that have changed anything?'

'It might have changed the way the others felt.' But he knew that wasn't true. Nothing would ever change that, and rather than tell her that, he only shook his head.

'You've given them enough. You've given them three years of your life which is more than anyone has a right to ask from you, for God's sake. I've done the same damn thing at my mine, and they won't thank you for it. When you die, they won't even care.' But Sabrina knew that wasn't true. She remembered the men lined up five deep when her father died and she brought him home.

She spoke in a sad soft voice. 'They remember it.'

His eyes met hers and held. 'It's too late then. Who cares? Your father didn't care.' He remembered it too. 'It meant nothing to him. You know what mattered most to him? You. Maybe that's something you'd better think about. You are what meant everything to him,' John Harte felt a lump rise in his throat, 'just as my children meant everything to me.'

She looked at him and felt for his pain. 'Is that why you never married again? Because of them?'

He didn't deny it to her. He wanted to be honest with her. He liked her too much not to be. 'That's right.' He knew that she must have heard about Spring Moon, but he didn't want to discuss that with her. There was too much impropriety involved, and he respected her. 'I didn't ever want to care that much again. I just wanted to be comfortable. But I couldn't bear to feel that way again, to lose someone I loved.' His eyes filled at the memory, and it had been twenty-three years since Matilda and Jane and Barnaby died.

'I think that's how my father felt about his first fiancée. That's what Hannah says. He didn't want to get married again for another eighteen years.'

'And I don't think I ever will,' he looked hard at her, 'but at least I had that once. You never have, and you never will, if you lock yourself up here.'

She looked angrily at him again. 'You're trying to talk me out of the mine again, aren't you?'

'No, I'm not, dammit. But I'm trying to tell you something that's important for you, or at least it should be. Don't give these people everything you've got, Sabrina. They'll never give it back to you. Give it to someone who deserves it. . . .' He felt a lump catch in his throat again and he wasn't sure why. 'Give it to someone you love . . . find someone you care about. Go enjoy your beautiful house in San Francisco, live your life. Don't just waste it here. Your father couldn't have wanted that for you, little one. It just isn't fair.' She was touched as much by the look in his eye as by his words, and she nodded slowly at him, and then she went to see about her men with his words ringing in her ears.

Chapter Twenty-Four

The worst fire in more than fifty years of mining history swept the Harte Mine in August of 1909. The ravages of the fire almost defied description as the inferno continued to burn and blaze underground for five days. Men were dragged out burned to a crisp and there was almost no way to rescue them. The gas fires burned so hot that the rescue teams were forced back each time they attempted to reach the trapped miners. But for five days, John Harte struggled to do what he could. He burned both arms badly, and his back as well, but he saved more than twenty men himself, and by the end of the second day, Sabrina Thurston was there. She worked along with his men, with rescue teams from other towns, with doctors who came from as far away as Napa to help, and Spring Moon who applied salves and herbs to burns. It was a gruesome, endless, agonizing five days, and when the last flames were finally put out, they were all staggering from lack of sleep, and the food lines for the rescue teams began to pick up. The last of the wounded men had been taken away, and the dead had been removed as well. Sabrina sat on a charred log, her face smeared with soot, one hand badly burned from helping to put out the flames on a miner's back. She looked up exhaustedly at John Harte, as he came toward her. Her eyes were so red she could barely see, but she saw him smile at her, his own face as filthy as hers.

'I can't thank you enough for what you did.'

'You would have done the same for me, John, wouldn't you?'

He nodded. They both knew he would. And she had sent for hundreds of her men to help as well. There had been no grumbling and no protests from her men. They were always willing to help their brothers in desperate times, and they had instantly answered Sabrina's call to them. They had come in droves, and now along with the rest, they were packing up.

'Your men were wonderful.' And so had been Spring Moon. She

242

had a gentle, knowing way with the men, and she had caught Sabrina's eye more than once as she moved from one wounded man to the next. And she had seen something more as well, something growing between Sabrina and John, which they didn't understand yet themselves. But she had seen how they looked at each other more than once, with a compassion and tenderness which Spring Moon recognized as the first seedling of love, and she wondered how long it would take for the seed to grow. And it was not of Spring Moon that John was thinking now. He turned to Sabrina with concern in his eyes. 'Go home and get some rest, little one. I'll come to see you later on. I want to make sure that hand is all right.' He glanced at it again and she smiled tiredly at him. He seemed to have endless drive. He hadn't rested in five days. She herself had gone home once to change, she had been so filthy from the soot and the ashes and the fumes of the mines. Even now it pervaded everything she wore, everything that touched her flesh, her hair reeked of it, and she was anxious to get home and take a bath. The prospect of stretching out between the clean sheets on her bed was more than she could resist. She could barely stay awake as she rode her roan mare home. But all the way home she thought of him again, and what a remarkable man he was. He was forty-nine years old, one of the most handsome men she'd ever seen, and as she crawled into her bed that afternoon, she suddenly envied Spring Moon. She was still dreaming about him after sunset that night, when Hannah knocked hard on her door. Sabrina sat up in her bed, her hair tumbled about her face, and squinted at the elderly housekeeper.

'Did the fire come up again?' She had been dreaming of the fire and John Harte and Spring Moon and all the wounded men, but Hannah shook her head. She still looked tired too. She had been cooking for the men for days, and sleeping not at all after she rode back.

'John Harte's downstairs. He says he came to see how your hand is. I told him you were asleep and he wanted me to come have a look.' She glanced at Sabrina's hand, but it looked all right to her. It seemed funny to her too that he was worried about such a small burn. His own looked a lot worse, and suddenly Hannah began to wonder about him. She didn't think much of him. Hell, he'd been living with that Indian girl for years. And he wasn't going to throw Sabrina in with her, not if she had anything to say about it. But it was probably just another ploy to make Sabrina sell her mines. 'You want me to just tell him you're all right?' Sabrina shook her head and hopped out of bed, grabbing her dressing gown from a chair. She ran swiftly downstairs to where he stood in the front door. He looked absolutely exhausted, but he smiled when he saw her.

'Are you all right, Sabrina?'

'I'm fine. Do you want something to drink?' He began to shake his head and then changed his mind.

'I wouldn't mind a little shot of something stiff to perk my backbone up again.' She smiled at the term and poured him a whiskey straight up and handed it to him.

'You should be asleep, instead of "perking up." '

'There's too much to do.' It was a familiar song to both of them.

'And who'll do it if you drop in your tracks, you fool?'

He grinned at her. 'You're beginning to sound like me lecturing you.'

'I do, don't I?' She grinned, and then sobered again, thinking of the men who had died. It was the worst disaster she had ever seen, but they had saved a remarkable number of them. 'I wish we'd saved more of them, John.' She looked up at him, but he shook his head.

'It couldn't be done, Sabrina. We tried . . . all of us did . . .' But the conditions had been worse than any human could withstand, and with the gas fumes rampant in the mines death had been quick. The explosions were incredible. 'We're lucky we didn't lose more. I'm grateful for that.' But she was worried for him anyway, and then suddenly she had a funny thought, and she turned to him.

'Hell, John, you've had your share of problems now, why not let me buy you out?' She was teasing him. It was the sort of thing he would have said to her a year before.

'I have a better idea.' He smiled strangely at her. 'Why don't you marry me?' Her heart stopped as she looked at him. He was teasing her. She knew that much, but it was odd that he said the words . . . and before she could say anything, he kissed her gently on the lips. No man had ever kissed her before, and she felt her whole body melt as he took her in his arms. It seemed a lifetime before he let her go. She looked at him in total amazement as he smiled at her and kissed her again and this time she pushed him gently away so that she could come up for air, and stared at him.

'Did the gas fumes get to you?'

'Must have,' he laughed, and then kissed her again, but she leapt to her feet, the dressing gown showing off her pretty ankles and graceful feet.

'What are you doing, John Harte?' Was he out of his mind? He had an Indian mistress living with him and he was proposing to her. He had to be teasing her, but the look in his eyes said that he meant everything he had said to her, and as usual, Sabrina was direct with him. 'What about Spring Moon?'

He seemed to hesitate briefly, but his eyes never wavered from hers. He had been thinking of this for days. Spring Moon knew him well. 'I'm sorry you know as much about that as you do, Sabrina. It's not something I would have wanted to discuss with you. But you have a right to know, I suppose. After I met you in San Francisco this Spring, and I began to call on you.' Sabrina stared at him in astonishment. She hadn't realized that he considered it that. 'I asked Spring Moon to move out two months ago. She's been living in a separate cabin near the mines, and she's going home to her people in South Dakota at the end of this month. I was going to wait and ask you then . . . but I couldn't stand it anymore, working for the past five days with you, all I wanted to do was hold you in my arms and keep you safe, and tonight . . . I can't live without you anymore.' His eyes suddenly seemed damp, and she wondered if it was from the smoke. 'I didn't think I'd ever want to do this again. I never wanted to put my heart on the line again after Matilda died.' He looked at her, and the memory of the wife and children he had lost stood between both of them, but his voice was soft when he spoke, 'That was twenty-three years ago, Sabrina . . . I can't close my heart because of them, and Spring Moon has been good for me for all these years, but there's more to life than something like that.' It was exactly what Jeremiah had discovered twenty-three years before when he met Camille and abandoned Mary Ellen Browne. But Sabrina had still not answered John. She was staring at him in disbelief. 'She understands.' They had had a long, sad, honest talk that night before he had ridden over to ask Sabrina to marry him. He honoured the years he had shared with Spring Moon and he wanted to tell her first. They had both cried, but he knew that what he felt for Sabrina was right.

'Why would you want to marry me?' She seemed amazed, much more so than Spring Moon had been, and the thought of her mine had crossed Sabrina's mind . . . now that his mine had been so badly burned . . . but she shook the thought from her head . . . 'I don't know what to say . . . how would I . . . would I . . . what if . . .' He could imagine all the questions running through her head, and he gently pulled her close to him.

'I could run your mine for you, or you could continue to run it yourself, if that's what you want to do. I won't stand in your way, and I won't take anything from you. The Thurston Mines are yours until the day you die, just as you said they were. I will never try to change that again, what I want is something much more important than your mine, Sabrina.' He looked down at her from his great rugged height and held her close, the smell of fire still clinging to them both but neither of them caring. 'I want you, beloved girl . . . and that's all I want, for the rest of your life. Maybe I'm too old for you, and I know you deserve much more than this, but everything I have is yours, Sabrina Thurston, my land, my heart, my mine, my soul . . . my life . . .' He looked at her and tears filled her eyes, and then she was kissing him again, and his beard tasted of smoke, but she didn't give a damn. Suddenly she began to laugh and he looked at her and she could barely speak as she explained.

'I used to think you were my enemy . . . and now . . . look at us . . .' He kissed her again and swept her off her feet in her dressing gown just as Hannah walked in with cookies and tea. And she glared at John Harte and looked at Sabrina pointedly.

'I'd thank you both to behave yourself in this house, Sabrina,' she sniffed and wagged a finger at her, 'I don't care if you do run a mine and five hundred men, in this house you'll behave ladylike, and with a little dignity.'

'Yes, ma'am. Does that apply after I'm married, too?' She looked angelically at her old nurse and the old woman went right on.

'After you're married you can do anything you damn well please, that is if . . .' And suddenly she stopped and looked at them. 'What?' She stared at John as he nodded happily at her, and with that Hannah gave a long, loud, ear piercing scream, as Sabrina threw her arms around her and John Harte hugged them both. And then Hannah suddenly backed off and glared at him again. 'Now wait a minute here.' She put her hands on her hips and looked at him. 'What about that Indian girl?' John blushed and laughed as he answered her.

'I'm so glad that we're all so terribly discreet.'

'Discreet my foot. If you think you're going to keep her around and marry my girl . . .' Sabrina was touched by the term and laughed at her as she answered for John.

'She's leaving for South Dakota next week.'

'And not a moment too soon. Ten years too late if you ask me.' And then, hands on hips, she smiled at them. 'I never thought I'd see this day, I gave up hope when you started running that damn mine of yours.'

'She's going to run mine for me now,' John grinned and Sabrina laughed as Hannah shrieked.

'She'll do no such thing! She's going to stay home with me and bring up your children, John Harte. There'll be no more of that mine nonsense around here!'

'What do you say to that?' He whispered to his future wife and she smiled at him and whispered back.

'We'll see. Maybe you could run the mines for me.' It was an amazing turnaround for her, and she wasn't yet completely sure of it. 'It would give me more time to deal with the vines.' But she liked Hannah's idea best of all so far . . . to stay home and raise his sons . . . what an intriguing thought that was. He saw the look in her eyes and bent to kiss her lips.

'All in good time, my love . . . all in good time.'

Chapter Twenty-Five

There was no one for John to ask for her hand, but when she talked to Hannah that night the old woman cried and hugged her tight.

'I'd given up hope, little girl ... I never thought I'd see this day.' Sabrina looked over her shoulder into John's eyes and they exchanged a smile.

'I didn't think you would either.' She pulled away and smiled into Hannah's eyes, but she could still feel a ripple of fear run up her spine. She hoped she was doing the right thing. She was sure she was ... but it was such an enormous step, and there were so many things to decide now, about her mine. There was of course the possibility of merging the two companies, but she didn't want to do that. She wanted to keep all of his business separate from hers. She was marrying him, but not intertwining her holdings with his. One of the best things about it though was that if he ran her mines for her, as he had said he might, it would leave her more free time to work with her vineyards and her wines, and she had wanted more time for that for a long, long time.

'Don't you suppose you could just stay home and sew?' He teased her once as they sat on her front porch. He had been waiting for her when she got home, galloping up the road on her old horse.

'Where are we going to live?' She had thought of that before, and she wasn't anxious to live in the house where his wife and children had died, and where he had lived with Spring Moon for more than a decade. She was leaving for South Dakota in a few days, and Sabrina was careful not to mention her. She didn't want to be indelicate with him, it was bad enough that she knew. But they hadn't as yet solved the problem of where they would live, and she wasn't sure how he would feel about living in her house. 'What about living here?'

He thought about it for a time, stroking his beard, and then he looked at her. 'I'm a little old to be living in another man's house,

Sabrina. Somehow that would always feel like your Daddy's house to me.' She nodded, she understood, but it was a difficult dilemma to resolve. And John looked at Sabrina now, with a boyish smile. He looked far younger than his years to her, and it seemed remarkable that he was twenty-eight years older than she. 'What about living at Thurston House. That would be fun, wouldn't it?' He looked like a mischievous child, and she laughed. It was her house, but no one had lived there in so long, it was almost like common ground.

'That would be fun. But what about the mines?'

'We could manage something, I suppose. We don't have to live in town all the time. But it might be a nice change for both of us,' he smiled at her, 'once I get those mines of yours shaped up. Lord only knows how badly you've run them into the ground.'

She swatted her hand at him and he laughed at her. He had already seen some of the logs she kept, and he was amazed at how impeccably her business was run. He wondered how she had managed to learn it all, and there were even some pointers he could learn from her, although after twenty-seven years of running his own mine, he could almost do it in his sleep. But he was mightily impressed with her. 'You're not exactly the run of the mill bride, little one.' He leaned forward and kissed her cheek, took her hand in his so much larger one, and she leaned against him in the night air. She had never dreamed of loving him in all these years, and suddenly there he was, and she felt as though she had been born for him.

It was over dinner later that night that she brought up the subject of Dan at the Harte Mines.

'I'd already thought about that the other day.' John knitted his brows and frowned at her. 'I won't deny you the fact that he's good at what he does. But I don't want him anywhere near you.' John looked unhappily at her.

'How important is he to you, John?'

'Less important than you, my love.' He looked down at her. It was strange how deep his feelings ran for her. It had come upon him all at once, after all these years. And he had been so certain that he would never feel that way again. 'I'm going to let him go.'

'Are you sure you want to do that?'

'Yes.' His voice was firm. 'I don't have to explain why to him. And he hasn't been with me for all that long.' It was only three years since he had left the Thurston Mines, and he had worked hard for John, but he couldn't stay on with him now. John was sure about it as he thought it out. 'I'll give him notice next week.'

Sabrina frowned and looked at John. 'That's going to be hard on him.'

'He should have thought of that a long time ago, when he gave you such a hard time.'

Suddenly she laughed. 'The funny thing is it all started over his wanting me to sell out to you, and here I am marrying you instead.' Which they both knew was not the same thing. 'All he ever wanted was to run Daddy's mines, without Daddy hanging around, or me.' She smiled.

'I haven't given him as much free rein as he wanted either. I'm just not that kind of man. I've run that mine for too long myself.'

She understood perfectly. She felt the same way about her own and it had only been three years. She liked doing everything herself, in her own way, and it would be difficult to turn the reins over to John now. She was well aware of that, but she trusted him, and in time she would trust him more. They had already agreed that for the first six months she would stay on, and work part-time, and show John the systems she used, introduce him to the men. She wasn't going to drop everything at once. She couldn't do that. And he was going to rotate between her mines and his own. He insisted that it would work. 'And in the midst of all that, you want to stay at Thurston House?' She didn't see how they'd find time to leave Napa at all, but he insisted that they would. And when he kissed her as they left the porch that night, she was sure that he could do anything.

The damage from the fire at his mines took several weeks to repair with every man at the mines working overtime to help out, and even Spring Moon changed her plans, and decided to stay for a few more weeks. She kept to herself now, and she seemed to accept her fate, knowing that the affair with John Harte had come to an end. She never spoke to Sabrina when they met, but her eyes would reach out to her and seem to hold her fast, and Sabrina didn't feel any hostility from her. There was a kind of fascination, and each of them would fight not to stare, and then suddenly John would come along and take Sabrina away. It made him uncomfortable to see them anywhere near each other on his land.

'I want you to stay away from her.' John scolded Sabrina first, and Sabrina's voice was shy when she spoke.

'She's so beautiful. I always thought she was.' And then, 'I think my father did too.'

John started at her words. 'Did he say anything to you?'

She laughed and shook her head. 'No. I tried to ask him about it once, but he wouldn't talk about it, he said it was not something he would discuss with me.'

'I should hope not.' John flushed to the roots of his hair, and looked at her. And then he said something he knew he shouldn't say. He didn't want to discuss Spring Moon at all, and certainly not with her. 'You're much more beautiful than she is, little one.'

'How can you say that?' She looked shocked. 'She's the loveliest woman I've ever seen.'

He shook his head and took a step closer to her. 'No, my love, you are.' She was even lovelier than his first wife. With her black hair, and big blue eyes, she looked up at him now and he felt his insides melt. Side by side, he, with his broad shoulders, still dark hair, sparkling eyes and jutting beard, they made a handsome pair, and he looked down at her with pride. He could hardly wait until their wedding day. They had begun to tell their friends in the past few days, and Hannah had spread the word all over town. The news had finally reached his men, and after his, hers, and there was talk of nothing else in the mines, particularly at the Thurston Mines, where the miners wondered what kind of impact it would have on their jobs. But there was one other man who wondered the same thing when he heard, and he was furious at the hand Fate had dealt him again when John told him that he couldn't stay on. John didn't tell him why he was letting him go, but there was no doubt in Dan Richfield's mind. She had done him in again. And he was going to get her this time. John Harte had given Dan two weeks to organize himself and pack up his things, and he knew he would have to be leaving town, because there were no other mines nearby except hers and his. The silver mines in Napa were long since defunct, and had been since Jeremiah's time, and there was nothing left now except what Sabrina and John controlled. There was nowhere left for Dan to go. He was thirty-five years old, and most of his children were half-grown or damn close. He didn't even want to take them with him, and was talking about leaving them in Saint Helena with some friends. But it wasn't the children he thought of now, as he sat around and drank, wandered in and out of bars, and told the other

251

miners whatever rumours he had heard. 'She's been sleeping around with him . . . hell, they even go at it with that Indian Squaw of his, you notice she ain't left yet . . .' and by the end of the week, he had both mines all abuzz with the filth he spread.

'You've been talking about my future wife?' John Harte grabbed him by the collar one day as he left the Harte Mine. Sabrina was still buried in work at her own. More so now, because in two more months she'd be married and starting to turn the reins over to John. She had to get everything in order for him. And because of that, he hardly even saw her now. But Dan Richfield stared at him now, the stench of whiskey was on his breath as he looked at the bigger, broader man, but he looked unafraid.

'It's nothing you ain't heard before, Mr. Harte. She's not been real kind to me.'

'That isn't quite what I'd heard.'

'Or what you'd believe.' Dan Richfield was bold, and for an instant was unsure what John Harte would do to him, and then with a sudden gesture, he let Dan go.

'Get the hell out of here, Dan. As I remember it, you've only two days left.'

'I'll be gone by then.' And no one would be grieved, least of all John. He was glad that he had fired him. He had never realized how much he drank until recently.

'Where are you going by the way?'

'Down to Texas, I think. I've got a friend who owns a ranch, and some oil wells down there. I thought that might be a nice change from these rotten mines.' He glanced over his shoulder at the mine where he had worked for more than three years, and then back at John.

'You taking your kids?' Richfield shrugged, and John glared at him. 'Just make sure you're out of here on time.' He had no kindly feelings toward him. It was obvious how much Dan hated John's future wife, and John didn't want him around anymore. It was high time he left, and he put him out of his mind as he walked back to his office to go through the papers on his desk. He still had plenty of his own work to do.

And so did Sabrina at the Thurston Mines until almost seven that night, and then in panic, she looked at her watch. She had promised John that she would ride over and have dinner with him. It was odd to her sometimes how she had a whole other life now. There was someone waiting for her at the end of each day, she had someone to tell her troubles to, share her victories with, be kind to her when she was tired, rub her neck, kiss her face, and she was happy to share the tales of his day with him. She wondered now why she had resisted the idea for so long. She had never even thought of getting married one day, and she had particularly avoided John because she thought he was after her mine. But she had no more fears about that now. The suggestion he had made sounded perfect to her. He would run her mines for her, but the mines would still belong to her. He no longer even suggested a merger to her, he knew how strongly she felt, and perhaps in time it would make sense to her, but if not, it was no longer important to him. She meant much, much more to him.

And as she swung into her saddle now, her thoughts were filled with him. She rode quickly through the night, and taking all the fastest trails she knew so well, she sailed past her own house and into the night, taking almost no time at all to reach the Harte mine. Just as she passed the main shaft, her horse threw a shoe.

'Damn!' She was already late enough, and as he limped along she had to dismount. She thought of leaving the horse tied to a tree, but you never knew who would come by, and she felt safer walking him the rest of the way to John's and tying him up there. He could always drive her home in his fancy motor car or lend her a horse. She loved riding along with him. She liked everything about the life they had already begun to share.

'Need a ride?' Sabrina almost jumped out of her skin as she heard a voice from behind a tree, and an instant later Dan Richfield appeared, slightly drunk, and leering at her. 'Or would you like me to carry your horse for you?' It was a smart aleck remark and she had no inclination to respond but she didn't want to start something with him now. She knew he was leaving in a day or two, and she had successfully avoided him until then. There was no point starting something now.

'Hello Dan.'

'Don't give me that polite shit, you whore.' At least he wasn't pretending to have changed his views about her. She eyed him now, and then pulled at the horse's bit and moved on, but he followed her. She noticed that he had no horse, and no car. He had probably been sitting there, drinking behind a tree.

'Why don't you just go on, Dan? We have nothing to say to each other now.' It was remarkable to think that she had known him all her life. It was incredible that he had turned out to be so rotten and disloyal. She was glad that her father hadn't lived to see that, and she thought of it now as she turned to him. She wanted to keep him in sight. She wouldn't have wanted to turn her back to him.

'You cost me another job, didn't you, you little bitch?'

'I didn't cost you anything.' She wasn't the young girl she had once been, and her voice was hard, as it often was with the men at her mine. She had learned that lesson long ago, when so many of them had walked out on her. She never treated them like her friends now. They were miners who worked for her, nothing more. She paid them well, and kept up her end of responsibility toward them. But there was a hard edge to her whenever she had to deal with them. A hard edge which belied the softness in her soul. But only John knew that side of her. And Dan never had. He had only known her as a child, but she was a woman now. It was the woman who turned and looked scornfully at him. 'You've cost yourself everything you've ever lost. And if you don't stay off the booze now, you'll lose it all again.'

'Bullshit. That has nothing to do with why Harte's throwing me out of here. And you know that as well as I do.' He tripped, which startled her horse, and they both lurched at the same time. Sabrina pulled sharply on the horse's rein and Dan righted himself and doggedly continued to follow her. She was approaching the first of the cabins now, but no one seemed to notice them and she still had a long way to go to reach John's house. She was wishing that John would materialise and get rid of Dan, but no one did, and Dan went on, following breathlessly. 'He's throwing me out of here because of you.'

'I know nothing about that.' She looked straight ahead and he grabbed her arm and almost pulled her down.

'Like hell you do. I know you've been whoring around with him, and that Indian whore of his . . . I can just imagine what it's like . . . the three of you. . . .' She looked horrified at his words and her jaw dropped, secretly she was still very young.

'How dare you say such a thing! What a disgusting. . . .' But he only laughed and went on.

'What's he giving you for a wedding present, whore? Spring Moon?'

'Stop calling me that!' Her voice quavered as it rose. 'And don't speak of him like that. You're damn lucky he hired you at all after I threw you out.' Her eyes were blazing at him now and he seemed pleased. He had waited three years for this.

'You didn't throw me out. I quit. Or did you forget? About three hundred men and I walked out on you.'

'They may have, but as I recall, you acted like a damn fool.' She didn't have to remind him how, and he looked anything but remorseful as he looked at her. 'Why don't you just take yourself off now? There's no point in all this, Dan.' She didn't want to discuss any of it with him. It was just painful to recall and he was upsetting her, but he was determined not to leave.

'Why? You scared?' He seemed to like the idea and he took a step closer to her, blocking her path and blowing whiskey fumes in her face as she almost reeled.

'I have no reason to be afraid of you.' She was determined to sound calm, but they were in a particularly dark part of the path on the way to John's house, and there was no one around and she felt suddenly very ill at ease. It was one of the rare times she hadn't brought her gun with her as she'd been in a hurry when she'd left and forgotten it in her desk.

'Why not? How come you ain't scared, little whore? Or is this what you like?' He grabbed at his belt as though to pull it off, and off to her right, Sabrina heard a faint rustling in the trees. She wondered if it was an animal, and she felt her horse stir at her side, but she never took her eyes from Dan's.

'You don't impress me, Dan. And if you don't stand aside, I'm going to walk right through you.' And then she smiled. She had taken a shot at him once before, and she knew he would remember it, even if she didn't have the pistol with her now. He couldn't know that. She slid her hand into the pocket of her skirt as though it were there, in her hand, and she watched his eyes travel to her skirt.

'You don't scare me. You ain't got the guts to shoot me from this close up, do you, little girl? Hell no!' He laughed and pulled at her arm, ripping it from the pocket of her skirt and he saw that she had nothing there, and with that he pushed her back and pinned her against a tree. His face was close to hers, and his body was suddenly grinding against her skirt and she could feel her heart pound in her ears. She attempted to jerk a knee into his groin, but he anticipated her and grabbed her by her shirt, flinging her to the ground. A moment later he was on top of her, pulling at her shirt, and tearing at her breasts with one hand, as the other pulled up her skirt. She screamed and he silenced her with a slap so hard across her face that blood ran down her cheek and she looked at him with wild eyes as she felt his hand at her crotch as she tried to roll away from him and he pinned her down again. 'I should have done this years ago, little whore. You've screwed me out of everything I could have ever had, and now I'm going to screw you. . . . I worked for that bastard father of yours for years, ever since I was a child, and what do I get for it . . . you, you little bitch, doing everything I wanted to do.' He was half crying as he rent her skirt in two, revealing the pantaloons Hannah had made, as Sabrina scrambled through the dirt and cried out again, but there was no one close enough to hear, and he wrestled her to the ground again. It was incredible that on the edge of the compound surrounding the Harte Mines, she was about to be raped by a drunken lunatic and there was no one to help.

He had torn her blouse and her corset off by then, and her firm young breasts were icy cold in the breeze, her nipples rigid with fear as he tore at them. She struggled to her knees again, and this time he grabbed her by the hair as he had once before, and forced her face into the dirt as he tore her pantaloons in half, leaving an opening more than wide enough for him, as he began to tear at his belt again. Suddenly he stopped as though he weren't sure that was what he wanted to do. He stared at Sabrina unseeingly, dropped his hand from her hair, and then from his belt as he still stared at her and she looked up at him unbelievingly, unable to understand what had happened to him, as he pitched slowly toward the ground, where he fell face first. Then, with a gasp, Sabrina saw the reason he had lost interest in her. There was a long evil-looking knife with a ferocious-looking blade sticking out of his back with a delicately carved ivory handle, and behind him stood Spring Moon, silently looking down at her.

'Oh! . . .' She covered her breasts with her hands, and struggled to her feet. Dan was dead. Sabrina knew it from the way he looked, and she stood in front of the Indian girl she had watched for so many years, half naked, in torn clothes, one shoe off, one shoe on, her face streaked with tears, the blood from her face dripping onto her bare breast. Spring Moon beckoned to her. She didn't come too close, and she never touched the trembling girl. There were sobs caught in Sabrina's throat and she couldn't speak, she was making frightened gurgling sounds. Spring Moon picked Sabrina's skirt up out of the dirt, and handed it to her to wrap around herself, and then she gently took the horse's rein and beckoned again.

'Come. It is cold here. I will take you to John.' Sabrina stumbled behind her, wondering what would happen to Dan where he lay, what they would do. She couldn't even begin to think about what had almost happened to her, or of what Spring Moon had done, or the good fortune that had put her on the same path tonight or had kept her from leaving for another week. Sabrina realized now that it was she that she must have heard behind the tree, not an animal. The only animal had been Dan, and she shuddered from head to foot, as Spring Moon stopped in a dark place and turned to Sabrina again. 'I will go to John Harte and bring him here. You stay.' She pointed to her, but Sabrina began to shiver harder than before and began to choke on her own tears.

'Don't leave me here . . . I can't . . . Don't . . . please . . .' Her eyes were young and wild as the Indian woman watched, and then with a long gentle hand, she reached out to her.

'He is there.' She pointed to a house only a few yards away, but she didn't want to risk leading her past any of the men. She wanted to bring John here, to Sabrina, and then she herself would disappear. Spring Moon was, above all things, discreet. 'We will hear you now, if anyone comes to you. You are safe.' Her face was so gentle, her voice so soft, as Sabrina stared at her. She wanted to be held in the smooth brown arms, to be cradled and rocked. She could easily see the comfort John had found there for so many years, and then she remembered the things Dan Richfield had said and wondered if anyone else thought that. She began to cry again. She was no longer a woman now, only a frightened child and she didn't want John to see her like this. She sank to the ground on her knees, with the skirt pulled over her as she sobbed and Spring Moon knelt beside her. 'You are safe now. You will always be safe with him.' They were powerful words and Sabrina looked up at her. She knew it was true, but it reminded her of all that Spring Moon was giving up, and she seemed to be leaving him so peacefully. 'You must always be very kind to him.' Sabrina looked at her with enormous eyes as she nodded her head through her tears.

'I will. I promise you.' And then her voice broke and she could barely speak. It had been the most difficult evening of her life, except perhaps the night that her father died. 'I will be good to him . . . I'm sorry . . . you have to go. . . .'

Spring Moon held up a hand. 'It is time for me. I was never his wife. Only his friend. You will be a wife to him. He needs you very much, little one.' It was the same thing John called her. 'You will be a good wife to him. I go to call him now.' And before Sabrina could stop her, she disappeared, and a moment later, she started at the sound of running feet. There were half a dozen of them, and then a shout. 'Stop dammit! Stop, all of you!' She recognized John's voice, some garbled words, and then, 'Where? . . . All right, the rest of you go back . . . oh my God. . . .' And then the pounding of feet again, and then suddenly he was standing there, looking down at her, as she shivered, and knelt huddled beneath her skirt. He had a blanket in his hands, which Spring Moon had given to him before leading the men away. She had told them where Dan Richfield lay with the knife in his back, and they had gone to look for him. 'Oh my God. . . .' John's voice was gentle in the night air, and she lowered her eyes, she could not look at him. . . .

'No . . . no . . . please . . . don't . . .' She wanted to tell him not to look at her, but she couldn't say the words. She could only sob and cling to his legs, and suddenly the horror of what had almost happened came down on her with its full force. The tears washed the blood from her cheek, and he wrapped her in the blanket like a very small child and swung her up in his arms, cooing softly to her as he had to his little girl long, long ago, and he walked her into his house and set her down on the leather couch in the living room. He looked at the damage to her face then, and the look in her eyes, and if Spring Moon hadn't already done it for him, he knew he would have killed Dan. But Spring Moon had told him quickly and bluntly that the girl hadn't been raped, not yet, and he was grateful for that. But had her knife missed its mark or taken a moment longer to pierce his flesh . . . he shuddered at the thought, and knelt on the floor beside where she lay.

'Little one, how could I let this happen to you? You'll never go anywhere alone again. I promise you that. I'm going to send a bodyguard everywhere with you. I'll be your bodyguard . . . this will never happen again. . . .' But the main reason that it never would was that Dan Richfield was dead. The knife had gone right through his heart and he had died instantly. Spring Moon had an extraordinary hand with a knife as he knew full well.

'If it hadn't been for her. . . .' Sabrina began to catch her breath as she took a sip of the whiskey-laced tea he was forcing her to drink, and she tried not to think of how she looked. She was still hunched beneath the blanket he had brought out to her. Spring Moon had gone to retrieve her clothes and soon brought them to John before disappearing again. He was looking at her now as though he had almost lost what he cherished most. What if Dan had killed her, the thought was more than he could bear, and there were tears in his eyes as he turned to her again. 'I'll never let anything happen to you. Never. Do you understand that? I'll never let you out of my sight. . . .' She stretched a trembling hand out to him and took his hand.

'It wasn't your fault, it was mine.' She was regaining her composure now, but she would have been unable to stand up, her knees were still shaking so hard. 'It was an old fight he had with me. It could have happened anywhere. It's a wonder he didn't come to find me at the mine long ago. He hated my guts, that was all . . . and you know yourself, this almost happened before. I was lucky it didn't happen then, and luckier still that Spring Moon happened along tonight.' And then she looked at John. She knew that some of his men had come to the door to speak to him a short while before. 'Is he dead?'

John nodded his head. 'He is. The knife went through his heart.'

'Will anything happen to her?' Sabrina knew it could. Spring Moon had been defending her, but she was an Indian girl and the law could take a dim view of it. But John had already thought of that before Sabrina did.

'She'll be on the train to South Dakota tonight. And his body was found on the path . . . he wasn't well-liked. . . .' John sounded convincing to her and she knew he wouldn't be questioned by the law. They would take his word for it, and the knife would have disappeared. 'You have nothing to worry about.' He sounded stronger and quieter than she had ever heard him before, and she had never felt so protected in her life. 'And neither does she. You're both safe, and he deserved exactly what he got. I'm only sorry I trusted him once.'

259

'So did I.' A thousand memories flashed through her mind at once, followed by the hideous image of him tearing her clothes off her back, and a sob caught in her throat again as she squeezed her eyes shut, but John came to her again and held her tight in his arms.

'I'm going to take you home now.' He left the blanket wrapped around her and carried her gently out to his car. Then he drove her home and carried her upstairs to her bedroom. Hannah was waiting for her, her lips pursed, and her eyes wide as she saw them come in.

'What happened to her?' She was like a worried mother hen.

'She's all right.' He told her about Dan then, and she was horrified.

'The sonofabitch. I hope he hangs.' He didn't tell her he was already dead, she'd find out soon enough.

'Thank God someone stopped him in time.'

'You've got good men.'

'And good friends.' There were other women who would have let Sabrina be raped. Spring Moon was losing the man she had loved for many years, but she had protected his bride like her own child, and he was grateful to her. There would be a handsome gift to her, there already had been, and he would put her on the train himself that night. It meant driving 'til dawn to make the connection for her, but it was important to get her out of town in case someone talked, and once she was gone, there would be no harm done. He looked down at Hannah now and patted her arm. 'Take care of my little girl.' And she was almost that to him, twenty-eight years younger than he, she seemed almost like a child to him, except that he also knew how powerful she was, how capable and strong. She would be alright again, and he would keep her safe for the rest of her life. It was what he had promised her, and promised himself before that.

And what he promised again on their wedding day, two months after that, as she stood in the church in Saint Helena, looking happily at him, with their men eight hundred strong almost hanging from the rafters of the church, crowded in, pressed together like sardines, some unable to get in at all and watching the ceremony through the open windows as they exchanged their vows. Even those who had abandoned her years before had come today, if not for love of her, then for love of John. Hannah cried openly throughout the ceremony, and both Sabrina and John had tears in their eyes more than once.

There was an enormous open air reception planned in the

compound of the Thurston Mines. There was nowhere else that would accommodate them all, especially with their children and wives, and Sabrina had wanted to include them all.

'You only get married once, you know.' She had smiled happily at him when they were making their plans, although she knew it wasn't true for him. But it was hard to realize that he had been married to someone else before. She had never known his wife, as Matilda had died more than two years before she was born. It was strange to think of him that way, married to someone else, with two children. It was almost as though he were a different man back then. She could envision him more easily with Spring Moon, because she had so often seen him with her over the years, but even that seemed hard to remember now. It was more as though he had never belonged to anyone but her, and as they took the steamer to San Francisco that night, he smiled down at her and took her hand.

'What did I ever do to deserve a child like you at my side, Sabrina Harte?' She liked the sound of her new name, and she smiled happily up at him.

'I'm the lucky one, John Harte.'

'I know better than that.'

He had offered her a trip to anywhere she wished, as their honeymoon, but she had surprised him by saying that all she wanted was to spend time with him in Thurston House, and they planned to do just that. He had arranged to spend a month in town with her there. They would stay until the Christmas holidays, and then return to Napa to take their businesses in hand. But they had no business on their mind that night, as they arrived at Thurston House well after midnight. She had asked her banker to hire a small, temporary staff for her and the house was ablaze with light. When John followed her upstairs, they found the enormous canopied bed turned down in the master suite and a fire roaring in the hearth. There were candles lit and flowers in enormous vases everywhere. The house had never looked more beautiful to her, and as she looked at the bed that had been her mother's so long ago, and hers after that, she realized that it was her marriage bed tonight, and with a shy look in her eyes she turned to John.

'Welcome home.' Her voice was whisper soft, and he took her hand and led her back downstairs. They drank champagne in front of the fire in the living room, and at last he saw her suppress a yawn. He carried her upstairs, and deposited her in her dressing room. She had already shown him his portion of the master suite and his bags had been unpacked. He appeared a while later in his dressing gown, smiling gently at her. She looked like a fairy princess in a pale pink satin dressing gown, and when it fell from her shoulders beside the bed, her hair looked like ebony as it draped over the ivory silk of her flesh. Swiftly he blew the candles out and the room was lit by the warm glow of the fire.

'Is it very strange to be here, alone with me?' He asked her as they slid into bed.

'A little bit. I am so used to being here alone. . . .' But it was not only that. She had had no contact with any man, had kissed no one but him, and the only other man who had ever approached her had, of course, been Dan. Now she was John's wife, and it was her wedding night, and all the seriousness and skill she had, the strength with which she ran the mine meant nothing at all. She was delicate and vulnerable, and more than a little bit afraid of what was in store for her, and he realized that there had been no one at all to talk to her about what was about to happen between them except the old housekeeper, and perhaps no one had said anything at all. It touched him to the quick to realize that and he cradled her in his arms like a child, but the longing that he felt for her as he held her close to him was not what one felt for a child.

'Sabrina. . . .' He didn't know how to begin to ask her what he wanted to know. Spring Moon had been so wise when she had come to him, and there had been other women before and after her, but they were none of them young girls . . . Matilda had of course been a virgin so long before . . . but they had both been eighteen years old . . . and now he lay beside this child . . . this girl . . . and she belonged to him. He looked down at her tenderly, 'Has anyone spoken to you?'

She smiled softly up at him, her face turned to a pale rose by the fire's glow. 'I think I know. . . .' She trusted him, and she knew she always would, and should have years ago.

'But has no one explained it to you?' She shook her head, and he kissed her lips, her cheeks, her eyes, and then her lips again. He had to restrain himself, she brought something out in him that he had never known before. 'Sabrina, I love you so.' He whispered the words in her hair, and she arched her body up toward his.

262

'Then that's all I need to know.' And with the utmost gentleness he took her hand and slowly kissed her palm, her waist, the inside of her arm, until at last he reached her breast, and the silk of her flesh as he followed it down to the inside of her thigh and then back again, and by morning, as they lay side by side in the master suite of Thurston House, he had taught her all she would ever need to know.

Chapter Twenty-Six

They returned to Saint Helena on New Year's Day, and by then they had resolved where they would live. It seemed simpler to move into the house Jeremiah had built so long ago for the girl who died. The honeycomb of bedrooms on the third floor would be perfect for them when the babies began to come, and Sabrina insisted that she wanted two or three of them or more, and John would groan and then laugh at her.

'At my age? They'll think that I'm their grandfather! How will I keep up with them?'

She smiled knowingly at him and touched his ear with her lips as she whispered to him. 'You seemed to have no trouble keeping up with anyone last night.'

'That's beside the point.' He looked delightedly at her. She was a dream come true in every way.

'I didn't think it was, myself.' They laughed together a great deal of the time, and talked constantly about the myriad interests they shared. She showed him everything about the Thurston Mines and introduced him to all her men. They spent three days together every week in her office there, while she joined him at his own mines for the rest of the week. He had an excellent new foreman at the Harte Mines, and now he only wanted to get hers in hand. He had a foreman in mind to run hers too, so that he, in turn, could become a sort of overlord, overseeing their joint domain.

'And eventually, we might even be able to spend most of our time in town.' He seemed to like the idea and she did too. She had no particular hunger for the social life they could have shared there, but she was very fond of all things cultural. They had gone to the opera, a visiting ballet, and several plays during their honeymoon, and they both enjoyed the splendor of the magnificent house her father had built.

'It always made me sad when I thought of it . . .' she told him one night. 'He built it all for her, and then two and a half years later she died. Somehow it didn't seem fair.'

John nodded, thinking of the distant past. 'He was an enormous help to me when Matilda and the children died,' it no longer hurt as much to think of them, it had been so long ago, and he had Sabrina now, and perhaps more children one day. That was their fondest hope. 'I was so sad for him when I heard that it happened to him, but he wouldn't see anyone then, you know. I went to see him once and he brushed me off. I think it was still too painful for him, and I understood.' John smiled and shook his head, thinking back on his youth. 'I wasn't very nice to him in those days, and your father was such a decent man. Kind and wise, and terribly modest, given all he had,' and he had taught the same virtues to his child, John had been pleased to find, but he had known all that about her before he married her. 'I was so determined to make it on my own back then, that I insisted on keeping my distance from him. It's too bad, I had an awful lot to learn.'

'I think he liked you anyway.' She smiled. 'In a funny way, you're a lot like him.' She had noticed that before she married him, but she saw it even more now, the patience, the gentleness, the tender ways, combined with the sharp mind. They were enjoying being at each other's mines and she was trying to teach him about her wines, but he didn't have much time. He enjoyed drinking them, but there were fewer bottles to drink now. There was a blight in the vineyards, and that summer she had lost more than half of her vines, and others had lost even more. 'It's rotten luck,' she had been very upset, but they had so many other things to do, the house in Napa to change subtly for him, the changes to make at the mines, Thurston House to open and keep staffed with a small crew for when they chose to visit there, and they had to learn each other's ways. They were both surprised at how easily they adapted to each other, and the only disappointment that they shared was that no matter how often they made love, or how energetically, by the following summer there was still no baby on the way, and Hannah questioned her about it one day.

'You're not using anything, are you?'

'What do you mean?' Sabrina looked confused. Despite her marriage to John, she was still innocent, and she knew only what he had explained to her. There was no one else to tell her those things, and never had been. Amelia might have perhaps, but Sabrina hadn't seen her in two years, although she had sent a spectacular wedding gift to them and was thrilled for her. So, Sabrina had no idea what Hannah was talking about.

'You know, you're not preventing the babies from coming, are you?'

'Can you do that?' She looked stunned, and Hannah narrowed her eyes at her, and then realized the girl really didn't know. She was pleased. She was a decent girl, not like her mother before her. She still remembered the gold rings she'd found. 'I didn't know . . . can one . . .' She had always wondered what certain women did . . . like those who made a profession of it, or . . . 'What do they do?' She was intrigued by the knowledge she was about to gain, although she had no desire to stop anything. On the contrary, she and John both wanted a child very much.

'Some use slippery elm, like the girls up here, but there are fancier things.' It sounded repulsive to Sabrina. Slippery elm? She made a face and Hannah laughed. 'Them what can afford it use gold rings.' She paused and decided what the hell. She was a grown woman now. 'Like your mother did.'

'My mother did that?' Sabrina looked surprised. 'When?'

'Before she had you. Your Daddy thought she wanted a baby as much as he did, but he was a lot older than her.' The age difference was even greater between her and John. 'She told him she couldn't understand what was wrong. They'd been married for more than a year by then, and I found one in her bathroom one day . . . one of them damn rings . . . and I gave it to him.' She grinned almost evilly. 'And then you came along pretty quick after that. She was sicker'n a dog by the time they went back to town.' And somehow what Hannah said really bothered her. It sounded so unkind. As though her mother had been trapped into having her. Her heart suddenly went out to her.

'What did my father say?'

'He was mad as fire, and then he never said much after that. He was satisfied as soon as he knew you were on the way.' She seemed almost proud of what she'd done, and for an instant, thinking of poor Camille, caught in her perfidy, Sabrina hated the old woman for foiling her. It wasn't fair. She should have been allowed to wait if that was what she wanted to do. But then again, since she had died so

266

soon after that, perhaps Destiny had chosen well . . . but twenty-three years later, her daughter felt sorry for her. Sabrina had just turned twenty-two that spring.

'What did my mother do?'

'Mope . . . sulk . . .' Hannah thought back and knew that she had never forgiven him, but she didn't tell Sabrina that. 'She was a young fool, he married her after all, he had a right to babies if that was what he wanted from her . . . damn gold rings . . . he got them all from her and broke them and threw them out and she cried like a child . . .' Sabrina felt her heart turn over inside her at the thought . . . poor girl . . . and she told John about it that night.

'It sounds so brutal of him. And wrong of Hannah to interfere. She shouldn't have told him. She should have told her, and let her go to him.'

'Maybe she was fooling him.'

'That's what Hannah seemed to think, but I'm not sure I believe that. Hannah has always said unkind things about my mother from time to time, there must have been some kind of jealousy between them. She had worked for my father for twenty years before my mother arrived. I suppose that was part of it.'

'Anyway, I'm personally very glad she found that ring.' He smiled at his wife, and then wondered something. 'What made her tell you that?'

Sabrina blushed and smiled at him. 'She asked me if I was using something to keep from . . . I didn't even know you could.' She looked less embarrassed then. There seemed to be nothing she couldn't say to him. He was her very dearest friend. 'You never told me that.'

'I didn't think you cared.' He seemed surprised that she did now.

'No, but it's interesting.' And then he laughed at her, and pinched her cheek.

'My little innocent. Is there anything else you want to know?'

'Yes,' she looked sadly at him for a moment or two, 'but you don't have the answer, I'm afraid, my love,' and they knew that he had had two children before so the problem wasn't his. 'I wonder why it hasn't happened yet.'

'It will, in time. Be patient, my love. We've only been married for nine months.'

She looked woefully at him. 'I should have a baby in my arms by now.'

He smiled at her. 'You have me instead. Will that do for a while?'

'Forever, my love.' He pulled her into his arms again and their lips met and she forgot everything that Hannah had said to her that afternoon, but she thought of it again once or twice over the next six months, but it took even longer than that for her to conceive. It was their second July when she got up one day, and felt ill almost instantly. They had been married for nineteen months by then, and Sabrina had just turned twenty-three years old. The heat was overpowering that day and she had worked at the mine with him the day before, insisting still that she didn't want to merge the Harte and Thurston Mines and they could still run the two enterprises separately. One of their rare quarrels had ensued, and between that and the stifling heat, she had barely slept all night.

'Are you all right?' He glanced over at her as she got out of bed.

'More or less.' There was still a relative chill between them from the night before, and then slowly she turned to him, but before she said another word, he watched her sink slowly to the floor, and as he leapt from the bed, he found her unconscious there.

'Sabrina . . . Sabrina . . . darling . . .' He was horrified, and always the spectre of the dreaded flu haunted him. He sent for the doctor at once who found no particularly frightening sign of anything.

'She's probably just tired, or maybe she's been working too hard.' John delivered her a lecture that night, it was time she left the new foreman alone. He would oversee him himself, and she could amuse herself with her vines, although that wasn't much fun these days. The blight had got worse. But she didn't seem to be listening to him, picking at her food. She fell asleep instantly as they sat in the swing that night, and he carried her up to bed without waking her. He was worried about the way she looked and even more so the next day when she fainted again. But this time he took her straight to Napa and booked a cabin on the steamer into town. The next morning he had her at the hospital, and a team of doctors went over her while John Harte paced the halls.

'Well?' John pounced on the first man to leave her room, and the doctor smiled.

'I'd say March myself, although one of my colleagues thinks February.' For an instant, John didn't understand, but from the cryptic smile on the man's face, he suddenly realized.

'You mean . . .'

'I do. She's expecting, my friend.'

268

You could have heard his shouts halfway across town, and he bought Sabrina an enormous diamond ring and gave it to her that night at Thurston House when he took her home. They had already decided to have the baby born there and John wanted her near all the fine doctors in town. But they had told him that she didn't have to leave Napa until December, so they had lots of time. And the delirious pair spent the night talking about it, the names for a son . . . those for a little girl . . . how she wanted to do the baby's room, and time and time again she threw her arms around John. 'I'm the happiest woman alive.'

He smiled. '. . . married to the happiest man.' And Hannah was ecstatic for them when they returned to Napa the next day. Now Sabrina did exactly as she was told. She stayed out of the mines almost every day, and even gave the new foreman her horse to ride. She spent long afternoons resting on her bed, and waiting for John to come home, sitting comfortably in the swing. When autumn came, the baby began to show just a little bit, and John would put his head on her at night, hoping to feel it move, but it was still too soon. She felt it first as the leaves began to turn, and he hadn't felt it yet, a week later, when one of his men came pounding on the door one night.

'Fire at the mine!' The words rang out in the night, and Sabrina heard him first and had the presence of mind to hang out the window and ask,

'Which one?'

'Yours!' the unfamiliar figure said, and she threw on her clothes as quickly as John did, but he put a firm hand on her arm.

'You stay here, Sabrina. I don't want any nonsense from you. I'll handle it.'

'I've got to come.' She had never stayed home when she was needed before. She could nurse her men, or at least be there, but John was firm.

'No! Stay here!' And without saying another word and only a quick kiss he left her there, to pace frantically for the next six hours. By morning she saw the dark smoke filling the sky and there was still no word from them and she could stand it no more. She took out the car and headed quickly for the mine as Hannah shouted from the porch.

'You'll kill yourself! Think of the child!' But she was thinking of John. She had to make sure he was all right, it was her mine after all, and her responsibility. When she arrived she saw the destruction that had been wrought and he was nowhere in sight. The foreman told her that he was in one of the shafts, rescuing men with a team and they had been down for more than an hour. She watched frantically as no one emerged, and a fresh explosion filled the air. Unable to bear it anymore, she rushed into the mine, and saw them trapped. She went back outside for help, and a dozen men went inside to pull the trapped miners out as she felt the smoke fill her lungs. She saw John emerge and sank to her knees gratefully, the smoke overcoming her as she fell. They carried her into the office where she had worked for more than three years and the doctor came to her at once. She seemed all right after a little while, and John berated her. He had one of the men drive her home, and that night, filthy and reeking of the pungent smoke, he came home himself, but he found Hannah grimfaced on the porch, and with tears running down her cheeks she told him the news. He rushed upstairs and found her there, sobbing, pale, heartbroken as she clung to him. She had lost the baby only an hour before.

'And I know I'll never have another one . . .' Her despair was bottomless and he pressed her to him, covering her with the soot that covered him but neither of them cared and his tears mixed with her own.

'Did the doctor tell you that?' She shook her head and sobbed again. 'Then don't think that, my love. There will be another one.' He looked gently down at her. 'And next time you'll do as I say.' But he didn't want to press the point with her as she felt guilty enough as it was. It was a full two months before she was herself again, before she laughed at something he said, before that look of constant sorrow left her eyes like a gnawing pain which she could not escape. It was a difficult Christmas for them both, but in January he took her to New York with him. They saw Amelia several times and stopped in Chicago to see friends of his on the way home. It was the first time John had seen her happy in weeks and he was relieved although he was disappointed for her that she was slow to conceive again this time. It was another two years before he saw her look just that way again . . . pale, and somehow ill, without actually being sick. They had both stopped talking about it, and Sabrina had abandoned all hope. They had been married for exactly four years, and it was on their anniversary that he thought she looked peculiar, and when he offered her a glass of champagne, she turned green.

'I think it's something I ate . . .' She looked at him and ran from the room, and the next day when he disagreed with her, she burst into tears, slammed out of the room and was sound asleep when he came to bed that night. He had seen it all before, but wasn't quite sure when, and then instinctively within a matter of days he knew, long before she did, or at least long before she would allow herself to hope. Finally, when there was no doubt whatsoever in his mind, he mentioned it to her. 'I think you're wrong.' She tried to brush him off, reading the reports he had brought home from the mine. She was very bored these days. He was handling everything and the mines were doing very well.

'I don't think I am.' He looked pleased with himself, and with her, certain that there was good reason to be.

'But I feel fine.' She looked at him, annoyed, and then stalked out of the room. It wasn't until they went to bed that night that he mentioned it again.

'Don't be afraid, little one. Why don't we find out? I'll go with you.'

But she shook her head and tears filled her eyes. 'I don't want to know.'

'Why not?' He held her close, and he already knew what the answer would be.

'I don't want to get my hopes up again. What if . . .' She choked on the words, and her tears spilled onto his arm. 'Oh John . . .'

'Come on, little love. We have to find out, don't we? And everything will be fine this time.' He smiled reassuringly at her and the next day he took her to the hospital again, and he had been right. The baby was due in July, and they were both ecstatic. They couldn't believe their good fortune, and this time John all but confined her to bed, and she cooperated fully with him. She didn't want to take any chances with this baby, and John practically wrapped Sabrina in cotton wool. They went back to Napa in January, but by April he brought her into town for the last three months. He wanted the expectant mother close to the doctors there, and she was comfortable at Thurston House, while he commuted to the mines several days a week. He bought a Dusenberg and hired a chauffeur to drive her around town as he didn't want her driving herself. She was following the news in Europe avidly, and they both wondered if there would be

271

a war there. Things seemed unpleasantly tense, but John was almost certain that things would calm down again.

'And if they don't?' She lay in their enormous bed one morning in June, looking over the paper at him, and he smiled at her. She looked like a large round ball, and he loved to put a hand on her and feel the baby kick. It was an active one this time. Barnaby had been like that thirty-two years before, and he still remembered it now. But he was even more elated about this child. It was difficult to be serious and listen to the political questions his wife was posing to him. 'What if there's a war?'

'There won't be. Not for us anyway. And,' he smiled at her, 'now you can discover the benefits of being married to an old man, my love. I don't have to worry about that anymore. They wouldn't take me.'

'That's good.' She smiled. 'I want you right here with me, and our son.'

'What makes you think it's a boy?' John grinned at her, he had that feeling, too, and they both wanted a boy, at least the first time. After that, they wanted a girl, if there was another one. But after all their fears, it had been a surprisingly easy pregnancy. She was still young. She had just turned twenty-six, and even though she insisted that she was practically a crone, she was young enough to have an easy time with the birth and John hoped she would. He had wanted her to go to hospital, but she insisted on having the baby at home, but he wasn't sure yet if he'd give in to her. He looked at her now, and repeated his question with a smile. 'Why a boy?'

'His big feet.' She pointed at the protruberance pushing out on the right side of the enormous balloon that was her mid-section now. 'You know, sometimes I wonder if he'll stay in there right until the end. He's been feeling awfully impatient to me.' But when her due date came and went on the twenty-first of July, she was proven wrong, and she began to grow impatient to see their child. 'Why doesn't he come out?' She was strolling through the gardens of Thurston House with John one night. 'He's already six days late.'

'Maybe he's a girl. Ladies are never on time.' Her husband smiled and patted the hand she'd tucked into his arm, noticing that her step was slower than usual tonight. As she climbed the stairs to their room, she seemed more out of breath than she had before. She was growing more enormous every day, and he was getting worried about her. 'What if the baby's too big?' he had secretly asked the doctor the week before. 'Then we take it out. It's very simple these days.' John wondered if she would have to have a Caesarean in the end, he hoped not, but the baby looked huge to him, and in comparison Sabrina seemed so small. She had narrow hips and a small back, and it terrified John to think of the baby tearing through her on the way out. It had been difficult with Matilda thirty years before and she had been a big, healthy, country girl. Sabrina looked more frail to him, and he was older and wiser now. He was fifty-four years old, madly in love with his wife, and he was worried about everything. 'Can I get you something to drink?' He noticed that she was squirming in bed as she sat reading a book later that night, and she had been restless all day. It was seasonably warm, and the stars were out in full force. It was unusual for the fog not to have come in. And she looked at him with a smile and then she sighed.

'I'm getting tired of this, my love.' She pointed at her giant belly, and he touched it gently with one hand, which met with an immediate and very hearty kick.

'At least he's in good form tonight.'

'That's more than I can say for me. My back hurts, my legs ache, I can't sit up, I can't lie down, I can't breathe.' He remembered hearing all that a lifetime before, but she really looked miserable as he rubbed her back just before they turned off the lights. He knew that most men no longer shared their wives' beds at this point, but he hated being away from her, and she insisted that she didn't mind sleeping with him. 'Do you suppose people would be shocked if they could see us now?' They were lying with his arm around her, and her head on his chest, but it was comforting for her.

'So what if they would be. I'm happy, aren't you?'

'Yes.' She smiled as he turned off the light, and she looked out at the stars beyond. It was a beautiful night, the twenty-seventh of July, 1914, and, just as she began to fall asleep, awkwardly on her side, turned toward John, she felt a sharp kick, and then a slow, unpleasant twinge. She opened her eyes, looked at John, sound asleep at her side, already snoring softly, and snuggled closer to him. Her back hurt more than it had before, and as she tried to shift her weight, she felt another twinge again. Within an hour, she felt as though she had the kind of cramps she hadn't had in months, and when she sat up to catch her breath, there was a sudden gush of water between her legs

273

and the bed was suddenly drenched. She was mortified when John woke up, and turned on the light, looking sleepily at her.

'Did you spill something?' And then suddenly, as he looked at her he knew what had happened, as she shook her head, blushing to the roots of her hair, but he covered her awkwardness and pulled her gently toward him. 'Don't you worry about that. Everything's going to be just fine.' He beamed at her, got up, brought her an armful of towels and rang for the maid, as he tied his blue silk robe around himself. 'I'll get Mary to change the bed. Why don't you sit over here?' He helped her to a chair nearby and watched her face as the cramps pulled at her again. 'What do you feel, love?'

She blushed again. He was so open with her, and it seemed odd to be telling him, but she was more comfortable with him than she was with anyone. 'Rather like monthly cramps.'

'Is that normal?' Matilda had never been as descriptive with him, and he remembered the baby Sabrina had lost, but it was too late for that to happen now.

'I don't know. I'm not sure. The doctor just said to call when the pains began. Do you suppose this is it?' He looked at the flooded bed and smiled at his wife.

'I'd say it is. Just think,' he tried to take her mind off the pain he saw furrowing her brow, 'in a few hours, you'll have our baby in your arms.' It was a wonderful thought, and as Mary arrived to change the bed, he went to call the doctor they'd engaged, returning a few minutes later with a cup of tea. The doctor was sending both nurses that he had hired for her, and he had told John to keep her calm, to keep her in bed, to keep her lying flat, and to feed her nothing at all. But she didn't look interested in food when he returned to the room and found her leaning against a chair, holding her huge belly with both hands and her teeth clenched. 'The doctor's on the way, sweetheart. Let's get you into bed.' She was grateful to lie down, and more grateful still to be having the baby at home. She hadn't wanted to go to hospital, and it meant a great deal to her to give birth to their child at Thurston House, so John had finally indulged her whim, but he was prepared to rush her to the hospital if need be. But when the two nurses arrived in less than an hour, they announced that all was going well and shooed John from the room. Sabrina cried when he left, 'Can't you stay?' She trusted him more than anyone else, and she wanted him there, it was her house after all, but the two nurses wouldn't hear of it.

'I don't think I should.' He looked gently down at her damp face, her eyes already slightly glazed. The pains seemed to be coming very quickly from what he could see. He heard her cry out as he left the room, and he began to pace outside, listening for her sounds, and he stood riveted to the spot when an hour later, he heard her scream. He pounded nervously on the door and the elder of the two nurses scolded him.

'She mustn't have any noise!' she whispered loudly at him with a stern face beneath her starched coif.

'Why not? There's nothing wrong with her ears.' But suddenly he heard her groan again, and he couldn't bear it anymore. Pushing his way into the room, he found her lying there, her nightgown pulled up to reveal the enormous abdomen, but it didn't seem shocking to him and he reached across the bed for her hand and spoke to her soothingly as the next pain came. The nurses were appalled, and the doctor arrived just then and looked more than a little startled to see John in the room.

'Well, what have we here?' He attempted to pretend that he wasn't surprised by what was going on, but it was obvious that he wanted John out of the room, although he wasn't at all anxious to leave, and Sabrina seemed to be clinging to him. She didn't even seem to care that she was only covered now by a thin sheet, and the sheet seemed to part company with her frequently when she was in pain, but she appeared to notice nothing at all. She had a hunted look now, and she was panting desperately as each pain came. Then suddenly she jerked forward and attempted to sit up, screwing her face up horribly, as the nurses pushed her back. The doctor, totally forgetting John, went to her, pulled back the sheet, looked at her most private parts, as she shouted John's name. As the doctor examined her, she screamed hideously. There was suddenly a film of sweat on John Harte's face as he watched his wife, and he wanted to clutch her to him but there was nothing he could do at all as she writhed on the bed, and finally the doctor indicated that he wanted to talk to him, and they left the room. But Sabrina panicked as they left, and it was only after another pain that John joined the doctor in the hall, and he wanted to know what was going on.

The doctor spoke in a quiet voice. 'It's going very well, Mr. Harte. But you're going to have to leave her alone with us. It's just too much for you to see. I can't let you do that, for her sake as well as yours.

You've got to leave the room now, and let us get to work.'

'Doing what?' John Harte looked at him angrily. 'She's doing all the work, and she doesn't mind having me there. You don't understand, I'm the only family she has, I'm her closest friend . . . and she's everything to me. I've been on farms before, I know how calves and foals get born.'

The doctor looked shocked. 'This is your wife, Mr. Harte.'

'I'm well aware of that, Dr. Snowe. And I don't want to let her down.'

'Then leave her to us. That's why you hired us, I believe.'

John hesitated, not sure what to do. He wanted to be with Sabrina, if she wanted him, but not if it embarrassed her. He didn't care what anyone thought, he was too old for that. To hell with Dr. Snowe, but he looked into the man's eyes now. 'If she asks for me, I'm coming in. This is my house, and my wife, and my child being born.' The doctor looked outraged, but he only pursed his lips.

'Very well.'

'Is it going well?'

'I'd say it is, but I also don't think it will be soon, and she has to marshal her strength. It could be a very long night,' he glanced outside at the sun coming up and almost smiled, 'a long day, I should say. I don't think your baby will be born before dinnertime.' He glanced at his pocket watch and there was a stirring from the room.

'How can you say that?'

'Because I know how things are. And I know how babies are born.' And you do not, were the unspoken words.

'But she seems so . . . so far along . . .' John was suddenly worried about her again.

'I'm afraid not.'

He felt like banging his head against the wall as the doctor disappeared into the room again, and for the next five hours, John thought he would go mad as he paced up and down the hall, up and down the stairs, up and down the house. He drank two brandies and then a scotch, and he wished he could give one to her but that really would have caused an uproar. At two o'clock, he sat forlornly on the stairs, beneath the stained glass dome, with his head down, thinking about her. The nurses had come in and out several times, and the doctor had only come out once to give him a report that things were going well but it would still be a while, and finally at four o'clock in the afternoon John thought he heard her voice, saying something in a loud, sharp tone, and then she groaned and he ran to the bedroom door and stood just outside as he heard a terrible moaning sound and a stifled scream. He wanted to pound on the door and call her name, but he was afraid he would frighten her, but more than that he wanted to hold her in his arms, and then as he stood there, he heard her voice again and this time there was no stifling the scream, and he couldn't bear it anymore. He let himself quietly into the room and no one saw him at first. The blinds were drawn, and the curtains blocked all light from the room. There was a bright light on the table beside her bed, another on a table near her feet, and there seemed to be a stifling heat everywhere, and she lay in their bed, her legs spread apart, a sheet over her, her face drenched in sweat, her hair matted to her head, her eyes rolled back, clutching the sheets as another pain seized her. Her voice rose agonizingly again, and the doctor lifted the sheet and John could see hair and a little round head, and his jaw dropped as he watched silently. He wanted to cheer her on as she pushed instinctively, and there was blood spurting from a wound between her legs, but John couldn't even think of that now, all he could think of was that tiny head, and the miraculous woman who was pushing it out. She screamed again and the nurses encouraged her to go on, as the doctor turned the shoulders of the child and the tears rolled from the father's eyes. Suddenly there he was . . . a perfect little boy, lying bloody and wet in his mother's arms, as John went to her and cried and held them both. The doctor was shocked, but as he looked at them, he really couldn't feel this was not natural. It was the most unusual delivery he had ever done, but perhaps they weren't so wrong these two. The child had been conceived of their love once upon a time, and now he was born into their hearts, into their hands, as they held him close, both of them, not just one, and the child cried lustily, at five fourteen pm on the twenty-eighth of July, nineteen hundred and fourteen, as Europe went to war.

Chapter Twenty-Seven

Jonathan Thurston Harte was christened in Old Saint Mary's Church on California Street when he was six months old, in January of 1915, when all of Europe was at war, and his parents had a small reception for their friends at Thurston House. The Crockers and Floods were there, the Tobins, the Devines. It was a small but select group that raised their glasses and toasted him with champagne, and that night his mother and father quietly and privately toasted him in the room where he had been born, and John smiled down at his wife happily.

'How lucky we are, little one.'

'Indeed we are.' There was nothing else she wanted with her life. She had a husband she loved, a child she adored, their respective mines were doing well, although she had refused to merge them again. She insisted that they had separate identities and it might hurt them to change that now.

'Everyone knows that we're married and I run both mines. What difference does it make?'

'It makes a difference to me.' She belonged to John, but the mines did not, and for some deepseated reason she couldn't explain she wanted to keep it that way, although he ran the mine for her and he did a stupendous job of it. She had no complaints, and, in fact, she wasn't even interested in the mine now that she had tiny Jon. Even the continuing blight on her vines didn't seem such a tragedy to her now. Nothing did. All she thought of were happy things, and she insisted that the baby looked like John. He had dark hair and great big violet eyes, but in truth, he didn't look exactly like either of them. Hannah knew who he looked like. He was the spitting image of Camille, but she never said that to either of them.

They stayed in Napa for most of that spring, and celebrated her twenty-seventh birthday by going to the Grange Dance, and that summer was the prettiest she remembered since her youth. John turned fifty-five years old, and the only sadness was a letter saying that Spring Moon had died in an accident, falling off a bridge. She had hit her head on the rocks and died instantly. Her brother had written to John, through someone he knew who could write. He felt that John ought to know, and he was touched. She had been good to him, and when Sabrina heard she was saddened too. Spring Moon had probably saved her life six years before, and certainly her virginity. It was difficult to believe that it had already been six years. It seemed to have flown by, and yet at the same time she couldn't imagine a life without John Harte now. It seemed as though she had spent her whole life with him.

And her predictions had come true. On the day Jonathan was born, Europe went to war, but there was no sign of America entering into it, and even when Jonathan was two years old, there seemed no real threat that the United States would get involved, or so the politicians said, but once again Sabrina didn't believe what they said.

'How can we not, John? They're dying by the thousands over there. Do you really think we won't lend them a hand? And the trouble is that if we do, we're fools, but if we don't we're the most heartless creatures that ever walked. I don't know what to think.'

'You worry too much about politics. That's the trouble with women who used to work, they don't know what to do with themselves after that.' He loved to tease her about her inquiring mind. She had plenty to do with little Jon, so much so that although she wanted to go very much, she decided not to go to New York with her husband. He had business to do for both of them in Detroit, and some investments to see about in New York. 'We could come back slowly through the South if you like.' John was tempting her, he hated to travel alone. He enjoyed her company so much, and they were inseparable most of the time.

'How long would we be gone?' He thought about it for a minute.

'Probably three weeks. Maybe four.' They lost two weeks just getting across the country and back, or almost. It was a long time to be separated from her husband, but Sabrina shook her head now.

'I just can't. Could we take Jon?'

John thought about it and then shook his head sensibly. 'Can you imagine ten days with him on the train?'

She groaned and they both laughed. 'I can, but I can't imagine

279

ever regaining my sanity.' He was two years old and into everything in sight. He was a lively, healthy, happy child, and Sabrina was sorry she hadn't got pregnant again. She had hoped to ever since he was born, but it hadn't happened again. Fortunately, it seemed less important now that they had Jon, but for some reason, and the doctor had no idea why, she didn't get pregnant easily. However, they were both more than happy with their only son. 'I hate to let you go alone, sweetheart, and for so long.'

'So do I.' He didn't look pleased. 'You sure you don't want to leave Jon with Hannah here?'

'I really don't think I can. He's too wild for her just now.' And there was no one at Thurston House that she would trust him with, although they were often there. 'I just can't this time.'

'All right.' He went ahead and made his plans, and on September nineteenth, she went to the station with little Jon and they kissed him goodbye. He waved from the private car he had availed himself of for the trip, and headed East as Jon and Sabrina went back to Thurston House to wait for him there. She had some business to do in town, with her bank, and she wanted to order new curtains and some new upholstery and rugs for Thurston House since they were there so much. She had enough to keep her occupied while he was gone, but it seemed terribly lonely there after he left. She rattled around in the enormous house, anxious for news of him, and more anxious still for him to come home, but it would be weeks before he did. And she sat in the garden playing with little Jon, and went downtown to select some of the fabrics she needed the next day, and wondered where John was at that point in time. She stopped on the street and watched the paperboy hand out the newspapers, and suddenly her heart stopped. 'Train Wreck on the Central Pacific Line. Hundreds die,' the headline read. She felt dizzy as she pushed her way through the crowd to see what the newspaper said, yanked it from the boy's hand and pressed a dollar bill in it, and stood there trembling with the paper in her hand. There were no names, no list of casualties, but it was the train her husband had been on. The wreck had happened in Echo Canyon, east of Ogden, Utah. She stood in a numbed state, and without thinking, went to her bank, not even sure how she had arrived there, and stood numbly with tears of terror running down her face until someone realized who she was.

'Mrs. Harte . . . may we help you? . . .' She was ushered into the office of the president and she handed the paper to him with a look of horror on her face.

'John left on that train yesterday. Is there any way to find out . . .' She didn't even dare say the words. It was possible that he was unharmed, or that he was among the casualties they talked about. And if he was, she would go to him at once. Jonathan would have to stay with the help until she returned, there was no question about that now. Her mind was already racing ahead, as she looked imploringly at the bank president. 'Can't you find out?' He nodded worriedly.

'We'll cable our corresponding bank in Ogden, and have them get the information for us.' The train had stopped there and had not gone on. It was too disabled to continue the trip, and an empty train had gone out from San Francisco that afternoon, to pick up the survivors of the wreck.

'What if we call the railroad line? They must have a list of casualties.'

The bank president nodded again. 'We'll do everything we can, Mrs. Harte. Where will you be?'

'I'll wait to hear from you at home, or should I stay here?'

'No, I'll have one of my men drive you home, and I'll let you know the moment we hear something.' He was terribly upset. The Hartes were their biggest customers, as had been Mrs. Harte's father before that. He only hoped that Mr. Harte had been unharmed in the wreck. He helped her into the car of his vice president, saw to it that she was taken home, and hurried back to issue frantic orders to everyone. Cables were sent to the Central Pacific with a request for an immediate response, he sent a messenger to the head of the railroad office, waited himself for the news, and when it came it wasn't good. John Harte was on the list of casualties. He had died in one of the six cars that had been totally crushed when the train jacknifed on the tracks, and fell hundreds of feet into a ravine below. His body had been recovered from the canyon only hours before and his identity had been unknown at first, but it was evident now who he was, and the corresponding bank answered the inquiry with regret and sympathy extended to the family. It did nothing to soothe the bank president's nerves as he drove through the gates of Thurston House late that afternoon and sounded the knocker somberly. A man answered the door, and he asked to see Mrs. Harte, if possible. She came instantly, the moment she was told who it was, leaving Jon with one of the maids upstairs, hurrying downstairs with a hopeful look on her face. Surely they had discovered that John was helping everyone. He was so accustomed to disasters at the mines over the years, that he was marvellous in times such as those. Sabrina looked down the broad staircase with a nervous smile, but the look on the man's face stopped her where she stood.

'John? . . .' It was barely a whisper beneath the great dome. 'He . . . he's all right isn't he?' She walked a few more steps and then stopped as the man shook his head, and then she ran to him. 'He's not . . .' He had wanted to tell her differently, wanted her to be sitting down so she wouldn't faint in his arms. And for nothing in this world did he want to be the one to tell her the news, but he had no choice. The task had fallen to him, and he looked at her now with a stricken face. It shouldn't happen to people such as these, people who loved each other so much, who led such decent lives, who had found each other after so long. 'I'm so sorry, Mrs. Harte. We just got word . . .' He took an enormous gulp of air and went on. It wouldn't get any easier, it could only get worse now, for her anyway. 'He was killed last night in the wreck. They recovered his body,' he hated to tell her this but there was no turning back now, 'from a ravine just this afternoon.' There was an almost animal moan of pain from her. And now there was no more John. She looked up at the bank president with more pain in her eyes than he had ever seen before, and he had no idea what to say to her as they stood on the stairs of Thurston House, beneath the dome her father had built, and which she had replaced after it was destroyed in '06. But neither of them saw it now. They saw nothing but each other's eyes, and he saw hers fill with tears, and then she walked him slowly to the door. She didn't scream, she didn't cry, she didn't faint, or have hysterics in his arms. She simply walked him to the front door and looked as though the world had just come to an end. And for Sabrina Harte, it had.

Book III

Sabrina: The Later Years

Chapter Twenty-Eight

There was no way to explain to two year old Jonathan Harte that his Daddy had died. He could barely talk, and there was no way to make him understand. But everyone else knew, and when John's body was returned to town there was a memorial service in Old Saint Mary's Church and a funeral in Napa, where they buried him. Sabrina felt as though she had died beside John. She had them open the casket when his body arrived, and she sat alone in the library of Thurston House, looking at him, the bruises and the broken neck. There was still sand on his face from the ravine, and she sat there, brushing it off for him, waiting for him to wake up at her touch, to tell her that it was all a mistake. But there was no mistake. John Harte didn't stir, and her brief life with him had come to an end. They had been married for seven years, and she couldn't begin to imagine how she would go on. She was more devastated than she had ever been by anything in her life, and she would sit for hours on her front porch, staring into space. Finally Hannah would come to tap her arm and remind her of some chore she had to do, or that Jonathan needed her. But it was as though her mind had gone blank when he died. She felt nothing, saw nothing, said nothing to anyone, and could even give nothing to her child.

She had already been told several times that there was a stack of things she had to look at, at both mines, but she couldn't bring herself to go to either one, neither his nor her own, and she couldn't imagine now why she had fought so hard against the merger he had sought for so long. What reason had she had? What point had she wanted to make? She could no longer remember it, nor could she muster the desire to tend to their businesses now.

'Mrs. Harte, you have to come,' her own foreman begged her half a dozen times, stopping by at the Saint Helena house, and she would nod at him, but the next day and the day after that, she still didn't go.

A month rolled by, and finally, in desperation both foremen came, and this time she knew that she could avoid it no longer. She got in John's car with them and drove to her own mine first, but as she walked into the office that had been hers so long ago, it was as though she had gone back in time. She could remember the first day she had gone there after her father had died, the brave speech she had made with the megaphone, and the men leaving her in droves . . . the ugly scene with Dan . . . She felt as deserted as she had then, it was as though the pain were that of yesterday, not a decade before, and as she looked at the two men who had brought her there, her face melted and she began to cry until she sobbed openly, and her own foreman took her awkwardly in his arms.

'Mrs. Harte . . . I know it's painful for you to come here now . . . but . . .'

'No, no,' she shook her head, looking desperately at him. 'You don't understand. I can't do it again . . . I just can't . . . I don't have the strength I had then . . .' He didn't understand what she meant, and she sighed and tried to regain control of herself, and then finally she sat down in the chair John had sat in so often when he worked at her mine. 'I can't run this mine again. I have a son to think of now.' They both knew that she once had run the mine singlehandedly, and considered it remarkable, what's more they had heard that she had done a damn fine job, but no one expected her to now.

'We didn't think you would, Mrs. Harte.' She looked surprised and relieved at their words, and suddenly realized that was one of the things she had feared in the past month, that, and the loneliness of seeing the mines where John had worked so hard. They would be so empty without him now. She couldn't bear the thought, and she stood up with a broken sigh.

'I want you both to run things as you have been. I will consult with you regularly, and I want to know everything that goes on. And,' she took them both by surprise, 'I want to merge all of our mines.' She knew she should have done it while John was alive, and she felt guilty at having resisted him for so long, as though she didn't trust him with her mines. She still felt sick when she thought of it, but she was going to do it now. 'Everyone knows the two are run as one. I want them called the Thurston-Harte Mines.'

'Yes, ma'am.' They all knew that it would take a while for the papers to be drawn up, but at least they could start doing that, and

286

there was a faint hint of her old self, as she wrote down a series of things on a memo pad and handed a piece of paper to each of them.

'Other than that, I want the mines run as they have been up until now. Continue everything my husband did. I want nothing changed in either mine.' But what she discovered in the ensuing months was that there were problems in both mines, particularly his. The profits of his mine had been going down radically for the past several years, but he had never complained to her, and he had been honest to a fault about how he ran the Thurston Mines for her, never applying her profits to his loss. She had even more reason to be grateful to him than she had known then, and she was sorry for the worry he must have had over his own mine. But those worries of what had been the Harte Mine altered radically when the United States entered The Great War in 1917, and suddenly the need for bullets and war machines created an insatiable need for cinnabar, and business at all of the mines boomed. They were known as the Thurston-Harte mines by then, and Sabrina was making money hand over fist, not that she really cared. All she cared about was her son Jon, and she still hadn't got over the loss of the man she had so greatly loved. Now, as though seeking some lost part of him, she began working again several days a week at the mines. It took her mind off all else, and once Jonathan was in school, it kept her busy while he was gone, but eventually, with increased demands put on both mines, she began to stay longer and longer each day, and she began to work as she once had, staying late into the night. Often when she came home at night, too tired to eat or do anything, it was too late to see her son.

She seldom went to San Francisco now. Thurston House was closed again, and she only went there from time to time, managing it herself as she did in her years alone, whenever she went there with Jon for a few days. They spent one Christmas there, but it was more than she could bear, remembering her time there with John and the night their son had been born. She knew how her father had felt after her mother died, and she had been married to John for far longer than he had been married to Camille. She really couldn't bear being there, and she would go scurrying back to Napa again with Jon, to lose herself at the mines all day long.

And in time she came to realize how much the boy hated it. 'That's all you do is work at those dumb mines, you're *never* here!' And she knew he resented her for it, but by then it was 1926 and there were problems with the mines again, with both of them this time, there was simply less need now for cinnabar, and she had had to let a great many men go and close some shafts at the mines that had originally been hers. As Prohibition had already been in effect for seven years, her vineyards were useless to her, and for the first time in her life, she began to worry about her finances. It was important to her now that she hang on to everything she could for Jon. He was only twelve years old and she wanted to give him everything she herself had had. He was a difficult boy in some ways, and he not only resented her hard work and long hours at a man's job, but the fact that his father had died. He seemed to blame her for it.

'It's not my fault, Jon!' She had said it to him a thousand times when he shouted at her, but the trouble was that she still felt guilty somehow for John's death, as though she should have been on the trip and died with him, and yet if she had, where would that have left Jon?

'My friends all think you're weird. You work harder than their fathers do.'

'I can't help that. I have a responsibility to you, son, and right now, it's a difficult time.' In 1928, with a breaking heart she sold what had been John's mine, and put the entire amount she received into the stock market, hoping to watch it grow so that, one day, she would have a fortune to give to Jon. That dream turned into a nightmare on Tuesday October 29, 1929. She lost every penny she'd got from selling the mine and she was consumed with guilt over what she'd done with it. In another three years, she would have to face sending Jon to college, and that made her shake in her shoes. She told him nothing of the money she had lost, and he talked about going to Princeton or Harvard all the time, and maybe going to Europe with her and wanting a car before he left. He seemed to make constant demands on her, but he didn't realize that she was having a hard time, and he had always been a demanding child, and she had allowed him to continue to be a demanding young man, giving him everything he wanted as though to repay some guilt, as though it could make up to him for the fact that she worked too hard and his father had died when he was two years old. But indulging Jon didn't bring his father back, it only made Sabrina's life impossible as the time for college drew near, and still worse when he was accepted at Harvard, Princeton, and Yale.

'Well,' she held her breath, trying to look perfectly at ease, and not let the panic show. But she was getting good at that, had been for the past two and a half years since the market crash, 'Where do you think you'll go?' And how do you think I'll pay for it? The mine had all but run dry on her, and she'd been thinking of selling the house in Saint Helena for a long time. They had moved into San Francisco when Jon began college prep, and had forced Hannah to come with them, almost against her will for a time, and now she had moved back to the house in Napa again. She was happier there, and Sabrina hated to sell the house out from under her, but she had almost no choice. She would have to sell the Napa house in order to send Jon to college in the fall, which ever one he chose.

'I think Harvard maybe, Mom.' He grinned at her with a self-satisfied air, and she was amused by him.

'You're pleased with yourself, aren't you?' He was a decent lad beneath it all, and if he was spoiled, it was her own fault, and she knew it full well. 'Actually, I'm pleased with you too. Your grades were wonderful, and you deserved to get into all of those schools. You really think Harvard is the one for you?'

'I think so.' He frowned. He had almost decided on Yale, but New Haven sounded almost as grim as he thought Saint Helena was. He wanted more action than that, and everyone said that Boston was fabulous, and Cambridge was only an extension of that. He was as interested in his social life as he was in the academic opportunities, which was hardly surprising or unreasonable in a lad of eighteen. What was unreasonable was the request he made of Sabrina shortly before he finished school that year. He was almost eighteen years old, and Sabrina was forty-four but in his mind she might as well have been a thousand and two. She was remote and mature, and often distracted, for reasons she didn't share with him. 'You don't mind if I buy a car and have it shipped East on the train, do you, Mom? I'm going to need it in Cambridge all the time.' He smiled angelically at her, it never dawned on him that she might say no to him. She seldom did, even if she had to deprive herself, which she often did. But this time, she couldn't even think about a car. She hadn't sold the Saint Helena house yet, and she was getting desperate. His tuition for the following year had to be paid by July first, and if the house in Napa didn't sell, she had no idea what she was going to do. 'I think a little Model A, with a rumble seat. It's really the perfect car, and if it gets too cold . . .' She held up a hand with a look in her eyes he had never seen before, but he didn't recognise it this time as the panic it was anyway. He was thinking of himself and she was thinking desperately of the dwindling funds. They were almost strangers now. She had kept too much from him.

'I don't think a car is a very good idea right now, Jon.'

'Why not?' He was surprised as he looked at her. 'I need a car.'

But something deep inside her just wouldn't let her tell him the truth. Pride probably. 'You can get around without a car at first, Jon. You'll only be eighteen in July for goodness sake, and not everyone arrives at college with a brand new Model A.' Her nervousness made her voice sharp and he looked horrified.

'I'll bet most of them arrive with some kind of car. My God, how do you expect me to get around?'

'You can bicycle for the first term,' she gulped almost visibly, 'or walk. We'll talk about a car next year.' Maybe by then things would be better at the mine, but she didn't see how they were going to be, and her vineyards had been useless for thirteen years now. She had all but given up on them, and was thinking of selling the land. The one thing she knew she'd never sell was Thurston House, but she wanted to sell as little land as possible. She knew how much that land had meant to her father when he'd built his empire so long ago, and one day she wanted to have as much of that as possible, to give to Jon.

'I just don't understand how you think.' He was pacing the room and glaring at her. 'What do you think I'll look like on a bicycle? Everyone will laugh at me!'

'That's ridiculous.' She was tempted to tell him just how things stood with her, but she would never do that. She didn't want to frighten him, and she had too much pride. 'Jon, half the country is out of work. People are saving money everywhere. It won't shock anyone to see a little economy. In fact, it would be far more shocking to arrive with a brand new car. There's a Depression on, you don't want to look like some showy bumpkin from the West, arriving with your car.'

'Now you're being ridiculous, and who gives a damn that there's a Depression on? It hasn't affected us, has it? So what do we care?' She knew as she listened that she had been wrong to always have painted such a rosy picture for him; in some ways it had made him unrealistic and insensitive, it was her fault if he didn't understand their plight.

How could he? She had explained nothing to him. Yet she still didn't want to tell him now. She had carried on the bravado for too long to stop now.

'That's an irresponsible attitude to take, Jon. We *have* to care . . .'

He cut her off. 'Well I don't, dammit. All I care about is my car.' He was still sulking at her when she put him on the train to Boston when he left for school. She had her heart in her throat as she always did, putting him on a train to anywhere, ever since John had died. She would have gone with him, but there was much to do at the mines these days. And mercifully, she had sold the Napa house just in the nick of time. The money had come through to pay Jon's way through Harvard for his first two years, and she only prayed that things would improve by the time that money ran out and she had to come up with his tuition again. It had broken her heart to sell the house. Her family had owned it for more than sixty years, and it was the house Jeremiah had built for the fiancée who had died of the flu, and where he had brought Camille after he married her and the house Sabrina herself had been born in. Jonathan had seemed to feel it was no great loss for them, he thought Napa was boring anyway, and Sabrina was grateful that Hannah had died just before and so couldn't see the house she loved pass into other hands. She had never thought much of Thurston House, it was the house in Saint Helena she loved, and now there were strangers living there, but Sabrina did not begrudge that to Jon. She wanted to give him the best education he could get, Depression on or not, which was why she got furious with him when she saw his midterm grades. He was failing everything, and apparently he appeared in class as seldom as possible, for which she gave him hell when he called her on Thanksgiving Day. Amelia had invited him to New York, but he had stayed in Cambridge with his friends.

Amelia was eighty-six years old, and although Sabrina still thought her elegant and remarkable, Jonathan thought her unbearable. 'She's so old, Mom.' She was undeniably that, but she was so much more too. Sabrina was sorry that he was still too young to see that. She was disappointed that he didn't appreciate her, but there was no arguing with him, except now, about his grades. 'If you don't get serious about this, Jon, I'm cutting your allowance off.' It would certainly have been a relief to her, and she knew that she had frightened him. She knew he still wanted to work on her about the

Model A, but he couldn't now. 'You'd better get yourself to all your classes too. If not, you'll have to come back and work in the mines with me.' A fate worse than death to him, she knew. He hated everything about the mines, except the money that they made for him, so he could have the things that made him feel important and secure, which was what the fuss over the car was all about, and she knew that. But she couldn't help him this time. He wanted the car so he could be like everyone else; he didn't have a father after all. But how long could she feel guilty about that? She had for years, but that didn't bring her husband back. 'I want you to get serious about your work. And we'll see how your grades look when you get home, young man.' She was having him come home to spend the holidays with her, which was hardly economical, but she didn't want him to be alone for Christmas, and she wanted to see him too. It was all she had to look forward to.

There was nothing in her life except Jonathan, and the endlessly depressing reality that she couldn't hold onto the mine for much longer now. If she got an offer for the vineyard land now, she knew she'd sell, although who would buy from her? It was useless to everyone. She had grown prunes and walnuts for a while, but there was no profit in that, apples . . . table grapes . . . what she wanted to grow were grapes for wine. She had always had a dream about making exquisite wines, but it had never materialised, and now she wondered if they would ever be able to make wine again.

When she saw Jon again in December, 1932, it struck her forcibly that sometime, somehow, in the past few months, at Harvard, or somewhere along the way, Jonathan had become a man. He looked adult and seemed surprisingly mature when they spoke. Everything about him was grown up, including his taste in girls. She noticed that he stayed out awfully late at night when he went out with his friends, but there were still some attitudes that hadn't changed. He still expected her to supply all of his needs and wants, all of his delights and indulgences and the only thing he paid for himself were his girls.

He had wrestled his grades up again, and she was relieved by that, but now he could again tackle the subject she dreaded most. Only two days after he got home he began to badger her, and he only waited that long because he was busy until then. 'All right, Mom, what about the car?'

'The keys are downstairs, sweetheart.' She smiled at him. She had no objection to his driving her car, she never had before, and she was startled by the look on his face now.

'Not that car. A new one for me.' Her heart sank. She had just been looking at the mine figures again; it was desperate. What they needed to get out of the hole was a good war, and she felt guilty for even thinking that, but it was what the whole damned country needed just then. She knew that women weren't supposed to think like that, but she knew the economy too well. And she was beginning to worry seriously that she was going to have to close the mines as she couldn't carry the expense of them anymore. It was already eating into the money she had made from selling the Napa house, and she needed the rest of that to pay Jon's tuition the following year. For herself she needed next to nothing now. She bought the minimum for herself, had sold all but one car, kept no servants at Thurston House, and she was holding onto her old vineyard land, some other acreage she still had left and the mines her father had left her for dear life. All her other investments had gone in the crash of '29.

'I don't think you need a car right now.' She couldn't even consider it.

'Why not?' He looked at her furiously, eighteen and a half years old, and certain that he was a man by now.

'Do we have to discuss it right now? Can't it wait?'

'Why? Are you running off to work as usual?' In fact, she was going to Saint Helena, to see someone at the mine. Her foreman still handled almost everything for her. But she was there a lot of the time, trying to put things to rights herself. She couldn't pass on that responsibility to anyone else, and she looked unhappily at Jon now.

'That's not a nice thing to say, Jon. I've always been here when you needed me.'

'When? When I was asleep? When you were too tired to even talk to me when you came home?' She was shocked at the things he was saying to her. For the rest of his holiday, he badgered her, but to no avail. When he left for the East at last, she was exhausted by his attacks on her and she felt guiltier than she ever had before for what she wasn't giving him. In revenge, he wrote to her, and said that he wouldn't be coming home again until July that year. He had been invited to Atlanta by one of the 'men' he had met at school, and his family was inviting him, but he didn't offer the boy's name or tell her anything about the family, and she saw the game he was playing with her. He was punishing her for not giving him the toy he wanted from her.

He came home that summer in mid-July, but this year there was nowhere for them to go. The house in Napa was gone, and all she had left was Thurston House. She talked of going to Lake Tahoe with him, but he was so annoyed with her when he discovered that she still wouldn't buy him the Model A that he went to the lake alone with friends. After all, he was nineteen years old, and she couldn't run after him, but she was disappointed not to see more of him and it seemed only moments later that he was gone again and she was left alone at Thurston House.

But not for long. That winter things simply got too rough for her, and there was no income at all coming in from the mine to pay her own expenses and Jon's. They were beginning to run in the red at the mine and all but one main shaft was closed. At Christmastime, Jonathan returned to Thurston House to find four other people living there. His mother had begun to take boarders in, and when Jon realized what she'd done, he almost went mad.

'My God, are you crazy? What will people think of me?' She cringed at how he felt and what he said, but she had been desperate that year and she didn't know what else to do. The vineyard land was up for sale, but no one had bought it yet, and there was no money coming in at all. It was finally time to explain it to him.

'I can't help it, Jon. The mine is all but closed. I had to do something to bring some money in. You know that yourself. And your expenses are a great deal higher than mine.' His life was one endless party in Cambridge now with his fancy friends, and she never complained about it, but this was the price they had to pay.

'Do you realize I can't have any of my friends here now! My God, it looks like a brothel for chrissake.'

She couldn't take much more. 'I assume, from the kind of money you've been spending back East, that you've seen a lot of those.'

'Don't make me speeches about that now.' He roared at her late one night. 'You've turned yourself into the Madam of Thurston House, haven't you?' She slapped his face for that, and she felt sick when she did, but things were impossible between them now, and she was almost relieved when, the following summer, he told her he wasn't coming home at all. He was going to Atlanta again, to stay with 'friends.' She assumed they were all right, and she was disappointed not to see him for so long, but she had so much on her mind that she wouldn't have enjoyed him anyway. And she couldn't have stood him badgering her about a car. She had made up her mind to sell the mine, even if it broke her heart, and it almost did. Worse, it was almost worthless now. She sold it for the value of the land, but it paid Jon's tuition again, although this time for only one year, but it also allowed her to get the boarders out of the house, so that when Jon came home at Christmastime, at least they didn't have that between them again. It was more peaceful this time, but he seemed to have grown away from her, and he said nothing about a car this time. He had something else on his mind, which presented as great a problem for her. He wanted to go to Europe with a group of friends in June, and she had no idea how she would pay for it. There was nothing left to sell, except her mother's jewelry, and she was saving that to pay for his last year of school, and was afraid to spend it on anything else, but the trip seemed to be desperately important to him. With an exhausted sigh, she sat and talked with him one night.

'Who would you be going with?' He never seemed to do anything with her anymore, but he was almost twenty-one years old and it wasn't really reasonable to expect that of him. It made her nervous at times that she didn't know any of the people he spent his time with at school, however. She only hoped they were respectable, but she assumed they were. There was so much that she didn't know about him now. Things which his father would have quizzed him on, but Sabrina wasn't sure how much was her place and she didn't want to pry into his life inordinately. He wasn't interested in chatting with her either. These were difficult years for both of them. He wanted what he wanted from her, and he wanted it when he wanted it . . . his whole exchange with her was based on want and need, and nothing had been said of love for years. She missed that part of him, the tiny child who had climbed into her lap and clung to her. She thought of that as she sat eyeing him in her library.

'Well, can I go?'

'Where?' She was so tired she had forgotten what they were talking about, and she felt a constant strain. She had absolutely nothing left except the house they were sitting in, her vineyard land and the jewelry that had been Camille's, and there was no income, no promise of a better time. She had been thinking of getting a job for the past few months, but she had another idea which might be more immediately

295

profitable. There were developers who wanted to buy the extensive lands around Thurston House, to build other houses where her gardens were. It might be an answer to her plight, but she was not yet sure. Jonathan was looking at her exasperatedly. Christ, she couldn't be senile yet, she was only forty-six years old.

'To Europe, Mom.'

'You never told me with whom.'

'What difference does it make? You don't know their names anyway.'

'Why not?' But perhaps Amelia did. She remembered everything, and seemed to know everyone on the East Coast and beyond, everyone who was anyone or had once been. 'Why haven't you told me your friends' names, Jon?'

'Because I'm not ten years old anymore.' He growled and sprang from the chair across from her. 'Are you going to let me go or not? I'm tired of playing this game with you.'

'And what game is that?' Her voice was very calm, it always was, and told him nothing of the grief she'd known nor the strain of recent years. Nothing ever showed on her, except that the pain of it was there, in her eyes, in her heart, in her soul, if one looked hard enough. Amelia had seen it there the last time and had felt sorry for her. There had been no man in Sabrina's life since John Harte had died eighteen years before, but no one had ever measured up to him, and no one ever would as far as she was concerned. She looked up at Jonathan now. He was actually unlike all of them. He resembled neither his father nor her own, and he wasn't very much like her either. He lacked the discipline, the passion for hard work. Instead, he liked to play, and always wanted to acquire things the easy way. She worried about that for him sometimes. He had to learn to earn things for himself, and perhaps now was the time. She thought of that as she looked at him, stalking about the room unhappily. 'Jonathan, if you want to go to Europe so desperately, why don't you get a job in Cambridge for a while?'

He looked at her in astonishment, unbridled fury in his eyes. 'Why the hell don't you get a job, instead of crying about how poor you are all the time?'

'Is that what I do?' Tears filled her eyes; he had cut her to the quick. She tried so hard not to complain to him, but he always knew how to hit just where it hurt. She stood up then, tired. It had been a

296

long day, too long, and maybe he was right. Maybe she should get a job. She'd thought about it often enough. 'I'm sorry you feel that way. And maybe you're right. Maybe we should both go to work. These are hard times for everyone, Jon.'

'It doesn't look that way at school. Everyone has everything they want, except me.' The car again. She had sent him everything else, and he had a handsome amount of spending money, as they both knew. But he didn't have a car . . . and now there was the trip to Europe . . . she really did have to do something about starting some money coming in. . . .

'I'll see what I can do.' But when he left for school again, she racked her brain about what she could do to bring some money in. It was almost impossible to get a job these days. It was 1935 and the economy had been impoverished for years. What's more, she couldn't type, couldn't take dictation, had no skills as a secretary, and jobs running quicksilver mines didn't exactly fall off trees, she laughed to herself to keep from crying in despair. That was the only thing she knew how to do. In March, she got a letter from Amelia in her now tremulous hand, explaining that a friend of hers was coming to California to buy some land, a man by the name of Vernay . . . de Vernay to be exact, Amelia had explained as Sabrina smiled at the precision she still insisted on. He grew the finest wines in France, and now that Prohibition had been repealed, he wanted to bring some of his vines to the United States, and grow grapes there. She apologized for troubling Sabrina with all this, but since she knew so much about the area, she wondered if she would mind terribly advising him.

In fact, Sabrina didn't mind at all, and she idly wondered if he'd want to buy her vineyard land from her. There was nothing she could do with it now. It was desperately overgrown, and she could no longer handle it herself. Prohibition had gone on for too long. Fourteen years had all but killed her dream of making her own wine someday. It had been a crazy idea anyway, even John had always teased her about her wines, although he had admitted once that they were good. At one time, she had known quite a lot about all that, but she had forgotten most of it now. All she knew anything about was cinnabar, and who gave a damn about that? No one, she knew only too well, and from time to time she would allow herself to remember the old days . . . the times when she had run the Thurston Mines

. . . when all those men had walked out on her . . . when she had built it up again, and then she would scold herself. She was still too young to dwell in the past like that. She would be forty-seven years old that spring, and remarkably, in spite of all she'd done she knew she didn't look it yet. But she felt every year, she thought to herself as she worked in her garden one day, trimming the hedges with an enormous pair of shears. She noticed a tall gray haired man at the gate, signalling to her. It was probably a delivery of some sort, she assumed, and she approached the man, holding one roughly gloved hand aloft to shield her eyes from the sun. She noticed then that he was well dressed, which was more than she could say for herself. She looked terrible, in rough work clothes that were her son's, but she had rolled up the pants, and put an old jacket over them. Her hair was tied in a knot high up on her head, but long wisps had escaped from it. She looked at the gray haired man in the well-cut suit and wondered what he was doing there. Perhaps he was lost, she thought as she opened the gate.

'Is there something I can do for you?' She smiled at him and he looked at her. He seemed surprised, and then amused, and when he spoke, she noticed that the accent was French.

'Mrs. Harte?' She nodded and he smiled.

'I am Andre de Vernay, a friend of Mrs. Goodheart in New York. I believe she wrote to you?' For a moment her mind was blank, and then she remembered the letter from Amelia weeks before, and she laughed up into his eyes, almost the color of her own.

'Monsieur de Vernay? Please come in.' She held open the gate for him, and he stepped inside, looking at the gardens that extended for almost a full block toward the house. 'I almost forgot . . . that was weeks ago . . .'

'I was delayed in France.' He was terribly polite and he looked suavely elegant and fresh as Sabrina led him toward her house, while he apologized for not having telephoned her first. Then he couldn't help asking her. 'Do you do all of this yourself?' He looked shocked and she smiled.

'Everything,' she shrugged. There was a certain pride in it, but it had been easier when she didn't do it all. 'I suppose it's good for me.' She laughed. 'Builds character.' She pretended to flex a muscle at him and he laughed. 'Biceps too. I can live without both.' She dropped her jacket on a chair and looked down at the ridiculous pants she wore and laughed again. 'Maybe you should have phoned after all.' He laughed too. 'Would you like a cup of tea?'

'Yes. No . . . I mean . . .' His eyes seemed to burn into her. It was as though he had come all this way just to talk to her, and she was amused by him. He was so electric, so intense, so obviously excitable. He was exploding with his idea and he wanted to share it with her. He sat down on a kitchen chair as she made tea for them both. 'What I want from you is advice, Madame. Madame Goodheart tells me that you know this area better than anyone, the area of Napa.' He said it like a part of France and Sabrina smiled.

'I do.'

'I want to grow the finest of French wines there.'

She smiled gently at him as she poured him tea and sat down across from him to pour her own. 'I used to want to do that.'

'And you changed your mind?' He looked concerned, and she looked at him, wondering why Amelia had really sent him to her. He was a very striking looking man. Handsome, tall, aristocratic, obviously very bright, but she had a strange sense as he sat in her kitchen drinking tea as though there were a reason for his being there, a reason she didn't yet know, and she was searching for it as she talked to him.

'I didn't change my mind, Monsieur de Vernay, I just did other things. There was a terrible blight in the valley several years ago, and it spoiled all of our vines. Then Prohibition came, and that made it pointless to even think about growing grapes for fourteen years, and now . . . my land is so overgrown, and . . . I don't know . . . it's too late for me. But I wish you luck.' She smiled at him. 'Amelia says you want to buy land. I should try to sell you mine.' He raised an interested eyebrow and set down his cup of tea but she shook her head. 'I wouldn't do that to you. It's so overgrown, it would take dynamite to clear it again, I'm afraid. My interests in Napa were in mines for many years. I'm afraid my vineyards suffered because of that. I never had time to do what I wanted to do. I made a few nice little wines, but nothing more than that.'

'And now?' There was something so dynamic about the man and he expected everyone else to be too.

She smiled and shrugged. 'I've sold the mines, those days are gone.'

'What kind of mines?' He was intrigued. Amelia had told him

something about her, but not enough. She had almost been mysterious with the introduction she made. 'She's a fabulous girl, and she knows everything anyone could possibly know about that valley. Talk to her, Andre. Don't let her get away.' It had been an odd thing to say about her, and yet he could sense something elusive about her even now, as though she were hiding from everyone. 'What kind of mines did you have, Mrs. Harte?' He pressed on.

'Quicksilver.'

'Cinnabar,' he said with a smile. 'I know very little about that. Did someone run them for you?' Obviously they had, but she laughed and shook her head, and she suddenly looked very young. She was a pretty woman, even in her gardening disarray, and it was difficult to tell how old she was.

'I ran them myself for a while. For a little more than three years when my father died.' Andre de Vernay was impressed. That was no small feat for a woman to accomplish. Amelia was right. She was a fabulous woman and she must have been a fabulous girl. He could sense it about her even now. 'And then my husband ran the mines for me after that,' there was a sudden sad cast to her voice, 'until he died, and I wound up with them again, and his as well. I've finally sold them all in the past few years.'

'You must miss the work.'

She nodded, admitting it easily to him. 'I do.'

He took another sip of his tea and then he smiled at her. 'When are you going to show me your land, Mrs. Harte?'

She laughed and shook her head. 'Oh no, I wouldn't do that to you. But I'll be happy to tell you who to see up there about buying some good vineyard land. There should be a fair amount of it for sale.' Her face grew serious as she looked at him. 'People are hurting economically here.'

'They are hurting everywhere, Mrs. Harte. Things are no better in France. Only in Germany, under Hitler's regime, is there a show of improvement in the economy, but God only knows what that lunatic is going to do.' Andre didn't trust him, no one did, even though the Americans thought he would do no harm, he didn't agree. 'But I have wanted to do this for many years. For me, the time is now. I've just sold my vineyards in France, and I want to start new ones here.'

'Why?' It seemed a remarkable leap to her and she couldn't help but ask.

300

'I don't trust what is happening in Europe now. I see Hitler as a real threat, although very few people agree with me. I think we're heading for another war, and I would rather be here.'

'And if there's no war? You go back again?'

'Perhaps. Perhaps not. I have a son, and I would like him to come here too.'

'Where is he now?'

'Skiing in Switzerland.' He laughed. 'Ah, the difficult life of youth!' And Sabrina laughed too.

'How old is he?'

'Twenty-four. He has been working with me at the vineyards for two years. He went to the Sorbonne, and then he came back to Bordeaux to work with me. His name is Antoine.' He seemed proud of his son, and Sabrina was touched.

'You're very fortunate. My son will be twenty-one this year, and he's in college in the East. I seriously wonder if he will ever live in San Francisco again. He seems to be in love with the East.'

'That will pass. Antoine was that way about Paris at first, and now he argues with me that Paris is a dreadful place, he's much happier in Bordeaux. He's so provincial that he wouldn't even come to New York with me. They all have their own ideas, but eventually,' he grinned, 'they become human again, more or less. My father always said that he enjoyed his children very much . . . after they turned thirty-five. We still have a few years to wait.' She laughed and poured them both another cup of tea, and then suddenly she had an idea, and she looked at the clock on the kitchen wall. He saw her do that and was suddenly concerned. 'Am I keeping you from something, Madame Harte?'

'Sabrina, please.' She insisted on the informality. 'No, not at all. I was just thinking that maybe we have time to drive up to Napa now. I'd like to show you some of the areas myself. How is your schedule today?'

He looked touched. 'I would be very pleased, but surely I must be keeping you from something else.'

'Only from trimming the hedge, and I haven't been in Napa for a while, I'd really enjoy going with you.' She could at least do that much for her father's old friend. Amelia had been so kind to her for so many years. 'How is Amelia, by the way?' She put their cups in the sink, and Andre walked into the main hall with her.

'Very well. Getting older and a little more frail of course, but considering that she just turned turned eighty-eight, she is remarkable in every way. Her mind is as sharp as a fine blade,' he laughed, 'I always love arguing with her. I can never win, but it's a challenge I have always enjoyed. We have very different political ideas.' He smiled at Sabrina . . . He blushed and she smiled.

'I think my father was always secretly in love with her. And she was very dear to me as I was growing up. She was like a mother to me in some ways. My own died when I was two.' He nodded, taking it all in, and she excused herself and went upstairs to change, and when she came down she was wearing a pretty gray and blue tweed suit, with a jumper the color of her eyes and comfortable flat shoes. Her hair was pulled back, and she had a certain innate style about her which struck him at once. She looked very different than she had only a few minutes before, and the term 'fabulous girl' flashed through his mind again. Amelia was right. She always was. About everything . . . except politics, he grinned to himself as he followed Sabrina outside. The garage was concealed by trees and hedges near the main gate where he had come in, and she took a six year old blue Ford out, opened the door for him, and locked the main gate behind them once she had driven out, and she looked at him in amusement as they headed North. 'And here I thought I was going to trim my hedges today.' Instead, she was delighted to be going to Napa with him.

Chapter Twenty-Nine

They reached Saint Helena two and a half hours after leaving San Francisco, and Sabrina took a deep breath of the fresh air, looking at the brilliant green on the hills, and she felt a renewal that she hadn't sensed in a long, long time. Since she had sold the house and the mines, she hadn't come to Napa at all, and now she realized how much a part of her it was, and how good it felt to be back. She felt Andre de Vernay watching her, and she turned to him with a sigh and a smile. She didn't need to say anything, he seemed to understand perfectly.

'I understand how you feel. I feel precisely that way about Bordeaux . . . and the Médoc. . . .' It meant everything to him, and this valley meant a great deal to her. It had been an important part of her life for such a long time. It was exhilarating just driving along, and she pointed things out to him as they went . . . Oakville . . . Rutherford . . . some of the new vineyards that had sprung up. She pointed to the hills where her mines had been, and then after turning off the Silverado Trail, she stopped the car, and pointed to a vast expanse of land. It was dense and overgrown, and nothing had been trimmed or planted in years. There was a 'for sale' sign that had been knocked down. She hadn't pursued selling it, and she didn't know what to do with it now. She had once had such rich dreams for this land, for the grapes she would grow there. She turned and looked up into Andre's deep blue eyes, and shrugged apologetically.

'It was beautiful here once.' She waved a hand, defining the different vines she had grown, and told him more about the blight and how Prohibition had completely shut them down. 'I don't suppose I'll ever do anything with it now.' She had two thousand acres of land sitting there, and more vineyards further on, and Andre said little. They walked into the fields, pushing branches from their faces, as he looked at what she had, stooped more than once to feel the soil with

303

his hands, and then he looked up at her with a serious face. He sounded terribly French when he spoke which made her smile.

'You have a gold mine here, Mrs. Harte.' He was serious and she shook her head.

'I might have once, but not now. Like everything, it's less valuable than it once was.' She was thinking of the mines she had had to close, and once these vineyards had been so well kept. They were barely recognisable now, and it saddened her to remember what had once been. It was a double-edged sword coming here, feeding her soul to return to the land she and her father had loved, yet reminding her of all that was no more; her father . . . John . . . even Jonathan was almost gone. She felt her lost youth weighing on her as they walked slowly back to her car. She was suddenly sorry they had come. What difference did it make? What point was there coming back to cry over the past. 'I really should sell all this one of these days. I never come up here anymore, and the land is just sitting here.'

'I would buy it from you,' he held the car door open for her, 'but it would be like stealing from a child. I don't think you really understand what kind of land you have, my friend.' It was like the rich soil of the Médoc, and he knew instinctively from the climate and the warmth and the feel of the soil, the look of the overgrown vines that he could produce wonders there. 'I want to buy land here, Sabrina. . . .' His eyes narrowed as he looked out over the hills. It wasn't Bordeaux, but it was beautiful and he could be happy here. If Antoine would come, and a few of their best men, they could do wonderful things, but first he had to find some land.

'Are you serious about this?' She could see in his eyes that he was, and she had offered to help him after all. He wasn't pressing her for her land, and she knew everyone around. She took him to the best office of agricultural real estate, and he talked to several men, and discovered that there were more than three thousand acres for sale next to her land. The price was low, and there was a great deal of work to be done, but Andre was anxious to see it before dark, and Sabrina drove him there. They had been there before, but they hadn't known about the acreage for sale, and now they drove past her property and he seemed to walk miles by himself, out in the fields, looking around feeling the soil again, breaking vines, touching leaves, he almost looked to Sabrina as though he were sniffing the air. And she was suddenly amused by him as she watched from the road. He was so intense about everything he did, so quiet and serious, and yet when she talked to him there was almost something mischievous in his eyes, but not when he discussed vines with her, or his 'recolte', or the land he was considering as they drove back to the real estate office again and when they got back to the office, he turned and smiled at her. He looked enormously pleased, and his excitement was contagious as she watched the spark in his eyes.

'What would you say, Sabrina, if I asked you to sell me yours?'

'Instead of what we just saw?' She looked surprised.

'In addition to that, and I have a better idea still.' She waited to hear as he went on. 'We could be partners you and I. I will cultivate your land for you as well. It would give us an incredible vineyard . . .' For a moment, Sabrina's eyes danced. It was what she had always wanted to do. But now?

'Are you serious?'

'Of course I am.' And with that the salesman returned to them and, in the blink of an eye, Andre negotiated the price, and settled the deal, much to the man's relief. His family would be eating well now on the commission he was going to make, and he had four children to feed at home.

Andre turned again to Sabrina then. 'And what about you?'

There was an endless pause, as they both held their breath and she felt a thrill she hadn't felt in a long time. The excitement of business, of industry, of ownership, buying and selling. Solemnly, she shook her head, 'I won't sell to you, Andre.'

Instinctively, he had expected that. 'Will you let me cultivate your land and become partners with you?' Together, they would have six thousand acres, an enormous chunk, and now she nodded her head, her eyes ablaze like his.

'I will.' He stuck out a hand, and they shook hands, as the salesman watched, feeling somehow that history had just been made, and he wasn't far wrong. A moment later, Andre wrote him a check as a deposit on the land he had just bought. And it was only then that it occurred to him he needed a house.

He hadn't even thought of that, and he looked at Sabrina in surprise now. He needed a place for himself and his son to stay, but they didn't need much, he could rent something small at first. He was leaving a small elegant chateau in France, in the Médoc, on the terrain he had now. But he was willing to leave everything. Every fiber in his soul told him that Europe was heading downhill. And this was a new country, a new world, a new opportunity for him. It was far more exciting than sitting comfortably in a well carved niche, long since established for him. And this would be exciting for Antoine too. They stopped at a roadhouse for something to eat shortly after eight o'clock, and they were both ravenous as they ate hamburgers and drank beer, and she told him about the Napa Valley of long ago, as best she remembered it.

'I was born here, in Saint Helena, in my father's house.'

'Do you still own it now?'

'I sold it,' she looked at him honestly, she had nothing to hide, 'to put my son through school. When the stock market crashed in '29, he was fifteen, and three years after that I sent him to college back East. I was losing the mines, I lost all of my investments in the crash, and I didn't need the house in Napa anymore, we've been living in town for years.' She wasn't too proud to admit her problems to him. He was a very unassuming man, and since they had shaken hands on the vineyard land they would annex and cultivate, she felt a peculiar bond with him. It was as though instantly they had become friends, and because of Amelia she trusted him. 'I still have to get my son through one more year.' And then, she heaved a small sigh of relief, 'At least I'll know he had the best I had to give.'

'And you? What does he give you?' She wanted to say 'love', but she wasn't always sure of that. He gave her something she supposed, a sense of comfort when he came home, a feeling that there was someone who loved her somewhere in this world, but he certainly never expressed it that way. He was more interested in what she could give him.

'You know, I'm not sure, Andre. I'm not sure children give one anything, except the joy you have just knowing they're yours.'

'Ah,' he nodded his head looking very French again. He smiled at her and set down his glass. 'Give him a few years.' She laughed, remembering some of the run-ins they had.

'It may take at least that long. Now, what about that land, what do you think you're going to do?' She was fascinated by the earnestness he showed every time they spoke of it. He was determined to leave Bordeaux and move here. 'Do you really think things will get that bad in France, Andre?'

'Worse. I am absolutely certain of it. I argued about that with

Amelia all night in New York. She says the French are too smart to ever be pulled down, but I think this time she might be wrong. Politically, we're sick, economically, we're not strong, and there's that madman to the East, waving his Nazi flag at us. I sincerely think it's time to leave, at least for a while.' But she wondered if he was panicking. Perhaps it was his age. He had told her earlier that he was fifty-five, and John had got more conservative too around that time and far more worried about politics than he had been before. For a time, he had seen doom everywhere, and she remembered that her father had been that way too, so she didn't put that much stock in what Andre said, but he was looking at her now pensively, and over coffee, he began to speak hesitantly. 'You know, Sabrina, perhaps you think I'm mad, but I keep thinking about that piece of land. Yours and mine. It is perfect for what I want to do, and you mentioned that you were interested once in your vineyards too. Rather than just leasing it and me cultivating it for you, could you not be an active partner and start the business with me?'

'I think those days are past for me. I'm not a business woman anymore, Andre.' And she had paid a high price for that, in the anger of her son.

'I don't know. I just see you as involved as I in this. Does that sound crazy to you?'

'A little bit.' She smiled as the waitress poured fresh coffee for them. Andre seemed to drink a lot of it, and murmured tactfully that it was not quite like the coffee in France, an understatement which made Sabrina laugh, but she was intrigued to hear his idea now.

'What are you thinking of, Andre?'

He took a quick breath, and set the coffee cup down again. 'How would you like to buy just enough of that piece of land with me so that we are indeed equal partners on this. Fifty-fifty all the way.'

She laughed right out at the American term. 'Buy with you? Andre, you don't understand. I can barely keep my son in school, I have hardly anything left at all, except my house in town and that piece of jungle in Napa that you saw. How could I possibly buy part of that parcel of vines with you?' It involved a purchase of eight hundred acres for her, an expense she could hardly afford, to say the least.

He looked disappointed but not defeated yet. 'I didn't know . . . I just thought . . .' There was a Gallic twinkle in the blue eyes, and she noticed again that she liked his looks. In many ways, he was a handsome man, and his lean, lithe good looks made him seem younger than he was. It was easy to imagine him twenty years younger than he was. 'Have you no other resources then?' It was rude to ask, but he wasn't being mean. He was desperately anxious to start a business with her. He had been comfortable with her from the moment they met that day, and Amelia had said extraordinary things about her, about how she had run the mines for years and had a brilliant mind. He suspected that her abilities were the only reason she stayed afloat now, and somehow he sensed that if she wanted to, she could find some way to buy the property with him. And she knew more about making wine than she'd admitted to him so far.

'It's been years since I paid attention to that sort of thing, Andre. When I was very young, I imagined that I was going to grow fine French wines right here, but,' she laughed at herself, 'how many years ago was that? Fifteen? Twenty-five? I would be no use to you at all.' She was amazed that he had even suggested a partnership, but she had to admit that she was intrigued by the idea. Much more so than just leasing him her existing land. 'You know, I'd almost like to do something like that with you. But I should be selling my land, not buying more.' She sighed, just thinking of it. She had another year's tuition at Harvard to come up with in the next few months, and all she had left to sell was the Napa acreage, the garden lots around Thurston House, and her mother's jewels, which she never wore. She had been mulling it over now for a while, and she thought of it that night again as she lay in bed. Andre was going back to Napa himself the following day, to go over the parcel he had first bought more extensively and talk to the owners about the deal and he had to find a place to live as well.

And as Sabrina thought of him, she realized that she liked the man, and hoped that he would do well with his wines. One had to admire a man his age, abandoning a country where he was comfortable and had everything he wanted already established there and coming to a place six or seven thousand miles away to start again. It took more than a little spirit to do something like that, and she admired him. Almost as much as he admired her. He had sensed an extraordinary inner strength about her that day, and Amelia had hinted at it before they met. She had a lot on her back even now, he suspected accurately, although the only hint of that was what she had told him when he had offered to buy the land in partnership with her. And she was still thinking about his idea, regretting that she couldn't buy the land, when she sat bolt upright in bed the next day . . . if she sold all the gardens around Thurston House, she could have enough to pay for Jon's last year at school, but there would be much more than that. She had planned to put it away for herself, and perhaps make an investment or two, but what better investment was there than land? Her father had always told her that, and if she joined Andre in the purchase of the acreage, she wouldn't have a dime left for herself, but if he knew what he was doing, they would make money in time. It was an outrageously risky thing to do, especially given the economy, but there was a feeling in her heart just thinking of it that made her blood race again as it had years ago as she pushed the mines on to greater things than they had done before, and this was what she had always wanted to do, right from the first. Even as a very young girl, she had loved the vineyards more than the mines. She thought about it all day, wondering if Andre had bought something else, and she made two or three calls about her garden lots. When he called her that night, she was so excited that he could barely understand what she said.

'I can do it with you, Andre!' The broker felt that there would be an offer on her Nob Hill lots by the next day. Two developers had been waiting for years, and they were willing to pay a decent price. It meant that she would have to live with construction all around her for a while, and she would never have the same seclusion she had had before, but she didn't care. If she could go into business with him. . . . He barely understood anything she said and was totally confused at his end of the line.

'What? . . . what? . . . what did you say? . . . slowly, slowly . . .' He was laughing with her, certain that something marvellous had occurred but he had no idea what.

'All right, I'm sorry. First of all, how did it go today?'

'Fine. Marvellous.' He sounded excited too. 'And I had this perfect idea. I buy the land, I sell the 800 acres to you, and you defer payment to whenever you want. Pay me in five years if you want. By then we'll both be rich from our wines.' He laughed and she beamed.

'You don't have to do that. I came up with an idea.'

She started to tell him and then instantly thought better of it. 'I have an excellent idea. Would you like to come here for a brandy perhaps, there's something I want to discuss with you.'

'Ahh . . .' He sounded intrigued, and the brandy was a fine idea. 'Are you sure it's not too late? It's already after ten o'clock.' She couldn't have stood waiting to discuss it 'til the following day; she had been like an excited child all afternoon. Andre agreed to take a cab from his hotel and five minutes later, he was outside knocking on her front door and she flew down the stairs and opened it to him. She had brandy and a snifter already waiting for him upstairs beside the fire in her library, and as she raced upstairs like a puppy dog he laughed at her. 'What in the world have you been up to today, Sabrina?' When he said her name it sounded French and she laughed at him, swiftly poured him the brandy, and indicated a comfortable chair facing her own.

'I had an idea . . . about the Napa property.'

A spark from her eyes caught his, and he looked at her, barely daring to hope. He wondered if this was why she had brought him here. Maybe she was going to wreak a miracle. 'Sabrina, don't keep me in suspense.' He whispered the words at her, and she looked at him, instinctively knowing that her life was about to change, as it had only a few other times . . . when her father died, she had to run his mines . . . when she married John . . . when Jonathan was born . . . and now suddenly, her life was going to take a dramatic turn again. She knew it as she looked into Andre's eyes. She had thought that her days of power had come to an end, but she knew now that they had begun again. She wanted to go into partnership with him. She wanted it more than anything. And she also knew with every ounce of her business acumen that there was something special about this man. Andre de Vernay had walked into her life. And now she was going to walk on with him.

'I want to buy the property with you.'

Their eyes met and held. 'Can you do that? I thought. . . .'

'I thought about it all last night, and I made some calls today. What I have to do is sell my garden lots here, surrounding Thurston House. I still need the money for my son's Harvard tuition next year.' She was being painfully frank with him, but she had no reason to hide anything from him, and she never would, if they went into partnership. 'But if I get a healthy price for them, and I think I might, I might just be able to squeak through to buy part of that acreage with you. We could be equal partners, right from the start.' Her eyes blazed and he looked at her, as though he also knew that something very important to both of them was about to begin. She narrowed her eyes and looked at him, her mind turning just as it had when she ran the mines. 'I really see it all.'

'So do I.' He looked at her for a long moment and then lifted his glass to her. 'To our success, Madame Harte.' There was a seriousness in his eyes she had rarely seen and she lifted her glass to him.

Afterwards, her brows furrowed again, well aware that they would have a lot of work to do, but she thrived on that. 'Who'll cultivate the vines? Will you bring people from France?'

'I'm bringing three with me, and my son, of course. The five of us will do everything that needs to be done, and we can hire local labourers as we need them. Why? Are you volunteering to pick the grapes, my friend?' He reached out and took her hand in his and smiled into her eyes. 'Do you really mean all this?'

'I've never been as serious before. I feel as though I've come alive again.' The stagnant waters of her life had begun to flow again, and she realized now how much she had missed working, running the mines, building something. All she had done in recent years was watch the remains of all that drift away. And now, all at once, she was in the midst of it again, thanks to him. 'If this works, I will owe you an enormous debt, Andre.'

'Ah, non!' He shook his head. 'There you are totally off the mark, Sabrina. It is I who will be indebted to you for life if we buy this land.' With his eyes narrowed like hers, he saw his dream growing in his head. 'It will be an enormous success one day . . . I know it in my soul . . . the finest wines grown anywhere, including France . . . perhaps even a champagne or two. . . .' She wanted to cry, she was so happy listening to him. It was everything she had wanted to do for years, and now he was offering it to her, and Amelia had sent him to her, like a messenger of fate to bring her alive again. He was the greatest gift of all.

For the next three days, they both went mad, speaking to banks, juggling their respective real estate, going back to look at the property again, speaking to the owners, and then the banks once more and finally the two developers who wanted her garden lots. Miraculously, within a week, both deals were closed. She had sold everything on Nob Hill except Thurston House itself and a tiny garden directly behind the house, and they had bought three thousand, eight hundred acres of land in Napa, adjoining her property of two thousand and one which gave them almost six thousand jointly-held acres of vines, and legally they each owned precisely half. Her lawyers had been busy for days, her bankers had insisted on checking Andre out, with cables flying everywhere. She had called Amelia twice herself to thank her for everything she'd done. It was the most frantic week Sabrina had ever survived, and when she put Andre on the train to New York at the end of the week, the two shook hands again and this time he kissed her on both cheeks.

'You know, we're both as crazy as hell, aren't we?' She looked and felt like a young girl again, and he was handsomer than ever after several afternoons, walking the property with her, in the Napa sun. But she didn't even see that side of him, she was so excited about what they'd done, and she still had to find a house, big enough for him and Antoine, with perhaps a cabin close by, for the three labourers they were bringing from France. 'How soon will you be back, Andre?'

He had promised to call her from New York, and cable her from Bordeaux. He had a lot to do there now but he hoped to be back in a month. 'Four weeks; five at most.'

'I'll find you a house by then, and if worst comes to worst, you can all stay at Thurston House.'

'That might be very nice.' He laughed at the image of his labourers from the Médoc moving into the elegant mansion on Nob Hill. 'We'll turn it into a farmhouse for you yet.'

'It's all right with me.' She waved at him and wished him luck, as the train pulled out. For just an instant, her heart sank, remembering the other train nineteen years before that had never reached Detroit.

But life couldn't be that cruel again, and it was not this time. Five weeks to the day, Sabrina was at the station again, this time to meet Andre, Antoine and the three men. She had found a small, simple farmhouse to rent for them on a piece of land adjacent to the acreage they'd bought, and in time Andre and Antoine could build a house for themselves. However, there was no need for that now. They all drove directly to the Napa Valley that day, and all of the men chattered excitedly in French when they saw what Andre and Sabrina had bought. And Sabrina was surprised at how charming Antoine was. He was a tall, lanky, strikingly handsome young man, with his father's blue eyes and a mane of thick blond hair. He had fine features, a gentle smile and his father's endless legs, and a kind, thoughtful way about him. His English wasn't very good, but he managed to say everything appropriate to her, and by the end of the second day they all spent examining the vines, she felt as though they had become friends. He was strikingly different from her own son, which she put down to his maturity, but what struck her most about Antoine was what a good sport he was. He seemed to want to make everything easier for everyone; he relaxed the atmosphere when it got tense, which it often did, given the Gallic tempers involved; he seemed to enjoy his father's company and he was exceedingly polite and at the same time humorous with her and she found herself wondering how he would get on with Jonathan when he got home. She wanted them to meet and to get along.

But that didn't happen until June when Jon came home. Six weeks had passed since Andre and Antoine had arrived, and they were staying at Thurston House with her for a few days, to attend several meetings at her bank about some loans they were hoping to take out. The racket outside was unbearable, as the construction people tore up the garden lots for the houses they were going to build. She had kept only one tiny garden behind the house, but even that was totally unusable now. Concrete flew everywhere, dust descended on them in clouds, and trees hung overhead, pulled out by cranes. It pained Sabrina to see them at work, and she tried not to think of it. It was sad to realize how much things had changed, but there was no fleeing from it now, and at least she was planning something exciting with Andre and Antoine. She had been able to pay Jon's tuition for his senior year and she was grateful for that, but now she had hardly a spare penny left. She wanted to sink everything she had into the vineyards with Andre and she went up to Napa several times a week, surveying their domain with glee. Andre came into town at least once a week, and stayed in the guest suite at Thurston House. They were ensconced there when Jon arrived. He looked at them with open hostility as he set down his bags in the front hall.

'More boarders, Mother dear?' She wanted to shake him for the tone he had used, and she looked at him angrily.

'Hardly, Jon. This is Andre and Antoine de Vernay. I told you about the vineyards in Napa we've invested in.'

'Sounds like nonsense to me.' He stood out in sharp contrast to Andre's son, who had welcomed her into their lives so openly. But it was obvious that Jon was threatened by them. His mother was flirting with business again, and it reminded him again of how much he had hated her working in his youth. Antoine held out a hand to Jon now, which the younger boy shook uninterestedly. He had other fish to fry now that he was in town. He had two friends from Harvard arriving the following week, and he was going to Lake Tahoe, and then La Jolla with friends. It wasn't exactly the summer he had planned. He would have rather gone to Europe with his friend Dewey Smith, but since his mother had insisted that she wanted him to come home, he was going to get even with her by forcing her to send him to Europe after he graduated the following year. He deserved The Grand Tour; everyone else went to Europe all the time. Why should he spend the summer at home? And he wanted to go on the Normandie when it was launched. She owed it to him after all; one didn't graduate from Harvard every day. But he didn't say anything to his mother now about his plans, he had plenty of time to work on her, and right now he needed a car for when his friends arrived.

'You can use mine when I'm in town, dear. I'll take the cable car.' Andre was listening to them with one ear while he made some calls in the library. He was surprised at her endless patience with the boy, but he was her only son, and that explained a lot. His father had died when he was two, and she had told Andre as they sat up late one night and talked, that she had always felt guilty toward Jon for the long hours she worked at the mine.

'But you did it for him. I had the same problem with Antoine when Eugenie died, but he had to understand. I was only one man. And you had an enormous responsibility on you, Sabrina. Surely now he must understand that.'

'When it suits him, he does.' She had smiled at her partner and friend. She knew her son well, and although it embarrassed her at times, she also knew how spoiled he was. And it bothered her that he was badgering her now in front of Andre about the car.

'Can't we buy another one for God's sake?'

'You know I can't afford it right now, Jon.' She attempted to keep her voice down but he refused to do the same.

'Why the hell not? You buy everything else, land in Napa, vineyards, God knows what else.' It was brutally unfair, she had bought nothing for herself in years, and although her clothes were obviously well made, they were noticeably out of date. Andre had noticed it too, and was well aware of the sacrifices she made. And she already had almost nothing left from her real estate sale as she had plunged it all

314

into the vineyards she bought with Andre and the tuition for Jon. There was no more money, even for her, but Jon seemed determined not to accept that and to continue to pressure her.

'Jon, you're being unfair. Just drive my car, for Heaven's sake.' She kept it in a garage across the street now, which she rented from friends. Her own garage had been torn down along with that entire part of the property in the grips of the construction people now.

'How do you even expect us to stand it around here with all that noise?' He was shouting at her over the din, and it was only when they stopped at night that she actually realized how loud they were. She had grown used to it in the last month, and would have to live with it for at least a year, from what she heard.

'I'm sorry, Jon. It won't last forever, and you'll be away part of the time.' She smiled gently at him. 'And when you finish school next year, they'll be all through.'

He sighed audibly and looked at her. 'I hope so. Now, what about the car? Can I take it this afternoon?'

'Yes, you may.' There was a girl he wanted to take out, she was a friend of a friend, and was a sophomore at Mills.

'Would you like to have dinner with us tonight?' She was accustomed to dining often with both Antoine and Andre, and she wanted Jon to get to know them both, but he already had other plans and shook his head as he stood up.

'Sorry, I can't.' And then he glanced over at his mother's friend. Andre was still busy on the phone, and Jon thought he couldn't hear him. 'Is that a new lover?' He looked pointedly into his mother's eyes and she blushed beetroot red. He could tell by the set of her mouth that she wasn't pleased.

'Hardly, Jon. He's my business associate. But I'd like you to get to know him and his son.'

Jonathan shrugged. For all he knew, they were a couple of bumpkins from France and he wasn't interested in them. He was judging by their interests in land, the fact that they came from Bordeaux, the simple way they dressed. The fact that they were both of noble birth had gone completely over his head as they never mentioned the chateau they had just sold. But Jon had other concerns, especially now that he had his mother's car, and half an hour later he was gone again and didn't return until late that night. The next morning, Sabrina left the house with Antoine and Andre shortly after dawn and she didn't come back again until late at night, having driven herself back from the Napa Valley again. She seemed to spend all her time in her car now, going back and forth between Thurston House and her new vineyard land, but there was a great deal to do.

'Why did you ever do a crazy thing like that?' Jon asked her again when they met that night and she saw something accusatory in his eyes, as though she had spent something she shouldn't have or she was failing him by being out so much as she had when she ran the mines. But he was twenty-one years old and he was at college three thousand miles away now most of the time, and she had a right to something that excited her as this did. It was something she had wanted to do all her life, and she was only forty-seven years old. She didn't plan to just roll over and die because he'd grown up. It was the best thing that had happened to her, but it was very threatening to Jon and he was unpleasant about it each time the subject came up, as though it were taking something away from him.

'Jon, it's going to do well. I promise you. We're going to have the finest wines in the States.'

He looked at her and shrugged again. 'So what? I'd rather drink scotch anyway.'

She exhaled in exasperation. Sometimes he was impossible. 'Fortunately, not everyone agrees with you.' And that reminded him, he turned to her with a particularly nonchalant air.

'By the way, I have some friends coming through town next week.'

Sabrina frowned as she thought and then looked at him. 'But you're going to Tahoe, aren't you?'

'Yes. I just thought that maybe they could stop by and say hello to you.' It was the first time he had ever suggested that and she suddenly wondered if it was a girl. She smiled shyly at him.

'Is this someone special to you?'

'Yes.' And then he realized what she thought and quickly shook his head. 'No, no, not like that . . . it's just a friend . . . never mind, you'll see . . .' For an instant she thought she saw guilt in his eyes, but this time she wasn't sure.

'What's their name?' He was already running off, and Sabrina called after him.

'Dupré.' She didn't even know if his friend was a woman or a man, and she forgot to ask him before he left for Tahoe the following week.

Chapter Thirty

After Jon had gone to Lake Tahoe with friends, Sabrina spent most of her time in Napa with Andre and Antoine and the French labourers. There was an enormous amount of work to do. There was land to be cleared, and, on her old land, vines to be cut down, others to be stripped, still others Andre had brought from France. It would be a full year before he'd be satisfied with the condition of their land, if then, but they were all prepared for that, and their project was well underway. They had already chosen a label for the wines they would make; they would call their ordinary brand Harte-Vernay, and their finer wines Chateau de Vernay. Sabrina was delighted with all of it. She returned to San Francisco after a week in the blazing Napa sun, dark as tar, her eyes like patches of bright blue sky, her hair plaited down her back. She was wearing the espadrilles Andre had brought her from France and trousers, and she was just going through her mail at Thurston House, when the phone rang on her desk. An unfamiliar female voice asked to speak to her.

'This is she.' She wondered who it was, but was more interested in the stack of bills in her hand. There always seemed to be more to pay, and she could see from these that Jon hadn't denied himself anything in the past few weeks . . . three restaurants . . . his club . . . the tailor he preferred . . .

'I am the Comtesse Dupré. Your son suggested that I call . . .'

Sabrina knit her brows, and then suddenly remembered the name. Dupré . . . but he hadn't mentioned a Countess. Perhaps she was the mother of a girl he was particularly fond of. Sabrina sighed away from the phone. She really wasn't in the mood, particularly not for a woman who announced herself in just that way. She sounded American, Southern almost, but her name was clearly French and her accent was excellent. It was too bad Andre and Antoine weren't in town. But they weren't, and she had promised Jon.

'Perhaps Jonathan told you that I would call.'

'Indeed he did.' Sabrina tried to sound welcoming on the phone while continuing to flip through the enormous stack of bills.

'He's a darling boy.'

'Thank you very much. Are you visiting San Francisco then?' Sabrina really didn't know what to say to her, or why she would call her now.

'I am.'

'It's unfortunate that Jon is out of town. He's at the mountains with some friends.'

'How nice for him. Perhaps I'll see him when he comes home.'

'Yes . . .' Sabrina steeled herself. She had to do her duty to Jon. 'Would you like to come to tea sometime this week?' With all she had to do, it was the last thing she wanted now, but she had no choice. Jon had warned her, and the woman had called now.

'I'd like that very much. I would like to meet you, Mrs. Harte.' She seemed to pause strangely on Sabrina's name, and Sabrina jotted a note to herself. She might as well get it over with.

'Perhaps this afternoon?'

'That would be perfect, my dear.'

'I'm delighted,' she lied politely. 'Our address is . . .'

But there was a charming peal of laughter in the phone. 'Oh there's no need . . .' And then, 'Jon gave it to me a long time ago.' Sabrina couldn't figure out if the Comtesse Dupré was old or young, a madam or a girlfriend, or simply a woman he had met. It was really the damnedest thing, and when Antoine called later that day and asked her to run to the bank for him to do an errand for him, she had to tell him she couldn't go.

'Damn Jon has stuck me with some woman of his. She's passing through town, and I've got her coming to tea,' she glanced at her watch; the tea tray was all set and she was wearing a grey flannel dress with a velvet collar and a string of pearls her father had given her when she was very young, 'she was supposed to be here ten minutes ago, and from the sound of her, I don't think she'll leave soon enough for me to get out. I'm really sorry, Andre.'

'It's all right. It can wait.' He thought of her pushing her way through the jungles of her own land the day before, her hair wild, her face burned, her eyes almost a Mediterranean blue and it amused him to think of her serving tea. He laughed and she made a face.

'I can't imagine what she wants, but Jon made a point of it, so I did the correct thing. Frankly, I'd much rather be up there with all of you. How is everything?'

'Fine.' But before he could say more, she heard the knocker on the front door, and then the bell rang.

'Damn. There she is. I have to go. Call me if anything special comes up.'

'I will. By the way, when are you coming back?'

She wanted to go on working with them, and Jon wouldn't be home for another week. 'Tomorrow night, I think. Can I stay at the farmhouse with all of you?' She was always the only woman there, and she was the consummate good sport about sharing their discomforts and rustic lifestyle. And at night she helped them cook, although it wasn't her best skill. 'I run a mine better than I cook,' she had grinned as she burned all their eggs before they went to work one day. From then on they cooked for her, and she did a man's share of work, as she always had. Andre admired her for that. He admired her in many ways.

'Of course you can stay there. We really have to build a decent house soon,' he mused. The plan was to build a simple house for the men, and a nicer one on one of their hills, for him and Antoine, but that wouldn't come for a while. They had other priorities first. 'I'll see you tomorrow night then. Drive carefully.'

'Thanks.' She hung up and ran down the stairs to pull open the door for a woman who stood looking at her. She wore a black wool suit, which clung to her form, and her hair was as black as coal. Sabrina suspected the hair was dyed, but she had a handsome face in spite of it, and eyes of brilliant blue which seemed to be examining Sabrina inch by inch. She took one step into the house and looked up at the dome as though she had known it would be there.

'Good afternoon . . . I see Jon told you about the dome.'

'No.' She looked at Sabrina and smiled. And Sabrina had a sudden, eerie sensation as she looked at her, but she wasn't sure what it was. It was almost as though she had seen this woman before, but she didn't know where. 'You don't remember me, do you?' Her eyes never left Sabrina's now, and slowly she shook her head. 'There's really no way you could.' Sabrina heard the Southern accent again. 'I just thought that maybe you saw a photograph . . . a sketch . . .' A chill ran down her spine as she stood immobilised and the woman's voice was a whisper now. 'My name is Camille Dupré . . . Camille Beauchamp . . .' Sabrina felt a wave of fear sweep over her as the woman went on whispering. 'Camille Thurston once, but not in a very long time . . .' It couldn't be. Sabrina stood rooted to the spot staring at her. It was a joke. It had to be. Her mother was dead. Sabrina fell back as though she had been slapped.

'You have to leave . . .' She felt as ill as though someone were choking her and her voice was strained, but she couldn't move from where she stood and Camille stood watching her, barely able to imagine what she felt, or the enormity of the blow she had dealt. It was like seeing her back from the dead, though Sabrina had never seen any picture of her at all, thanks to her father's care, but now she saw who Jon had looked like for all these years. He was the image of his grandmother . . . the hair . . . the face . . . the eyes . . . the mouth . . . the lips . . . Sabrina felt an overwhelming urge to scream but instead she took another step back from her. 'This is a very cruel joke . . . my mother is dead. . . .' She was almost breathless now, with fascination and fright; she had always wondered what her mother looked like for so many years, and now . . . perhaps possibly . . . she had needed a mother so much back then . . . but suddenly here was this woman now . . . how could it be? Sabrina sat down heavily in a chair and stared at her, as Camille Beauchamp Thurston Dupré looked calmly down at her. She was pleased at the effect she had had.

'I am not dead, Sabrina.' She spoke in a firm voice and looked at her. 'Jon told me that was what Jeremiah had told you. That wasn't fair of him.'

'What should he have said?' Sabrina couldn't take her eyes off her. It was almost impossible to understand what had just happened to her. Her mother had walked right out of the grave into her life and now stood calmly there. 'I don't understand.'

Camille acted as though it was something that happened to her every day. She wandered slowly beneath the dome, explaining to Sabrina what had occurred as Sabrina continued to stare at her. 'Your father and I disagreed a long time ago.' She smiled apologetically, almost charmingly, but Sabrina was too shocked to be charmed. 'I was never really very happy here,' the memory of Napa returned to her and she almost winced, 'particularly at the other house. Napa was never exactly my cup of tea,' it was the understatement of the last five decades, 'and I went home to Atlanta, because my mother was ill.' Sabrina stared at her, she had never heard this story before and it puzzled her. Why would her father lie to her? 'We had argued terribly about my going home, and he wrote to me while I was there, and told me never to come back. It was then that I discovered he had a mistress here in town.' Sabrina's eyes grew even wider than they had before. Could that be true? 'He refused to allow me to come home, or to see you again . . .' She began to cry, 'My only child . . . I was so heart-broken I went to France,' she sniffed and turned away for an instant as Sabrina watched. If the woman was lying to her, she was good at it, she would have convinced anyone of how genuine her pain had been. 'It took me years to recover from the shock. My mother died . . . I stayed in France for more than thirty years, and since then I have wandered aimlessly . . .' Actually she had wandered into her brother Hubert's house as soon as Thibaut Dupré had died, and she had lived there ever since, far more handsomely than she had with Dupré, but Fate had brought Jonathan into her life.

The name Beauchamp had meant nothing to him. He knew he had had a grandmother by that name, but she was long since dead, or so he thought. But when he went home from Harvard to Atlanta with Hubert's grandson in his freshman year, he had discovered his grandmother living there, and for two years they had discussed her coming to California with him. At first he had thought his mother would be pleased, and then, instinctively he knew she wouldn't be. But something urged him to arrange for the surprise, something he fought for a long time and then finally had lost. And he was angry at her now. She was being difficult and demanding with him, he thought; she hadn't given him the car he'd wanted for so long. He didn't owe anything to her, or so he told himself, and finally he told Camille the time was right. Sabrina deserved it for all the times she had left him alone to work at the damn mines. He knew what Camille had in mind, and she had promised him that he could live on in the house for as long as he wanted, once she moved back in. It was her house after all, not Sabrina Harte's, but she didn't point that out to her now. She was going to wait a few days for that. And Camille had also promised Jon a car. But she had other things to think about just then. Sabrina was looking at her suspiciously.

'Why would my father lie to me?'

'Would you have loved him if you knew the truth, that he had chased your mother away? He wanted you to himself, Sabrina, you and that old witch who brought you up.' Jon had filled her in on that; the long-hated Hannah had stayed on but was now dead at last. 'And he didn't want me interfering with his affairs. He had a mistress in Calistoga, you know.' Warily Sabrina wondered about that again. She had heard tales about him and Mary Ellen Browne a long time ago, but supposedly that was before he married Camille, even though someone said they had a child, but Sabrina had never put much stock in it. 'And he had another woman in New York.' A faint chord of what she said rang true, as Amelia swiftly came to mind, but somehow she had never really thought that her father had had an affair with her . . . perhaps at the very end of his life, but not before. Their relationship had seemed so chaste . . . though warm . . . Sabrina looked into the woman's eyes with total confusion now.

'I really don't know what to think. Why did you come here now? Why now?'

'It's taken me all this time to find you again.'

'I haven't gone anywhere. I'm still living in the house he built for you.' There was an accusation there, but Camille seemed not to notice it. She was very smooth. 'You could have found me long ago.'

'I didn't even know if you were alive. And for all I knew, Jeremiah still was and would keep me from you.'

Sabrina smiled at her cynically. 'I am forty-seven years old. You could have got to me, if you chose, whether my father was alive or not.' He would have been ninety-two years old that year and hardly a threat to anyone, surely not this brazen woman standing there. And Sabrina couldn't bring herself to feel anything for her, except suspicion of all she said. And why had Jon led Camille to her without warning? That puzzled her. Did he hate her that much? Or was this his idea of a joke? 'Why did you come here now?' She wanted to get to the crux of this, and get it over with.

'Sabrina, you're my only child, my dear.' She looked near to tears.

'We've been through that. And I'm not a child anymore.'

Camille draped herself across a chair like an ingénue and smiled at her. 'I had nowhere else to go.'

'Where have you been living till now?'

'With my brother, and he just died, so I've moved in with his son, the father of our Jonathan's friend,' Sabrina cringed at her possessiveness of her son. 'But things are a little awkward there. I've had no home since my husband died . . . er . . . my friend . . . that is . . .' She blushed, but covered the faux pas as quickly as she could, but Sabrina had instantly picked it up.

'You married again, Madame Dupré?' She stressed the name, and raised an eyebrow as she waited for Camille to speak. And something told her that she wasn't going to like what she was going to say from now on.

But this time Camille managed to stun her again. 'Don't you realize, my dear . . . your father and I never divorced. I'm still his wife, and I was when he died.' Jonathan had assured her that Jeremiah had never married again, not that he knew of anyway, although he had never known the man as his grandfather had died eight years before his birth. 'Technically,' Camille was smiling evilly at Sabrina now, 'I own this house.'

'What?' Sabrina looked as though she had received a massive electric shock as she sprang to her feet.

'But I do. We were married right 'til the end, and he built this house for me, you know.'

'For God's sake, how can you say a thing like that?' Sabrina wanted to throttle her. After all she had been through, now this woman wanted to take it all away. 'Where were you when I needed you? When I was five years old or ten or twelve? . . . where were you when my father died? When I had to run the mines for him? . . . when . . .' There was a catch in her throat and for a moment she could not go on. 'How dare you come back now? I used to lie awake at night and wonder what you had been like, I used to cry thinking of how you had died, and I still remember how grief stricken he was . . . and now you come here and tell me that you went to nurse your mother and he wouldn't let you come back. Well, I don't believe a word of it, do you hear me? Not a single word! And this house does *not* belong to you, it belongs to *me*, and one day it will belong to Jonathan. My father left it to me, and I will leave it to him when I die. But none of that has anything to do with you.' She was crying openly as she stood shaking beneath the dome, and Camille watched her carefully. 'Do you understand? This is *my* house, *not* yours, damn you! And don't malign my father to me in this house. He died here thirty years ago, and this was a sacred place to him . . . and you're right, he built it for you, but somehow, for some reason I apparently don't know, you disappeared, and it's too late for you to come back now.' Camille had been gone for almost fifty years and suddenly she had returned, but she seemed strangely calm now. She hadn't come unprepared for this, although she was startled by Sabrina's vehemence.

'You realize, don't you, that you can't force me to leave?' She looked sweetly at the woman she claimed as her child and Sabrina was seized with rage.

'The hell I can't.' She took one step closer to her. 'I'll call the police if you don't leave.'

'Fine, then I'll just show them this marriage certificate, and a few papers of my own. I am Jeremiah Thurston's widow, whether you like it or not, and Jonathan and I are going to reopen his will, and after that you'll have to ask me if *you* can stay here, not the other way around. And in the meantime, you can't force me to leave.'

'You can't be serious.'

'I am. And if you lay a hand on me, *I'll* call the police.'

'And just exactly what do you intend to do? Live here for the next fifty years?' She was being sarcastic and Camille didn't let it bother her. She was used to getting her way and was extraordinarily gifted at seeing that she did. She had planned this for a long time, with Jonathan. For months, he had hesitated, but finally the time was right. She knew it would be eventually, and she had waited patiently 'til then. Sabrina wasn't going to get rid of her easily now.

'I'm going to live here for as long as I like.' But she had another plan after that, one she hadn't mentioned to Jonathan yet. First she had to make Sabrina uncomfortable, and she had no guilt about that. Sabrina was a stranger to her after all, and what harm was there in it? She would stay with her for a few months, long enough to take over the house and make her acutely ill at ease, and then perhaps there would be a pleasant little settlement which would allow Camille to return to the South victoriously, with dignity, and purchase a house of her own. She had no desire to live in the North again, but it suited her purposes now just perfectly, and she was indeed within her rights. She had checked extensively, Jeremiah had never filed for divorce, from what she could tell. They had still been married when he died, and if she contested his will even now, it would take quite a while to settle it. Long enough to get the point across.

'You can't just move in here.' Sabrina was looking at her in horror now. 'I won't let you move in here.' But as Sabrina spoke, Camille moved toward the door, and signalled to a boy waiting outside, who swiftly trundled in, awkwardly carrying half a dozen bags. There were two large trunks still waiting outside. Sabrina advanced swiftly on him. 'Get that garbage out of here.' She was referring to both Camille and her bags, and she pointed at the door and raised her voice again. 'Right now!' It was the tone she had used at the mines thirty years before, but it didn't work on the boy. He was even more afraid of Camille than he was of Sabrina. 'Did you hear me, boy?'

'I can't ... I'm sorry, Ma'am.' He shivered in his shoes as Camille directed him nonchalantly upstairs. She still remembered everything, the master suite, Jeremiah's library, her own boudoir, and she directed the boy to deposit the bags in Sabrina's dressing room. Sabrina made to drag them out again, but Camille looked deprecatingly at her as though she were indeed a child.

'It's no use. I'm staying here. I'm your mother, Sabrina, like it or not.' And this was the mother she had dreamed of for so long, and so tenderly. It was beyond anything, she thought, and tears of rage filled her eyes and she did feel like a child. She couldn't believe this was happening to her. No wonder her father hadn't let her come back. She was a witch, an absolute monstrosity, but how was she going to get rid of her? She went into her father's library, frantically called Andre and explained her plight to him.

'Is she mad?'

'I don't know,' Sabrina was sobbing now, 'I've never seen anything like it before. She just moved right into my house as though she'd been away on a short trip.' She blew her nose loudly into the phone and he was sorry that he wasn't there to comfort her. 'And my father never told me. ...' She sobbed louder than before, 'I just don't understand ... he said that she had died when I was a year old. ...'

'Perhaps she ran away. You'll find out eventually. Someone must know.' And they both thought of the same solution at once, but Andre said her name first. 'Amelia. Call Amelia in New York! She'll tell you everything. And in the meantime, throw her out.'

'How? Bodily? Andre, she has moved right into my dressing room.'

'Then lock the door on her. I mean, she can't just march in on you like that. Can she?' Suddenly he sounded nervous too, and Sabrina was anxious to hang up and call Amelia at once. At least she wanted to know what had happened between her father and this woman who said she had remained married to him. 'Do you want me to come in?' Andre offered before he hung up. Now with the Bay Bridge making the trip so much easier, it was a shorter trip, but even if it hadn't been, he would have come in for her. Antoine could take care of things while he was gone.

'Don't do anything just yet. I'll call you back. I want to call Amelia, and then my attorney.' But it was to no avail. Amelia had a terrible sore throat, the housekeeper said, and couldn't come to the phone, and Sabrina didn't want to frighten her by saying how desperate she was. Her attorney was away on holiday; 'He'll be back in a month,' the secretary said non-commitally, and Sabrina felt almost hysterical as she went to confront Camille again. 'Madame Dupré . . . Countess . . . whoever you are, you simply can *not* stay here. If indeed you have some claim on my father's estate, and that claim is still good, then we can discuss it with my attorney when he returns next month, and in the meantime you will *have* to stay at a hotel.'

Camille looked over her shoulder at her daughter as she hung up her clothes. She had already dumped an entire rack of Sabrina's things onto a chair, and Sabrina had a strong urge to strangle her. She grabbed her own clothes, pushed Camille's aside, and threw them on the floor, screaming at the top of her lungs.

'Get out of here! This is my house, not yours!' But Camille only looked at her as if she were an errant child.

'I know this is difficult for you. And we haven't seen each other in a long, long time. But you must control yourself. When Jon comes back, he'll want to find us here living happily. He loves both of us, you see, and he needs a peaceful home.'

'I don't believe you're doing this,' Sabrina stared at her, she felt completely helpless for one of the rare times in her life. There were few things she hadn't been able to deal with before, but this was one of them. 'You *must* get out of here.'

'But why? What difference does it make? It's an enormous house. There's lots of room for all of us.' She looked carefully then at the murderous look in Sabrina's eyes and made a wise decision gracefully. 'All right, I'll stay in the guest room then, and you won't even know I'm here, my dear.' She smiled cheerfully, scooped up her things, and the boy, whom Sabrina had forgotten by then, ran behind Camille carrying all the bags and trunks again. Her memory was excellent. She directed him to the correct door, and a moment later, he hurried out.

When Andre called Sabrina later that afternoon, he still detected the same hysterical tone in her voice. 'What did Amelia say?'

'She couldn't talk to me. She has a fever and a terrible sore throat.'

'Oh my God . . . of all times . . . did you get the woman out? You know, she may be an impostor anyway. I thought of that after we talked before.' But Sabrina shook her head silently.

'I don't think so, Andre. She knows this house perfectly, even after all these years.'

'Perhaps someone prompted her. Some old disgruntled employee of yours.' But there was another reason why Sabrina believed that she was indeed Camille Beauchamp, and that was that she looked exactly like Jon. She told Andre, who grunted. 'Why do you suppose she's come back now?'

'She's made no secret of that.' Tears filled Sabrina's eyes again. 'She wants the house, Andre.'

'Thurston House?' He sounded horrified. Even in the short time he had known Sabrina, he knew how much it meant to her, and he had come to love it too. 'That's preposterous!'

'I hope the courts think so. And my lawyer is out of town 'til next month. What in God's name am I going to do? She's as stubborn as a mule, and she moved right into the guest suite, as though I'd been expecting her.' If it hadn't been so awful, she would have laughed. 'How can she do this to me?'

'Apparently easily.' And then he said something that he felt rather cautious about. 'What part exactly does Jon play in all this?'

She didn't understand that yet herself, and she didn't want to accuse him falsely to Andre, but just from the little she had heard from Camille, she suspected that there was something very ugly afoot. 'I don't know that yet.' And it was obvious that she didn't want to say more about it to him at that point.

'Isn't there something I can do for you?'

'Yes.' Sabrina smiled miserably. 'Throw her out. Make her disappear, make her never to have come back.'

'I wish I could.'

There was silence between them for a moment or two. 'You know, for so many years, I used to dream about her . . . to wonder what she

327

was like . . . once I broke into this house when I was about twelve years old, or maybe thirteen, and I went through some of her things that I found . . . and now she turns up, and she's an evil, awful woman, out for what she can get . . . I wish I'd never seen her, Andre, if she really is who she says she is.'

'I hope she's not.' Or perhaps it would put the ghost to rest at last. It was hard to tell. But it was too late for that anyway. She was there and she had dug in her heels, and now Sabrina had to get her out. She spent the entire night awake in her room, thinking about it, wanting to run into the guest suite and shake the woman out of her bed, but instead they met in the kitchen over breakfast the next day, and for a woman of her age, Sabrina had to admit to herself that Camille was still beautiful, and she must have been extraordinary fifty years before when her father married her . . . fifty years . . . or forty-nine anyway. It was amazing to think about and Sabrina sat for a moment, staring at her, wondering what had gone wrong, why she had left, why she had never come back, who Dupré was, and if perhaps that was the key. But she said nothing at all to her. She just stared at the table and drank her tea. It was impossible to believe that this had happened to her. As when John had died, she had a feeling of the whole world being upside down, but Camille floated around the kitchen happily, as though she was happy to have finally come home. Sabrina looked up at her again in astonishment. At last Camille sat down again, and the two women looked at each other, mother and daughter brought together at long last by circumstances or perhaps greed, having met the last time forty-six years before when Sabrina was a year old. What had Camille been like then, she asked herself, and then suddenly she remembered something Hannah had said a long time ago, about gold rings that Camille had used for birth control, and Hannah finding them . . . and her father being irate . . . and Sabrina coming along after that. She suppressed an urge to ask her mother if they'd wanted her, but she knew the answer to that in her heart, so what difference did it make? She was forty-seven years old and had a grown child of her own, her father had loved her very much, and her mother was . . . dead, she had been thinking to herself. But she wasn't dead. She'd been gone.

'Why did you really leave him?' The words sprang from Sabrina's mouth almost involuntarily. 'Tell me the truth about that.'

'I told you.' She avoided Sabrina's eyes. 'My mother was sick. She died shortly after that.' Camille didn't seem anxious to discuss it with her.

'Were you with her when she died?'

'I was in France at the time.' Why lie to her? What difference did it make now? She was back in the house. She was still Jeremiah Thurston's wife, and Sabrina was terrified. Jon had been right, Camille was tougher than his mother. The fort had been taken, almost without a fight. Camille was proud of herself. It had gone much better than she had planned, and when Jon came home, it would be even easier. An ally would help her a great deal. And he had promised her all his help.

'Did you live in France for long?'

'Thirty-four years.'

'That's quite a while. Did you marry again?' She was trying to trap Camille, but her mother only smiled at her.

'No. I did not.'

'You're not a countess by birth . . . and the Dupré? . . .'

She looked Sabrina straight in the eye. 'He was my patron in France.'

'I see. You were his mistress then.' Sabrina smiled sweetly at her. 'I wonder how that affects your claim. Thirty-four years is a long time.'

'I was legally married to Jeremiah Thurston the entire time, and still am. You can't change that fact, Sabrina, no matter how hard you try.'

'I just think it's interesting that you went on with your life with your . . . er . . . patron. . . .' She particularly stressed the word wanting to make Camille blush, but there was no hope of that, 'and now you come back for this house. It's certainly convenient at any rate. Have you made your Thanksgiving plans yet? Or are you going to redecorate? I mean after all, why waste a moment's time?' There was a bitter, vicious tone in Sabrina's voice which was unusual for her.

Andre arrived shortly before noon. Camille was sweeping down the main stairs, and she smiled at him. He was an extremely attractive man and she was delighted to find that he was French, although her delight lessened when she realized that he was in Sabrina's camp and he was going to do everything he could to get Camille out of there. She attempted to chat with him about France, she seemed to have lived most of the time in some very small town in the South, but she had spent a little time in Paris too. She attempted to pretend that she had led a glamorous life there, but he knew it for a lie and brushed her off. He wanted to speak to Sabrina alone.

'Have you locked up the silverware and the jewels? She could be a very clever common thief, you know.' But Sabrina laughed at that.

'The only jewels I have were hers, or most of them anyway. At the rate she moves, she'll demand them back anyway.'

'Well, for Heaven's sake, don't give them to her. And I think you should call the police.' He didn't like the look of her. But when he called the police himself and tried to explain, they told him that they didn't get involved in family affairs, and a call to another attorney they knew was discouraging. He said they would have to fight it out in court, and now that she had moved in, it would be almost impossible to get her out until then, unless they threw her out bodily and then she could easily sue. 'You shouldn't have let her in yesterday.' Andre sounded matter of fact and she stared at him.

'Are you crazy? How was I supposed to know? She moved in here like a division of Russian tanks and the next thing I knew she was throwing my clothes on a chair. I'm just lucky she agreed to move into the guest suite, or I'd be sleeping in there.'

'What?' He tried to make light of it, but it was difficult to do. 'She's sleeping in my room! Get her *out*!' Sabrina laughed but there were tears again.

'I just don't understand, Andre.' It had been a tremendous shock. 'Why didn't my father say anything?'

'God only knows what passed between them. From the sound and the look of her, she's a tough customer, and I don't believe the story she told you. It's a damn shame Amelia won't come to the phone.' But he tried her again and this time she did, croaking horribly and complaining about her throat, but at least she set them straight, and she told them what Camille had done about the affair with Dupré and that she had abandoned her husband and her baby daughter.

'I'm sorry she's come back to haunt you now. She was a terrible, selfish, mean-hearted young girl then, and it doesn't sound as though she's improved with age.'

Sabrina smiled sadly at her friend's words. 'I don't think she has.' And then she thought back over what Amelia had said about Camille's flight. 'My father must have been heartbroken.' Now she understood even better his unwillingness to talk about her. He had never recovered from the shock.

'He was very hurt. But he had you.' Amelia smiled, thinking back. 'You were the joy of his life. In later years, I don't think he missed her very much. He got on with his life. But for the first few years . . . it was very rough.'

Sabrina decided to ask her then. 'Is it true that he had a mistress and maybe that was why she left?'

'Not at all!' Amelia sounded outraged on behalf of her old friend. 'He was totally faithful to Camille. I would vouch for it myself. In fact, he was very upset that you took as long as you did to come along,' she didn't want to tell her about the perfidy with the rings although she still remembered that, and she didn't know that Sabrina knew. 'It turned out that Camille had something to do with that herself, and your father was very upset about it, but we won't discuss that now, my dear. Be a good girl now, and don't let all this worry you, just throw her out.'

'I wish I could. Apparently we have to go to court first.'

'What a dreadful ordeal for you, poor child.' At forty-seven, Sabrina was no child, but she was touched by her words. 'The woman ought to be shot. Actually, Jeremiah should have done that long ago, it would have made things a great deal simpler for you now.'

'It would that.' Sabrina smiled, grateful that there had been someone to phone. 'I'll tell you how it turns out.'

'You do that. And how is Andre, by the way? I take it you two are rebuilding the world and plan to fill it with drunks.'

'One of these days.' Sabrina laughed at Amelia's description of their plans. 'Are you all right?'

'Fine. Except for this throat. I seem determined to live forever, in spite of myself.'

'Good. We need you around.'

'Well, you don't need her. And you never did. So throw her out.'

'Amen.' Sabrina thanked her and hung up and turned to Andre again. There was absolutely nothing they could do until they went to court, and with that Camille floated through the room in a white chiffon dress, with diamond earrings Sabrina suspected weren't real. She looked at Andre in despair. 'What am I going to do?' The prospect of living with her until they went to court almost drove her mad, and when Jon returned the next day, things did not improve. He greeted Camille like his long lost friend and beloved grandmother, honoured and expected guest, and Sabrina went straight to his room and closed the door. She stood facing him as he sat on the bed. He didn't look as though he were in the mood to talk, but she wasn't offering a choice.

'I want to talk to you, Jon.'

'What about?' But he was playing with her. He knew, and it amused him to think of how angry she would be. What the hell? Why not? She never gave him what he wanted anymore, the Grand Tour, the car he had been begging for for three years. She just cried poor all the time, and whined about Thurston House. Well, now Grandmother would take it off her hands, and she could go live in Napa with the French farmer she was so busy planting grapes with. And he and his grandmother could live in splendor at Thurston House. And Grandmother had promised him a car, once she got things worked out. That was definitely his style, and he could hardly wait. It was going to be a very amusing senior year, with a car of his own, if they worked things out soon enough, and The Grand Tour at the end, a graduation present, Grandmother had said. After that he was moving to New York to find a job so he didn't care who lived in the house anyway. He probably never would again, not for any serious length of time. He thought San Francisco a pathetic, provincial little town. He was ready for New York after three years at Cambridge, although they were certainly nice to him everywhere . . . Boston . . . Atlanta . . . Philadelphia . . . Washington. . . .

'I want an explanation from you.' His mind was torn back from pleasanter thoughts by his mother glaring down at him. She was almost shaking with rage, and there would be no avoiding her. But she couldn't do anything to him now. Grandmother was already in the house, and she had got in all by herself. Originally, she had wanted Jon to let her in while Sabrina was away, but he had refused to go quite that far, and she had agreed to handle it herself. He knew she could. She was even tougher than Sabrina was, but somehow she seemed to have more in common with Jon, they thought the same way, as Sabrina feared now, and that was something else she wanted to discuss with him. 'Just exactly what role did you play in this?' Her eyes were relentless as they bore through him.

'What do you mean?'

'Don't play games with me. She tells me she's known you for almost three years. Why didn't you ever say anything to me?'

'I thought you'd be upset.' But he averted his eyes and, without warning, she reached out and slapped his face.

'Don't lie to me!'

He looked up at her, shocked. She had never looked at him that way before. Her eyes hurt more than her hand, but she had never felt more betrayed, and the more she had thought about it, the angrier she got. 'Dammit, what difference does it make who I know! Do I have to tell you everything I do?'

'She's my mother, Jon, and you met her three years ago. Why did you help her do this?'

'I did no such thing,' and then as he looked at her he shrugged. 'Maybe she has as much right to this house as you do. She says she was married to Grandfather when he died.'

'You could have warned me of that, couldn't you?' He didn't answer her, and her voice rose again. 'Couldn't you?' And then, 'You know what the worst thing about all this is, Jon? It's what you did to me. She's never been a mother to me, but you are my son, and you not only let this happen, you helped her set it up. How does that make you feel about yourself?'

He looked right into her eyes, belligerent and hostile to the end, and something inside her began to die as she looked at him. 'I feel fine,' he shrugged.

'Then I feel sorry for you.'

'I don't need anything from you.' He said it as Sabrina left the room. She couldn't control herself anymore, and she couldn't bear what she was seeing in him. He was so much like Camille, and for so many years she had wondered about him. He was different from her father, from his own, from herself, but now she had traced the genes back to their source inadvertently. He was exactly like Camille; evil to the core. He had no loyalty to Sabrina at all, after all she had done for him. Somewhere, sometime, something had got twisted in him and it had never got straightened out again, and it was almost too late now. Particularly if Camille stuck around to bring out the worst in him. In the next few days, she watched the two of them collaborate and conspire, whisper and go out. Sabrina felt totally abandoned by her son, and she couldn't concentrate on anything now, but she didn't dare leave the house and go to Napa to see Andre and their lands. She was afraid that if she left, they would do something even worse to her, like pillage the house, or steal her things, or maybe even change the locks and not let her back in.

'You can't sit there terrified for the next few months.' Andre was genuinely worried about her.

'Do you think it'll take that long?'

'It could. You know what the lawyer said.'

'I think I'll go mad before that.'

'Not until you come up here and make some decisions about the wines.' And then he had an idea. 'I'll tell you what. I'll send Antoine down, and he can stay there at the house and keep an eye on things while you come up here, and when you go back, he'll come back up here.' It was an elaborate system, but it worked. And for the next two months that was exactly what they did. By then her attorney was back, and he had the matter in hand. He also agreed that there was very little they could do. It would have to go to court, and that might take another two months. In the meantime, Jon had to go back to college, but the chill between him and his mother hadn't warmed. He went out to dinner with Camille the night before he left, and Sabrina went out to dinner with Andre and Antoine. The bitterness between them was almost irreparable now, and she almost felt sometimes as though she had lost her son. And in a sense she had, to Camille. So far, Camille had won nothing else, but the loss of Jon was a major defeat in itself to Sabrina. Camille was promising Jon the moon, once they got Sabrina out of the house. And through it all, Sabrina still felt as though he were wreaking vengeance on her because his father had died, and because she had worked at the mines. He would never forgive her for those things, and now he was going to make her pay for the rest of her life. She said as much to Andre one day as they were walking through the vines.

'I must have failed him terribly.' She sighed. 'If his father had lived, I wouldn't have gone back to work of course. And I didn't work full time, but I think he wanted more than I gave.'

'Maybe he's one of those people who would have always wanted more than you had to give. You can't do anything about that.'

'I'd like to save him from Camille now. He doesn't see her for what she is yet, but he will, and he'll be badly disillusioned by then.'

Andre didn't think that was such a bad thing, and he thought he deserved it for his perfidy. He was a rotten kid. Andre hadn't liked him from the first, but he would never tell Sabrina that. He was the only one she had, and despite her pain, she still loved him after all. He was her son. But she got comfort now from Antoine too. Knowing what she was going through, he was particularly kind to her, and he brought her flowers and baskets of fruit, and little thoughtful gifts from time to time. They meant a great deal to her and she always mentioned it to Andre, telling him what a fine boy he had. He was proud of him, and she envied them the closeness they shared. She hoped that in a few years, when Jon was the same age as Antoine, he would have matured as much and grown closer to her, but some deep inner part of her told her that would not be the case, so she turned her mind to other things, the vineyards she was building with Andre, and the suit she was going to bring against Camille. Camille knew the date was coming close, and she appeared unmoved by it, playing her cards tight and well, and only a week before the court date, she knocked on the door to Sabrina's suite. It was December ninth, and they were going to court on December fifteenth.

'Yes what do you want?' Sabrina stood in her robe and bare feet, still unable to believe that Camille had inflicted herself on her. She had been there for more than five months now, and it was like a nightmare without end, a terrible dream from which Sabrina never seemed to wake up. Camille was always there, wandering around the house with a possessive air, putting on her cheap clothes and ratty furs and putting on the dog around town. Sabrina had heard rumors of it, and now and then some valuable object would disappear from the house and Camille would insist she had had nothing to do with it, but Sabrina knew otherwise. She couldn't seem to stop her and she couldn't watch her all the time. As Sabrina had predicted to Andre, Camille had attempted to reclaim her jewels, but Sabrina wouldn't hear of it. By a sheer quirk of fate, she had to tolerate the woman in her house, but that was all she would do. And as the bills began to pour in, incurred by Camille and her son, she took a stand and refused to pay for them. They seemed to be trying to do everything they could to bankrupt her, and she would have been if she had tried to pay the bills for the mountain of things they charged to her. But Sabrina let Camille's bills pile up without touching the stack, and she mailed Jon's to him at school.

'I thought we might talk.' Camille always sounded very Southern when she had a plan in mind. And the only thing Sabrina really hated

335

about her was that for the rest of her life she would think of that voice, and see the face and worry that in some way she might look or talk or think or act like her ... even a single gesture in common would have been a repulsive thought, and it was still worse to realize how much like her Jon was. But none of what she felt showed in her eyes now.

'Talk about what? I have nothing to say to you.'

'Wouldn't you rather talk than go to court?'

'Not necessarily.' Sabrina was hardened now, and she was calling her bluff. Why not? Her lawyer said that the more he looked at it, the less he thought Camille had a case. Jeremiah's will had been written in such a way that he had excluded her without actually saying her name, 'any persons I might have been married to. . . .' Sabrina remembered thinking that strange at the time of his death but she had been so upset at the time she hadn't dwelled on it. And now it had to be fought out in court, no matter how good her chances were. Unless Camille backed down and left, but that seemed unlikely after she'd dug her heels in for so long. 'I don't mind going to court.'

Camille looked at her and smiled. 'I don't want to take your house away, child.' Sabrina wanted to slap her face or beat her head into the ground. After almost six months of torturing her, invading her life, stealing her son, now she didn't want to take her house away from her? And she dared to call her 'child'.

'I'm almost fifty years old, and I'm not your "child", and never was. I have nothing to do with you. You make me sick. And if I had my way you'd be thrown out of here on your ass tonight.'

'I'll go this week,' her voice was an insidious whisper, 'if you pay my price.' Without saying another word to her, Sabrina slammed her bedroom door in her face.

For Andre it was agonising watching Sabrina go through what she had to for six months, and there was nothing he could do to help. He went to court with her on December fifteenth, and for once Camille actually looked frightened and pale. She had gone too far, and she knew it as she attempted to wheedle her way around the judge, who was shocked by the tale, and her brazen act of moving into the house and tormenting Sabrina for so long, after abandoning her as a child. A sworn statement had been taken from Amelia in New York. Despite her age, her memory was excellent, and she had been more than articulate about the events of some forty-six years before. Camille almost shook as she looked around the court. She was alone, and she was a fool. She had never meant for it to go this far. She thought Sabrina would buy her off, and now they were talking about having her pay damages and back rent for the past six months. The matter of her extensive bills was brought up, and those she had encouraged Jonathan to incur, and when it was all over, she was grateful to receive only a sound scolding from the judge. He had actually threatened to put her in jail, and he gave her exactly one hour, with a sheriff's deputy standing by, to pack and be out of Thurston House.

Sabrina couldn't believe the nightmare had come to an end, and as Camille walked down the stairs for a last time, Sabrina looked at her from beneath the magnificent dome, and there was no longer hatred in her eyes. There was nothing there at all. She had lost too much in the last six months to feel anything for Camille now. She had lost her peace of mind, and more importantly, she had lost her son.

'I thought when it was all over, we might be friends.' Camille spoke to her in a nervous, hesitant voice. She had played her hand too far and got badly burned. And now she had to go back to Atlanta with her tail between her legs, to stay with young Hubert again, and she hadn't been kind to him either when she left.

Sabrina spoke in a clear strong voice as the deputy stood by. 'I don't ever want to see or hear from you again, and if I do I'll call the police and report it to the court. Is that clear?' Camille nodded silently. 'And stay away from my son.' But that battle she had lost, for when she called Jon the next day, after regaining her wits and her calm, he told her he wasn't coming home for Christmas after all. He had been planning to take the train West on the eighteenth. He was going to Atlanta instead, and his voice was accusatory again.

'I talked to Grandmother yesterday. She says you bought off the judge.' Sabrina was stunned and for the first time since the judge had ordered Camille out of her house, she felt tears on her cheeks. Was it possible that Jon would never understand, that he would hate her always, was he that much like his grandmother?

'Jon, I did no such thing.' She was fighting to stay calm. 'I don't even think one could. The judge was a decent man and he saw her for what she was.'

'She's an old woman looking for a place to live, and God only knows where she'll go now.'

'Where was she before?'

'Living on people's charity from hand to mouth. She's going to have to move in with her nephew again.'

'I can't help that.'

'And you don't care.'

'No, I don't. She tried to take this house away, Jon!' But he refused to understand. He hung up, calling her a bitch, and that night she lay alone in her bed, in the house that was finally hers again, knowing that she hadn't won after all. Camille Beauchamp Thurston had. She had won her son away from her.

Chapter Thirty-One

It would have been a lonely Christmas for her that year, without Jon, if it hadn't been for Antoine and Andre. They refused to let it be lonely for her. They arrived on the doorstep of Thurston House, with a Christmas tree and egg nog Antoine had made, and they teased her and amused her and cajoled her all day. They all went to midnight mass together and sang carols as the tears rolled down Sabrina's cheek, and Andre put an arm around her shoulders and smiled at her. They were a good threesome and she was grateful to them. Without them she would have sat alone in the house and cried at the miseries Camille had brought, but with the two Frenchmen around, it was impossible to remain depressed, and by Christmas Day, she was in good spirits again. Antoine went back to Napa to rejoin the men, but Andre stayed on with her, so that they could go to the bank together the next day. They wanted to take out another loan for some equipment they would need, but things were going well for them. Andre was brilliant at running the vineyards for her, and they had cleared all of the land by then.

'Even my jungle looks wonderful now,' she teased, 'I hardly recognize it.'

'Wait 'til you taste our wine!' But instead he had brought her a bottle of Moët and Chandon and they sat and looked at the Christmas tree after Antoine left, and Andre glanced at her admiringly. She had been through so much that year, but Amelia had been right long ago, she was made of remarkable stuff, Sabrina was. She was extraordinary, gentle and kind and stronger than any woman he knew. Even more so than Amelia perhaps, and Sabrina would have been stunned to hear him say that. Amelia was what she would have wanted her mother to be like. But she couldn't pretend anymore. She knew exactly what her mother was. A bitch and a whore, and a woman who had tried to take everything from her dishonestly. She had even stolen a small painting in her suitcase when she left, but Sabrina was grateful to be rid of her at almost any cost. She sat staring at the tree, thinking of that.

'It's been an amazing year, hasn't it?'

'I would say.' He laughed at the words she used and her look of surprise, but she smiled at him.

'It's been good as well as bad. You and Antoine have been the best gifts of all.' And aside from all that, he had given her a beautiful red cashmere sweater with a matching hat and she had bought him a warm jacket and warm gloves. 'So, it wasn't all bad.'

'I hope not.' But they both knew that she was sad about her son. It would have been impossible for her not to be, although she said little about it, even to him. It was just too painful to talk about, and she concealed it by joking with him.

After their meeting with the bank the next day, she went back to Napa with Andre, and she spent the rest of the week there. She wasn't afraid to leave Thurston House unguarded now. She had had the locks changed the day Camille left and even Jon did not yet have the new key. She had her own room in the large farmhouse Andre had rented eight months before. He and Antoine were already making plans to build their other house, but for the moment they all still lived in the large communal arrangement, and Sabrina was happy there. The men were friendly to her, and she was beginning to speak halting French.

And after the New Year, Andre drove her home again. They came across the Bay Bridge, up Broadway, and then south to California Street and right on Taylor to Nob Hill. He parked the car on the street outside Thurston House, and carried her bags inside for her. He wanted to stay in the city again for a day or two, Antoine could easily carry on for him, and he and Sabrina could do some work in town. They spent long hours in her library that night, going over some of the paperwork. They shared the responsibility of that, and in some ways it reminded her of the old days at her mines after her father died, except that she would have been grateful to have Andre then.

'It must have been so difficult for you.'

'It was.' She smiled. 'But I learned a lot from it.'

'I can see that. But that's not an easy way to learn anything.'

'Maybe I wasn't destined to learn the easy way.' She was thinking of Camille and Jon again, and what a disappointment he had been to her, and Andre watched her eyes. He asked her an odd question then, about something he had wondered about for a long time. They had been good friends for ten months now, but there were certain things they never talked about. She rarely mentioned John Harte to him, and he seldom spoke of his wife. She had died when Antoine was five, and he had been lonely for a long, long time. There had been a woman he had grown fond of in France, but now that was over with. He knew from a recent letter from her that she was involved with someone else. And he wasn't heartbroken over it. He had expected that when he left France and she hadn't wanted to come to America with him. But now he wondered about Sabrina's previous life and he was comfortable enough to ask.

'What was your husband like?'

She smiled at her friend. 'Wonderful.' And then suddenly, she laughed. 'Actually, at first we didn't like each other very much. He kept trying to buy me out. He owned the rival mine.' Andre laughed, imagining the sparks of that. 'But eventually . . .' She smiled nostalgically, 'we settled down. You know,' her face sobered again, 'I never let him merge our mines even in later years. And afterward, I was so sorry about that. I gave him such a bad time . . . and for what?' She looked into Andre's eyes. 'In the end, after he died, I merged them anyway. I was stupid not to have done it before that.'

'Why didn't you?'

'I think I wanted to prove something to him, that I was still independent and not just a part of him. But he humoured me, and kept things the way I wanted them, even though he must have known that it was a lot more trouble that way. He was so patient.' She looked into Andre's eyes, 'It has made me a better partner to you in the past year because of what I learned from him.'

'You've been wonderful.' He smiled at her, and then he grinned, 'Except your cooking and your French!'

'How can you say that?' She began to laugh. 'I cooked everyone an omelette last week.' And she had been so proud of herself and they were laughing now, at one in the morning in her library, tired, but comfortable, side by side.

'Didn't you see how sick they got?' He loved teasing her, and he pulled gently now at one of the plaits she wore. She looked like a very young girl to him, and someone who didn't know her well would have lopped a dozen years off her age. 'You know, you look like an Indian squaw.' And at his words she suddenly remembered Spring Moon, and she told him about her fascination with her, and that she had saved her from being raped by Dan. 'You certainly didn't lead a boring life, my dear. Are you sure the vineyards aren't too tame for you?'

'They're perfect now. I don't think I could stand all that excitement again. One day, more than three hundred men walked out on my mine. I don't ever want to live through something like that again.'

'You won't. Your life will be peaceful from now on. I promise you.' She had certainly earned that much and she smiled ruefully at him.

'I wish you could promise that, for all of us.' She was also thinking of Jon. 'What about you, Andre? What do you want out of life, other than a huge success with our fancy wines?' She tweaked his ear and he pulled her hair again.

'Don't get fresh with me, ma petite . . . what do I want?' His face grew serious, and he would have had a good answer to that, but he didn't dare. 'I don't know. I suppose I have everything I want. There's one thing lacking here.' She was surprised to hear him say that. He seemed so content.

'What's that?'

'Companionship. I miss someone to share my life with, I mean other than Antoine, because that won't last for long. He should move on, and he will in time. But don't you miss that too?' He had had companionship far more recently than she, only a year before, and she thought about it now. She had missed it too of course, but she had grown accustomed to being alone for so long. There had been no man in her life since John, and she had told Andre that before. He thought it remarkable but he wasn't surprised. 'I always suspected that.' By now, they knew each other very well, and he would have known if there was someone in her life. 'How could you stay alone for so long?' He was impressed. Two years after his wife had died he had had a serious affair, and there had been several in the years since, not excessively, but he enjoyed having a woman in his life. 'Don't you find your solitude unbearable?' He was intrigued by her and she laughed at him.

'No. I don't. It's actually very simple and pleasant sometimes. It's lonely too. But after a while, you don't think of that. You know,' she teased, 'rather like being a nun.'

'What a waste.' He looked very French as he looked at her and they both laughed. 'It really is, you know. You're such a lovely woman, Sabrina, and you're still young.'

'I wouldn't say that, my friend. I'll be forty-eight in May. That's not exactly like being a young girl.'

'You're in your prime.'

'Now I know you're crazy, Andre.'

'I'm not!' The woman he had been involved with in France had been older than she, and not nearly so beautiful. Sabrina would have been a rare gift for any man. She was a very special woman, as Andre was aware. And he wouldn't have dared approach her just for fun. She meant too much to him for that. They parted company at two o'clock in the morning and met again at breakfast the next day, fully dressed and businesslike, but they were closer after their late night talk. She was freer about mentioning John to him now, and he talked about some of his women friends to her, almost as though they were sounding each other out without realizing it, and he startled her when he decided not to return to Napa on Friday night as planned and invited her out to dinner instead.

'Is there something to celebrate?' She looked surprised and she was tired. It had been a long week, and she was still exhausted from her legal ordeal with Camille the month before. The relief from that had left her almost weak at the knees and she hadn't gone out much since then. He thought it might do her good.

'Why not just go out for the hell of it?'

'How decadent.' But the idea appealed to her, and she retired to her rooms to dress for him, and when they met downstairs beneath the dome, she was wearing a black dress he had never seen before.

'You look very elegant, Madame.' He smiled at her playfully and she noticed again how handsome he was. She didn't notice it very often now, they were so used to each other and they were just friends, but tonight she curtsied to him with an impish grin. 'Merci, monsieur.' He drove her to the restaurant and they had a drink at the bar, and then took their table after eight o'clock, and they had a lovely time, he telling her about things he had done in France, she telling more stories of the mine and about herself, and as usual, they wound up back at Thurston House, but tonight, she invited him into her

343

private sitting room. Usually, they sat in the library, but this was smaller and cozier and more intimate, and she built a fire and lit it when he went downstairs to get drinks for them. He poured two small brandies, and they sipped them by the fire, looking into the glow as the embers rolled and kindling caught. She looked at him then. 'Thank you for tonight, Andre . . . thank you for everything. You've been good for me. And very good to me, as well.' He was moved by what she said and he reached out and touched her hand.

'I would do anything for you, Sabrina. I hope you know that.'

'You already have.' And then, as though they had both expected it, he leaned over and kissed her lips; it just seemed so natural, and they sat side by side, holding hands and kissing by the fire. After a while she laughed gently at him. 'It's like being kids again, isn't it?'

'Aren't we?' He smiled.

'I don't know . . .' He muffled her words with his lips and she felt a hunger for him rise up in her like an unfamiliar sweet pain. He took her in his arms, and as they lay by the fire, he felt his body warm beside hers, and his hands began to move on her flesh; it was as though they were both ready for what was happening.

He whispered gently to her, he didn't want to do anything they'd both regret or that, more importantly, she would. She was too important to him as a human being, as well as a friend. 'Should I go away, Sabrina?'

'I don't know.' She smiled at him. 'What are we doing here?'

'I think I'm in love with you.' He whispered back. And remarkably it didn't surprise her at all. She realized that she had been in love with him for a long, long time, maybe even from the first time they had met. They had built something beautiful together, with their hearts and their hands, courageously, energetically. He had brought her alive again, and now this was only an extension of that, and she reached out to him, and he carried her to her bed, and they made love there as though they had always done, and at last they lay in each other's arms sleepily as he smoothed the silk of her hair beneath his fingertips and fell asleep with his arms round her.

When they awoke the next day, he was relieved to see that there was no regret in her eyes. And he kissed her on the eyes, the lips . . . the tip of her nose, and she giggled at him and they made love again. It was almost like a honeymoon, and everything about it was comfortable. She couldn't imagine how it could all happen that easily. It

344

had been twenty years since she had made love to a man, and yet here she was, as happy as could be with him, and he was obviously crazy about her. A floodgate had suddenly opened in him, and he seemed to engulf her with his love.

'What happened to us?' She looked at him sleepily after they'd made love again. It was Saturday, and they didn't have to go anywhere. They were alone and happy and in love.

'It must have been something we ate last night . . .'

'Maybe the champagne . . . we'll have to remember to grow ours like that.' And then with a smile, she drifted off to sleep again and awoke at noon as he arrived in the bedroom with a tray of things to eat.

'To keep up your strength, my love.' And she needed it, when they made love again the moment after they finished eating.

'Good Heavens, Andre!' She was laughing, and happy and enjoying herself, 'Are you always like this?'

'No.' He answered honestly and snuggled closer to her. He couldn't get enough of her. It was as though he had waited a year and now had to press it all into one day. 'You do something wonderful to me.'

'May I return the compliment?' They slept and made love all afternoon, and at six o'clock they finally got up and bathed and dressed and went out again, this time to the Bal Tabaria on Columbus Avenue, and it really was like a honeymoon.

'How did this happen to us?' She smiled at him over a fresh bottle of champagne with dessert.

'I don't know.' He looked serious as he looked at her. 'I think maybe we've earned it, my love. We've worked awfully hard this year.'

'What a nice reward.' And he thought so too as they went back to her bed that night, and made love again, this time with a fire in the hearth of her bedroom. It was the room where Jonathan had been born almost twenty-two years before, but she wasn't thinking of that now. She was thinking of Andre, and they slept soundly in each other's arms and awoke just after dawn. They looked at each other, kissed and went back to sleep, and made love when they woke up again the next time, and this time, afterwards, Andre looked at her in concern. He had thought of it the day before as well and then forgot.

'Would it be rude to ask you if you're worried about birth control, my love?' He realized he had done nothing about it for two days, but she was unconcerned.

'By the time I might get pregnant, Andre, I'll be eighty years old. I don't get pregnant easily to say the least. It took me more than two years each time I got pregnant before. I am the least dangerous woman you know.'

'That's convenient at least. But you're sure that's all right?'

'I'm positive. I probably can't even get pregnant at my age.'

'You can't be sure of that.'

'I'll do something about it next week. And in the meantime, don't worry.' By Sunday night they were so content that they decided to spend another night at Thurston House before going back to Napa again. Neither of them was anxious to end the impromptu honeymoon. Their whole lives had changed in two days and neither of them regretted it. It added a new dimension to all they'd had before, and when they drove to Napa the next day, Sabrina began to laugh, her long hair falling down her back, her blue eyes as bright as a young girl's. She was wearing the red cashmere sweater he'd given her, with a pair of grey flannel slacks. 'What'll we do in Napa now? The men will be shocked.' It was none of their business anyway, and she didn't think Antoine should know, at least not yet.

'It looks like I'll have to build my house a little more rapidly. Tomorrow I'll call the architect!' They both laughed and that night he tiptoed from his room to hers and then tiptoed back again at dawn with a happy smile on his face. He was fifty-five years old, and he had never been so happy in his life as he was now.

Chapter Thirty-Two

They crept back and forth between each other's rooms for the next few weeks, going to the city at least once a week, but she was in Napa most of the time with Andre and Antoine. A different look passed between Sabrina and Andre now, a secret message understood only by them, although once she thought she saw Antoine watching them, and then he quickly turned away, as though afraid to intercept what was not meant for him. Later she thought she saw him smiling at them.

'Do you think he knows?' She asked Andre late one night, as they lay whispering in her bed in the Napa farmhouse. He had indeed gone to the architect that week, and his new house would be started in the spring. But they would still have to tiptoe back and forth between their rooms for a long time before the house was complete.

'I don't know.' Andre smiled at her in the moonlight as he touched her face. He had never loved a woman as he loved her, and she felt something for him she had never felt before, not even for John. She had been so much younger then, and there was more depth to what she felt for Andre now. 'I think he would be happy for us, if he knew. I almost told him yesterday.'

She nodded. She could not imagine telling Jon. He had already accused her of having an affair with Andre long ago, and she didn't want to prove him right now, even though there had been no other man in her life for years, not since his father died. She knew he wouldn't understand. And there had been no news of him in almost a month, nor of Camille, who had retreated to Atlanta again, but Sabrina certainly didn't want to hear from her anyway. Now she forced her thoughts back to Antoine. 'You don't think he'd be upset?' He was so different from Jon, and she was already so fond of him.

Andre smiled at her in the moonlight again. 'What would he be upset about? He'll be pleased for us.' And Sabrina suspected that too. He was unusually kind to her these days, helping her in the fields when they all worked side by side, which she liked best. And it was Antoine who was with her a few weeks after that, when she stood up in the bright sun for most of the day, then suddenly reeled toward him late in the afternoon and almost fainted in his arms. She was mortified, as they sat side by side in the dirt, and he made a cool compress from a handkerchief and the water from a canteen he had with him. 'You should have worn a hat.' He scolded her as though she were a child, and she looked up at him, feeling very ill. Everything seemed to be spinning round, and her stomach continued to heave, but she managed to control herself and walk slowly back to the house with him a little while after that.

'Antoine . . . don't say anything to your father. . . . please.' She looked imploringly at him, but he frowned at her.

'Why not? I think he should know, don't you?' And then suddenly he was frightened for her. His mother had died of cancer when he was five, and he still remembered her, and how sad his father had been. He looked at Sabrina with worried eyes. 'I will not tell him, if you promise to go to a doctor straight away.' She seemed to hesitate and he grabbed her arm, propelled by the distant memories he had. He looked fiercely at her. 'I mean that, Sabrina. Or I'll tell him right now.'

'All right, all right. It was just the sun.' But he didn't think she looked well now, and he noticed during the next few days that she wasn't eating very much. He questioned her about the doctor again. She was going to fob him off, but he wouldn't let her do that. 'Antoine, I'm fine.'

'You are *not*.' He actually shouted at her, but it was different than the fights with Jon. It was so obvious that he was worried about her, and she was touched. When it almost happened again, he almost dragged her back to the house at noon, though fortunately Andre was at the architect's office. 'Now, do you call your doctor, Sabrina, or do I?'

'For Heaven's sake. . . .' She was embarrassed but he wouldn't let her off the hook. He stood by the phone, looking at her menacingly until finally she laughed. 'It's a good thing you're not my son, Antoine, I wouldn't have stood a chance against you.' But she was teasing him and she looked at him gratefully as she went to the phone to call. It was nice knowing that he cared that much, and now two people did. Andre and his son. She called the doctor and made an appointment for the following afternoon. 'And do you know what he's going to say?'

'Yes.' Antoine looked intransigent. 'That you work too hard. Look at Papa, he works hard too, but he takes a nap each day.' It was a habit he had brought from France, but because of it he looked healthy and young.

'I don't have the patience for that.'

'Well, you should.' But he was pleased that she was going to see her doctor. At least he had accomplished that much. 'Do you want me to drive you into town tomorrow?'

'No. That's fine. I have some other things to do anyway.' And she didn't want to make a fuss of it, or Andre would wonder what was going on.

'You'll tell me what they say?' She saw the fear rampant in his eyes, and it was almost as though he were a little boy again. She went to him and looked up into his eyes. He was a great deal taller than she, but she felt protective toward him now.

'It won't be anything terrible, Antoine. I'm in perfect health, and I promise you, I feel fine I think probably all that strain with my mother turning up, and going to court, and. . . .' they both knew she had almost added Jonathan to the list, 'I think it all wore me out, and I'm paying for it now.'

'I was so sad they did that to you.' He looked down at her almost as though she were his mother now.

'So was I. But maybe it was just as well to clear it all up.' And yet through it she still felt that she had lost her son. She had seen a side of him she could not forget. Even now. 'And now, I want you to stop worrying about me. And I promise you, I'll tell you everything the doctor says.' But when she sat in his office the next day, she knew she couldn't keep her promise to Antoine. She sat staring at the doctor she had known for years, shock and disbelief stamped on her face. 'But that couldn't be . . . it's not possible . . . the last time it took . . . and I thought that by now. . . .' She stared at him. It was impossible to believe. But the doctor was smiling gently at her.

'It's true, Sabrina. That test doesn't lie. At least not when it's positive. And it was. You're pregnant, my dear.'

'But I can't be. In fact, last year I know I started the change of life.

I haven't even had my period since. . . .' She counted back and then stared at him. 'Oh no. . . .' It had been two months. He was right. She hadn't associated it with Andre. She was just happy not to be bothered with it. 'I never thought. . . . My God, if I hadn't almost fainted in the fields the other day. . . .' It would have been months before she'd known. And she still couldn't believe it was true. 'But both other times it took me years to get pregnant, and. . . .'

The doctor reached across his desk and patted her hand. 'It isn't always like that, my dear. And for all you know the problem then was John.'

'Oh my God.'

She was so distressed then, that a terrible thought occurred to him. 'You do know who the father is, don't you?'

'Of course!' She looked even more shocked than she had before. 'But I have no idea what he'll think of this . . . we're business associates and friends, but . . . at our age . . . we had no plans . . . we. . . .' Tears suddenly filled her eyes and spilled onto her cheeks. How cruel fate was. Why couldn't she have met him fifteen years before and then perhaps. . . . 'What am I going to do?' She cried openly into the handkerchief he handed her, and then blew her nose and looked at him. 'Will you take care of it?' It was a shocking thing to ask, and they both knew it was against the law but she didn't know where else to turn. He was the only doctor that she knew, except an old man in Saint Helena she'd gone to years before, but he looked sadly at her now.

'I can't do that, Sabrina. You know that.'

'I'm forty-eight years old. You can't expect me to have this child? I'm not even married to the man.'

'Do you love him?' She nodded her head and blew her nose again. 'Then why not marry him and have the child?'

'I can't do that. We both have grown sons. We'll be a laughing stock. He's fifty-five, I'm forty-eight. And at this age, he could still get away with it. He looks like a young man. But I could be a grandmother by now for Heaven's sake.'

'So what? Other women have done it before. I had a patient two years ago who was fifty-two years old. The same thing happened to her, except that she was married of course. And she and her daughter wound up in the hospital having a baby at the same time. You won't be the first one, Sabrina.'

350

'But I'd feel like a fool. And I refuse to force him to marry me. . . .' She smiled through her tears and laughed and cried at the same time, 'It's so ridiculous, at my age, to be forced into marrying a man because of a pregnancy.' She looked at the old doctor and started to cry again, and then looked at him pathetically. 'I'm sorry I'm such a mess.'

'It's understandable. It's quite a shock for anyone. And I have to admit, in your circumstances, Sabrina, it's not an easy situation. Is he a nice man, at least? Could you be happy with him?'

'Yes, I could.' But they had never discussed marriage and there was no reason for him to marry her. They were reasonably comfortable as things were. 'But still . . . a baby at our age. . . .' She thought of Jon, and the baby she had lost before him, and she hadn't even been considered terribly young then, but at forty-eight . . . it was inconceivable, and yet she had. She looked at the doctor again then. She knew what she had to do. She just didn't know where to go for it. 'Can't you help me find an abortionist? I just can't go through with this. It's not right.'

'You can't be the judge of that.' He frowned at her. 'If it happened, then perhaps it is. Perhaps one day, you'll find it was the greatest blessing that you ever had.' He refused to give her what she wanted from him. And he stood up to indicate that the visit was at an end. 'Now, I want to see you three weeks from now, Sabrina. And try to get off your feet as much as possible. There's no reason why, at your age, you can't give birth to a healthy child, but you want to be more careful than you might have been twenty years ago.' Twenty years ago . . . how ridiculous that this should happen now. She suddenly felt angry at him, and herself, and Andre, for getting her into this. For God's sake, she was pregnant and forty-eight years old, or at least she would be in May, and by then she would be four months along. Damn.

She left the doctor's office and went home, her mind full of everything he had said to her . . . about the baby . . . and Andre . . . that it could prove to be the greatest blessing of their lives one day, but she refused to even think of that. She had to find an abortionist and fast. She knew she had only a few weeks left before it became very dangerous for her. And she had no idea who to ask. How did one find an abortionist? She had never even thought of it before and she strained to think now, but as she did, the memory of the baby she had lost

351

kept haunting her. She remembered her own grief at the loss and John's. How could she think of killing a baby now, because that was what it was. But how could she not? She lay down on her bed, feeling sick, thinking of it, just as the phone rang. It was Antoine.

'What did the doctor say?' He had worried about her all day, and his father had just gone into town to buy some supplies, so he rushed to call Sabrina before Andre came back.

'Nothing dear, I'm fine. I told you, it's just fatigue.' But her voice sounded strained, even to her own ears, and he didn't sound convinced.

'Are you sure that's what he said?'

'I promise you.' She lied to him, but what choice did she have? 'I'll come back tomorrow or the next day.'

'I thought you were coming back tonight.' He sounded worried again, as though he had been her son, and she was moved to tears again. She had to fight to keep them from her voice. Suddenly everything that happened made her cry.

'I found that I have a little work to do here. Is everything all right up there, Antoine?'

'Yes, fine.' He told her what they had done all day. 'You're sure it's nothing then?' He sounded a little bit relieved at last. It wasn't cancer then. He always thought of that. And he had with her.

'Positive.' Positive was certainly the right word this time, and she smiled ruefully as she talked to him, and then Andre came back and took the phone.

'What are you up to there, ma petite?' He called her that sometimes, 'My little one', except when they were alone at night when he called her 'cherie' or 'mon amour', my darling and my love.

'Nothing much. I found a stack of mail I had to take care of sitting here. I really have to work something out about that. Maybe someone could send it to me when I stay in Napa for more than a few days.'

'That's a thought.' It was a relief just to hear his voice and she had an urge to tell him what the doctor had said, but she knew she couldn't do that. She didn't want to put that kind of pressure on him. What if he felt he had to marry her? It could ruin everything. It was better not to say anything. She would take care of it herself, and he would never know. 'When are you coming back?' There was an urgency in his voice which made her smile. She loved him perhaps more even now and she was sorry again that it hadn't happened fifteen years before. Maybe then she could have told him, and married him and let the baby live. But not now.

'I'll try to come back tomorrow or the next day. I was just telling Antoine, I found a ton of work to do here, in my mail.'

'Can't you bring it up here?' It was unusual for her to linger in town. 'Sabrina, is there something wrong?' He already knew her too well, but after a year of partnership and two months of sharing her bed, he knew her perfectly, down to the very depths of her soul. In some ways, he knew her better than anyone ever had, even in this short time. They were soul mates in every way.

'No, no, everything is fine.' She lied to him as she had to Antoine. 'Honestly.' She had to fight back tears again.

'Did you hear from Jon?'

'No. Nothing. I suppose he's busy at school. It's the end of his senior year. . . .' She always made excuses for him.

And Andre hated to ask, but he could hear something in her voice. 'Something from Camille?'

'No, thank God.' She smiled. She missed him so terribly, and it had been only a few hours since she'd seen him last. It seemed almost as though she needed him more now, but she couldn't let him see that need.

'Well, hurry home.' He would have offered to come to be with her, but he had too much to do just then, 'I miss you, cherie,' he whispered into the phone as the tears rolled down her cheek and she fought to keep normalcy in her voice.

'So do I.'

She lay awake for most of that night, alternating between tears and an iron resolve, and the next morning, she picked a directory, and selected a doctor's name in an unattractive part of town. His office hovered on the edge of the Tenderloin, and there were two drunks asleep on the street when she arrived there by cab at noon. She walked gingerly into the building which reeked of urine and cabbage, and went up the creaking stairs. She was relieved to see that the waiting room was immaculate, and when she was ushered in by an ancient nurse, she saw a short, fat, balding, spotlessly clean little man in a white coat. She wasn't sure if she was disappointed or relieved, but she took a deep breath before she spoke to him as he smiled reassuringly at her.

'Doctor . . . I . . . I apologise in advance if what I'm going to ask is an affront to you. . . .' Her eyes watered as she spoke and looked at him, 'I came to you because I'm desperate. . . .'

He looked at her wondering what would come next. He had seen everything in the past forty years at this address. 'Yes? I will do whatever I can.'

'I need an abortion. And I picked your name out of the directory. I don't know whom to ask, where to go. . . .' The tears rolled down her cheeks, and she expected him to leap to his feet and point to the door. Instead, he looked at her compassionately, and he seemed to weigh his words for a long time.

'I'm sorry. I'm sorry that you feel you cannot have the baby, Mrs. Smith.' She had made the appointment as Joan Smith and she suddenly remembered why he called her that even before she remembered what she had called herself, as he went on. 'Are you sure there is no possibility of going on with the pregnancy?'

He hadn't refused her yet, and she slowly began to hope. Perhaps she had come to the right place after all. 'I'm forty-eight years old. I'm a widow with a grown son, who is graduating from college this year.' That seemed enough reason to her but not to him.

'And the father of this child?'

'Is my business associate. We are good friends,' she blushed, obviously. 'He's seven years older than I am, his son is even older than mine. We have no intention of marrying . . . it's just impossible. . . .'

'Have you told him yet?'

She hesitated and then shook her head. 'I only found out yesterday. But I don't want to pressure him. I just want to take care of it and go home.'

'You live elsewhere?'

'Part of the time.' She was intentionally vague. She didn't want him to know who she was, hence the 'Mrs. Smith'. He would undoubtedly have recognized the name and he didn't need to know.

'Don't you think you owe it to him to at least discuss it with him?' She shook her head and he looked at her with kindly eyes. It wasn't the first time he had been asked for this kind of help, and he knew it wouldn't be the last. 'I think you're mistaken, Mrs. Smith. I think he has a right to know. And your age doesn't seem like an appropriate deterrent to me. Other women your age have borne children before.

354

It is a slightly greater risk, but this is not your first pregnancy, which reduces that risk considerably. I just don't think you should do this without giving it a great deal of thought. How pregnant do you believe you are?'

'Two months.' She knew it couldn't be more than that, because they had only been sleeping with each for slightly more than eight weeks. She had counted it out carefully the night before.

The doctor nodded. 'Then you don't have much time.'

'Will you help me then?'

He hesitated. He didn't do it anymore, although he had a long time ago, but a young girl had almost died, and he had promised himself not to do it again, and he never had. And for some reason, he felt that it would be wrong to do it for her. 'I just can't, Mrs. Smith.'

Sabrina gasped almost angrily. 'Then why did you . . . why . . . I thought when you listened to me. . . .'

'I'd rather convince you to have the child.'

'Well, I won't!' She leapt to her feet, crying openly now. 'I'll do it myself, damnit, if you won't.' And for an instant he thought she might and it frightened him.

'I can't help you. For your sake plus mine.' He could lose his license and never practice again. He could wind up in jail. But there was another possibility. He had given the name to someone before, and she had been pleased. He sighed and pulled his pad and pen toward him. He used a blank sheet, without his name, and scratched a name and phone number and handed it to her. 'Call this man.'

'Will he do it?' Her eyes were fierce as she looked at him. The doctor nodded somberly.

'Yes, he will. He's in Chinatown. He was a great surgeon once, but he got caught at this. I sent someone else to him. . . .' He looked sadly at Sabrina and told her what he thought again. 'But I think you should have the child. If you were poverty stricken, or diseased . . . or had been raped . . . or were a morphine addict . . . but you look like a decent woman to me, and probably your friend is too. You could give this child a home with love,' and he had noticed the fine wool of the black suit she wore. It was old but it had been expensive once. And even if her funds were slim now, a woman like this would find a way. 'Think about it, Mrs. Smith. The opportunity may never come again. And you may always regret not having this child. Think of that. Think about it carefully before you call that name.' He

355

waved at the sheet of paper she held in a trembling hand. 'Afterwards, there's no turning back, and even if you have another baby after this, you may always regret this one.' He reminded her of the one she had lost. Even Jon had never quite filled that void. It was a dream forever gone, as this would be . . . but she could not allow herself to think like that. She had no choice. She stood up then and shook his hand.

'Thank you for helping me.' She felt relieved. At least now she knew where to go.

'Think about it carefully.' His words echoed again in her head as she left, and when she got home she sat at her desk for a long time, feeling ill, trembling violently. She had to dial the number three times before she got it right, and a woman with an accent answered the phone at the other end.

'I'd like an appointment with the doctor please.'

'Who gave you his name?' The voice was suspicious, and Sabrina's hand trembled on the phone as she held her breath and then gave the name of the doctor she had just seen. There was a long silence then, as though someone else was monitoring the call, and then the woman answered her. 'He'll see you next week.'

'When?'

A pause again. 'Wednesday night.' That seemed odd to her, but she knew that it wouldn't be an ordinary office visit to a doctor downtown. 'At six. Wait at the back door, knock twice, then knock again. And bring five hundred dollars with you, cash.' The voice was as harsh as the words, and Sabrina almost gasped, not at the amount but at the image it conjured up.

'Will he do it then?' There was no point pretending now. They both knew what she wanted from him. Perhaps it was all he did. But why at night? What difference did it make, she told herself. She wondered how long it would take.

'Yes. And if you get sick afterwards, don't call us back. He won't help you then.' Their approach was certainly direct, and Sabrina wondered who she would call in an emergency. Perhaps the doctor who had referred her to him. She couldn't call her own, or could she . . . the questions raced through her head like bats, and when she hung up the phone again, she felt as though she might throw up, and eventually she did. She was violently ill as she knelt on the bathroom floor, thinking of the appointment she had made. Wednesday night.

At six. It was six days away, and she dreaded it. But there was no turning back now.

She drove back to Napa the next day, and pretended that all was well with her. She chatted a lot, worked too hard as usual, even offered to cook, in answer to which all the men teased and laughed. They were used to cooking for her now, but she ate almost nothing that night or the next day, and she saw Antoine glance at her once or twice, but he didn't ask her about the doctor again. And Andre seemed totally unconcerned. They made love almost every night, except finally on Tuesday night when Sabrina turned away and feigned sleep. The next morning when he awoke, she had left the room, and he found her downstairs, before dawn, just sitting there, staring out at the fields and hills, deep in thought. He tiptoed to her and sat down, and then she started and turned to him with a quiet smile.

'What are you doing up, Andre?'

'I was going to ask you that, ma petite.' Sabrina sighed. She glanced at the kitchen clock behind where he stood. It was five after six. Twelve hours from now she would be in Chinatown, paying five hundred dollars in cash to kill his child . . . the thought made her head swim and she felt ill just sitting there. 'What's wrong?' He sat down next to her and pressed her fingers gently to his lips. 'I know you've been upset for days, my love, and I didn't want to pry until you were ready to say something to me.' But she looked worse now than she had all week. She was almost green. 'What is it, my love? Is that woman tormenting you again?' He was afraid that Camille was bothering her. She shook her head, not sure what to say, fighting tears. She didn't want to lie to him, but she couldn't tell him what it was.

'Sometimes, Andre, there are things one has to take care of oneself. And this is one of those things.' This was the first time she had shut him out and it cut him to the quick, but he nodded understandingly and then looked at her.

'I cannot imagine anything I would not understand, ma petite, and I would do anything to help you if I could. Is it Jon?' She shook her head. 'Financial worries again?' They both had their share of those, but she shook her head again.

'It is something I must deal with alone.' And then, as she sighed and straightened her back, avoiding his eyes, 'I'm going into town for a few days.'

Andre asked, with a tone of fear, 'Is it us, Sabrina? You must tell me if it is.' He loved her so much. He had to know. He was too old for another heartbreak now. 'Are you sorry that we . . .' But she was quick to allay his fears with a kiss, a gentle smile, her fingers on his cheek.

'Never. Not that. It's something entirely unto myself.'

'There is no such thing. There is nothing we do not share.'

'Not this time.' Sadly, she shook her head.

'Are you ill?' She shook her head again.

'No. I'm upset, but I will be fine again. I'll come back on Saturday.' She had given herself three days to recuperate, and she hoped that was enough. Three days to ache and cry bitterly for the child that would die . . . for five hundred dollars cash . . .

'Why will you be gone so long?'

'Because I'm going to grow a beard and shave my head,' she teased him now as the sky turned to grey, then mauve, as the sun came up.

'Why will you not talk to me and tell me what it is?'

'Because I have to take care of this myself.'

'Why? There is nothing I would not share with you.'

She nodded. She felt the same. But not this time, and she forced both of the doctors' words out of her head . . . he has a right to know . . . ask him . . . tell him . . . give him a chance . . . 'Andre just let me handle this. On Saturday, I will be back and we can go on.' But she wondered now if it would stand between them anyway. She was deeply sorry that he suspected anything was wrong, and she had tried so hard to keep up a good front, but he knew her too well. And, just then, two of the French labourers came downstairs, and Sabrina went back upstairs to dress. There was a small problem with one of the machines after that, and a new piece of machinery arrived, Antoine needed Andre's help, and before they had the opportunity to speak again, Sabrina was ready to leave for town. It was two o'clock and she would arrive just in time to stop at Thurston House, bathe, change her clothes and go to Chinatown. She kissed Andre goodbye now, and Antoine, feigned enormous cheerfulness that fooled none of them, and got in her car.

'See you on Saturday . . . behave yourselves . . .'

'I'll call you tonight,' Andre called out to her, but he did not look pleased. It had been a dreadful day so far, and she was not helping anything. He was worried sick about her, and she saw it in his eyes and hated herself for it.

'Don't worry. I'll call you.' She just hoped that she could talk when she got home. She had no idea how long it would take, how she would feel, or even how she would get home. She planned to take the car and would have to drive herself home afterwards.

She drove off then and left them there, and Andre said almost to himself, 'Something's wrong.' And by then, Antoine had enough of it.

'I think she's sick.'

Andre suddenly wheeled to face his son. 'What makes you say that?'

'She almost fainted in my arms in the fields more than a week ago.'

'Why didn't you tell me that?' His voice was loud and sharp as he looked at Antoine. It was a relief though to have someone to talk to about her. They had both been worried for days, and her pretense only made it worse.

'She made me promise not to say anything. I told her that she had to go to the doctor, or I would.'

'Thank God for that, and . . .?'

'She said he told her she was fine.' But Antoine didn't look convinced and he finally dared to say the words, much as they hurt, and tears stung his eyes now, grown up or not, part of him was still a child. His chin trembled as he turned to Andre, 'I don't think she is Papa . . . I hear her getting terribly sick sometimes . . . vomiting . . . and she almost fainted again the other day . . .'

'Merde.' Andre's face went white, and he clenched his hands. 'Do you know where she's going now?'

Antoine shook his head. 'Maybe for tests? Or to see the doctor again . . . I don't know. She just told me everything was fine.'

'Menteuse.' Liar. 'You can see it's not. She's been worried sick all week and she wouldn't tell me anything.' And then, as he looked at his son, he knew what he had to do. He dropped the tool he held where he stood and strode towards his own car.

'Où vas tu?' Where are you going? Antoine ran after him, but he already knew.

'I'm going to follow her.' Andre pulled the choke and started the car, there was still earth on his hands but he didn't care. He didn't care about anything but the woman he loved, and he was going after her.

'Vas y, Papa . . .' Go on . . . Antoine waved, feeling relieved as his father drove off. She had only a twenty minute start on him. He had faith in his old man, he'd get to the bottom of it, and he'd make her take care of herself. And all the way into town, Andre kept his foot on the gas. He had to stop once for a small traffic jam, a truck had a flat tyre, and then he roared on across the Bay Bridge, grateful that it was open now, and they didn't have to contend with the ferries anymore. He roared across Nob Hill and saw her car parked outside Thurston House and felt a wave of gratitude and relief wash over him. She was there, he would find her now, and get to the bottom of it, but just as he turned into the street and glimpsed her car, he saw her hurry out of the house, somberly dressed, a scarf over her head and an old coat he'd never seen before with flat shoes. She dashed back out to her car as he watched, and some instinctive sense told him to follow her. He hung back, and then followed as she started her car, turned right on Jackson Street, and headed East. He kept a healthy distance from her, and was surprised when he saw her stop in Chinatown. What she was doing made no sense at all, and it was almost dinnertime. For an instant, his heart sank and he wondered if there were a man involved, but she didn't look dressed for that as she parked her car and hurried across the street to a shabby address. He saw her knock, then hesitate, then knock again, the door opened then. There was a brief exchange, and then she handed an envelope to someone standing behind the door, and as Andre watched he could see even from there that she was deathly pale and instantly he knew that danger was involved. Something was going to happen to her. Someone was threatening her, blackmail perhaps. He almost leapt from his own car, leaving it parked in a crosswalk, and ran to the door where she had disappeared. And if he made a fool of himself, he didn't care. Sabrina had been through enough in her life, and if now someone was trying to do something to her, he'd kill them before he'd let anything happen to her. He knocked on the door, once, twice, there was no answer and he began to pound, and then he began looking at the solidity of the door to see if he could break it down. He was sorry he hadn't brought Antoine. But just as he had the thought, the door opened a crack.

'Thank you.' He startled the woman on the other side, and shoved the door into her face as he walked in. It was a darkened hall, a narrow staircase just in front of them, and she almost leapt at him.

'You can't come in here.'

'My wife just came in,' he lied to the landlady, 'she's expecting me,' but he knew as he looked at her, in a filthy bathrobe and slippers that no one was expecting him and he couldn't imagine why Sabrina had come, unless his guess had been right. They were blackmailing her. 'Mrs. Harte. Where is she?'

'I don't know . . . there's no one here . . . you make mistake . . .'

And without another word, Andre took one of his huge hands and shoved the woman against the wall. 'Where is she? *Now!*' He roared at her and her eyes flew to the top of the stairs, but not as quickly as Andre's feet as she shrieked and followed him. She tried to keep him from opening the first door on the second floor, and that only made it easier for him. He pushed his way inside and found himself in a room the size of a cell with one long filthy table in it, and beside it a tray of instruments. Sabrina was standing half dressed in the corner of the room, and a tall seedy man reached for a gun as both Sabrina and the woman screamed. Andre didn't move further than he had come, but he glanced at Sabrina once as the doctor levelled the gun at him.

'Are you all right?' She nodded and he turned his eyes back to the man with the gun. 'Why is she here?' But he knew instinctively.

'She came of her own choice. Are you the police?' The gun wavered once and then held firm as Sabrina held her breath.

'No.' Andre's voice was strangely calm. 'She is my wife, and she won't be needing you. She made a mistake. You can keep the money, but I am going to take her home.' He spoke as though to a child, and he correctly sensed that the man with the gun was drunk. It almost made him ill to think of what he would have done to her, but he couldn't think of that now. He turned to Sabrina again. 'Get dressed.' His voice was harsher with her than with the man. He knew now why she had come. He had seen a place like this in Paris once, when he had been very young, with a girl he had fallen in love with when he was twenty-one. She had lived through it, but he had sworn to himself that no woman he loved would ever go through that again, and none had. He saw out of the corner of his eye that Sabrina was dressed at last. And he waved her toward the door, and looked at the man again. 'I do not know your name, and I do not wish to know. We will never tell anyone that we were here.' He pushed Sabrina toward the door, and the doctor hesitated and lowered the gun, letting her pass, but he looked at Andre. He admired his guts, and wanted to help them out.

'I'll do it while you wait outside, if you want. It won't take me long.'
Andre wanted to gag, but thanked him politely and then dragged
Sabrina down the stairs without a word. He tore open the door
through which they'd entered from the street, and pulled her outside.
There was no sound from the building they had left, and he took a big
breath of air and then pulled her wordlessly toward his car, still parked
crazily where he had left it ten minutes before. It had been no longer
than that, and if he had come five minutes later than he had . . . or ten
. . . he shuddered at the thought . . . and didn't look at her as he dragged her to his car, pulled open the door and shoved her roughly inside.

'Andre . . .' Her voice was shaking as badly as his would have, if he
spoke to her . . . 'I have my car . . . I can . . .'

He turned to her, deathly white. 'Don't say a word to me!' His voice
was as tight as wire, and she was too frightened to even cry as he drove
her back to Thurston House, parked, and walked to the front door.
Her hands were shaking so badly, she couldn't even unlock the door
and he took the keys from her, stepped inside, waited until she had
followed suit and closed the door and then suddenly his voice roared at
her as they stood in the hall beneath the dome. 'My God, what in hell
were you doing there?' No words were strong enough, there was nothing to tell her the full measure of what he felt, 'Do you know that you
could have died on that table in that filthy little place! Do you know
that he was drunk?! Do you know that? . . . Listen to me . . .' He
grabbed her shoulders with both hands and shook her until her teeth
rattled in her head.

'Let go of me!' She pulled away from him, sobbing now. 'What
choice did I have? What did you want me to do? Do it myself! I thought
of that! I don't know how . . .' She sank to her knees in the hall, her
head bowed, the full impact of what she had almost done crushing her.
She looked up at him, her face contorted in tears, her voice devoured
by sobs, and suddenly he bent down and pulled her into his arms,
pressing her to him, tears running down his face too, holding her,
crushing her, his hands in her hair.

'How could you do a thing like that? Why didn't you tell me?' So
that was what it was . . . he looked down at her, heartbroken that she
hadn't trusted him enough. 'Why didn't you tell me? How long have
you known?' He pulled her to a chair and sat her on his lap like a child.
She looked as though she were about to faint in his arms, and he didn't
feel much better than she.

'I found out last week.' Her voice was small and sad, and he could feel her whole body shake. She wondered if she would ever feel the same again, and wondered how she would have survived if he hadn't come . . . now she knew how wrong she had been . . . 'I just thought . . . I had to solve it for myself . . . I didn't want you to feel pressured . . .'

The tears rolled slowly down his face. 'It's my baby too, don't you think I had a right to know?'

She nodded, aghast, unable to speak. 'I'm so sorry. I . . .' She couldn't go on, and he held her tight again as she cried. 'It's just . . . I'm too old . . . we're not married . . . I didn't want you to feel . . .' He suddenly pulled away and looked at her.

'Why do you think I'm building that house? For Antoine? What did you think I was doing that for?'

She stared at him stupidly, 'But you never said . . .'

He rolled his eyes. 'I didn't think you were that dumb . . . of course I want to marry you. I thought we'd take our time, and do it sometime this year. I thought you knew that.'

'How could I know?' She almost choked. 'You never said anything to me.'

'Merde alors,' he stared at her in disbelief, 'you are the smartest woman I know, and also the most stupid sometimes.' She smiled through her tears and he kissed her eyes, and then he looked serious again. Neither of them wanted to look back to an hour ago. It was the most frightening experience of her life, and perhaps his as well. A life had almost been lost, a life they both cared about, and she would never have been the same again mentally or physically. He was sure of that. He shuddered to think of it. 'Tell me something now . . . do you really want that badly to get rid of it?' It was a problem that had to be faced. She must have wanted to get rid of it very desperately to go through that. It had been a nightmare for her.

But to his amazement she shook her head. 'No, but I felt I owed it to you . . .' It was true, even her age didn't seem to matter as much as it had a week before. She had given it a lot of thought and she had been doing it for him, so as not to complicate his life, put pressure on him, force him to marry her . . .

'You would do that for me?' He looked appalled, and felt his hands shake again, 'You could have died. Do you know that? Not to mention our child, whom you would have killed.'

'Don't say that.' She closed her eyes, and when she did, the tears were flowing down her cheeks again. 'I just thought that . . .' He stopped her right then. Enough had been said.

'You were wrong. Do you want our child?' The way he said it, who wouldn't have, and she nodded her head, keeping her eyes on him.

'Yes. You don't think it's ridiculous my being so old?' She smiled sheepishly at him and he laughed.

'I'm even older than you are, and I don't feel ridiculous. In fact,' he kissed her neck, 'I feel very young and strong.' She smiled at him and they kissed.

'Do you want the baby, Andre?'

'Absolutely. I must ask you sometime though why you felt so sure that this was impossible . . . it seems to me I recall your telling me that there was no chance of this happening, hmmm . . .' He was teasing her now, and the nightmare in Chinatown seemed light years away.

'I was wrong,' she grinned. She almost looked victorious now.

'Apparently. I'll bet you were surprised. Serves you right.'

She rolled her eyes. 'You will never know how much.' The memory sobered both of them, and he sounded stern when he spoke to her again.

'Whatever happens to you in this life, Sabrina, no matter how ugly or frightening or sordid or sad, I want to know about it. There is nothing you have to hide from me. Nothing. Is that clear?'

'Yes. I'm sorry . . .' She began to cry again and he held her close. 'I almost . . .' She began to shake again, and he rocked her like a child.

'Don't think of it. We were fortunate. I followed you from the house.' She looked stunned. 'I don't know why. I jumped in the car a few minutes after you left. I just had a feeling that something was terribly wrong, and I was right. But that's over now.' He smiled and looked at her. 'We're going to have a baby, my love. Doesn't that make you feel proud?'

'Yes, and a little silly too. I feel like a grandmother.'

'Well you're not.'

And that reminded her. 'Do you suppose Jon and Antoine will be horribly upset?' He suspected that Jon would but perhaps not Antoine, but he wasn't sure, and he didn't really care. All he cared about now was her, and their child.

'If they are, tant pis for them. This is our life, our child. They are both grown men with their own lives to lead. When they have babies, they won't ask us what we think, so we won't ask them.' She laughed at the simplicity of it in his mind.

'That's simple enough. Well, I guess that takes care of everything.'

'Not quite,' he laughed at her, 'you're forgetting one detail, a small one, I'll admit, but nonetheless . . . perhaps we should do our child the favor of making it legitimate. Sabrina, my darling, will you marry me?'

She grinned at him. 'Are you serious?'

He laughed again, and pointed at the still flat tummy as she continued to sit in his lap. 'Is that serious?'

'Yes.' She was laughing too now, her eyes still red from her tears, but she looked happier now by far, 'Very serious.'

'Then so am I. Well?'

She threw her arms around his neck again. 'Yes, yes, yes . . . yes! . . .' He kissed her hard on the mouth, carried her upstairs to her bed and deposited her gently on the side where she slept. She had given birth to Jon in that bed, but they both knew that wouldn't happen this time. She was too old to give birth at home, and he wanted every precaution taken for her. But it wasn't the birth but the wedding on their minds now.

'When do you want to get married, my love?' He smiled down at her and crossed his arms, and he had never looked more handsome to her.

'I don't know . . . shouldn't we wait for Spring Vacation for Jon? It would be nice if he were here.' But at that, Andre laughed out loud and pointed at her tummy again.

'Aren't you forgetting something?'

She laughed too. 'Hmmm . . . you may be right . . . I don't suppose we should wait.'

That reminded him. 'When will it be born?'

'The doctor said October.' It was only seven months away, and they might still be able to pretend that the baby was legitimate in the years to come. At her age, a baby born two months early was possible . . . but not much more than that . . .

'How about this Saturday?'

She lay back against her pillows and smiled at him, looking lovelier than any woman he had ever known. 'That sounds wonderful . . . are you sure that's what you want to do though?'

'I've wanted that since the day we met. I'm only sorry we waited this long . . . sorry that we didn't meet twenty years ago.' She had thought of that too. They had wasted so much time, but perhaps that was the way it was meant to be. 'Saturday almost isn't soon enough.'

She was smiling happily. 'Shall we call and tell Antoine?'

'I'll call him later and tell him everything's all right, but first,' he scowled at her, 'I want you to rest. For a future Mama, you haven't exactly had the ideal day, and I'm going to take care of you now. Do you understand?'

He glanced at his watch. It was after eight. 'I'm going to make you something to eat. You're eating for two now, you know.' He bent down and kissed her again, and ran downstairs to make her one of the omelettes she loved, à la Française, but when he came upstairs again, she didn't even eat for one. Between the exhaustion of what they had been through and the baby growing in her womb, she was sound asleep on their bed.

Chapter Thirty-Three

When Sabrina and Andre drove back to Napa on Thursday afternoon, they left her car in town. Andre had picked it up earlier that day and put it in the garage they had rented across from Thurston House, and they drove up in his. Antoine saw them arrive, as he left the fields and walked toward the house. It was a beautiful sunny day, and Sabrina looked as happy as a young girl as she walked toward Antoine. It was difficult to believe she was the same woman who had left the day before. But Antoine had already heard the relief in his father's voice the night before when he'd called. He hadn't explained anything, but Antoine knew instantly that everything was all right and he was sure of it now, and they told him that night as Andre poured his son a glass of champagne.

'We have something to say to you.' Antoine was amused, they were like two kids, and he guessed ahead of time what the news would be, or at least part of it. They weren't going to tell him about the baby yet.

'Should I guess?' He teased. 'Let's see . . .' Sabrina was giggling like a girl, and Andre grinned broadly at his son.

'All right, you smart aleck, never mind . . . We're getting married on Saturday.'

'So soon?' That was the only thing that did surprise him, he thought they were going to tell him that they were engaged, and then suddenly something dawned on him. He looked at Sabrina guardedly but he could see nothing there. Perhaps it was too soon, he thought, but if that were true, he was happy for them. He hadn't even thought of that when she had seemed so ill. And he beamed at them now and kissed them both on both cheeks. Andre asked him to be the best man, and that Saturday, at the little church in town, Antoine stood beside Andre as Sabrina walked down the aisle alone. Their workers were there and no one else, and the minister said the words solemnly as tears ran down Sabrina's cheeks, and she became Andre's wife. Afterwards they shared a sumptuous meal that the men themselves had prepared and a whole case of champagne, although Sabrina only drank one glass, and Antoine took her aside and gave her a warm hug.

'I'm happy for you and Papa. You will be wonderful for him.'

'I'm the lucky one to have both of you.' She wished that Jonathan had been as kind. She had called to tell him in his dorm, and there had been a long silence on the phone followed by a few chill words.

'What's the rush?' He would know soon enough.

'We just thought . . . Darling, I'm sorry you can't be here . . .' She was agonized, forgetting the pain he had caused her with Camille.

'I'm not. Why in hell would you want to marry a farmer like him?'

'That's not a nice thing to say, Jon.' She was hurt by his words but he had planned it that way.

'Anyway, good luck.'

'Thank you. Do you want to come home for Easter, sweetheart?' She would have sent him the fare.

'No, thanks, I'm going to New York with friends. But you can send me to Paris if you want, in June.'

'That's not quite the same thing, is it? I just thought that you might like to come home and see all of us.'

'I'd rather see France. A whole group of us are going on the Grand Tour when we graduate. What do you say?' He had dismissed her marriage to Andre and was already thinking of himself again.

'We'll discuss it some other time.'

'Why not now? I have to make arrangements if I'm going with them.'

'I don't want to be pressed. We'll discuss it later, Jon.'

'For Chrissake . . .'

'You have to go to work when you graduate. What about that?' If he was going to push her, she was going to push him. Turnabout was fair play, although she seldom applied it to him. But she was mad about his comment about Andre . . . a farmer from France indeed.

'I'm pretty sure Johnson's father is going to give me a job in New York.' She felt her heart sink but she had expected it. 'Five of us are going to rent a townhouse.'

'Sounds expensive. Will you be able to afford that?'

'Why not? You have Thurston House.'

'I don't pay rent.' Although if Camille and he had had their way, perhaps she would have by then. 'How's your charming grandmother, by the way?'

'She's fine. I got a letter from her last week.' Sabrina didn't say anything, she just sighed. It annoyed her that Camille stayed in touch with Jon, and he seemed to have such an affinity for her.

'Well, we'll see you at graduation then,' and she hoped Camille wouldn't be there. She never wanted to see her again, but her great nephew would be graduating as well and perhaps she would come. Sabrina didn't ask Jon, and he asked her about the trip again. 'I'll think about it and let you know.' But he figured she would ask Andre and he might say no.

'Make up your mind soon.'

'And if I say no?'

'I'll find some other way to go.'

'Maybe you should.' Her voice was very calm. She recognised all the mistakes she had made with him now, and she wouldn't make them again with her next child. It warmed her heart to think of that . . . she had a baby on the way . . . another child . . . she wondered what it would be . . . who it would look like . . . she smiled to herself.

'God damn it, Mom. I need that trip.'

'That you do not. You want it, there's a difference.' And with that, he hung up on her, without congratulating her again, or sending his regards to Andre. And she didn't hear from him again for another month, when he phoned to press her again about the trip, and this time she did discuss it with Andre, and he expressed his views to her, although he knew they wouldn't be popular with Jon.

'Do you really want to know what I think?' He had restrained himself until then. He felt that how she dealt with her son was her own affair, and he didn't want to tread on delicate ground.

'Yes, I do. He's making me feel as though I owe it to him, but I'm not sure it would be good for him just to give him the trip. On the other hand, he's graduating from Harvard in June, it would be a beautiful gift . . .' She looked helplessly at Andre.

'Too beautiful a gift, I think. I think if that's what he wanted, he should have begun saving for it a long time ago. He never thinks about how difficult it is for you. He thinks he has a right to it. That's a dangerous way for a man to think, and sooner or later reality is going to hit him hard. You won't always be there to put money into his open hand. Once he leaves school, he should stand on his own two feet.'

'I agree.' She was slowly hardening herself to Jon's constant demands. He was the ultimate spoiled child and it had gone too far. 'And the trip?'

'I would tell him no.'

She sighed. 'That's what I think, but I dread telling him.' Andre nodded sympathetically. He knew what a hard time Jon gave her and he felt sorry for her. He was a rude, selfish little sonofabitch, and he didn't think it was just because he had been spoiled. There was something more to it than that. He was too much like his grandmother for his own good, and Andre felt that he must have been born like that.

He was certainly different from Antoine, who was nothing but nice to her. He was almost twenty-six years old, and very much involved with a girl in town, and each time he looked at Sabrina now, he thought that his suspicions had been correct, but neither of them had said anything to him, and he didn't want to ask. Finally one day in May, he looked at Sabrina and smiled.

'Can I ask you something?'

'Of course.' She smiled at him, she loved him as her own son, and in many ways, he was easier to love than Jon. The explosion over the trip had caused an enormous rift, and she hadn't spoken to him in a month, although they still planned to go to Cambridge in June to see him graduate.

'I know it's rude to ask . . .' He blushed beneath his deep tan, and she noticed once again how handsome he was. He was a magnificent-looking young man, and she wondered how serious he was about his current girl and if that was what he wanted to talk to her about now. But he took her by surprise instead. 'Are you . . . am I going to have a little brother or sister? . . .' He couldn't stand the suspense anymore and she smiled at him, blushing herself now. She nodded and he swept her up in his powerful arms, kissed her cheek and put her down again. 'When?'

She began to tell him what she and Andre had agreed to tell everyone, and then thought better of it. She could tell Antoine the truth. In a way, he had been the first to know, when she had almost fainted in the fields. And he was no fool, he would figure it out eventually. They just didn't want other people to know. 'October,' she smiled at him, 'but officially, it's two months later than that.'

He grinned, and appreciated her honesty, 'I thought that too, but I didn't want to ask.' And in his heart, he knew that his father would have married her anyway. 'Does Jon know?'

'Not yet. We'll tell him next month when we go East.'

'Papa is thrilled, I can tell. He's been strutting around here like a boy since you came back from San Francisco, a few days before you two got married.' He didn't ask her what had happened then, but he knew it had changed everything, and all to the good. It was as though they each knew how much the other meant to them after that. And he envied them that. He would have liked to have found a girl he loved as much as his father loved her, but so far he knew he had not. The girl he was seeing now was fun, and he cared about her, but he already knew it wouldn't last. She wasn't bright enough, and she never laughed at the same things, that was important to him. He looked at Sabrina now, 'I'm happy for both of you.' And then with an extra smile, 'I hope it's a girl.'

She whispered to him as they walked hand in hand to the house, 'So do I.' The baby was just beginning to show in the trousers she wore around the farmhouse. Their other house was supposed to be finished in two months. She wanted to move in in time for the baby to come, but she was going to go to San Francisco for the birth. Andre was insistent about that. He wanted her to have the best care she could have, but so far she had had no problems with the pregnancy. Even the train trip to the East didn't bother her, and when they saw Jon the atmosphere between them was tense. He ignored Andre, and looked at his mother with hostility.

'I suppose you're pleased at the news.'

'What news?' She looked blank.

'I wrote to you last week.'

'I didn't get anything. The letter must have arrived after we left.'

There were tears in his eyes as he spoke to her, and she was stunned. 'Grandmother was hit by a bus last week and was killed instantly.' It took her a moment to register the fact that he meant Camille and then she stared at him, amazed at the grief he seemed to feel. She felt nothing at all, except, in some remote way, relief.

'I'm sorry to hear that, Jon.'

'No, you're not. You hated her.' He sounded like a child again, as

Andre watched from where he sat on the windowsill in Jon's room in his dorm. Sabrina was sitting on the bed, and she was obviously flourishing. She had gained weight and she couldn't wear her old clothes anymore. She had had to buy some loose dresses like the blue silk dress she wore now. It was the same color as her eyes and Andre thought she looked even prettier than she had before.

'I didn't hate her, Jon. I barely knew her. It's true that what I knew I didn't like very much. You'll have to admit she wasn't exactly decent to me. She tried to put me out of my house, after abandoning me as a child, and staying out of my life for forty-six years.'

He shrugged, it was a difficult accusation to deny. And then he seemed to look Sabrina over with surprise. 'You've sure got fat. Marriage must agree with you.' It was hardly a tactful remark and she laughed.

'It does, but that isn't why I've gained weight.' She had to tell him sometime and it was as good a time as any, or so she thought. 'I know you'll be surprised. And to be honest with you, so were we.' She took a breath and went on, 'We're having a baby at Christmastime, Jon.'

'You're *what*?' He looked at them both and jumped to his feet. 'You're not!' He looked horrified.

'I am.' She sat calmly where she was and looked at Andre and then her son again. 'I know it's a bit of a shock initially, but . . .'

'How can you make such fools of yourselves? Christ . . . of *me*? My God, everyone I know will laugh me out of town! You're nearly fifty years old, and God only knows how old he is . . .' He was less than gracious to them both, and Sabrina couldn't help smiling. He was so enraged that he looked like a little boy again, and it was certainly different from the reaction they had had from Antoine, who had rushed out and bought the baby its first Teddy Bear, 'and remember to tell her it's from me!' He had insisted that it was going to be a girl, but Jon obviously didn't care what it was going to be as he stormed around the room.

'These things do happen you know, old boy.' Andre tried to calm him down. He was sorry to see the boy behave this way to his mother, but it didn't surprise him at all. He was totally immature and completely spoiled, and he always seemed to have an axe to grind against her. 'You'll get used to it eventually. We did. And so did Antoine. And he's even older than you are. Four years older in fact.'

'What the hell does he know? All he does is plant grapes. I'm a

372

man for God's sake!' Andre got to his feet, controlling himself with difficulty.

'So is my son. And he is your stepbrother now. I will thank you to speak of him with respect, Jonathan.' For an instant the two men exchanged a long look and then Jon backed down. He was no fool, and he could see that Andre meant every word he said. Andre looked at Sabrina then, and indicated that it was time to leave. Jon had plans for that night, but they would see him at graduation the next day, and then they would dine with him and a friend, and the next day Andre and Sabrina were leaving for New York with him. He was sailing on the Normandie three days after that. He had come up with the money for the trip himself after all, quite a lot of it in fact, and Sabrina was impressed. And she and Andre wanted to see Amelia anyway.

'We'll see you tomorrow, Jon.' She went to kiss his cheek but he avoided her and his back was turned when they left the room.

'I'm sorry he took it so hard,' she said to Andre as they took a cab back to their hotel.

'Did you really expect otherwise? He's still very immature,' he patted her hand, 'four years makes a big difference at this age. Antoine is already a man. Jon isn't quite yet. It'll come. And it's probably a threat to him, in terms of what he'll inherit from you . . . the house . . . the Napa land . . .' She hadn't thought of that, but she nodded now, wondering if Jon had.

'You may be right. Strange about Camille, isn't it?'

Andre looked at her. 'It's just as well. She was an evil, greedy useless woman, and she should have died years ago, as your father claimed she had.' He had never forgiven her for what she had done to his wife.

'It's odd. I don't feel anything.' It was a strange thing to admit. She had just learned that her mother had died, and she didn't care at all. 'Jon certainly does.'

'He's known her for four years, and apparently, they had "atomes croches".' She smiled. She loved that expression of his, 'hooked atoms', something in common.

The graduation went off without a hitch the next day and Sabrina cried as she watched Jon participate. No matter how difficult he was, she was proud of him, and she had got him through school, selling the mines, the Napa house, the gardens around Thurston House . . .

she had done it, and so had he. They had a lot to be proud of and to celebrate, and they dined out that night. Jon got more than a little drunk, but Sabrina and Andre understood and he was actually nicer than he usually was, far nicer than he was on the train to New York. He was embarrassed to be seen with her.

'My God, what will people think?' He whispered to her and she smiled, and whispered back.

'Just tell them I eat a lot.' They asked him about his job. He was going to work in September for the father of a friend, when he came back from Europe. The boy's name was William Blake, and when they saw Jon off on the ship, he introduced Sabrina to Bill, who had a radiantly pretty young girl with him. She never took her eyes off Jon, and Sabrina learned that she was only eighteen, Bill's sister, and it was obvious that she had a ferocious crush on Jon. She introduced herself to them as soon as she discovered who they were.

'Hello, my name is Arden Blake.' She shook hands with Sabrina, and then Andre, glanced only casually at the loose red dress Sabrina wore, and then went on to tell them how wonderful Jon was, although he seemed totally indifferent to her. 'And Daddy thinks he's going to do just fabulously. That's why he's sending him to Europe with Bill, as a sort of bonus before he even starts . . .' Sabrina was furious hearing about it, but nothing showed in her face. Jon had told her that he got up the money himself, not that he was travelling for three months as someone else's guest, and First Class on the Normandie, not to mention the hotels they would be staying at. She knew who William Blake Sr. was, everyone in the country did. He was the biggest banker in New York, and she had had some dealings with him before she'd sold John's mine, with some investments John had had. She looked at her son now, wanting to throttle him, but it was too late to discuss it with him before they sailed. Instead she went on talking to Arden innocuously, remembering with amazement that she had been running her father's mines at the same age. It was incredible to think of that, particularly with this sweet, innocent girl, who was so totally gaga over John. 'Mummy and Daddy and I are going over next month and we're going to meet them in the South of France,' she practically swooned at the thought and Sabrina smiled.

'Just be sure he behaves himself,' she warned the pretty little green eyed blonde. 'I don't always trust my son.'

374

'Mummy says he's the nicest boy she knows. He's going to be my escort at my coming out party in December.' She absolutely glowed, and when the boat horn sounded for them to get off, Sabrina saw Jon kiss her on the lips first and then three other girls after her. There were four of them sailing on the ship, all classmates from Harvard, and Sabrina hated to think of the mischief they would get into. But she hated more to think that someone else was paying for the trip. He had very effectively forced her hand and now she was going to have to send a handsome check to William Blake Sr. to cover the expense of the trip. She would not allow Jon to go as someone else's guest, and God only knew what sob story he had told them.

'I want to discuss that with you when you come back.' She looked meaningfully at him and handed him an envelope that she had meant to be a graduation gift. She had been so proud of his paying for his own trip, she was giving him a thousand dollars to spend, but now, it was just an additional expense and she wasn't pleased. 'Be nice to Arden Blake,' she whispered to him, 'she's a sweet girl.' Sabrina had the uncomfortable feeling that Jon was going to take advantage of Arden.

'She's my ticket to success,' he winked and whispered back, and Sabrina almost felt sick. Later, Sabrina saw her waving frantically from the dock as her own mother watched. Sabrina almost wanted to warn her of what her son was like, but how could she do a thing like that? He stood on the deck outside his suite, smiling down at them all, looking more handsome than she had ever realized he was. He was a tall, thin, fiery-eyed young man with jet black hair and blue eyes like Camille's and a face for which any woman would have died. It was almost painful to look at him. And Sabrina turned to Andre with a sigh as they left, and told him what Jon had said about Arden Blake. She also told him about how he had financed the trip.

'At least you know he'll never starve. He's too clever for that.'

'Too clever for his own good.'

'Sometimes I wish Antoine were. He's so damn impractical he couldn't fight his way out of a paper bag. All he thinks about are principles and ideals, and intellectual mumbo jumbo most of the time.' Sabrina smiled tenderly. Andre wasn't too far off, but Antoine was such a decent boy. He was intelligent, but somehow above the practical side of life. He would have rather read philosophy than eat, would rather pursue some vague, abstract idea than conquer a technical one. He was a dreamer in a way, and yet a brilliant one.

'He's a lovely man, Andre. You should be proud of him.'

'You know I am.' He helped her into the cab and then smiled at her and glanced at the small protruberance as she sat down. 'And how's our little friend?' She had felt it move for the first time a few weeks before, and now it seemed to be moving a lot. He could feel it too and it delighted him. 'Jumping up and down?'

'She's going to be a ballerina, I think. She jumps around a lot.' More than Jonathan had or the baby she had lost.

'Or a soccer player.' Andre smiled. And that afternoon they went to visit their old friend, and she was delighted for them. She thought it nonsense that they were sensitive about their age.

'If I could, I'd have one now!' She was exactly ninety years old and Sabrina thought she looked terribly frail. 'Enjoy every moment of it . . . it is the greatest gift of all. The gift of life.' And as they looked at her, they knew it was true. She had lived ninety full, wonderful, rich, giving years. She was an example to everyone in sharp contrast to Camille. Sabrina talked to Amelia about her for a while, and then finally they left when Amelia's nurse came in. It was time for her nap, and they both noticed that she looked tired. She kissed them both goodbye, and as she did, she looked deep into Sabrina's eyes. 'You're just like your father was, Sabrina. He was a fine man. And you're a fine woman. There's none of her in you.' But there was in Jon. Sabrina knew it to her very soul, and she regretted it bitterly. But she said nothing now. 'Be grateful for this child.' She smiled tenderly at them both. 'And may she bring you great joy.' And then she laughed. 'I think it will be a girl.' She put a hand on Sabrina's tummy, and then kissed them again.

The next day they took the train home again, and Sabrina settled in to Napa for the summer. In August their new house was ready and they moved in and the following month they moved into the city, so that Sabrina could be close to the hospital. They called Jon from San Francisco when he got home. He had had a marvellous time, and he mentioned Arden Blake once or twice. He had already started his new job, and it seemed to be mostly play, thanks to Mr. Blake. Sabrina had indeed sent him an enormous check with her thanks, to cover Jon's trip, and, although it had gone back and forth once or twice, he had finally accepted it. He had told her that he was very fond of Jon, as were they all, and Jon seemed to like them too.

'I'm going to Palm Beach with them for the holidays.' He crowed, and Sabrina was disappointed.

'I thought you'd come home then. The baby will have arrived . . .'

But he had no interest in that. 'I won't have time. I only have two weeks. I'll come out next summer probably. The Blakes are renting a house in Malibu, and I'll probably stay with them for a while.'

'Don't you have to work?'

'No more than Bill does. I get the same vacations he takes. That was the deal.'

'Sounds awfully cushy to me.'

'Why not? I work as hard as he does.'

'I'd say he has an inside track, wouldn't you?'

'Maybe I do too.' Jon sounded very confident. 'Arden is crazy about me, and Mr. Blake thinks I'm tops.'

'Sounds like you found yourself a lucky job.' And of course he had. And when she attempted to discuss the sneaky way he had arranged the trip to Europe for himself, he brushed her off.

'You didn't have to pay for it, Mr. Blake said he would.'

'I couldn't let him do that. And you shouldn't have either, Jon.'

'Oh Christ, if you're going to give me a speech on morality, Mother, I think I have to hang up.'

'Maybe it's something you should think about, Jon. Particularly in regard to Arden Blake. Don't use that girl, son. She's a sweet person and a very innocent child.'

'She's eighteen years old for Chrissake . . .'

'You know exactly what I mean.' He did, but he wouldn't admit it to her.

'Never mind. I'm not going to rape anyone.'

'There's more than one way to do that.'

She worried about him a lot, although he seemed happy in New York, from the cards they got from time to time, and as October wore on, Sabrina lost interest in everything but herself, as the baby got big and she got increasingly uncomfortable. She could scarcely walk up the stairs of Thurston House as her due date approached, and when the big day arrived and the baby's head didn't move down, she and Andre began to take long walks.

'She must like it in there,' Sabrina sighed, 'I feel like she's never going to come out.' She looked at Andre woefully as he laughed. She could barely walk now. And she had to sit down every few steps. She felt a hundred years old and as though she weighed three hundred pounds, she claimed, but she was in good spirits too.

'What are you going to do if it's a boy? You keep calling the poor thing "she"!'

'He'll have to get used to it, poor thing.' But three days after the baby was due, she woke Andre out of a sound sleep at four o'clock with a broad smile on her face. 'This is it, my love.'

'How do you know?' He was still half asleep, and hoping for a reprieve until the next day. Or morning at least.

'Trust me, I know.'

'Okay.' He wrestled himself out of bed, and woke up with a start as he saw her double over suddenly. He leapt out of bed and held her in his arms, and then led her gently to a chair as she looked at him with a slightly panicky look.

'I think I may have waited too long' she was panting a little bit and she looked more than a little uncomfortable. '. . . but I didn't want to wake you up . . . and I wasn't sure at first . . . ohh . . .' She grabbed his arm, and he felt suddenly terrified.

'Oh my God . . . did you call the doctor yet?'

'No . . . you'd better . . . oh Andre . . . oh my God . . . call . . .'

'What's happening?' He led her back to the bed with a panicked look and grabbed for the phone. 'What do I say to him?'

She gave a moan and fell back on the bed. 'Tell him I feel the head . . .' She lay there panting as he dialled, and gave a small shriek suddenly. He had never been through anything like this before. He had waited politely in the hospital lobby for several hours when Antoine was born, and he had never seen his wife in labour at all.

The doctor answered the phone and Andre told him what Sabrina had said, and he asked Andre hurriedly, 'Does she feel like bearing down?' He tried to ask her, but she wouldn't listen to him, she was grabbing his sleeve, her face was contorted with pain. It had gone so rapidly he couldn't understand anything.

'Sabrina, listen to me . . . he wants to know . . . Sabrina . . . please . . .'

The doctor was listening to her at his end, and he shouted down the phone at Andre. 'Call the police. I'll be right there.'

'The police?' Andre looked horrified, but he had no time to think

378

of anything or call anyone. Sabrina was literally crawling across the bed, sobbing now.

'Oh God . . . oh Andre . . . please . . .'

'What can I do?'

'Help me . . . please . . .'

'Darling . . .' There were tears in his eyes and he had never been so desperate in his life. It had even been easier wresting her from the abortionist's hand at gunpoint seven months before. That had required only a little bit of sangfroid and some bravery. This required skills he knew nothing about, but as she turned to him now and looked at him helplessly, writhing in pain, he suddenly forgot all that he didn't know and instinctively reached out to her and held her hands, speaking to her soothingly. He knew now that he would never get her to the hospital. She had woken him too late, and it had all moved too swiftly ahead. She had pulled her clothes off, and lay there covered only by a sheet, just as she had lain there once before, so long ago, and there was something familiar to it now. It was as though she had forgotten all of it before, but now she remembered it perfectly, like a distant dream. She looked at Andre and for the first time in an hour she almost smiled at him. Her face was damp, her eyes were dark, and she suddenly pushed with all her might as he held her shoulders for her, and when she stopped she looked up at him and smiled this time.

'I told you . . . I wanted . . . the baby . . . born . . . in this house . . .' And as she said the words, she pushed again, and he held her in his arms again, holding her from behind where she lay, so that he had the same perspective as she and he was not quite sure what was going on. There was nothing to see, and all he could feel was the tremendous straining of her entire body as she pushed, and then slowly she began to scream, a low deep ancient agony, as her whole body tensed and she almost sat up this time. 'Oh Andre . . . oh God . . . oh no . . . Andre . . .' It seemed an endless sound as he cooed meaninglessly to her, holding her in his arms, tears running down his face, and this time she gave a sharp cry, and then another one, and she fell back against him each time as the pain began to ebb and then she would tense again, and now he sensed a quickening of the pace. He knew . . . he knew . . . it was as though he felt just what she did and he talked to her.

'Go on . . . go on . . . go on, darling . . . yes, you can . . .'

'I can't! . . .' She was screaming in pain and he wanted to tear the baby from her to end her pain.

'You *can*!'

'Oh God . . . oh no . . . Andre . . .' She tore the sheet back as she writhed, gripping him, gripping the bed, pushing until she could not breathe or move or cry, and as she watched, a round head pushed its way out and he screamed with her.

'Oh my God . . . Sabrina!' He could not believe what he saw, the face was turned up toward them, and as though he had always known what to do, he went to the other end of the bed, and held the tiny head as she pushed again, and the shoulders pushed free as the baby began to cry for the first time. He helped it gently out from its mother's womb as he cried with her. She was crying and laughing now, and he urged her on again. A moment later, the brand new child lay in his hands as he looked miraculously at his wife, and held the baby up to her. 'It's a *girl*!' He was crying unashamedly and he had never seen anything as beautiful as the baby he held or the woman he loved. He went to Sabrina's head again as she lay back now, and he held her shoulders as she began to shake, covered her with the sheet again, and placed their baby in her arms. 'Oh, she's so beautiful . . . and so are you . . .'

'I love you so much . . .' The cord still throbbed between the two, and Sabrina looked exhausted but proud. She looked up at him with newborn love, and he kissed first the mother and then the child.

'You're incredible.' It was an experience they would never forget, and as he looked at her he knew that he would never love her more than he did now. She was the loveliest sight he had ever seen, with their baby in her arms.

And then slowly, she smiled at him, still shaking, but looking so pleased. 'That wasn't so bad for an old girl, was it, Andre?' He was totally in love with her, and with their child. When the doctor arrived with an ambulance ten minutes after the baby was born, Andre opened the door with an enormous grin.

'Good evening, gentlemen.' He looked so happy and so proud that they knew they had come too late. And the doctor flew up the stairs to find Sabrina happily nursing her child.

'It's a girl!' She announced to him with delight, and both father and doctor laughed, and then the doctor closed the door, looked at them both, cut the cord, and made sure that Sabrina was indeed all right.

He looked at her with astonishment. 'I must say, I didn't expect this from you, my dear.'

'Neither did I.' She laughed at them both, and reached for Andre's hand, and looking at him with gratitude in her eyes, said, 'I couldn't have done it without you.'

He was amazed at the undeserved praise from her. 'I didn't do anything but watch. You did it all.'

Sabrina looked down at the baby lying peacefully asleep at her side. 'She did it all herself.' What a miracle she was, lying there.

The doctor looked at her again. He was satisfied that mother and baby were doing fine; a good seven and a half pounds from the look of her, maybe more. 'I really ought to take you to the hospital and let you rest there,' but there was no reason to disturb either of them as it had been a perfectly normal birth, 'What do you think?'

Sabrina did not look pleased. 'I'd rather stay here.'

'I thought you would.' The doctor did not look surprised. 'Well . . .' He looked at them both so peaceful there, 'I'll tell you what, I'll let you stay at home, but if there are any problems at all, any fever, any discomfort you think is unusual,' he turned to Andre, 'then call me at once.' He wagged a finger at Sabrina then, 'And don't wait until it's too late this time!' She beamed at them both.

'I thought I could wait a while. I hated waking everyone in the middle of the night.' And both men looked at her and laughed. She had anyway, and far more dramatically. It was only five fifteen now, and it was still dark. And Dominique Amelie de Vernay had made her entrance into the world. The first name 'Dominique' had been difficult to find, but they had long since agreed on the middle name.

When the doctor left with the ambulance, Andre brought her a cup of tea, and the maid, who had been waiting patiently for the baby's birth, came upstairs to wash Dominique and return her to Sabrina as soon as possible. The bed was changed, Sabrina was bathed, and as she lay in her bed again, sipping tea, with Dominique at her breast, Andre looked at her unbelievingly, as the sky paled and the sun came up. Suddenly he laughed. 'Well, what shall we do today, my love?' They looked at each other and laughed and laughed. How long they had waited and how swiftly it had come, and as Sabrina drifted off to sleep in their bed, she remembered back to the hideous place she had gone to in Chinatown . . . and she still saw Andre speaking quietly to the man with the gun . . . and how they

381

had fled downstairs . . . and now here she was with a tiny baby girl asleep beside her, and her husband at her side.

They called Antoine when Sabrina woke up again. He had been just about to leave for the fields, and he answered the phone distractedly. Andre came right to the point. 'It's a girl!'

'Already?' Antoine was thrilled. 'My God, how wonderful!'

'Her name is Dominique, and she's very beautiful, and she is two hours and,' he checked his watch, 'fourteen minutes old.' He beamed and Antoine was incoherent with delight.

'Oh my God . . . Papa . . . c'est formidable! . . . How's Sabrina? . . . is she in the hospital?'

Andre laughed at his older child. 'The answers to that are yes, and fine, and no. Yes, it is "formidable," she's fine, and no she isn't in the hospital. The baby was born at home.' Sabrina beamed at him as he explained. She would never forget how he had held her up, that he had been with her. It meant everything to her to have shared that with him.

'What?' Antoine was stunned. 'At home? But I thought . . .'

'So did I. But your stepmother pulled a fast one on me. She didn't want to disturb my sleep, so she woke me too late. And . . . voilà, Mademoiselle Dominique arrived about twenty minutes after I woke up. And the doctor arrived here after that.'

'That's incredible!'

Andre sounded as though he were still in a dream, and his eyes were damp again. 'Yes, mon fils, it is incredible. It was the most beautiful thing I've ever seen.' He wished that for Antoine one day; a woman he loved as much as Andre did his wife, and the birth of a much-loved child, shared with his wife if possible. He was glad that he had been there with her after all, now that everything was all right. It had been at the same time much more difficult and much easier than he realized. It was much harder work than he had ever known before, more painful, more frightening, more beautiful, and in effect Dominique had delivered herself. But he realized that Sabrina was one of the lucky ones. When Antoine had been born, his mother had been in labour for more than two days.

'You do that awfully well, you know.' Andre teased her that afternoon as they lay in bed side by side. She was eating lunch, and Dominique was sound asleep in the cradle that had been Jon's, draped with white organdie and new white satin ribbons now.

'Maybe we ought to do that again sometime.' He was teasing her and she looked at him in astonishment.

'Now just a minute here . . . it wasn't as easy as all that : . .' She was understandably terribly sore, but none of the danger signs the doctor had warned them of had happened to her. 'I don't think I want to do that again.' And they both knew that it was unlikely she would have the chance at her age, but Dominique herself was a gift they were both grateful for.

They were both disappointed that Jon was out to lunch when they called him. She left a message with the secretary he shared with young Bill Blake, and he called her back later that afternoon, sounding a little drunk and not very interested in why she called at first. Then when he heard the news, there was dead silence at his end and she thought they'd been cut off.

'Jon? . . . Jon? . . . Jon? . . . Jon . . . oh damn . . . Andre, I think . . .' And then he came alive again.

'I can't believe you really went through with it.' He hadn't seen her since four months before. 'Somehow I thought you'd come to your senses before it was too late. Mom, I guess it looks like you're stuck with it.' He laughed tipsily and Sabrina was annoyed at him.

'Her name is Dominique, and she's tiny and very beautiful. We hope you see her soon.' She went on as though he were as pleased as they, and then Jon realized something as he counted backwards on his hands.

'Come to think of it, weren't you supposed to have her in December, Mom? Seems to me you only got married in April or something like that . . .' He was no fool, her boy.

'Something like that. She came two months ahead of time.'

'Don't tell me he knocked you up before you married him. No wonder you two were *surprised*, as you put it in June. I'll bet you were.' He was laughing openly and Sabrina wanted to throttle him.

'Come home soon, and see your sister, Jon.'

'Sure, Mom. Oh . . . and congratulations to you both . . .' How different from the call to Antoine, she thought as she hung up. Antoine had been wild with excitement for them, near tears, overwhelmed, Jon had been cynical, nasty, and had pointed out that he knew the baby had been conceived before their wedding day. Sabrina felt disappointment in him wash over her again, and she looked at Andre with tears in her eyes.

'He wasn't nice.' She looked like a little girl, and Andre patted her hand and kissed her cheek.

'He's jealous. He's been an only child for a long time.' He always made excuses for him, for her sake. But she agreed with him less often now.

'So has Antoine. You know, he's rude and selfish and he's going to get his comeuppance one day. You can't go around treating people like that and not pay a price for it.' And as she said it, she remembered Arden Blake and hoped that she wouldn't get hurt by Jon.

They didn't see him again until the following year. He arrived in June when Dominique was eight months old, and he scarcely looked at her as he walked into Thurston House. He looked around as if he owned the place, and his mother looked at him. He was even more handsome than when he'd graduated a year before. He was not quite twenty-three years old, actually a month shy of it, and he was tall and lean and looked very debonair. There was something so sophisticated about him that he almost looked decadent, and Sabrina put her arms around him and smiled into his eyes. It had been a year since she had seen him off on the Normandie and she was so happy to see him again. She had the cooing baby in her arms who laughed at him, but he seemed almost not to notice her.

'Well, what do you think of Miss Dominique?' Sabrina looked proudly from the baby to her son.

'Who? Oh . . . that . . .' He pretended not to be amused and his mother scolded him.

'Now come on, don't put on that grown up stuff with me, Jon. I remember when you were this age, and it wasn't that long ago.' He smiled at her, and looked warmer this time.

'All right . . . all right . . . she's cute. But she's not quite the age I like girls best.'

'And what age is that?' She was teasing him as they walked upstairs and he looked around his room. Nothing had changed. She always kept the room for him, no matter how seldom he came home.

'Oh between twenty-one and twenty-five.'

'I guess that leaves out Arden Blake.' Sabrina hadn't forgotten her or the comment he had made that Arden was his ticket to success, which had irked her so terribly.

'She can't be more than nineteen by now.'

'You have a good memory, Mom. She is. I make an occasional exception for her.'

'Poor child.' His mother rolled her eyes.

'Never mind that. She and Bill are coming up from Malibu next week. Can they stay here?'

'You can even come up to Napa, if you and Bill share a room. We've got two very nice guest rooms you can use. In fact,' she smiled happily at him, it was so good to have him back, no matter how impossible he was sometimes, 'we'd love to have you come up.'

'I take it you're not living in that dump anymore.'

'Jon!'

'Well, it was.'

'It was temporary. No, Andre built us a lovely house. There's a separate cottage for Antoine.'

'Is he still hanging around?' Jon seemed annoyed.

'He runs the vineyards with Andre. That's no small property and things are beginning to roll very pleasantly. Andre couldn't do it without him.' She remembered Jon calling Andre 'that farmer from France,' but he said nothing derogatory now.

'Maybe we'll come up for a few days if we have time. They want to spend most of their time here.'

'There's a lot to see. But they might enjoy Napa too.' And when they arrived, they were thrilled with it. Jon was noticeably blasé and bored, but Bill was fascinated with the enormous vineyards they ran. He said that his father had, at one time, invested heavily in wines in France and had made a fortune with it.

'I know,' Andre smiled at him, 'your father and I did very well in that deal.' He laughed and Bill was thrilled to realize who he was. He turned to Jon and explained that Andre and his father had known each other years ago. Bill Blake Sr. hadn't come to the ship and Andre hadn't seen him at the Harvard graduation the previous year, he realized now. 'Next time I'm in New York, I will phone him. But in the meantime, please send him my regards.'

'I will.' Jon seemed suddenly more interested in Andre after that, although he ignored Antoine totally, and Sabrina and Arden had gone for a long walk with Dominique in the buggy Sabrina had found in an antique store somewhere. They walked for hours along paths Sabrina had known as a child, and when they returned at last the four men were lying around the pool. Arden shook hands with

Andre and Antoine, whom she hadn't met before. And Sabrina saw Antoine's eyes almost fall out of his head as she shook hands with him. He had stared at her for the rest of the afternoon, and they had talked for hours that night while Bill and Jon went out to play pool in town. They were used to leaving Arden behind, and neither of them thought anything of it. Bill had asked if Antoine wanted to come along, but he said he had work to do at home, which he seemed to forget the moment they were gone.

Sabrina smiled as she mentioned it to Andre that night, after she put the baby to bed. Antoine and Arden were sitting in the dark, in earnest conversation on the porch. 'He's very taken with her. Did you notice that?'

'I did.' Andre thought about it. 'Will Jon object? I thought he had a soft spot for her.'

'I'm not sure he does.' Sabrina sat down on their bed. 'He said something about her I didn't like last year, that she was his "ticket to success," and I hope he wasn't serious. Marrying her would certainly give him a permanent place in Bill Blake's bank, but I don't ever want him to take advantage of her like that.' Not that anything she said had any influence on him, and she didn't delude herself about that, but Andre didn't take the comment seriously.

'I don't think he meant any harm by that. It was probably just a smart thing to say at the time.'

'I hope that's all it was. He doesn't seem particularly interested in her.' They had been in a hurry to run away and play pool that night.

'I can't say the same for Antoine.' Andre smiled. Antoine had broken up with the girl in town and he had looked lonely for the past few months, but not tonight with Arden Blake. The two of them had played with the baby endlessly, cooing and laughing and holding her. Antoine seemed enchanted with her, unlike Jon.

The next day, Arden took the baby into the pool with her and played with her carefully, and when Antoine came back from a meeting in town with some important distributors, he changed into his swimming trunks and joined Arden in the pool. They chatted and laughed quietly, played gently with the baby, and at last returned her to Sabrina. They went on talking endlessly, as Sabrina watched approvingly. They had looked almost married as they had played with the child. And they were both old enough. There was something so quiet and warm about both of them. It was almost as

386

though they were out of the same mould; even their hair was the same blonde. They looked like a perfectly-matched pair, although no one remarked on it, but Jon seemed to notice it as he dove into the pool once Dominique was out and swam right between Arden and Antoine. That evening they took Arden to the cinema with them, but didn't ask Antoine to go along. Sabrina found him sitting on the porch alone, lost in thought, smoking a cigarette and drinking a glass of their own wine.

'Don't you know better than to drink that stuff?' She teased as she sat down in the rocking chair next to him. 'Everything okay with you, love?' She always worried about him, he was so quiet, one didn't always know if something was troubling him, or what he had on his mind. He never wanted to cause others pain, and he took too much responsibility on his back. Because of that, he was a wonderful operations manager for Andre and a help to both of them.

'I'm okay.' He still had the same melodious accent he'd had when he arrived and she smiled at him. 'Ça va.'

'She's pretty, isn't she?' They both knew who they were talking about: Arden Blake.

'More than that.' He spoke very quietly. 'She's a very unusual girl for her age. She has a great deal of compassion, and depth. Did you know she worked with a missionary in Peru last year for six months? She told her father that if he didn't let her, she would run away. So he gave in. She speaks fluent Spanish and perfect French.' He smiled at Sabrina again, 'And a lot goes on in that pretty blonde head of hers. More than Jon knows, I suspect.'

'I don't think he's really interested in her.' Sabrina still didn't think he was, but Antoine knew better than that.

'I think you're wrong. I think he's waiting 'til the time is right. Right now he wants to play, and she's still very young.' Antoine looked at her with something old and wise in his eyes which she hadn't seen there before, and it saddened her. 'I think he'll marry her one day. She doesn't know that yet, but I'm sure of it. He wants her kept on ice until then, and if anyone gets too close . . .' They both thought of how Jon had simply taken her along that night, even though they had no real interest in having her as a companion. But she had said too much about Antoine. 'I know I'm right.'

Sabrina was honest with him. 'If he marries her, it will be for the wrong reasons, Antoine.'

'I know that.' He smiled almost sadly at her. 'It's strange when you see into the future like that. It's so easy to predict sometimes what other people will do. You wish you could stop them sometimes, but you can't.'

'You could in this case, Antoine.' For once, she wanted him to have what he wanted out of life, and not worry about everyone else. He didn't owe a damn thing to Jon, who had never even been pleasant to him. And for some reason she couldn't explain she didn't want Jon to have Arden Blake. It was for the girl's sake, not his own. She knew it would be wrong for both of them. 'Go after her, if that's what you want.'

'She's too young,' he sighed and then smiled, 'and she's absolutely crazy about him. Apparently, she has been since she was fifteen. That's a tough one to fight. She'll have to grow out of it, and she hasn't yet.'

'She will in time. He isn't very nice to her.'

'That only makes it worse. There's something masochistic about girls that age.' He was wise for his years and Sabrina looked at him.

'Why don't you spend some time with her?'

'We did today. And she won't be here for very long, I think.' Sabrina had an idea then, and she mentioned it to Andre that night. 'Don't you think you should send Antoine to New York to see about that market plan we discussed?' Andre stared at her.

'Why? I thought we'd go this fall.'

'Why not let him?'

'Don't you want to go?'

'We can go another time.'

He looked at her strangely then, and suddenly grinned. 'Are you pregnant again?'

She laughed. 'No. I just thought it would do him good.'

'There's more to it than that. You're not fooling me. What have you got up your sleeve, you witch?' He came over and pulled her into his arms and her nonchalance disappeared as she giggled with him.

'Stop it, I'm serious.'

'I know you are. But what about?'

'All right, all right . . .' She told him about Arden Blake and Antoine's interest in her.

'Why don't you let him fend for himself? He's twenty-seven years old, he can take care of himself. If he wants to go to New York, he can afford to go on his salary.' They paid him a handsome wage, but that was beside the point this time.

'He won't go then. He's too much of a gentleman and he doesn't want to cut Jon out.'

'Maybe he's right. Shouldn't you stay out of this?' He looked concerned, but she didn't give a damn.

'Andre, she's perfect for him.'

'Then let him work it out.'

'Dammit, you're impossible!' But he had heard everything she said. He chatted with Antoine about Arden casually the next day and said nothing when Antoine vanished for the afternoon and then came home looking sunburned and contented after a picnic somewhere near a brook they had found. He had introduced her to some of their wines, presumably kissed her once or twice, and that night took her for a quiet walk while Bill and Jon went to town to chase a line of chorus girls they'd heard about. When Arden left Napa with Bill, to return to Malibu, she said that she hoped she would see Antoine again. Jon stayed on for only a few more days, and then went South to join them. He went back on the train to New York from Los Angeles with Bill. And Antoine discovered that there was something he had to see about there and went to see her once in Malibu before she and her mother left, but he said very little about it to Sabrina and Andre.

'Well, are you sending him to New York?' Sabrina was enjoying it all vicariously and her husband smiled mysteriously at her.

'Yes, but only because he asked me himself. He wants an excuse to go to New York and see her again, although he didn't put it that way.' But the next time Jon called, he sounded interested in Arden again and talked about her a lot. He had taken her here and there, to some cocktail party, to a play. Sabrina knew he was playing with her, and Antoine was right. He wanted to keep her on ice for himself, and she was young enough to fall for it. Antoine went to New York to see her anyway and seemed depressed when he came back.

'What happened? Did he say anything to you?' Sabrina pounced on Andre as soon as father and son had their first talk.

'Yes. That she's in love with Jon.'

'But she can't be. She looked crazy about Antoine when she was here.'

'He's been making a fuss over her, and she even thinks they might get engaged. She didn't think it was fair not to tell Antoine. And she

389

didn't even kiss him this time, but don't you dare tell him I told you that.'

'Of course not.' She looked as depressed as Antoine. 'Jon is as manipulative as Camille ever was.'

'Look, stay out of it,' Antoine advised her. 'It's between the three of them. If Antoine wants her badly enough, he'll fight for her. If Jon is playing games, he'll drop out eventually. And if she has any brains at all, she'll pick the one she wants. The best thing you can do is leave them alone.'

'I can't stand the suspense.' She laughed with him. But she knew that he was right.

Antoine didn't mention her again for months, and Sabrina saw no letters coming in from Arden, although they might have come while she was in town. And when they talked to Jon at Christmas she could have wrung his neck.

'How's Arden, dear?'

'Who?'

'Arden Blake.' The girl you were so busy keeping from Antoine, you ass. But she kept her cool. 'Bill's sister, your friend.'

'Oh . . . of course. She's fine. I'm seeing a girl called Christine now.'

'Where'd she come from?'

He laughed. 'Manchester, I think. She's a model here in New York, and she's English, and very tall and sexy and blonde.' As dark as he was, he definitely had a thing for blondes.

'Is she a nice girl?' Andre laughed as he waited to say hello, and Sabrina laughed too. 'Never mind.' She was pleased to hear that he had dropped Arden again, and she was planning to pass the information along. 'Do you see Arden at all?'

'Once in a while. I'm seeing her when I stay with them in Palm Beach this week.'

'When are you coming out?'

'Next summer probably. Maybe I'll bring Christine.' That sounded even more promising for Antoine's romance, and Sabrina was thrilled.

'That sounds great. Give her my love.'

Andre was outraged when she hung up. 'Whose side are you on anyway?'

'Who do you think?' She smiled. She wanted to see Antoine get what he wanted this time. He seldom did, and Jon always had. It was time he learned, and she knew that deep down he wouldn't care. She didn't want him to be hurt, but she also didn't want him to hurt someone else and she knew that he would hurt Arden Blake, given the chance. The next day she mentioned to Antoine that Jon was seeing someone new.

'That's nice.' He seemed not to hear.

'Antoine,' she looked for a delicate way to tell him Arden was free and then cast caution to the winds, 'he's not seeing Arden anymore.'

'That's nice too.' He smiled at her, but there was no sign of elation on his face.

'Don't you care about her anymore?' Bemused, she looked blankly at Antoine and he kissed her cheek.

'I care about her very much, Mother dear.' He called her Mother often now. 'But she's a very young girl, and she doesn't know her mind. And I don't want to get in the middle of this.'

'Why not?'

He looked at her honestly, 'Because I'll get hurt.'

'So what?' She was shocked. 'That's what life's all about. At least fight for what you want.' She was suddenly furious with him, but he wouldn't be moved.

'No. I can't win this one. Believe me, I know. She is totally blind to his faults,' he looked apologetically at Sabrina but she didn't seem to mind. She knew what Jon was, better than anyone. 'The more I would seek her out, the more she would run to him.' He was right but Sabrina couldn't bear the thought.

'How dumb can she be?'

'Very. It's called youth. She'll grow up.'

'And then?'

He was philosophical as he shrugged. 'She'll probably marry Jon. That's how it goes sometimes.'

'Don't you care?'

'Of course I do. But there isn't a damn thing I can do about it. I saw that when I went to New York. That's why I was so depressed and moped around for weeks after that,' he smiled sheepishly and she was touched that he would admit the truth so openly to her. 'But there's absolutely nothing I can do about it. I'm beaten in this. Your son is a very convincing, insidious young man, and Arden believes every word he says, superficially at least. Deep down, I think she has tremendous misgivings and suspicions about him, even now, he lies to her constantly about his other girls, but she pretends to *herself* that she believes what he says. I think there's a part of her that is never convinced but she's not old enough to trust her instincts and listen to those voices yet. She will one day.' He looked sadly down at Sabrina. 'Probably long after they're married and have a couple of kids. That's just the way life is sometimes.'

'And what about you?' That was her main concern. If Arden was that dumb, as far as she was concerned she deserved what she got. And Jon could take care of himself. But Antoine . . . 'What do you wind up with in all this?'

'A small scar,' he smiled, 'and a valuable lesson learned. Besides, I have other fish to fry. We have a business to run here, and I want to go back to Europe this Spring.'

But when he did, he was even more depressed. He was absolutely certain that there was going to be a war. Hitler was growing far too powerful and there was unrest everywhere. He and Andre discussed it for weeks when he came back, and for once even Andre was afraid.

'And do you know what I most fear?' He admitted to her late one night, 'I fear for him. He's young enough to go rushing off to war, convinced that he's doing the noble thing, for patriotism and all that crap, and get himself killed . . .' He felt a tremor in his heart just thinking about it.

'Do you really think he'd go?'

'I have absolutely no doubt. He told me as much himself.'

'God, no . . .' She thought of Jon then. She couldn't even imagine him in a war. But when she talked to Antoine herself, he put none of her fears to rest.

'France is still my country . . . it always will be . . . no matter how long I live here. If she is attacked . . . I go. It's as simple as that.' But nothing was that simple, and now each time they listened to the news, Sabrina and Andre felt the threat. She almost wished he would pursue Arden Blake. Maybe if he married her, he would be less liable to run off. And what he said was beginning to seem true. It seemed almost impossible that there wouldn't be war over there. They just prayed it wouldn't be soon, and that Antoine would have changed his mind about it by then. Maybe they could convince him that they absolutely needed him here. But Sabrina suspected he would go anyway, and Andre agreed with her.

392

And to take their minds off all of it, Andre gave her a magnificent fiftieth birthday party at Thurston House. There were four hundred people there. People she loved, people she cared about, some she barely knew, and it was an absolutely exquisite night. The nurse even brought Dominique in, toddling along in a pink organdie dress, her blonde hair in curls with a little pink satin ribbon, and her cherubic smile and big blue eyes. She was the joy of their life, and Sabrina and Andre loved her more every day, with Antoine as crazy about her as they were. He brought a very nice girl to Sabrina's birthday party too. An English girl who was studying in San Francisco for a year. She was a medical student, and a very serious girl, but she lacked the warmth and the spirit and the ingenuousness of Arden Blake, and Sabrina couldn't help wondering what was happening to her. Jon didn't come out for the party, but he had mentioned her last summer when he did. He just said he was seeing her again, and Christine too, and there was a new French girl now, another model, and an absolutely fabulous looking German Jewish girl he had just met. She had just got out of Germany before things got too hot, and Jon and Antoine had had a heated argument about politics the night before he left. He insisted that Hitler was great for the German economy and would probably do Europe a lot of good, if everyone else, Jews included, behaved themselves. Antoine was so irate that he broke two glasses and a cup and Sabrina cringed as she heard the abuse they hurled at each other.

'Leave them alone.' Andre kept her from going into the living room. 'It's good for them. They're both grown men.' Sometimes it was hard to remember that.

'They're drunk, for Chrissake. They'll kill each other.'

'No they won't.'

In the end, Antoine walked out in a huff and Jon went to sleep on the couch. The next day they parted friends, actually more than they usually did. Antoine even said he'd call Jon at the bank if he came to New York again, and he had never suggested that before. Sabrina was amazed and admitted to Andre he was right.

'You know, men are really very strange.' She was still stunned when they came back from seeing Jon off at the train. 'I really thought they'd kill each other last night.'

'Hopefully, they'll never do that.'

It was a busy summer after that. The grapes were growing

beautifully, and Antoine and Andre were busy overseeing the picking of the grapes in the fall. Dominique had her second birthday shortly after that. Then Christine came, and Jon was in Palm Beach with the Blakes again. Antoine never mentioned Arden anymore, and suddenly it was spring, and then summer again, and Jon called in July and said he'd be out in another month. He was planning to arrive around August eighteenth and he hemmed and hawed, and Sabrina couldn't understand why until he stepped off the train, and the most beautiful blonde girl she'd ever seen stepped out after him. As she walked toward them, Sabrina got another shock. It was Arden Blake, all grown up. She was twenty-one now, and Sabrina hadn't seen her in two years. And what a difference the short time had made. She was breathtakingly beautiful now, her hair arranged in a sophisticated style, her makeup perfectly done, her body leaner than it had been, more like Jon's. Side by side they were a truly spectacular pair, and Arden was as sweet as she had been before.

'Do you approve of my surprise?' He glanced from his mother to Arden with a smile as they all had dinner that night at Thurston House. Antoine had even come in. Sabrina saw him look searchingly at Arden more than once, but he seemed very reserved now, and she was sure the dinner wasn't easy for him.

'I certainly do approve of your surprise. We haven't seen enough of Arden out here.' She looked at her with a warm smile and she blushed innocently, in counterpoint to the very sexy black dress she wore which revealed just the appropriate amount of her creamy breasts. Antoine had had a difficult time with that as well, although Jon didn't seem to notice it at all. Sabrina silently hoped that he wasn't sleeping with her, though she didn't know why.

'Well, we have another surprise for you, Mom.' He grinned and Arden looked at him breathlessly as Sabrina almost felt her heart stop. Suddenly she knew, and without thinking, she glanced at Antoine, desperately wanting to protect him. Jon saw her look and he went on. 'We're getting married next June. We just got engaged.' Sabrina looked instinctively at her left hand, as Arden quietly turned a very pretty sapphire and diamond ring from out of the inside of her hand. She had been hiding it until Jon told them and now she beamed. 'Do you approve?'

Sabrina was silent for just an instant too long; she wasn't sure what to say. And Andre stepped into the gap. 'Of course we do. We're delighted for you both.' She would be twenty-two when she married Jon. He would be twenty-six, and Antoine would be out of luck. But nothing at all showed on his face as he toasted them and it was he who went to get a very fine bottle of champagne made from their own grapes.

'I congratulate you both, and wish you long life, long love . . . good years . . .'

'Hear hear!' Andre seconded his son's elegant toast, and Sabrina tried to make up for her initial shock, but the evening was a strain for her, and she was relieved when finally everyone went to their respective rooms and she could be alone with Andre to tell him what she thought of it.

'Antoine was right.' He had predicted exactly that. But he had also predicted divorce in another five years, and she thought he would be right again. No matter how beautiful they looked as a couple, Sabrina instinctively knew that it was wrong and she said just that to Andre. 'He doesn't love her. I know it. I can see it in his eyes.'

'Sabrina,' Andre looked firmly at his wife, 'there is nothing you can do. And your wisest course will be to go along with them. If it's a mistake, let them find out. They're not getting married for another ten months. That's what engagements are all about. You can pave a road from here to Siam with returned engagement rings.'

'I hope she opens her eyes and does just that.' And she hoped it more fervently later on in their stay, when a rumour reached her that Jon had been out with two chorus girls again the night before. She said nothing to him. He had just said that he was going out with some old friends, and he had left Arden at home. But Sabrina did not approve. He was no different than he had ever been. Nor was Antoine, or his feelings for Jon's fiancée. There was a smouldering look in his eyes each time he looked at her, and it was as though she knew. Their eyes would meet and hold, and she had to tear herself away. But the real shock came on September third, the day before they were to return to New York, and Antoine came home, having heard the news. He had had a meeting in town, and on his way home, he had heard the radio. His predictions had been right again! Europe was at war. He walked into Thurston House and Sabrina stood transfixed. She had just heard it too.

'Antoine . . .' Without his saying a word, the tears began to roll down her face, and Andre's face was grim as he walked into the house just behind his son.

'You heard the news?' Antoine didn't have to ask. They both nodded and stared at him, fearing the worst. But Andre surprised them both.

'Please don't go.' He spoke in a frightened, broken voice. He had been terrified when he heard the reports and he had rushed home to beg. He couldn't let Antoine go to war . . . he was a boy . . . his first born . . . there were tears in his eyes now and Antoine clung to him. As Arden walked slowly down the stairs, Antoine looked up at her. Sabrina never knew if he said the words to her or to them.

'I have to go. I have to . . . I couldn't stay here knowing that was going on.'

'Why not? This is your country too.' Sabrina spoke up.

'But that was my country first. It's my motherland. My home. I was born there.'

'You were born to me.' It was a frightened plea, and for the first time since she had known him, Andre looked old. 'Mon fils . . .' The tears rolled unrestrained down his face, and Sabrina saw that Arden was crying too. Her eyes were glued to Antoine and he walked to her and touched her face.

'One day I will see you again.' He sighed then and turned to the rest of them. 'I called the Consulate a few minutes ago. They've made arrangements for me to leave on a train tonight. It will go straight through to New York, and I'll take a ship there. There are already others going now.' He looked at his father then. 'Je n'ai pas le choix, Papa.' I have no choice. It was a matter of his self-respect. And it was all Andre's fault. He had brought him up too well, with too much integrity, too much pride, Antoine could never have hidden with them, six thousand miles from home, where they needed him.

And it was all like a nightmare after that. They took him to the station that night, after he packed his things. He talked for two hours with Andre, about the business matters he was leaving behind, and he apologized constantly for letting him down but he was not willing to wait so much as another day. Even Jon thought that was foolish of him.

'Why the hell don't you wait until tomorrow, old man, and go with us, on a decent train? What do you lose?'

'Time. They need me now. Not after I stuff my face for four days, and play cards in the parlour car. My country's at war.'

Jon looked at him ironically. 'They'll wait. They won't cancel it because you're a week late.' But Antoine wasn't amused, nor were they at the station at two in the morning, watching him board the train with a handful of others going East. There was a flurry of French being spoken on the platform, a sea of gray faces, a river of tears. And then suddenly, as they said their goodbyes, Arden was in his arms and he kissed her cheek and looked down at her.

'Sois sage, mon amie,' he whispered. Which could have been translated as 'be good' or 'be wise', it was an interesting choice for her and one she would have to make soon. She looked devastated as she watched him go and she called out his name as the train rolled away. Jon took her by the arm and pulled her toward the car. And Andre stood sobbing in Sabrina's arms. They had left Dominique at home. It was too much for a three year old child and she wouldn't have understood.

'I never really thought he'd go . . . even all this time when he said it. . . .' Andre was inconsolable, and he lay sleeplessly in her arms all that night. And the next day when Jon left was another kind of agony. It was like seeing the family smashed all within one day, and when Sabrina kissed Arden, they both cried though neither knew why. They were crying for Antoine, but there was nothing they could say. And then Sabrina kissed Jon again.

'Take care of yourselves . . . come back soon. . . .' Andre hadn't come to the train. It would have been too much for him, and that night when they drove back to Napa, Sabrina drove, and Andre said not a word during the entire trip.

Antoine phoned them once from New York the night before he sailed and they didn't hear from him again for four months, until January. He was well, he was safe, he was in London and temporarily assigned to the RAF. He was wild with admiration for De Gaulle, it was all he talked of when he wrote, and Sabrina ran to the mail box every day, as Dominique clutched at her skirts. When there was a letter from Antoine, they would run back twice as fast, and Sabrina would hand it to Andre. As long as they heard from him, everything would be all right. But it seemed as though they lived in constant fear. Even Jon's wedding to Arden paled in comparison to that. It was a magnificent wedding in New York. Andre and Sabrina went, Bill Blake was the best man, Dominique was the flower girl, there were twelve bridesmaids and ushers and 500 guests at Saint Patrick's Cathedral on the first Saturday in June, but Sabrina was distracted through most of it. She kept thinking of Antoine, and wondering how and where he was. It seemed as though he had been gone for a hundred years, and when he told them he was coming home on leave three months after that, Sabrina sat down and wept. He had been gone for thirteen long months and was now in North Africa with De Gaulle, when a chance for him to come to the States had come up. He would only be able to spend a few days with them, but with any luck at all, he would be there for Dominique's fourth birthday.

And he was. There was general rejoicing by all, and somehow it didn't seem quite so awful when he went back this time. Even Andre wasn't quite so depressed. And it was as though Antoine's aura was still in the air for a long time after he left. They had talked business about the vineyards endlessly, he had bounced Dominique on his lap from the moment he arrived until the moment he left, and he had told them all about the war, and especially about De Gaulle, whom he revered.

'And one of these days the Americans will be in it too.' He had been absolutely certain of it.

'That's not what Roosevelt says,' Sabrina said.

'He lies. He's getting ready for war, mark my words.'

She smiled. 'Still making predictions, Antoine?'

'Not all of them are right,' he smiled back, 'but this one is.' He also asked of Arden and Jon, but she could read nothing on his face. He was too busy with the war and De Gaulle and the rest of it. She told him how pretty the wedding had been, but she missed seeing Amelia when she was there. She had died a few months after Dominique's birth, at the ripe old age of ninety-one. She had lived a long, full, happy life and it had been time, but Sabrina missed her anyway.

Antoine was planning to look up Arden and Jon on his way back through New York, but as it turned out he didn't have time. They shortened his leave, and he left three days earlier than planned, in dark of night, on a troop ship. So all he did was phone, and he got Arden, since Jon was out. 'He's at a business dinner with Bill. He'll be sorry he missed your call.' And she wanted to tell him that she was glad she'd been there, but she was married now, and aware of what she said to him. 'Take care of yourself. How were Sabrina and Andre?'

'Fine. Busy. It was good to see them. And Dominique is huge.' He laughed into the phone, seeing Arden's face, and she closed her eyes and smiled, grateful that he was still alive. She often thought of him. But she was happy with Jon. She knew she had made the right choice. And they had been married for four months. She hoped she would be pregnant soon.

'You should have seen her at the wedding, she was adorable.' But it still hurt him to think of the marriage, and he had had to go, others were waiting to use the phones that had been rigged up near the ship.

'Tell Jon I said hello.'

'I will . . . take care. . . .' She sat staring at the phone for a long time after they hung up, and she wanted to wait for Jon, but as usual when he was out with her brother he didn't get home until three o'clock.

She told him about Antoine's call the next day, but he had a hideous headache and didn't seem to care. 'He's crazy to have got himself into that,' Jon snapped at her. 'Thank God this country isn't that dumb.'

'France didn't exactly have a choice.' She was annoyed at him. It was a stupid thing to say.

'Maybe not, but this country does, and we're a hell of a lot smarter than that.' He expressed the same views in Napa the following year and Sabrina almost bit off his head.

'Don't kid yourself, Jon. I think Roosevelt is lying. We'll be involved over there within a year, if the war isn't over before that.'

'The hell we will,' Jon growled. He had drunk too much wine but it was their annual visit, and Jon was glad they'd come this year. Arden had been depressed for the last two months. She had lost a baby in June and she acted as though it was the end of the world. 'It was only a baby, for Chrissake . . . hell, it wasn't even that.' But she had sobbed inconsolably and Sabrina knew exactly how she felt. She remembered how she had felt when she lost the first child she and John had conceived, and it had taken her so long to get pregnant both before and after that.

'You'll get over it . . . look at me, I had Jon . . . and look at Dominique.' They exchanged a smile as they watched her playing with a puppy on the lawn. She was almost five years old now, and to her parents she seemed the sweetest child that ever lived. She was the joy of her parents' life, as others had said she would be. 'You'll have another one, one day. But it's difficult at first. Why don't you keep yourself busy for a while?'

Arden shrugged, with tears in her eyes again. All she wanted to do was to be with Jon and conceive another baby but he was almost

399

never home, and when he was, he was either drunk or tired. He was hardly being cooperative, but she didn't want to tell his mother that.

'Give it time. Goodness, it took me two years to conceive again, and it won't take you that long.' Arden smiled, unconvinced. She still looked as though the end of the world had come and Jon left her in Napa for the entire trip, while he went to San Francisco to see friends, which Sabrina thought was inconsiderate of him.

'Does he do that a lot?' she asked Arden frankly one day, and Arden hesitated and then nodded her head. She seemed even prettier and sleeker this year, though she had lost a little too much weight. She was actually prettier than the models he chased.

'He and Bill go out quite a bit. My father said something to Bill about it a few months ago. He thought that maybe if Bill didn't go, Jon would behave,' she looked apologetically at her mother-in-law but Sabrina urged her on, 'but those two have been friends for so long, you can't separate them even for an evening. It would help if Bill got married, but he says he never will,' she smiled, 'and at the rate he's going, that's probably true.'

'The difference is that Jon already *is* married. Has anyone reminded him of that?' she said angrily to Andre that night, but he refused to get involved.

'He's a grownup now, Sabrina, a married man. He didn't welcome my interference as a boy, and I certainly don't think I should say anything to him now.'

'Then I will.'

'That's up to you.'

And when she did, Jon told her to go to hell. 'Has she been whining to you again? What a pain in the ass. Her brother is right. She's a spoiled, whiny brat.' He was fiercely annoyed and he had a hideous hang-over again.

'She's a warm, decent, loving girl, Jon, and she's your wife.'

'Believe me, I've noticed that.'

'Have you? What time do you come home at night?'

'What is this? A kangaroo court? What business is it of yours?'

'I like her, that's what. And you're my son, and I know what a horse's ass you can be, indulging yourself, chasing girls. You're married now, for God's sake. Act like it. You were almost a father a few months ago. . . .'

He cut her off. 'That wasn't my idea. That was her fault.'

'Didn't you want the baby, Jon?' Her voice was gentler now, and her voice was sad. She wondered if Antoine's prediction was right. Things didn't seem to be working out.

'No, I did not. I want a baby like I want a lame horse. For Heaven's sake, I'm twenty-five years old, we have plenty of time for that.' In a way he was right, but Arden was anxious for a child. And then suddenly, Sabrina couldn't stop herself from asking what was on her mind.

'Are you happy with her, Jon?'

He looked at his mother suspiciously. 'Did she tell you to ask me that?'

'No. Why?'

'It just sounds like something she'd want to know. She's always asking dumb questions like that. Hell, I don't know. I'm married to her, aren't I? What more does she want?'

'Maybe a lot more. It takes more than just a ceremony. It takes affection and understanding and patience and time. How much time do you spend with her?'

He shrugged. 'Not much, I guess. I have a lot of other things to do.'

'Like what? Other girls?'

He looked at her defiantly. 'Maybe. So what? It's not hurting her. There's still enough for her. I got her pregnant, didn't I?' His attitude made her sick.

'Why did you ever want to marry her?'

'I told you that a long time ago.' He looked Sabrina in the eye and never flinched, 'she was my passport to success. If I'm married to Arden, I have a job for life.' Sabrina almost cried at his words.

'Do you mean that?'

He shrugged and looked away. 'She's a nice kid. I know she's always been crazy about me.'

'But what do you feel for her?'

'The same thing I feel for any other girl, sometimes more sometimes less.'

'And that's it?' Sabrina stared at him, wondering who he was, who was this hideous, unfeeling, ungiving, uncaring man she had once carried inside her own flesh? Who was he now? . . . he was Camille, a voice inside her said . . . but he was also part of her . . . and yet, he had no heart. 'I think you've made a terrible mistake.' She spoke in a

401

quiet voice. 'That girl deserves better than that.'

'She's happy enough.'

'No, she's not. She's lonely and sad and she probably knows that you don't care about her any more than you care for the shoes on your feet.' He looked down and then up at Sabrina again. There wasn't much he could say.

'What do you want me to do? Pretend? She knew what I was when she married me.'

'And she was a fool. But she's paying a high price for it.'

'That's life, Mom.' He grinned lopsidedly at her and stood up, and she noticed again how handsome he was. But that wasn't enough, and she pitied Arden now even more than she had before. She held her tight for a long moment when she took them to the train.

'Call if you need me. . . .' She looked her in the eye. 'Remember that. I'm right here, and you can always come out.' She had been pushing for them to come out for Christmas that year, ever since her talk with Jon. But he wanted to go to Palm Beach, it was more fun for him, and Bill would be there for him to carouse with. San Francisco was beginning to bore him to tears. It was too provincial for him, after Boston and Paris and Palm Beach and New York. But Arden, who came from all that, was happier in Napa with Sabrina and Andre and Dominique.

'We'll see.' Arden clung to her and there were tears rolling down her cheeks as the train pulled away, and Sabrina felt a huge weight on her chest for weeks remembering what he had said to her. It took her that long to admit it to Andre and he was as horrified as she was.

'Antoine was right.'

'I thought he would be. He should have fought for her.'

'Maybe he was right about that too. Maybe he couldn't have won. She was so crazy about Jon.'

'She was dead wrong. He'll ruin her life.' It was a terrible thing for a mother to say but that was how she felt. 'I just hope she doesn't get pregnant again. That's all she needs. This way, if she sees the light one day, she'll be alone and free to start again.' It was an awful thing to wish, for one's daughter-in-law to divorce one's son, but she did. Although she didn't say it to Antoine when he came home on leave again. This time he missed Dominique's birthday, but not by much. He came at the end of November and stayed for a week, and they were on the way to the train station, with the radio on in the car, when news of Pearl Harbor hit.

'Oh my God,' she stopped the car and stared at him. They were alone. Andre never came to the station to see him leave anymore, it was too painful for him. 'My God . . . Antoine . . . what does that mean?' But she already knew what it meant. It meant war . . . and for her it meant Jon. . . . Antoine looked at her with sad eyes.

'I'm sorry, Maman. . . .' She nodded, choked with tears, and started the car again, she didn't want him to miss his train, although actually she wanted that more than anything. What was the world coming to? The whole damn world was at war, and they had two sons to worry about, one in North Africa with De Gaulle and God only knew where they'd send Jon now. But within a few days she knew. He had enlisted with Bill Blake after they got drunk the day they heard the news, and Jon was mad as fire. Bill was being shipped a few miles to Fort Dix. Jon was being sent to San Francisco, and after that he'd ship out. He was bringing Arden out with him, and she could stay with Sabrina and Andre while he lived at the base.

'At least we'll get Christmas together this year.' But the prospect didn't please him very much. He was in a hideous mood when he arrived, annoyed at everything, lonely without Bill, and taking it all out on his wife, even on Christmas Eve, which they spent at Thurston House. Eventually Arden left the table in tears as Jon threw his napkin on the floor. 'She makes me sick.' But not for long, as four days later, he got his orders and the following day he was shipping out.

Sabrina and Arden and Andre and Dominique went to the pier to see him off. There was a flood of humanity everywhere, crying, sobbing, waving handkerchieves and flags. There was a band playing music from the wharf, and there was a kind of unreality to it all, as though it were a game of 'Let's pretend', but there was no pretense as they kissed Jon goodbye, and Sabrina grabbed his arm.

'I love you, Jon.' She hadn't said it in a long time, and he wasn't an easy person to say things like that to, but in spite of everything she wanted him to know that now.

'I love you too, Mom.' There were tears in his eyes and then he looked at his wife with his irresistible lopsided smile. 'Take care of yourself, Kid. I'll write to you once in a while.'

She smiled through her tears and held tight to him. It seemed unbelievable that he was going now, but after they had said their goodbyes, they watched the ship pull out and Arden was convulsed in sobs as Sabrina put an arm around her and held her tight, and Andre looked down at them, with Dominique in his arms, and thought of his son so far away. They were terrible times, for everyone, and he only prayed that both boys would come home alive.

'Come on, let's go home.' Arden had decided to stay with them for a while, and when they went back to Thurston House, it felt so much like a tomb to all of them, and they left for Napa that afternoon. Somehow life was easier to endure there, there was the gentleness of the countryside, the fresh grass, the blue sky, it was hard to imagine that all wasn't right with the world up there.

And it was here that the telegram came, five weeks after he left. The man in the uniform came one day, knocked at their front door and handed it to Andre. He felt his heart stop and tore it open for her, but the tears blurred his eyes before he could see which name was there . . . It was Jonathan Thurston Harte . . . 'We regret to inform you that your son is dead . . .' The sound she made was an animal scream, the same sound she had made when he was born twenty-seven years before. He left the world as he had entered it, through his mother's heart, with a piercing scream as she reached out to Andre, and Arden stood by in shock. Then Sabrina went to her, and the three of them clung to each other late into the night. Even Dominique cried. She understood now. Her brother had died. He was never coming back.

'Which one?' she kept asking Andre, confused about who it was.

'Jon, sweetheart . . . your brother Jon.' And then he held her close to him, cradling her on his lap, feeling guilty that it was Jon and not Antoine, and at the same time relieved that it was not. He couldn't look at Sabrina all day, so great was the guilt he felt, but she saw it there, she knew him too well.

'Don't look at me like that.' Her face was almost unrecognizable she had cried so hard. 'You didn't make the choice. God did.' And with those words, he came to her arms and sobbed and prayed that God would not make that choice again. He couldn't have borne to lose Antoine. Maybe it had happened to Jon because Sabrina was stronger than he was, he thought. But however he turned, whichever way he looked, it made no sense anyway. God gave and He took, and He gave and then He took again until it made no sense at all.

404

Chapter Thirty-Four

'What are you doing today?' Sabrina looked over her shoulder at her daughter-in-law playing with Dominique. Arden had stayed on, without ever actually deciding to. She had just never gone home. And she had been in Napa with them for five months now. It was June 1942, and Antoine was due home on leave in July. He had been hit in the left arm a few months before, but it had not been a major wound. The only benefit of it was that he was working in De Gaulle's office now, and they were grateful for that. 'Do you want to come into town with me or stay here?'

Arden mused and then smiled at the woman she loved so much. 'I'll come into town. What are you going to do?'

'Just some things at the house . . .' She didn't want to upset her now. She had recovered very well. They had discovered after Jon's death that she was pregnant again, but she had lost the baby almost immediately this time. 'Maybe it just wasn't meant to be.' But they had been difficult words to hear, and to say when Sabrina said them to her. She would have loved to see Jon's child . . . her only grandchild . . . but it was too late to cry about that now, and they were all recovering slowly from the blow. The sun still rose every day, and the hills were green, and the grapes were beautiful, and each day it all began again, and somehow life didn't seem so painful after a while. She had felt as though she were stumbling along the ground for a long time, but Andre had helped her up, and she had Dominique to bring her joy and give her love to, and Arden as well.

'Any news from Antoine?' Arden sounded casual as they drove into town. She was holding Dominique on her lap, and the child was asleep. She loved riding with them in the car, and especially loved her Aunt Arden, as she called her.

'Nothing much. He's alright. Some funny stuff about De Gaulle,' she knit her brows, 'but I showed you that. He's still coming in when he said he was.' Arden looked at the passing countryside and then down at the sleeping child on her lap.

'He's a very special man.' It was the first time she had really talked about him since Jon died, and Sabrina had wondered if she had guilt feelings about that. Jon had been rotten to her, there was no denying that. Maybe she had even wished him dead once or twice. That would have made it harder when he died . . . 'I almost fell in love with Antoine a long time ago.'

Sabrina smiled as she drove. 'I knew that.' And then, she moved on to more delicate ground. 'I think he was in love with you then, too.'

Arden nodded. 'I know. But I was so crazy about Jon.'

'Antoine understood. He said you'd marry him long, long before you did.'

'He did?' She looked stunned. 'How did he know?'

Sabrina laughed this time. 'You said it yourself. He's a very special man.' The two women exchanged a smile and crossed the new bridge into town. Sabrina liked the Golden Gate. It had a majestic quality to it, much more so than the Bay Bridge. She remembered the days of steamers and trains . . . how swiftly time passed . . . it was hard to believe that she was fifty-four years old, hardest for her to believe it. She didn't feel that old. Where did it all go? And why so fast? Why didn't one have more time? . . . but thoughts like that reminded her of Jon. And that was why she had come into town. She had come to watch them install the plaque.

On the side of the house, where they had begun building so long ago, was the little niche her father had had put in. He had told her what he had wanted done, and now she was doing it for him . . . and John . . . and now Jonathan . . . all those who had lived in Thurston House, so that one day no one would forget . . . so that they were all there.

The men were waiting for her when she arrived with a small handsome piece of bronze, which she showed to Arden. They went out to the garden that was now so small, but had once been so large. Sabrina glanced at her plants, at the bright flowers, as the men drilled and then attached the plaque. There were three of them now . . . Jeremiah Arbuckle Thurston . . . John Williamson Harte . . . Jonathan Thurston Harte . . . it was sad seeing their names there, with the dates that framed their lives.

'Why did you do that?' Arden looked at her with big sad eyes.

'So no one forgets.'

'I'll never forget you.' The men were gone, and Arden looked at her. 'You will always be part of this house for me.'

Sabrina smiled and gently touched her cheek and then glanced at the plaque with the names of the men she had loved. 'As they are for me . . . my father . . . John . . . Jonathan . . .' The words brought their faces to mind . . . almost seemed to bring them to life again, and then Sabrina looked at her. 'My name will be there one day . . . Andre's . . . yours . . . Antoine's . . .' The only one who had disappeared was Camille. There was no plaque for her. She had chosen to abdicate, and she was erased from all memory. 'The past is an important thing. It is to me, it has been to this house . . . how it came to be here.' She thought of her father then. The people who loved the house, who brought it along from then into now. 'But the present is important too. That part belongs to you,' she dared to say the words she hoped for them, 'and perhaps Antoine, perhaps you will live here one day . . .' And then she looked at Dominique cavorting in the flower beds, and suddenly she stopped, as though she knew her mother was talking about her. 'And the future is hers. Thurston House will be hers one day. I hope it means as much to her as it has to us. She was born in this house,' Sabrina smiled remembering her birth with Andre at her side, 'and my father died in this house . . .' She looked back up at it, at the rooms she loved and knew so well, and then she smiled at Dominique again. It was a legacy she was leaving her, or would leave one day, of people who had come before, leaving their marks, and their hearts, and their love.

<u>ZOYA</u>

Danielle Steel

One woman's odyssey through a century of turmoil.

St Petersburg: one famous night of violence in the October Revolution ends the lavish life of the Romanov court forever – shattering the dreams of young Countess Zoya Ossupov.

Paris: under the shadow of the Great War, émigrés struggle for survival as taxi drivers, seamstresses and ballet dancers. Zoya flees there in poverty ... and leaves in glory.

America: a glittering world of flappers, fast cars and furs in the Roaring Twenties; a world of comfort and café society that would come crashing down without warning.

Zoya – a true heroine of our time – emerges triumphant from this panoramic web of history into the 80s to face challenges and triumphs.

WANDERLUST

Danielle Steel

At 21 Annabelle Driscoll was the acknowledged beauty, but it was her sister Audrey – four years older – who had the spine and spirit. She had talent as a photographer; she had the restless urge of a born wanderer.

Inevitably it was Annabelle who was the first to marry, leaving Audrey to wonder if life were passing her by. The men she met in California were dull, worldly. Even in New York, they failed to spark her. Only when she boarded the *Orient Express* did she realise she was beginning a journey that would take her farther than she had ever dreamed possible . . .

Time Warner Paperback titles available by post:

☐ Crossings	Danielle Steel	£5.99
☐ Family Album	Danielle Steel	£5.99
☐ Fine Things	Danielle Steel	£5.99
☐ Going Home	Danielle Steel	£5.99
☐ Kaleidoscope	Danielle Steel	£5.99
☐ Remembrance	Danielle Steel	£5.99
☐ Season of Passion	Danielle Steel	£5.99
☐ Zoya	Danielle Steel	£6.99

The prices shown above are correct at time of going to press. However, the publishers reserve the right to increase prices on covers from those previously advertised without prior notice.

timewarner
paperbacks

Handwritten:
```
60  00
 7  00
15  75
 7  00
89  75
```

TIME WARNER PAPERBACKS
P.O. Box 121, Kettering, Northants NN14 4ZQ
Tel: 01832 737525, Fax: 01832 733076
Email: aspenhouse@FSBDial.co.uk

POST AND PACKING:
Payments can be made as follows: cheque, postal order (payable to Time Warner Books) or by credit cards. Do not send cash or currency.

All U.K. Orders	**FREE OF CHARGE**
E.E.C. & Overseas	25% of order value

Name (Block Letters) _____

Address _____

_____

Post/zip code: _____

☐ Please keep me in touch with future Time Warner publications

☐ I enclose my remittance £ _____

☐ I wish to pay by Visa/Access/Mastercard/Eurocard

Card Expiry Date

☐☐☐☐☐☐☐☐☐☐☐☐☐☐☐☐☐☐☐

_____